I0779144

The Notch

Author: Brandon Zagst

ISBN: 979-8-9936750-5-3

Cover Illustration: Zoey Zagst, Copyright 2025, Notch Media, LLC

Book Design, Publishing, and Production: Notch Media, LLC

<h1 style="text-align:center"><u>The Notch</u></h1>

Part One: Project Zohar

<u>UUONE</u>

The Second Israeli Invasion into Lebanon had been difficult
for Ezekiel.   What some called the Lebanese Civil War, he saw
only as destroying his dream of advancing in the Israeli
Defensive Forces (IDF). Ezekiel had just turned twenty years
old, when on September 16, 1982, his life would be changed
forever. Completely out of his control, the Lebanese militia they
were supporting had decided to kidnap hundreds of residents
from the Sabra neighborhood in Southern Beirut. Israel had been
placed in a supervisory position over the militia, and they had

decided to turn a rather blind eye to what was occurring. What multiple commissions around the world may view as genocide.

As a relatively new IDF recruit, his job was to follow orders, not to think for himself. His family had close ties to Prime Minister Oren Levitte, and the Prime Minister himself had hand selected Ezekiel to participate in this unit. Ezekiel had no idea as to why he was selected, other than his father's prior time in the military with Levitte. His father had served on a unit that was originally founded and commanded by Ariel Sharon, the former Prime Minister. That group was called Unit 101. In 1955, Ezekiel's father, Joshua Barak, had served in Unit 101 in Operation Black Arrow against the Egyptian Army.

While the Unit had supposedly been absorbed into the 890th Paratroop Battalion, the original members of this secret unit were now all high ranking officers either in the Israeli government or the IDF. Ezekiel's father had served with valor that day against the Egyptians, saving the lives of many of the men involved in the invasion. His father's name had been included on the walls at the memorial site in Mefalsim which honored the brave heroes of the Black Arrow Operation. Another necessary mortal statistic for the protection of Judaism.

Joshua Barak would have been proud of his son's basic training achievements, and while he didn't know of his father's secretive past history or show up to his graduations from Paratrooper schools, his presence was always felt by his son. His father was a decorated soldier who had served with the Prime Minister. His father was a hero. Ezekiel remembered his father always calling him "EZ" instead of his more formal first name, and that nickname had stuck since his time in the IDF. He preferred this to some of the other nicknames his teammates had acquired, and he knew nicknames were earned, not personally selected.

His leave time to Tel Aviv with his fellow officers hadn't been that many years ago, and his success in picking up the ladies on Rothschild Boulevard had earned him the moniker. He apparently was easy on the eyes, easy to get the digits, and easy to pass out too early. He had to laugh as all of this was true, but these guys didn't know that his father had also used the same nickname for his son. He wouldn't change it for the world.

The Sabra Massacre, as it was being called, had resulted in nearly three thousand deaths. The Lebanese forces moved into the Sabra neighborhood with over three hundred men that faced no resistance from the PLO forces that had withdrawn the previous day. The ceasefire rules had now been broken. IDF radio communications indicated atrocities being committed by the Lebanese. And under Ezekiel's leadership, gates were blocked, and when asked, flares were shot into the night sky to illuminate the enemies of Israel. Palestine must never become a state his commanders had reinforced to EZ.

Ezekiel was simply following commands, and he had served admirably. Not realizing the complete slaughter that had occurred, all he had heard when he returned to his base was that he had done his duties without question and to the greater good of his country. He would be handsomely rewarded by those in charge. His country would never forget his actions to protect the homeland. However, Ezekiel began to question his actions during the mission. He hadn't felt that he was a hero. How could blocking gates, ignoring radio communications, and lighting flares result in a hero's welcome?

So it was with great disbelief, that the next day he was to be brought to Jerusalem to meet the Prime Minister himself-Oren Levitte.

Ezekiel put on his best dress uniform and entered the rear of the armored Mercedes SUV. He could not believe he was going to meet the Prime Minister personally. His commanding officer was incredibly pleased with his actions and was likely up for a promotion as well. Finally, all of his hard work was paying off. Perhaps he was his father's son after all.

Turning onto Smoleskin Street, he looked around the Rehavia neighborhood with pride. He was now amongst Israel's richest and brightest-doctors, lawyers, and judges. As the SUV curved through the neighborhood, it reached Balfour street. The heavy SUV slowed to allow the famous "Black Curtain", which kept the Prime Minister's residence from view, to open and the SUV to be inspected by the heavily armed security detail.

Hand selected by the Prime Minister and known to be more ferocious than the United State's famous Secret Service, Shin Bet was responsible for all intelligence and security for the Prime Minister. Loyal to the death, Ezekiel knew that very few made the cut to work behind the Black Curtain.

Ezekiel whispered to himself as the gates opened, "Beit Rosh HaMemshala". He knew most Jews called the house Balfour, or Beit Aghion. He felt Hebrew was more appropriate at the moment. The large Jerusalem stone construction projected the residence's current tenant, responsible for the protection of what some would argue, the most attacked country on Earth. He had heard his Mother tell stories of his Father being invited to the former Prime Minister's residence, Julius Jacobs House, and now here he was, following in his father's footsteps. He viewed three archways that shadowed over two doors. Shin Bet agents lingered in the shadows of both entrances. As the door opened, two more agents appeared and guided him through the archways to the door at the right of the building. As it opened, he couldn't believe his eyes. There before him was the Prime Minister, Oren Levitte, and a second man that he instantly recognized.

"Hello EZ. It's been a long time."

Joshua Barak had a soft commanding voice that put EZ in a complete stupor. It wasn't possible. His father had died during Operation Black Arrow. His passing was celebrated publicly. His name on the wall. There was no way that his Father would not have been around to support him through his teenage years, let alone his entrance into the military world.

"General-let's get this young man a drink. I think he's going to need it."

Levitte looked at Joshua Barak and laughed. Extending his hand to EZ, he pulled the young soldier in and gave him an intimate hug, almost as if he was a long lost family member.

Levitte released the hug, and EZ stood face to face with his father. His brought back from the dead father. He had grey hair now instead of the dark black hair which EZ remembered from his old family photo albums, and he was in incredible shape for his age. A gym was definitely on his daily priority list.

"EZ, I know you have a million questions, but let us first sit down for a drink. An old man must hear his son's stories once in a while, to beam with pride, to feel like his time on this Earth has had value. And from what I hear, you performed honorably, with zero doubt in the face of conflict, to protect your fellow soldiers, and to protect Israel. I'm very proud of you."

Joshua Barak's calm tempo captured his son's complete attention, just as it had done before his death. Levitte had referred to him as the General. But the last name Barak was synonymous with a biblical General. Was his father an actual General or was the Prime Minister making a joke? EZ knew that Barak was also Hebrew for lightning, and he could recall seeing a lightning bolt logo on many of his father's prior uniforms. It was a lot to take in all at once. EZ had yet to form a spoken word or even an opinion on his Father's surprise.

The Prime Minister turned back to EZ, once again extending

his hand. But this time, he had pulled something from his pocket. Reaching for EZ's hand, he placed a pin, made of what he could only guess by weight, solid gold. The gold pin was in the rough shape of a six sided rhombus, with smooth angles, its intersecting lines forming a lightening bolt, suspended over a flaming sword. EZ recognized the similarity to the Jewish Kabbalah Tree, with a military undertone.

"Ezekiel, welcome to Balfour. And welcome to UUONE."

Loyalty

Ezekiel's father's death had not been in vain. Out of Operation Black Arrow, a new Underground Unit 101, code named UUONE, was founded. An organization that wasn't known within the Mossad or Israel's other Intelligence agencies. UUONE had one mission-to protect the country no matter the cost. Morals, money, or men were irrelevant. The soul of the Jewish state must be preserved. Its members were only chosen by other UUONE or Unit 101 members of the past. A three man "Yes" vote was needed, and it was up to the recruit to decide acceptance into the secret unit-volunteers only-for God and country.

Politicians would come and go. Movers and shakers willing to concede to the highest bidders. No matter the country or reasons, large corporations would sway the most hardened beliefs or instill blackmail to achieve their desired outcomes. UUONE could achieve these dark outcomes, and allowed the country's long term goals to be achieved over decades at no risk of political shortcomings and capital influence. UUONE shaped the long term goals of Israel. It mattered not who was in power.

The most die hard Zionist's made up its ranks. Just as the United States's CIA and NSA were able to maintain order over secret projects like Roswell, the budgets of UUONE were nonexistent and known to only three people. None of which could ever be at the same location. Nothing could be left to chance, and nothing could ever be written down. Only an oral history. It had worked for thousands of years prior to the written word throughout Jewish and Christian history, and it was much safer in today's data driven world.

In the tradition of the Kabbalah, the Lightening-Flaming Sword represented the divine energy through the ten sefirot on the Tree of Life-the Order of Creation. Levitte recalled giving the oath to Barak years earlier. In Yiddish, Levitte stood before Barak, with the three UUONE members who had nominated him.

"Keter, Chochmah, Binah, Chesed, Gevurah, Tiferet, Netzach, Hod, Yesod, and Malchut. The Kabbalah Tree's principles have been held sacred and secret to the world. Are you willing to be exposed to the Universe's secrets, to the divine, to the mysteries of the world? Do you freely accept to keep the secrets of all souls? To the source of the light and the darkness? Are you willing to understand who God is?"

Levitte's voice filled with reverence. Solemn. Truth.

"I am willing to be exposed to the light." Barak replied.

"Then let the Universe of Crown, Wisdom, Understanding, Love, Strength, Harmony, Eternity, Glory, Foundation, and Kingdom be revealed to you now Barak. Let your eyes be opened to Shechinah, to our very essence in the Universe."

Levitte finished and placed the same gold pin he had just presented to EZ in Barak's hand. Levitte smiled, for he too had been in Barak's shoes once, and he knew what Barak was about to experience. A connection to the Universe only a few on Earth had ever experienced- over generations of warriors, religious figures, and politicians. God's existence was revealed. No more need for faith. An experience of pure, proven belief.

"Take this cup, and drink from it. May your beam of light shine upward towards the heavens, and may your third eye see the darkness below."

<u>**For Love of Country**</u>

On September 19, 1982, the truth finally had to be revealed, as the massacre in Sabra had taken a global stage, and if they were to use the powers of Levitte to place Ezekiel in consideration for UUONE, it must be now. The Prime Minister's image was being tarnished in the wake of the event. Now was the time to reveal to Ezekiel his Father's past, and his current work in Central America. His Father's secrets would continue on in the family, as they had been for generations. Levitte looked into EZ's eyes and spoke.

"EZ. You have been nominated for a special unit, UUONE. This unit serves no country. It serves only the future of the Jewish people. It can never be spoken of, and your existence in the country of Israel will never be again. From this day forward, you will not be allowed to step foot into the Holy Land unless you instill another into UUONE. Your existence will remain secret to all but a few, and you will be a member of the smallest, most powerful group known to the Universe. Should you accept, you will leave today and be transported away from all of your old friends, military history, and whatever future you may have valued throughout Israel."

"I'm a bit confused sir." EZ said.

"To see my Father here before me is a bit much on its own, but to be asked to right now, right at this moment, join a secret society of some sort, and abandon all of my military goals, all of my future here in Israel. I'm not sure how to respond. I'm not even sure why a very average Israeli officer like myself would be asked to join this supposed powerful unit." Barak spoke to his son lovingly.

"EZ, I know this is a lot to ask. To leave what family you have left, to just vanish into thin air as I did many years ago. That's a lot to ask of a young man. But you were chosen EZ, just as I was, and just as your grandfather was many years ago. Our family has been given the obligation to keep the existence of the Jewish secrets, its power throughout the world, intact. Have you ever asked yourself why so few have been able to fight off so many? Why are we able to place Jews throughout powerful countries, to employ the heads of banks and finance? Without people like yourself EZ, we will not be able to hold onto the dream of a promised land. Our last few years of research has placed us into a special position to insure that the dream will happen. Along with other Pro-Jewish countries throughout the world, our power will be revealed, just as it will be revealed to you should you accept the Prime Minister's offer. It is ultimately your own decision, and if you say no, I will once again disappear into the vastness of the world. If you are to say yes EZ, then you will work right by my side, continuing on with the implementation of my last twenty years of breakthroughs."

EZ considered the offer. What could be so secretive that his Father appeared out of nowhere, with the Prime Minister no less? What would he be leaving behind? A long, slow uphill battle within the political old boy's club of the IDF did not sound like a promised future that they were offering today. He had no serious relationships or close friends. He was quite tired of the club scene in Tel Aviv. No one of any real value seemed to present themselves. Was that because of the two before him he wondered? There had been many possible girlfriends that seemed to quickly lose interest without explanation. Had it been him? Or, had UUONE arranged this outcome? He really had nothing. As he examined his current situation, there was very little to actually value in staying in Israel.

"By the way EZ, I know a young man such as yourself is always worried about his financial future. I can see the wheels turning in your head on this offer. Let me put you at ease by saying that you will never search for the next paycheck. Your wallet will be forever full, and you will have whatever you could possibly ever want to own. A home, cars, vacations, yachts. And this is even if you WANT the materials of the common man. It's very likely that your mission will reveal the secrets of happiness, and the desire for nothing. While it may not make sense to you now, ask your Father here if he has ever longed for riches or conquests."

Levitte offered. The Prime Minister looked towards EZ's Father Barak.

"EZ, I can tell you honestly, you will be the richest man on the planet. You will want for nothing. You will be blessed with the secrets of the Universe. Join me. It's been my dream for years to bring my son back into my world. Today is that day EZ. Let's take this journey together."

His Father's voice held the power of truth and no shadow of regrets. With the two most powerful men in his lifetime offering what seemed to be the impossible, EZ made his decision in his mind's native Hebrew.

"Far liege fun land." *For the love of the Country.*

<u>Departure</u>

It had all been quite simple and rather undramatic, other than the oath to which he had committed himself. Not much different than any other oath he had taken in his past with say the Tzofim,

Israel's Boy Scout equivalent, or even his oath with the Defense Force. He hadn't raised his right hand. They had not cut his hand open to draw blood and mix with the others as the Mafia would have done. Just a simple Yes was all the two men EZ admired had requested.

His Father had given him a cell phone. One that most would refer to as a "Burner". He was told that over the next two weeks, to enjoy himself around Israel, say his goodbyes, and that a call would come shortly after, informing him of his next step for UUONE.

He was rather surprised in Tel Aviv when he was at the local dance club and used the ATM. When the receipt printed, he had checked to see if his last IDF paycheck had cleared into his checking account. When a balance of over 300,000 Shekels appeared, he thought there must be some mistake. At best, he usually only had enough to live month to month. With no one to call, he took his Shekels and continued on with the night, noting that he would have to ask his Father who he should speak to regarding the error.

Two weeks passed, and EZ carried the phone close. The goodbyes had come pretty easily. With no girlfriends, little family, and no home to tidy up, he had given what few things he owned to his teammates or neighbors. What was left would fit into his small used Honda Accord. Its four doors easily fit the few boxes and military duffels he had left to his name, and being that the car looked like it might break down at any point, he didn't worry about the items being stolen. When the phone actually rang, he was just going to bed at a mid level hotel in Tel Aviv. They had not told him where to stay or where to be, so he took it upon himself to stay near a bigger airport, assuming he would be leaving the country soon.

"Park in the covered parking at Lot 15 at Ben Gurion

Airport, Natbag, tomorrow at Noon. Pack one checked bag suitable for a one month stay in a climate for weather of 32-68 degrees Celsius. One pair of hiking shoes, athletic shoes, and sandals. Proceed on the Shuttle Bus to Terminal Three International departures. Sit in the chairs opposite the Air Europa Counter to await further instructions. Do not worry about your car or its contents. Leave the keys on top of the left driver's side tire. We will move it to a safe location at a later date. Destroy and dispose of your phone after this call. Please repeat these instructions back to me now."

EZ repeated the instructions back to the caller, including tomorrow's date and all other pertinent information. He heard the distinct click of the phone call ending and proceeded to pack his bag with the contents requested, having no idea of his future location. He focused only on the current task at hand as his military training had commanded him only a short two weeks prior. Should he take a carry-on bag? They had not mentioned it, so he decided that just the one checked bag would suffice. He quickly pulled up the average baggage weights of the airlines that flew into Tel Aviv using the hotel WiFi from his laptop as he had no Smart Phone to do research, and he also did a quick check as to what flights may be leaving between Noon and Nine the next day. Too many to guess.

Unsure as to whether he could bring his laptop, he decided to leave it in his car the next day as well. Whoever was planning this had to know the world worked off smart phones, and also that his old identity could somehow be traced back to his laptop. He scanned the few pictures and files he had on the computer, savoring what could be his last time to cherish the memories of his childhood and military days. Everything was out of his control now. Nerves were starting to set in. It was time.

<u>Dad</u>

EZ arrived at Lot 15 around 1145. Better to be early on the first day of his new job. He found the covered parking spaces, and picked one closer to the shuttle pickup.

"Pretty easy to find a spot at the cost of NIS 90 per day," he said to himself alone in the Accord. Grabbing his bag, he caught the shuttle after a short ten minute wait, and proceeded to Terminal Three with his one beat up suitcase tagging along behind him. The nerves had passed after his morning workout, and he had put on the most average tourist outfit he thought he owned-a white long sleeve Patagonia shirt with tan cargo pants, and his trusty worn down IDF Scout boots. He could pass for a college aged tourist heading out for any hiking destination around the world. Best he could do with such little information given.

He arrived right on time in front of the Air Europa counter and proceeded to the chairs discussed the day prior. He was alone. He scanned the people around his general vicinity and didn't see anyone that may fit a secretive, James Bond, type of persona. Not having a phone, he was unaware of the time, but guessed at least thirty minutes had passed when an older gentleman took the seat next to him, tapping an old worn wooden cane against his boot as he did so. Despite the beard and mustache, EZ could not immediately place the disheveled old man. He wore an older grey sport coat, common of so many that age, a plaid button down shirt, and khaki pants, with obligatory Dad-like white New Balance's to complete the outfit.

"EZ. It's good to see you again," Joshua Barak said.

"Dad? Unreal! I didn't even recognize you." EZ looked past the oval spectacles to now see his father. The disguise was insanely perfect as was his gait with the cane.

"Just who are you?" EZ asked as his father pulled his canvas travel bag up to his lap.   "You will know in time EZ. I'm proud of you. I wanted to be the last person you saw before your journey. I wanted to let you know that you are protected, and that you can completely trust all those you are about to come in contact with. Rest assured, should you need anything, anything big or small, UUONE will be there for you. I was once in your shoes. Unaware of my mission, my purpose, my destination. And yet, I am still here, just as you will be for your own son one day." Barak continued.

"Take these three boarding passes to the Air Europa counter. I also have a passport, cell phone, and book to help you pass the time. Study this passport before going to the counter and memorize your cover name as well as the date of birth and address. No need to memorize much more. Your address will be from your hometown in case any questions arise. Once you go through security, you will head to Terminal 3. Go to the Greeter's Hall. Once there, look for the Synagogue. A Rabbi named Malachi will provide you with further instructions."

EZ looked down at the boarding passes. Lying on top was a 405 PM flight to Madrid, Spain. Flight UX1302, Air Europa. Pulling forth the second pass revealed the airport code, LIM, on Air Europa Flight UX175.

"Where is LIM Dad?"

"Lima, Peru, EZ. You will love Peru. I've spent years there, and it's one of my favorite countries in the world. Also one of the oldest civilizations known to modern man."

Pulling out the third pass, EZ read a city code he had never heard before-CUZ-on an airline he had never heard of before-H8 Sky Airline Peru, Flight H25011.

"Before you ask, CUZ is the abbreviation for Cusco, Peru. This will be your final destination. Malachi's brief will get you up to speed in the Synagogue. EZ, you will lead this nation and this family into the next generation of UUONE. Your knowledge of what's to come starts in Peru. The book I have given you is a travel guide for the country and provides a history of all the ancient civilizations you will see there, and since you will have 33 hours in Economy, take the time to absorb its contents."

Shakily beginning his stand with the cane, Barak brushed the hair on EZ's head, the same as he had when he was a young boy.

"When will I see you again Dad? Now that I know you're alive, there is so much I want to hear about. So many things to catch up on. And since I'm now a member of UUONE, won't I be able to discuss what I've done, and what you've done all these years?".

"EZ, it's likely that after Peru, you'll be able to talk to me anywhere, anytime you put your mind to it."

And with a slow turn, his Father walked towards the airport exit.

Grabbing his tickets, he sat down to memorize the Passport as his father had instructed. Ezra Zaks. EZ laughed at UUONE's choice, likely his Father's. The initials EZ would get to stick with him after all.

The Rabbi

Once in Terminal 3, EZ followed his Father's instructions and went to the Greeter's Hall. After asking for some direction, he easily found the Synagogue. A smaller old man with a distinguished gray beard saw him, and motioned for him to sit near the rear of the room. They appeared to be the only two people there. This must be Malachi EZ thought.

"Ezra correct? I was told to be expecting you. And you are right on time. That's unexpected for a man from your generation," the old Rabbi laughed.

"I supposed I'm here to give you some prayers for your journey. I've been to Peru many times, and I have a carry on bag that may help you along the way."

Reaching behind the chair, Malachi produced a single-sling gray Maxpedition pack. EZ had always wanted one, but with his IDF salary, luxuries like these were for much higher ranking officers.

"Within this pack, you will find some items necessary for journeys of your type. I understand that you are seeking more meaning in your life. Mr. Barak used to visit this Synagogue. He flew quite often for business when he was younger. We have developed quite the friendship over the years. He tells me that you may be taking his spot in the business?".

Malachi looked into EZ's eyes, and EZ couldn't quite decide if Malachi knew of UUONE, or if he was just a conduit of the journey ahead. Perhaps this was his first test from his father. He was actually quite surprised as he thought members of UUONE could not return to Israel once joining. I guess some with more power might have to come back to deliver some type of intelligence or initiate new members. He decided to play down his position.

"Mr. Barak has blessed me for sure. It was quite a surprise to have the opportunity to venture away from Israel. I'm very unfamiliar with South America. It will be my first trip, and seeing that I don't speak Spanish, could be a difficult one." EZ tried to repeat back only facts that had been presented by the Rabbi.

"You will love Peru Ezra. It has a long history with Jewish settlers, and some say the Jews have traveled there much longer than is evidenced through the written word. Before the state of

Israel was ratified, there was a Jewish community in Peru that dated to the Incan Empire. Likely arriving with the Spanish, these Jews, along with many Lutherans and Muslims, were put to death or expelled during the Peruvian Inquisition in 1570. This lasted for 250 years. We Jews seem to be persecuted no matter where we go." Malachi paused after the last sentence, staring out for a few seconds before continuing on.

"Ezra, regardless of all of that, you like your Jewish ancestors, who showed much bravery in going back to Peru for the Rubber Boom that followed years later, have established a history of overcoming fear, just as Moses did when he led his own people. I believe that Mr. Barak has sent quite a few young men such as yourself to Peru. Always having them stop to see me prior to their departure. Maybe to pray with each other, perhaps also to give you some items that don't necessarily make it through security." The Rabbi said with a smile.

EZ looked straight into the man's eyes attempting to still read him. If he had done this many times before, then he had to know something, but how much. *Just play along for now* EZ thought.

"Rabbi, I would certainly love to pray with you before my journey. Perhaps we can first go through the bag to see what Mr. Barak may have thought would be helpful for this trip."

EZ, now Ezra, opened the biggest outer zipper. He first noted though that a one inch velcro patch had been placed on the outside of the bag, he almost didn't recognize the word-ZAKS-in all capital letters. His new last name.

Within the first pocket of the bag, Ezra found a small Apple laptop with a charger and a folding cell phone bag that he recognized as a Faraday Pouch from his military time. He wondered if he was supposed to put his phone into this after the synagogue. He continued on feeling frustrated at the lack of prior instruction.

He next found a small notebook journal with a pen, and a paperback book that stated on the front- *"Homework for Your Ayahuasca Journey" by Egle Schon,* as well as another book entitled-*"Stalking the Wild Pendulum: On the Mechanics of Consciousness" by Itzhak Bentov.* Having zero clue of either author, he favored the latter as at least it was written by a Jew rather than a German.

Opening the first side pocket he found two cans of nicotine pouches, a four inch red lens flashlight, and a zip lock that was weighted with currency labeled *"Nuevos Soles"* with reference to the Bank of Peru at the top. Someone was nice enough to provide him with some money up front as he didn't have an ATM card. There was an assortment of denominations as well as Euros and US dollars. The longer side pouch contained a tourniquet, and a black box, unopened, with a company and descriptor he didn't immediately recognize- Baker Forge Karambit. Now he knew why security was uninvolved. He may not recognize the company, but he knew that a karambit was a deadly curved fighting knife He next found an American Passport with his name and an address in New York City, with the same date of birth as the one his father had just given him. A Pelican bottle was attached with a carabiner in the bottle holder pouch on the side. That seemed to be all of the contents. Zipping up the pockets, he looked back to the Rabbi.

"You seem to be missing one quite important pocket, Ezra, turn the bag over."

The Rabbi was making a pancake flipping motion with his hand. He watched EZ flip the bag to its back side. Ezra hadn't noticed the rear, bag length zipper across the rear of the bag. This zipper would clearly be noticed once he threw the bag over his shoulder. Sliding back the zipper, he first noticed two double stack pistol magazines, held to the wall of the bag with circular velcro retentions. The next item was a Heckler and Koch VP9SK pistol.   The gun had an extended grip for his smallest finger, as well as swollen palm grips. Attached to the trigger guard was a plastic tie stating: Customized and Tuned by Cornbread Tactical, NC. Next to the tag he saw what looked like a skillet with various knife and gun shapes. Ezra now knew this was no ordinary Rabbi, but he would need his prayers to get through security now at the airport in Peru. Sensing his uneasiness, as he had seen on so many young men in his Synagogue opening the same bag, with the same items-Malachi eased Ezra with some advice.

"For all of your airport connections, please select the security entrances ALWAYS to the right. Your American passport is also a Diplomatic Passport should there be any other inspections along the way, but your connections as a Diplomat to Israel will not be validated by phone calls, whereas a call to the American Embassy will likely work like magic. Now let's discuss your journey."

"Mr. Barak wished for me to give you the knowledge of what has recently been labeled the Hummus Trail, as it appears more of our fellow Jews are discovering Central and Latin America. Young men and women like yourself receive a nice bonus after their mandatory military service is up. But rather than invest this money, they choose to travel to various destinations around the world-many where you are going, as well as Southeast Asia. Because there are so many Jewish Youth pursuing these travels, they often congregate together. Many even do drugs, sleep with prostitutes, or otherwise explore ideas that they have never had the chance to do in Israel before they return to the Homeland.

"There are a number of particular sites most wish to see

along this Hummus Trail in Peru. The book Mr. Barak has given you will be helpful for those. However, the books I gave to you will be your primary homework for the next two weeks. Memorize all the details, facts, ideas, and names. Try your best to understand the process of what is being mentioned. You will at first tour your choices along the Hummus Trail, a Chabad center will help you in Cusco, but eventually, your final destination will be an Ayahuasca Retreat in what's known as the Sacred Valley. You will head to a town that has a significant Jewish presence for those seeking a stronger connection with God. The town is called Pisac and has a special Chabad there where you will receive your final guidance before the ceremony.

"This Chabad will also enable you to make connections in the Sacred Valley with other young Jews your age, Kosher foods, internet connections, etc. It could be that many may attend the same retreat that you are booked for, so remember your dates and read up on their website. Your new name will appear in most military documents should former veterans look into you, but I think you should be able to adapt your conversations to avoid digging. Just tone down heavy questions with a response that reflects prior trauma from your time in service, and that's why you are here-to get your mind straight with the Ayahuasca. The laptop you are provided will also enable you to read the emailed preparation modules sent by the retreat. I have downloaded the community app so that you can get a feel for what and who you will be around at the retreat."

"OK Malachi. That's quite a lot, but it seems straight forward. Get to Peru, act like I'm just out of military service, perhaps drink with the locals, read all the books in the bag, read the Internet forums, see the sacred sites around Pisac, and don't reveal who I am. Does that sound about right?"   Ezra smiled.

"That seems about right, Ezra. You are a quick study just as

Barak had told me."

"But just one question for you Rabbi. Why is it that I would need to travel with a gun, knife, and a faraday bag? Why would there be a need around what seems to be a Hippie Jewish journey?" Ezra asked.

"Ezra, what you will learn during your time in Peru will show you that you are about to enter into an entire world of mystery that you did not know existed. A world that doesn't play by the rules that you learned in the military. A world in which Israel's enemies would love to enter, and that you must keep safe. What Barak has now entrusted you with cannot be revealed. *Ever.* You will be put through your first test. Trust the journey. Trust the Ayahuasca. Open your heart to these new ideas. But through all, you are a hand picked soldier of the faith. Paranoia and distrust will be needed for you to comprehend what will be happening in your mind. Your first test is the most important one. Will your mind be captured, or will you capture the mind?".

Malachi continued.

"I questioned all of this years ago, just as you have now, and everyone will have a different skill set that will befall them. Who knows? It could be that in your later years, it will be Rabbi Ezra at Ben Gurion helping other Jews preserve our future. A light will be revealed to you Ezra. God will be revealed to you, just as it was revealed to Moses. Hard for you to imagine how something in Peru will change the way you view the world, but this will happen. Now let us pray Ezra. Your Father asked that I do so before your trip." Ezra bowed his head. Malachi followed.

What is this light? Ezra wondered. *Could it be related to the ancient Incan civilizations in Peru? And how was there any way on Earth God could be revealed there and not in Israel?* The Rabbi stood, shook Ezra's hand, and continued on as if nothing had been said. It was time to start the journey. He was curious now. What exactly was Ayahuasca?

<u>Arrival</u>

EZ made the thirty three hour journey on time. He actually enjoyed the books they had given him to study, and it helped having a task to pass the time on his long flights. Even the trip time of thirty three hours seemed somehow symbolic. At least according to one of his books, stating that the number 33 held special meaning to many religious and cult organizations, but certainly, UUONE was no cult. He would never consider something his father had served in as one, let alone the Prime Minister of Israel. But nonetheless, fragments of special numbers and characters he started to take notice of after his readings.

He laid out a plan of the sites he would go to visit, and over what amount of time to achieve them. His notebook was starting to fill with religious sites from this ancient South American country. The comparisons with Egypt's pyramids, architecture, and cave paintings were all eerily similar.

From one book's suggestion, he had used the airline provided headphones to listen to the historian Graham Hancock's podcast comparing these coincidences. DNA linked to Australian lands dated the ancient Incan tribes. Going back thousands of years before the possibility of a Bering Land Bridge crossing would have been possible. He couldn't fathom how his high school textbooks could possibly be wrong. Was he to accept that these ancient peoples had somehow arrived by boat over thirty to one hundred thousand years ago? It all seemed impossible.

From the perfect construction of pyramid like societies

containing thousands of people, to perfect road construction far ahead of its time, the culture there would provide much intrigue, and all was somehow connected through design to the stars, constellations, equinoxes of the summer and winter solstices, and to God's that were replicated in the Middle East and Indian tribes of North America-with no genetic linkages whatsoever.

This Hancock fellow kept linking psychedelics, especially ayahuasca from the Amazonian rain forest, to the ability to have such knowledge and visions. How would these cultures even know how to derive such a special concoction without modern chemistry? And why had the Jewish population chosen only two to three areas within Peru to establish the Chabads? Peru was presenting more questions than answers.

His plane departed Spain and finally reached Lima, where he boarded a much smaller plane for his final destination of Cusco. He was fascinated by the first Peruvian he saw once in the country. Dark, maroon skin, short in stature, deliberate in tasks. The small people were adorned with bright colored clothing, and marketed paintings with tight, geometric shapes containing snakes, serpents, and intricate patterns and swirls. The people seemed connected, at least more so than Israeli's, to nature. Polite. Quieter and slower in their daily tasks, relaxed with the tasks at hand. Much more present and deliberate with listening, as if time was exponential, and to rush would be rude rather than seen as better service. The slowness didn't remind him of laziness, but instead, as a peaceful way to interact with the world. Almost as if the Peruvians knew something he did not.

He noticed his pace started to slow to their's. He felt as if his peripheral vision was expanding and that breaths came a little easier. Being away from the guns, missiles, and war may be a factor EZ also considered. This Hummus Trail might not be so bad after all. His mind could stand to be away from the chaos and division of the Middle East.

<u>Peru</u>

Two weeks was in no way enough time to discover all the wonders of Cusco. Ezra could not understand how a civilization so ancient had accomplished so much. Where did the information come from? Had they taught themselves over thousands of years? Did a lost civilization reveal these intricate techniques? Why were there so many similarities to Egyptian archaeology? Why was astrology so in sync with the Native Americans an entire continent away? How had these cultures created such precise calendars with no instruments?

He had concentrated on his Peru tour book focusing on sites to visit in Cusco. First on his list was the site most well known to the world, Machu Picchu, perhaps the most important archaeological site of the Americas which served as the heart of the ancient Incan spiritual empire. In the native language, he had learned that Cusco's translation came from the Quechua word Qosqo, meaning navel of the world, or the center of the Universe. From his perspective, the mystic nature of Machu Picchu felt as if it was used either for religious ceremonies or as a type of altar to the Gods of the sky. From his readings, he learned that this site had not been discovered by Westerners until 1911, by Hiram Bingham, and soon after became one of the Seven Wonders of the World.

Tour guides at the site presented that this was no religious site at all, but rather a summer home to the Incan Emperors to escape the summer heat. Whatever the case of its origin, Machu Picchu was vastly impressive.

At almost 8,000 feet, the landmark rose high above the valley of the Amazonian jungle. Without the use of mortar to connect the stones, which fit together with laser like precision, it towered above the Sacred Valley and was referred to as the Lost City of the Incas since its rather modern discovery. Believed to have been built around the 1400s-1500s, historians explained that it was abandoned as a royal summer retreat when the Spanish invaded and brought the societal devastation called smallpox. Rows and rows of terraces, called andenes, graced the side of the plateau around the structure, which were used for irrigation and farming.

Continuing on his self tour, he took a three hour bus ride to Rainbow Mountain. At 17,000 feet, he worried about altitude sickness and had purchased Diamox before departing Cusco, just in case he couldn't adjust to the elevation. There were no oxygen canisters available, but he figured he was in good shape from his military training.

The natives referred to Rainbow Mountain as Vinicunca and Montana Arcoiris, Rainbow Mountain. Seven colors were glowing across its elevation. Reds, greens, browns, whites, yellows, pinks, and purples. The levels of color were the result of contrasting layers of different minerals-oxides, silicates, muds, clays, manganese, copper, and more. He noticed that many of the colors he adored in Peruvian clothing and artwork arguably could have been inspired by Rainbow Mountain. From the deep greens of the Amazonian rain forest to the hues of the Andes, Peru held a painter's palate.

In between sight seeing excursions, Ezra attended Shabbat at the Chabad in Cusco. And just as he had been forewarned, many of the Jewish post-military hikers were planning on attending various Sacred Valley Ayahuasca ceremonies. With many different retreat choices, Ezra listened keenly to the similarities and differences of the retreats. Some priced too high and for celebrities, while some featured inadequate air conditioning or amenities. Many felt that Non Peruvian maestros and ceremonial leaders would be inauthentic while others had been led by word of mouth or social media.

Through his Ayahuasca Retreat prep literature, he was starting to attune to the lingo used to describe the ritualistic experience. Some hikers had attended multiple ceremonies, and now were returning for more. Traumas were healed, bad memories erased, and physical injuries had all vanished through this magical medicine lovingly referred to as Mother Ayahuasca. Always referred to in the feminine, she was said to hold magical powers. Page by page, he continued through his journal as he conversed and made connection after connection, using his prior military trauma to connect with other veterans as an excuse for attendance.

Being able to enjoy his own religion, food, and language at the Chabads was intoxicating. Ezra could see how the Hummus Trail was an addicting travel experience. One alluring aspect was with safety in numbers. There were always cultures that hated the Jews, but the Peruvians seemed to accept all with equal regard, allowing the secrets of their own spiritual past to be absorbed without judgement of one's current beliefs. Accept us for who we are, and we will in turn accept you.

As an ancient people, the Incas worshipped Inti, the Sun God, as the center of their Universe. Quilla-the moon Goddess, Viracocha-the creator God, Illapa-the rain God, and Pachamama-the Earth Mother God. Cusco was the center of all worship around these Gods. Ezra's last visit was to the Qorikancha-Temple of the Sun, the most sacred of Incan temples. At one point, the temple held over 4,000 priests within its solid gold covered walls. Shrines to the sun, moon, weather, and stars were all connected to this one temple.

The fascinating interlocking stone that Ezra witnessed at

Machu Picchu was also present at Qorikancha. He could only imagine how the Temple would have appeared before the Spanish conquest that confiscated much of the gold from the temple's walls and stole much of the perfectly carved stone to erect the Santo Domingo Convent. The stone was known to be so geometrically interlocking and durable that even large earthquakes had been unable to cause destruction.

The buildings in modern cities weren't earthquake proof. Ezra's mind continued to wonder at how such knowledge could have been attained, as no methods in existence today could replicate the stone wall's construction.

Ezra's journey continued daily to more sacred locations of the Inca: Saqsaywam, Tambomachay, Q'enco, and lastly viewing the Twelve Angled Stone, which was now placed at the palace of the Archbishop of Cusco on what was called the Hatun Rumiyoc. The stone was rumored to be the representation of twenty four families-twelve from the Hurin dynasty and twelve from the Hanan dynasty. Incan stones were famous for ashlar masonry that used hammers, chisels, sand, and rope levers to build to the millimeter, almost unthinkable for tools of that age.

From Chabad to Incan architecture, Peruvians to native mysticism, from Israeli drug infused raves to ancient ceremonial reenactments, Ezra tirelessly absorbed as much as possible over his two weeks. Laying in bed, reading about his pre ceremony diet, ayahuasca's organic structure, astrology, all while reading sacred Hebrew texts. Many were even bringing to topic the Kabbalah, which Ezra knew he wasn't supposed to read until age thirty three according to his Rabbi. But Kabbalah seemed to make more sense among this ancient culture than the traditional Torah.

He was in a mystic Incan heaven. Lost amongst the colorful people, the color filled landscapes, the Salvador Dali-like

animals such as llamas, alpacas, and ocelots. Ezra always smiled
at his Chabad's favorite animal reference-the Kinkajou.
Someone had even created an off spin sticker around the
Chabad. In big letters, it stated KinkyJew, with a picture of
Jeffrey Epstein's head attached to a kinkajou devilishly smiling
in a yarmkule.

He missed the dry Jewish humor of his old military unit and
found hope in hearing the other hikers describe ayahuasca's
ability to forgive, both one's self as well as those who have
caused harm in the past.

Maybe this was the Mother he never had. Maybe Mother
Ayahuasca would listen to his struggles. Perhaps she would
provide guidance as to what exactly he was to do for UUONE.
For now, he did as he had been instructed. Read, observe, fit in,
and remain healthy. His two weeks were coming to an end, and
it was time to depart for his retreat.

<u>Operation Northwoods</u>

General Lyman Lemnitzer sat in the briefing room at the
U.S. Joint Chief of Staff Office and pondered his options on what
to do with the current situation in Cuba. As Chairman, he knew
that Fidel Castro's takeover in Cuba three years earlier was not
making President Kennedy, his boss, look forward to press
briefings.

The Bay of Pigs disaster had also occurred under his watch,
but that had been for a much different President, Eisenhower, a
true military commander with a sense of authority and strategic
planning. Kennedy was a new kind of military man. A Vietnam
era Catholic Army man, whose interactions with the hippies and
the popular culture sometimes seemed more important than the
task at hand. Eisenhower was old school. Kennedy was the new

school. The former World War Two and Korean commandants were now growing grey or passing away. Replacements would soon lead to a shift in powers and strategy.

Being that the Bay of Pigs fiasco had embarrassed the entire United States government, Kennedy had tasked him, as well as the entire Pentagon, with developing a new plan to defeat and rid Cuba of the popular Communist hero, Fidel Castro, who was held in supreme Communist status with his defeat of the American CIA led invasion into his homeland. Lemnitzer's team had come up with quite the plan indeed.

In order to win support of the American people against Castro, he would have to steer the media and the populace to believe that the Cubans were committing terrorist acts against U.S. citizens on American soil. Once the three big television networks broadcasted nonstop stories that his department would kindly distribute, Americans would be begging for an invasion against Castro. Multiple false flags occurring at multiple locations, and too many to ever have been achieved by the CIA. The American people would need someone to blame.

With the support of every branch of the Armed Forces, the Joint Chiefs had invented a plan, Operation Northwoods. The first operation would be to place CIA operatives on a commercial U.S. jetliner, and while in the air, swap the plane out with an empty remote controlled jet making it appear as if a Cuban MIG fighter plane had shot down the aircraft. In the meantime, the original plane would be landing secretly at Eglin Air Force Base in Florida with the general public none the wiser.

If this failed to work, plans had been developed to make it appear as if Cubans had played a role in the failure of NASA's third space launch or even in astronaut John Glenn's death. Attacking the American base at Guantanamo Bay, killing our own troops, and also paying for a coup using US tax dollars were also on the table. Whatever tactics it took for the Joint Chief Chairman to defeat Castro, he was ready to deploy. Sometimes a few innocent people had to die to keep the industrial machine running.

Operation Northwoods fell under a bigger plan called Operation Mongoose. The CIA, Pentagon, and all heads of the military were coordinating covert actions to achieve the President's goals of freeing the Cuban people from the hands of Castro's Communism. 1962 could possibly be a much better year for his career than eleven months earlier with the Bay of Pigs. It was time to push for his next step up the ladder in Washington D.C. In all likelihood, if Operation Northwoods pushed the narrative to invade and destroy Cuba, he might possibly have a chance at the Presidency. He would have the support of the CIA, media, and military.

There were no current Generals with his long tenured record. He knew Kennedy was not fond of the CIA after the Bay of Pigs incident, and he also knew that the CIA was equally not fond of Kennedy's portrayal of the infamous intelligence branch. Kennedy was also openly calling for CIA cuts and demotions. What Kennedy didn't know was that the CIA was what really controlled the United States. If there was such a thing as a deep state government, then the CIA was as deep as one could dig. Now was the time to sell this to the President. This final visit to the White House would determine what so many had worked so hard to envision.

He sipped his coffee as he headed towards the Oval Office and wondered how much longer the President would make him wait, when he heard a door open to his left.

"Good morning Mr. President. How are you on this fine March day?" Lemnitzer asked as he snapped to attention outside the Oval Office.

"Please come in and sit, General. What have you and the boys come up with to help me get rid of this Cuban bastard?" President Kennedy stated with anything but a smile. He was sick of Castro's arrogance since the Bay of Pigs.

"Sir, I have prepared a simple outline of Operation Mongoose as well as Operation Northwoods for you here."

Lemnitzer passed over a folder that held several outlines, photos, and numerical projections about success for the mission. The nation's best agents had an untold number of man hours inside that folder. He held his breath as Kennedy read through the first two pages outlining in the simplest of terms what was to be done to entrap the Cubans.

"There is no fucking way I will ever order the attack of my own military bases, an American astronaut, or the downing of an American passenger plane. You guys are out of your fucking minds. I have already had to deal with one embarrassment, and that wasn't even an idea from my administration. Get the fuck out of my office. Come back when you have something that doesn't get me assassinated." Kennedy screamed.

Kennedy threw the folder at the General, sat into his chair, and spun around to look out his Oval Office window.

"Unfucking believable," he muttered.

Lemnitzer took the folder and walked out of the office revealing little expression. He had served as a General in three wars, and he knew that soon he would serve in another, regardless of what Kennedy had to say. He knew who ran D.C., and this wasn't the first time he had been turned down in the Oval Office. He headed back to his office and picked up the phone. He had two phone calls to make.

"Director Dulles, I know you are currently not the acting director, but I thought you should know. We are a No Go for our Operations."

Lemnitzer had respected the old school Dulles, placed in office by Eisenhower, both old school boys. Able to get things done, no matter the risks.

"OK Lyman. Thanks for letting me know. I'll continue with our second option. Please let Director McCone know."

Allen Dulles, the former director of CIA, and a close friend of Lemnitzer, replied. He had only recently resigned. Lemnitzer knew that he still was running the show for the time being as the transition occurred to the new director John McCone. Eisenhower had placed Dulles at the head of the CIA for a reason, the old school could get the job done. And not only had he positioned Dulles to take on the new threats from Russia, but he had also placed his brother John Dulles into the position of Secretary of State. This enabled Eisenhower to not only control the intelligence apparatus of the United States, but also the arm of the Executive Branch. Eisenhower understood that when the OSS was shut down after World War Two, and the CIA was formed, that long term goals of the country could not be threatened by the new school guys like the Kennedy's.

"Will do Allen."

He touched his finger to the phone base, hanging up, and dialed the second number from his secured, unrecorded line. Lemnitzer cleared his voice before he addressed his other close friend. "Bob. Kennedy has not gone for Operation Northwoods, I thought you might want to know immediately."

Robert McNamara's appointment to Secretary of Defense by Kennedy had been good news to him, as they both had similar career aspirations, and that's how you achieved things in D.C. where everyone was out for themselves.

"Lyman. Proceed as planned. Please let Dulles know if you haven't already. Our time has come to use our backup plan. You and I both know that we cannot let one man hold up an entire country's long range goals. Ensure that Bentov's U.S. citizenship is expedited by McCone. It's important that we also continue to watch the work of Gottlieb without drawing media attention."

"Secretary, would you like me to inform Sidney Gottlieb at MKUltra of this news?" Lemnitzer asked.

"Let Dulles call that freak. It was his idea to use Gottlieb almost a decade ago, and those two are not only physically disabled, but mentally disabled as well. That's his baby. If it fails or gets discovered, that's on Allen, not us. We all need deniability about what may transpire. Project Artichoke is turning into Project Fartachoke. I'm tired of giving this program any more attention. Either Bentov's ideas turn this around, or his theories are worthless. Bring him in as a citizen, watch him like a hawk, and see where his ideas take us. We don't have much time before all of this will get exposed, and then it will be up to a future director to think of a way to carry out an end to Communism. Thanks for the call."

McNamara ended the call. Lemnetzir had his approval to proceed.

Whatever this MKUltra plan was, it was highly classified and very few knew of its size. The budget was huge by CIA standards, and the Kennedy administration may not give it much of a go if they really knew what it entailed. It was causing as much damage to Americans as Operation Northwoods may have, but the administration didn't need to know that. He knew a plan of that size would eventually be exposed-too many egos and cogs in the wheel.

Just who was this Itzhak Bentov anyway? Lemnitzer thought.

He decided it was time for him to find out. It was risky looking into Israeli citizens, but today, Bentov would become a

U.S. citizen, and that meant he could now look freely, and legally, for the safety of America's future. Tomorrow, he promised himself to commit more investigation into this MKUltra Project. After all, there was to be no more Operation Northwoods, and he knew Kennedy's play on the CIA's plans wouldn't go well in the future. One could only decline that agency's ideas so many times before some form of retribution. If the CIA didn't get its way, there was no telling what they were liable to do. Lemnitzer reviewed what little he had on Bentov.

The CIA had been closely following this Bentov scientist since the British had departed Israel in 1948. Being a scientist for Hemmed, the Israeli Science Corps, Bentov had been at the forefront of numerous Israeli inventions such as the Loretta and Hollow Charges, weapons used to disable military vehicles during the attack by Egypt that same year. More importantly, Bentov had created the first Israeli rocket. With so many bright minds left in such a small country, the United States had been sure to keep an eye on what these new scientists could develop. After all, it was the best Jewish minds who had developed the atomic bomb.

Bacterial warfare was also being developed for use against Acre and Gaza. Lemnitzer knew of this secret project through his sources as Operation Cast Thy Bread. Israel's secret IDF mission would have violated the 1925 Geneva Protocols, and that was something the United States could not afford to have happen in a country they were partially responsible for creating. Instilling typhoid into the occupied Gazan wells was not an original concept, and although disgusting to him, he understood that the United States had used similar practices in its history. Bentov might even have knowledge of this covert act. Who was he to judge? He had just presented false flag attacks to the sitting U.S. President.

However, a scientist with the ability to create rockets on a limited budget just may prove useful, and since the Operation Paperclip new hires from Nazi Germany were creating numerous new jobs and technologies around the country, proof of the effectiveness of foreign scientist recruitment or abduction maintained value to the administration. They had kept a close eye on this gentleman since his arrival into the United States in 1954, and now it was time to offer him the wealth and a new start inside the world's greatest nuclear power. Not only could he be relevant in the laboratory, but it was Bentov's other theories that Lemnitzer relished. Bentov was now the leading scientist on human consciousness and mind control.

With only a handful aware of Project MKUltra, fresh ideas may reap huge rewards for the advancement of the most secret project against the Russians. This may not happen during his tenure, but at some point, under perhaps a different administration, they would make use of controlling the minds of the enemy. Project Artichoke's goal was to develop a Manchurian candidate, a soldier brainwashed to commit an assassination. What started as Operation Bluebird,

Artichoke had developed into an even bigger project, MKUltra. The CIA had evidence that the Russians were now in a race with the United States, much like they were with nuclear technology, to discover the ability to control the human mind.

Bentov had already opened a makeshift laboratory in Belmont, Massachusetts, and he was hired relatively quickly after his arrival to work for the Arthur D. Little think tank in Cambridge, Massachusetts. The think tank was known to be involved in the hiring of prior military and civilian minds in the development or management of biological and chemical weapons, laser technology, computer technology, oil and gas technology, aerospace, industrial products, telecommunications, or just about anything else that somehow might affect the future security and prosperity of the United States. What was developed for commercial use may also serve the military for more profits.

Lemnitzer wondered if Bentov had provided knowledge to the think tank from his rocket research, or God help him, Operation Cast Thy Bread bacterial weapon technology. The Arthur D. Little think tank only hired the brightest and most imaginative, so if they recruited Bentov, he was the type of scientist that might be able to push MKUltra's success.

Lemnitzer picked up the phone once again and dialed Allen Dulles.

"Allen, the Secretary has asked that you contact Gottlieb. Bentov is a go. Godspeed to us all."

Hanging up the phone, he wondered if someone could actually control his mind. He just didn't think it was possible, but then again, no one thought two bombs could end a war and the lives of over 200,000 people.

<u>Homework</u>

Around two weeks prior to his arrival at the Ayahuasca retreat, EZ had been asked to do several things by the retreat. The first was an intake phone interview. During the interview, it was to be decided if he was a good psychological candidate for the process as well as to check on his health history for any potential medications that might be contraindicated. Since UUONE had not said otherwise, he answered honestly during the interview and felt he could reveal much of his psychological and physical past. Since he was on no medication, this part of the interview went quickly.

The mental health questions focused on trauma from his

past, current life perspectives, and his attitude toward alternative plant medicines. He described stories from home, including war, death of his fellow teammates, struggles in childhood, his mother's depression, growing up relatively poor, and added, although untrue to some extent, that he was having difficulty finding meaning in today's current political climate. It almost felt like the interviewer was guiding him along a path to saying what they wished to hear with the interviewer providing rationale for his need to attend. He had sent in his medical forms by email prior to the phone call, so they now had a complete mental and physical evaluation of him to work with. All of this was provided to them of his own free will and consent. He had signed the release of medical information and injury forms that were necessary to proceed with the phone call.

A plan would be sent to his email soon which would include all of the goals, diet, and homework that should be done prior to his arrival. At the end of the phone call, he was told that he had the green light on registering for his flight, hotels, and where he could pay by credit card. The facility would require him to obtain emergency health insurance for his visit, and this travel insurance would have to be presented at time of arrival. Should he fail to present proof of this insurance, he would not be allowed to attend. He now was rubber stamped and cleared. It was now on him to do his research with materials sent, follow the diet, exercise, discuss his trip with family, and most importantly, complete all audio, video, and written assignments that would soon be sent to him after his interview. The possibility of dying during the ceremony had been repeated three times during his call.

As promised after his initial payment, the last of which, $1,000, needed to be at time of arrival in new, crisp bills, a very well done series of documents, references, exercises, and videos were emailed. EZ worked on this at night during his Peru excursions. He also questioned as many of the Israelis he met along the way about their experiences with the medicine. Many described heroic life altering changes to their lives while some felt as if they did not get out of it the miracles and visions that others had.

The coursework seemed to describe the same, and to understand that this was an adjustment process. Not all people would experience profound relief from trauma. Regardless of outcome, just by signing up, he would be starting the path to a better understanding of himself and the Universe. Mother Ayahuasca, as the medicine was lovingly called, had already spoken to him, just by signing up for the course. She would guide him. She was far smarter than he knew, and this would be revealed to him through ceremony.

His welcome email included all travel instructions, what to pack for the Amazon jungle, and a link to his homework. Since he was already in Peru, he noted where his bus pickup would be and who to meet. The packing list was quite extensive. It included clothing, shoes, jackets, sunscreen, notebooks, pens, and copies of his passports and medical insurance. Items that were in bold he observed were a strict requirement for the ceremony, including a red LED light, a lighter for smoking mapacho tobacco, and bug spray. He logged onto Amazon and purchased the recommended items to be sent to his hostel address in Cusco, hoping it would arrive on time.

The first part of his homework went into great detail on the chemical components of ayahuasca, its composition, and the pharmacokinetics of its effects on the brain, including why and what current medications would be dangerous related to its ingestion. EZ had heard many of the words and terminology used at the Chabad, but did his best to try and comprehend the science. The ayahuasca brew that he would be ingesting at the ceremony was composed of two naturally occurring compounds, both being found naturally in the Amazonian rain forest basin.

Banissteriopsis Caapi, Ayahuasca, was an alkaloid compound that inhibited the body's uptake of monoamine oxidase. In modern medical pills, these types of drugs were known as MAOIsMonoamine Oxidase Inhibitors and were used to treat depression and bipolar diseases. The second compound of the brew was Psychotria viridis, Charcruna. The main compound of this root was DMT, or N-N-dimethyltryptamine, the actual psychedelic within the concoction. He was informed that both were needed to produce a journey.

MAO was an enzyme responsible for degrading organic structures which held an amine group. This structure was found in monoamine neurotransmitters within the body as well as in certain foods. An MAOI would keep the body from being able to break down amine groups, resulting in an increase in MAO at receptor sites. Foods containing tyramine were therefore a concern when using an inhibitor as toxicity could occur. The MAO was also important for the regulation of the neurotransmitters serotonin, norepinephrine, and dopamine.

DMT was far different. It was what was termed an entheogen. An entheogen could invoke the feelings of God. DMT was metabolized by MAO. The brew's magic necessitated both chemicals. In order for the DMT to work after both were absorbed in the intestines, the MAOI needed to block DMT's uptake by the liver so that it could reach the brain for a psychoactive effect to occur. Whomever discovered this thousands of years ago was one of the greatest mysteries of the Amazon. To take the DMT on its own would do nothing, but combine them, and that's where medicine men were born. Although DMT was produced naturally in the body, it was not to the levels where the Universe would be revealed.

The involvement of MAO and MAOI's is where many of the health risks could evolve. Because MAO was needed to metabolize norepinephrine, dopamine, serotonin, and tyramine, to ingest the Charcruna might pose a risk of increased levels of any or all of these four chemicals.

EZ read through these significant dangers, including Serotonin Syndrome and TyramineMediated Hypertensive Crisis. Symptoms ranged from agitation, fever, increased blood pressure and heart rate, to psychosis and death. The medical history interview now made sense. Many of the people coming to the retreat were already taking SSRI's, Selective Serotonin Re Uptake Inhibitors, as well as MAOI's.

Ayahuasca retreats provided a means of plant medicine to hopefully make life long changes and rid the need of lifelong antidepressant medications. Many of the attendees wished to stop their lifelong dependence on pharmaceuticals. To not have a client stop their medications, especially these types, would be a catastrophe, and hence, why they were being so strict on presenting health insurance. EZ knew people didn't like to give up their drugs, especially the Americans who were so dependent on them. The possibility of overcoming past traumas without the need of prolonged medication was enticing to many of the participants.

Foods also posed a problem according to the notes. Fermented foods, such as aged cheeses and yogurt, milk, beer, chianti, vermouth, aged meats, preserved meats, sauerkraut, fava beans, soy sauce, tofu, miso soups, chocolates, yeasts, avocado, kombucha, and certain fruits were to be avoided prior to the camp. These were to be stopped one week prior and after the ceremonies due to their abilities to increase MAO.

Since the brew contained MAOIs, any increase through

these foods may lead to a hypertensive crisis through their effects on the sympathetic chemicals norepinephrine and dopamine. The possibility of a hypertensive crisis, internal bleeding, seizures, and stroke did not go unnoticed to him. Just what was UUONE expecting him to go through? With this fear, he turned to the page describing what diet was recommended and decided to pay a little more attention to lunch that day.

It appeared to be a diet that he was already following in Peru, maybe since he was traveling where the brew was created helped. They recommended a diet high in root vegetables, potatoes, yucca, spinach, cauliflower, kale, grains, rice, oats, beans, nuts, seeds, and olive oil. For protein, he was encouraged to eat chicken, fish, and eggs.

It was also recommended to avoid alcohol. Nicotine would be used in ceremony and could be continued, but harder drugs were revealed to also be lethal if continued for his journeys, including cocaine, amphetamines, lithium, ephedra, and MDMA. The list went on with drugs, foods, and chemicals he had never heard of before.

His homework also included over twenty lessons with timelines on diet and medications, and a plethora of other helpful items for before, during, and after the ceremonies. Questions he should ponder about his life, strategies to interpret his visions, exercises like yoga to get the body moving, descriptions about his ego and awareness, setting his goals for the ceremonies, how to avoid a bad trip, music selection for pre and post ceremony, and lastly, an enormous section on interpreting what was experienced under the medication. The spectrum of nothing happening to being overwhelmed was all covered.

The section on adapting to his return to family he did not read, as his family was now UUONE, and they had promised to take care of him for life.

Everything under the sun was covered in great detail. He listened to the audio and watched the videos. Took notes and did as much as time allowed as he toured Peru. Whatever this ayahuasca was, it was more serious than he imagined. He only hoped not to suffer a stroke, or some life long psychosis that many of the youth at the hostel described. He had been through worse in his combat in Israel, so he thought many were over exaggerating. He was healthy, on no medications, and already ate well.

If nothing else, he hoped to gain information that would make him more valuable to UUONE. After all, they were the ones telling him he had to go.

Camp Guides

EZ boarded his bus in downtown Cusco. He said goodbye to the beautiful elevation of the Peruvian mountains and headed to a plane back to Lima. From there, he started his long prearranged bus journey from Lima to the remote Amazonian town of Pucallpa on the Ucayali River. He was told to stay at a hostel and be ready at eight the following morning to venture by boat further into the depths of the Amazon. EZ loved Peru. It's people. It's food. He now would get to see the famed Amazon jungles to its east. His final destination would take another half day to the village of Bello Horizonte. While the majority of the other Chabad attendees were going to retreats within the Sacred Valley, they were all quite envious of the "real" retreat EZ was getting to attend.

The next morning, EZ went to the river's departure area and met his travel guide. The river's brown water changed from extremely shallow to deep and wide. Navigating a tiny canoe, the local Peruvian villager seemed to know which channels to follow as they changed frequently with constant flooding and heavy rains. A tiny, gas powered motor propelled EZ and three of the other attendees northward where they soon parked on a sandy outlet. The villager pointed towards their bags and to a trail bordering a stream.

"Vaya aqua." He said.

They needed no translation. A small sign in Spanish labeled the trailhead, and it was the same from his emails. *Retroceso del Pendulo*. The four grabbed their belongings as they heard the other two boats arrive behind them. It looked to be a total of twelve in attendance with the group almost evenly split with women and men.

They had all stayed at the same hostel the night before and had gotten the opportunity to get to know one another. A representative was present from Pendulo to make the Amazon a bit more welcoming. The backgrounds of those attending were a diverse collection from many parts of the world. The United States and Europe made up the bulk of the clients with EZ being the lone representative from Israel. Mosquitoes and rain kept them confined to a shared, netted space where a meal of chicken, rice, beans, and plantains was provided. As they got to know one another, the commonality of this shared journey became more relevant.

Many were going through the same difficulties. War, divorce, abuse, depression, and various stories of trauma were told after dinner around an introductory campfire. A few had been to the retreat multiple times, describing profound life changes. EZ couldn't help but wonder if the medicine was so effective and life changing, why repeat visits would be necessary, especially with the costs involved. Ayahuasca retreats were not for the poor.

As he emerged from the trail, a series of small wooden huts

presented themselves around a large ceremonial area which was termed the maloca. The building was in the shape of a large cone. Its roof covered in straw, mosquito screens forming a circle around the posts supporting the roof. In the distance, closer to the stream, he saw another set of buildings likely for the staff. Gas powered generators could be heard further into the distance which seemed to provide electricity for cooking, lights, and what appeared to be WiFi boosters hanging high in the canopy.

They were each issued a numbered hut and told to meet at the maloca for their initial class, rules, and further instruction. EZ walked to the closest of the huts, almost adjoining the maloca. Since routes of escape were zero in the Amazon, no keys were issued, and other than passports, no one had anything of real value to lock in their new homes. The hut was raised off of the soil to prevent water, snakes, and jungle guests from making a visit.

One pipe containing a thick electrical wire could be seen entering the bottom of the structure. On the inside, he noticed one outlet, a fan, small desk, armoire, bed table, and a single bed-surrounded with mosquito netting hung from the ceiling above. Plugged into the one electrical outlet, a walkie talkie and a small lamp. Simplistic Amazonian living at its best.

He unpacked his clothes, played with the walkie talkie, insured the fan worked, and went through the rest of his belongings before he headed up to the maloca. Gravel and concrete blocks formed paths throughout the compound's trafficked areas.

Arriving at the maloca, he was greeted by a short Peruvian who maintained a constant smile and beamed with happiness. He spoke English and instructed EZ to remove his shoes, then directed him to find a spot among a circle of back-jack floor chairs. While shaded from the intermittent sun, the maloca was humid and hot. Three staff were seated in the middle in front of twelve pens, notebooks, and what looked like ashtrays.

Around the edge of the maloca, under the meshed screens used as windows, were twelve single size mattresses, each with a single pillow, and something he found quite humorous at the time, the famed purging bucket. Through his conversations and reading, ayahuasca had a quite famous reputation for inducing vomiting, and if one were lucky enough, diarrhea. He looked back towards the door and was relieved to see a covered walkway which traversed to a set of nearby latrines

The twelve arrived in spurts with some taking longer than others. Many were taking as many photos as possible of the experience, likely for their social media, where it seemed the biggest celebrities had all recently gone on an ayahuasca retreat. Many attended the more luxurious air conditioned facilities in Costa Rica where reliable air conditioning and airports could be found. UUONE seemed to have found a retreat as far away as possible, probably wanting him to have more of a true Amazonian experience he thought.

Since EZ's job involved intelligence, it was his duty to note the layout of the camp, Escape routes, number of staff, water and food sources, and before him now, the instructors, which were the most interesting of all. They sat in front of the group. One male with short cropped brown hair, smoking a cigar, whispering to the other two females. He appeared in shape, almost military like. The two females were both very thin, but in perfect shape. They reminded him of the typical physique found in those that eat too well and practice too much yoga.

The three observed each of the students as they entered the maloca. Studying each individual, saying little. Perhaps reserving judgement from their health forms that they had already been presented weeks ago. He had taught many classes in the past, so he had been in their shoes before, and he knew teachers would always discuss their students. Once settled, the first to speak was the cross legged blonde on his left.

"Good morning everyone. How was your trip? Hopefully, you all arrived comfortably. We know you are anxious, but glad to be here. Let me introduce myself. My name is Kristin. I am one of the facilitators here at Pendulo. I have been here for over ten years, and I look forward to working with each of you on your journeys this week. I'm from Florida originally but have made Peru my home country for the last five years. Welcome."

She had mysterious, troubled blue eyes, and spoke with a voice just heard above the generators in the distance. He felt as if he had to lean in to hear what she was saying. He wondered if this was intentional, instilling a sense of calm over all of their anxieties. After an uncomfortable pause, the next teacher spoke.

"Hello everyone, I'm Daniel. From the accent I'm sure you hear a bit of Ireland. Dublin is my home. I am also one of your facilitators for the week. I work full time in biochemistry at Trinity College back home, and when free, come here to be near Mother Ayahuasca. I look forward to helping each of you this week."

His introduction was paused by the near continual smoking of a cigar. Large swaths of smoke that neither of the two women seemed to mind. His mannerisms seemed like that of a professor, but with a more sinister degree of sarcastic tone. EZ would have to watch this one further. He had no idea why he should be suspicious, but then he remembered that UUONE had sent him here for a reason, and that reason remained a secret.

"Hello," a European English accent began, "My name is Hanna. I am from Salzburg, Austria. I have dedicated much of the last few years of my life to the study of plant medicine. I currently live in Lima, so that I can access the airport to get back to Austria as well as fly to the Sacred Valley near Cusco. I am excited to be here and see what magic occurs for each of you in this mystical jungle."

Quietly eloquent, she spoke with purpose, but seemed to have a more motherly sense than the other two. He could already tell that she would be a good listener and that she was the most patient of the three, especially as she was downwind from Daniel's cigar smoke. There was almost no airflow in the maloca, and she appeared to not mind the fog that now surrounded her. Kristin continued.

"We are here for introductions, to lay out your schedule for the week, provide rules, and then to help you through our first exercise before tonight's ceremony. Who here knows what Vomitivo is?".

EZ heard a few groans in the crowd, as he too recalled what this was from his homework. An intentional purging of the stomach with forced ingestion of copious amounts of lemongrass tea. They would have to rapidly drink the tea until vomiting, then remain without food until the ceremony.

Described as a cleansing process for the medicine, he wondered if it was a test of some kind. Many would feel too embarrassed to vomit during ceremonies around strangers. Some may have a physical inability to purge, like those with a paraesophageal hernia, their stomachs literally in their chests. Whatever the case, they would have to do it as a group, and no one could proceed with a ceremony until they had been cleansed.

The session continued until a break was announced. Side groups were formed. Intentions, science, goals, fears, and questions addressed until they all went outside for the Vomitivo. It took him eight large cups of the lemongrass tea before Daniel told him to put his finger in the back of his throat. An immediate reservoir of tea spurted into the grass outside the maloca. Each student was cheered on by the other eleven until the Vomitivo was complete. Everyone had survived. If nothing else, it seemed to bond the group through universal suffering.

"You may all now head back to your huts, and rest before tonight's ceremony. Remember to bring a scarf, toilet paper, a lighter, your journal, pen, and most importantly, your red LED flashlight. You won't want to ruin your night vision when you go to the bathroom tonight." Hanna informed them.

As she finished the class, EZ looked at his classmates and then on to the instructors. The women were organizing the mattresses for the evening, placing them an exact distance apart around the wall of the circle. Daniel had stepped to the side, staring out into the jungle. The red tip of his cigar glowing with each puff.

EZ's sixth sense kicked his gut. His street level instincts on alert. There was something more to the Irish instructor. He could feel something out of place. His senses never lied to him, and neither had those at UUONE. He knew his mission would involve Daniel.

Heading back to his hut, the jungle was loud with the sounds of its monkeys, birds, insects, and reptiles. He could hear them calling out to each other across the night. Leaves rustling as unseen creatures crawled across the canopied floor. Laying upon the bed in the small hut, he closed his eyes and focused on the sounds of the jungle. Falling into a deep sleep, resting before tonight's ceremony.

MKUltra

Sidney Gottlieb didn't feel all that blessed by God. He

stuttered, had a club foot, and because of the latter, was turned down for military service when all the men around him were headed off to perform acts of heroism in Europe. Three surgeries had not helped his foot, and the teasing throughout his school years only added to his suffering. But those days were long ago. Jewish kids in the Bronx were known for overcoming challenges, finding success one way or the other in the tough neighborhood.

He had found his own way to serve his country. The knowledge of a special kind of warfare was now tasked by one of his heroes-Allen Dulles-who also happened to have a club foot. Dulles seemed to understand what Sidney had endured with his disability. The constant jokes, bullying, and harassment of peers. Dulles had experienced the same degradation throughout his life, and so it was through this shared understanding that a new form of service would be found. What others could achieve physically, they would do mentally.

His agricultural degrees were what his country valued now. While his parents had immigrated away from Hungary as Orthodox Jews, he could not seem to find any spiritual relevance in the Jewish faith. His parents had been less than thrilled about his wife's Presbyterian roots and marrying outside the faith was frowned upon. Mr. Dulles had seen his worth, and that was all the faith he needed going forward. All the hard work, all of the nights practicing chemistry, meaningless experiments, were now being rewarded.

He was to be awarded by Dulles an untraceable, unlimited budget to accomplish one task, to develop mind control to defeat America's enemies.

Dulles informed him that the Soviets already possessed the technology. The CIA was capable of infiltrating the thickest forests of Communism. It wasn't possible for an all knowing Dulles to be wrong, and if these Russian imbeciles could do it, so could the greatest minds of the United States. After all, the top scientists in the United States now had even better resources thanks to Operation Paperclip.

With the approval of President Truman after World War Two, General Eisenhower, on April 26, 1946, with an order from the Joint Chiefs of Staff, was instructed to confiscate any and all German scientific journals, lab studies, and papers related to the Nazi's military research efforts. Not only was the science and materials to be brought back from the defeated Germans, but also the scientists who had conducted it. There was now a new military goal, and that was to insure that Stalin didn't win the intelligence, arms, and nuclear race, and so, Operation Paperclip began. Germany prior to World War Two had the most advanced scientists and Universities in the world. A University seat in Germany guaranteed working around the brightest minds-no matter the field. Chemistry, biology, physics, rockets, aviation, math, engineering, and psychology-the subject did not matter. Germany was the ultimate home base of all the brightest minds, and for many of those minds, Sidney was now granted privileged access thanks to Paperclip.

President Eisenhower had enforced the bill militarily, and now was insuring it executively. No one in United States history had been given what Sidney Gottlieb was given, and since he had never been given any power in his lifetime, this disabled, poor Jewish kid from the Bronx would not let Mr. Dulles down.

Sidney had been briefed on the history of MKUltra. Going as far back as the concentration camps of Dachau and Auschwitz in Hitler occupied Germany. Nazi's had been interested in using various drugs and torture techniques to break the will of prisoners as well as instill involuntary mental suggestions, such as assassinate political enemies. Barbiturates, mescaline, and other narcotics were given to prisoners, without consent, to research the effects on temperament and decision making. The search for a truth serum would be a powerful tool in time of war, and the ability to control a subject's mind to perform devious acts of the state, with deniability, was also seen as worthy of funding.

The United States began experiments in 1943 through the Office of Strategic Services (OSS), and continued in 1947 within the Navy. After Operation Paperclip's successful recruitment of Nazi scientists, and with the uncovering of scientific experimental research throughout Germany after the war, the once OSS, now called the Central Intelligence Agency (CIA), began a continuation of efforts to secretly unlock the mind.

There was an urgency to beat the Soviets with the information acquired with Paperclip, as Russia had also discovered the Nazi's attempts at mind control through the acquisition of their own Nazi scientist defectors. Because this was now considered crucial to United States security, the Eisenhower administration increased funding and raced forward with a new operation, the MKUltra Project, in 1953. Sidney was now in charge of this ultra secret program with many hospitals, universities, and corporations wittingly or unwittingly participating in the experiments. Whether it be to create a Manchurian candidate, or to invent a truth serum for use in interrogation, Sidney's approval was necessary.

Programs had been created to distribute viruses, such as dengue fever, to foreign soil, to spread disease through animal migration, to erase memories, to drug and control foreign leader's minds, and to steal new pharmaceutical technology around the world. Any techniques that could possibly manipulate human behavior and thought regulation were at the forefront of the race against Russian dominance. For if the Communists discovered the techniques first, then the free world democracy espoused by the now powerful United States would be at risk. With Eisenhower at the wheel, and with the former power of Nazi research's best and brightest to assist, the United States was in a race for the next game changer as its nuclear dominance was no longer. Mind control was the new Manhattan Project.

Dulles had decided that mind control would be the next way to conquer the world. Sidney's starting budget of $300,000, and with no need to keep receipts or records, was proof that the United States was committed to the victory over the human psyche.

First Ceremony

Jungle sounds were eerily mysterious. Unseen animals amplified the night, and the sounds of swaying trees were unfamiliar to those waiting anxiously in the maloca. Arriving at dusk, there was no light pollution, and the stars and moon were the brightest EZ had ever seen. He could tell the moon was close to being in its fullest stage. Its light reflected on to the top of the dense canopy, where only darkness awaited those brave enough to enter below. They were all scared. Attempting conversation and laughter to hide the fear of the unknown. The darkness of the jungle floor might be more enticing than the fear before a ceremony that many had never undergone.

Tonight would mark their first ceremony. Each participant had arrived nervously, one hour early, to a yoga session designed to loosen up the mind and body. Facilitators were on their padded chairs in the middle of the room. Two chairs sat empty, these would be for the maestros, the ancient Peruvian experts, who trained for over twenty years in Amazonian plant medicine. What Western culture ridiculed, the maestros had perfected and passed down over thousands of years. Hundreds of plants within the Amazon were studied and prescribed for ailments. In evaluating happiness, life expectancy, and lifestyle choices, one couldn't say they were fairing much worse than their Western counterparts.

Mattresses encircled the facilitators like the numbers on a clock. Puke buckets, flashlights, toilet paper, and ashtrays all located within arms reach of each participant. EZ had learned that the cigar Daniel had continually smoked was called mapacho. This native South American tobacco was sacred to the ancient maestros. It held higher contents of nicotine than American cigarettes, and it was valued as a spiritual protector and healer during rituals. Its use went hand in hand with ayahuasca ceremonies. The maestros and participants used the plant to offer protection before, during, and after the ceremonies.

The practice of soplada had been explained to the group by Hanna. Soplar in Spanish means "to blow", and that is what the group was taught to do. Inhaling the mapacho heavily, we were advised to set intentions, and purposely blow the smoke over our bodies. This smoke would provide protection, instill better connection with Mother Ayahuasca, dispel unwanted spirits, and offer blessings over the event. Maestros would blow the smoke "four directions", over the ayahuasca, and meditate with it prior to beginning the ceremony. We were encouraged to smoke as we felt the need, as often as we wanted, before, during, and after the ceremony. This explained the ashtrays EZ had seen throughout the maloca. Kristin handed a fresh rolled mapacho to each in attendance.

EZ looked to the center of the room and guessed correctly. Daniel was there with his cigar, surrounded in a cloud. As the darkness overtook the jungle, it became difficult to see across the maloca, with only four candles placed at each edge of the facilitators in the center. Looking up, he could make out the reeds and straw forming the cone top of the structure. The building now took on a reverent tone as nervous giggling and conversations decreased to silence. Those who had attended before smoked the mapacho, blowing its smoke intensely over their bodies, hoping for its protection on the journey ahead. They were waiting for the maestros to arrive.

EZ could hear a four wheeled ATV in the distance moving about, likely farmers or fisherman moving equipment at day's end. Working to keep their homes separated from the never ending takeover of the Amazon. The ATV seemed to increase in sound and stop at the perimeter of the compound. Night animals chirped across the jungle, carrying on uninterpretable conversations. Monkeys, once howling, began to grow weary, fading into the distance, likely needing their rest. He felt as if he heard a constant humming in the distance which he had not noticed before, but he wrote this off to the river currents or perhaps generators from far away camps.

The two maestros arrived in their ceremonial gear. A husband and wife team, Luis and Aruma, who had performed ceremonies for years. Both approaching only five feet tall, they continued to the center of the room, speaking in whispers to the facilitators. Cups and the ayahuasca brew were next to Daniel and Luis.

Sitting at their respective edges of the circle with backs against the maloca's wall, the participants bathed in the silence that took over the room. It reminded EZ of men about to go into combat. The fear of death, the unknown, possibly not returning home unchanged, weighed heavily upon the group. Every participant had heard the stories of someone who was never the same after a bad journey, and yet here they were, about to jump out of a plane, hoping that their parachute would open.

They waited for what seemed like twenty minutes, listening

to the jungle's voice. The maestros would not begin their dosing until they had offered prayers for the ceremony, and for Mother Ayahuasca's guidance. What EZ had not known was that the maestros and team would also be taking the plant medicine for every ceremony. He wondered how they could possibly function under such a strong drug, but he thought it likely they would consume a lower dose, or had built up a tolerance. Maestros felt they should be connected to Mother Ayahuasca's presence in the maloca, just as much as the rest of the participants. When the time was right, Aruma got up from her position and headed over to Daniel. It was time for them to take their first dose.

The ceremony would proceed in a specific order. First, each person would go to the center of the maloca and take their dose. Each person would then sit in silence as the maestros waited for the medicine to work. After the maestros felt the medicine was taking effect, the two would begin their Icaros, spiritual songs that would offer protection and guidance over the maloca. The maestros would then split the room in two. Luis sitting before a participant and singing a personal Icaro, while Aruma, one hundred and eighty degrees away across the maloca, would offer a follow up Icaro to another. Once the circle had been completed, each participant could take a second dose of ayahuasca should they wish, and the whole Icaro process would be repeated again around the circle.

No one could leave the maloca except to go to the bathroom or outside to a cleared grassy lawn. Security had been brought in to keep an eye on all participants should they stray during the journey. Once the maestros felt all journeys complete, they would close the ceremony, and only then could the group head back to their huts for the night.

The dosing circle approached EZ, and he rose to take his first dose of the medicine.

He approached the center of the maloca, and sat on a pillow before Daniel and Aruma. They whispered to each other, discussing what dose felt right for him. The maestro drawing on years of knowledge, and the facilitator attempting to predict a dose based on prior conversation, medical records, and weight. Together, a formula was made.

Daniel spoke in a whisper.

"EZ, we will start with one full cup. One full dose, and see how you do. Try to drink the medicine quickly, in one full swallow."

EZ did as he was asked as Aruma studied his reaction from her pillow, intently smoking her mapacho. Her aura felt like that of a disappointed mother. The ayahuasca brew had a chalky earth consistency and tasted like a foul form of bitter beet juice, hinted with wood. He swallowed in one gulp, and returned to his mattress. Aruma seemed pleased. Around the room they went until everyone had their dose.

They watched from their mattresses as Luis, Aruma, and each of the three facilitators drank their own cups of the medicine. They then returned to their respective seats, and each sat quietly smoking mapacho. Aruma could be heard spitting into her bucket occasionally, likely fighting off the nausea caused by the plant. EZ heard one person vomit into their bucket, another dry heaving, but the darkness revealed nothing as to who it was. He could feel his stomach expanding. Churning similarly to how the lemongrass had done during his Vomitivo.

Many began to hiccup, and a few moans could be heard across the room. People began to shift on their mattresses, attempting to avoid nausea. A generalized restlessness took over each mattress. Their was no longer stillness, but an increasing sense of anxiety over what was to come.

EZ lit his mapacho, took a puff, and felt that it settled his stomach. After what seemed like forty five minutes, he heard a bird call outside the maloca. The bird had a distinctive call. One that he had never heard before. The bird's call was consistent, distinct, and loud. His hearing seemed amplified and was where the ayahuasca decided to work first.

EZ's ears searched for what else he may hear in the jungle. It was as if hearing aids had been placed in his ears. Insects. Crickets. Limbs blowing and touching. The sounds were far away, but almost overtaking him at the same time. The ATV that he had heard earlier came to life again; and all at once, the bird near him had flown away. Perhaps making its way across the dark of night to a mate. A few seconds later, there it was again. Far away from him. Closer it seemed to the ATV in the distance.

Shortly thereafter, the maestros started their Icaros. He had never heard such beautiful songs. Luis's high voice layered onto Aruma's with persistent octave shifts and pitch changes. It reminded him of the American Indian songs he had seen on old Western shows, but with purpose. More spiritual and with more meaning. The sounds induced an almost ancient tribal sense in his soul. With the silence that preceded them, the Icaros overwhelmed the coned roof maloca. The sounds seemed to echo in every direction. Although they were on opposite sides of the structure, he could make out each maestro's part independently, and together, at the same time. He was baffled at this new ability.

He had listened to the melodic jungle bird and now felt hypnotized by the Icaro. The medicine was working.

He could feel a vibration begin to crawl over the skin of his legs, and slowly work its way up through his chest and arms before entering his mouth, ears, and eyes. Each inch of the crawl was felt as the medicine worked its way up his spine.

A complete overwhelming vibration and tingling began, and he experienced more auditory effects. One note of the Icaros would become ten, then a hundred. He could zoom into Luis with accuracy, then zoom back out to Aruma. Combining the two together into a full one hundred piece symphony, or choosing to only hear one of them, but he seemed to be able to hear all of this at once. One symphony developed into twenty.

The Icaros took on more meaning, seemingly making more sense, as if he could travel across the room to have a discussion with Luis, or fly back to talk to Aruma. He tuned out more of the crowd's hiccups. They seemed to be everywhere.

Feeling more at ease, he noticed that he didn't like looking across the room. His vision started to double, triple, quadruple shapes. Small movements of his eyes produced massive shifts in sounds, feeling, and visualization. He began to hear visions, and see sounds. His sense of smell could relate to colors. They had advised if this became overwhelming, it was a good idea to ground yourself closer to the Earth. Closer to Mother Ayahuasca. So, EZ slid himself quietly down the wall, placing himself flat on his mattress.

Staring up at the ceiling, it had come alive with movement. Moving colors, lightening bugs, symmetrical patterns. Closing his eyes, the brightness increased. Colors he had never seen before were directly behind his eyelids. Two, three, four dimensional patterns emerging above, below, behind, and to the sides. It was as if he was at the heart of a sphere and could see in every dimension. Even through dimensions. Words would never describe his ability to travel instantly, globally throughout this world behind his eyes.

Without warning, an image of three skulls appeared in what he perceived as the right side of his mind. The skulls reminded him of instructions that might pop up on a video game or a computer program. A red arrow below the second skull's tilt displayed that it was time to turn his head to the left, so he did so. The last skull indicated that the head's final position should be horizontal. EZ felt he needed to push his body further into the ground. Grinding into the mattress, the Icaros changed. He could hear Luis in his right brain and Aruma in the left. When the two combined in the center of his mind, a green light appeared at the center of his brow. After this happened, he was able to travel across the room encountering those who were struggling. He felt it necessary to help them. They communicated in chirps, code of some sort, that he was able to understand. A language of some type for which he didn't have the code. Insects, trees, and whatever he turned his attention to, was now available for personal discussion.

He tried as hard as he could in this new green light pathway, to purge their pain, to help ease their burdens. A clear vision of his brother appeared as the green light took him across the world. A voice that wasn't talking, a voice that was within his mind, was guiding this journey. The voice took over his mind, and he instantly knew whose voice this was. She was in control now.

This was Mother Ayahuasca.

She told him that his brother had a sickness in his lungs, and to reach out to him after the retreat. As he focused on helping his brother, Mother told him his Father would die soon, but to let this emotion go. There was much more she needed to show him and not to be distracted by death. There was nothing to fear in death.

His future daughter Zoey appeared. She was the most beautiful thing he had ever seen.

"She will be on top of the world one day EZ. She will marry someone from Asia. She will have more success than you can imagine. Never worry for her future."

EZ was then carried on to his future youngest daughter, Stella. He felt an immediate need to protect her. He sensed from himself an immediate anger at Mother Ayahuasca. His feelings told him that this beautiful, loving child, who inspired the world around her, was to have something inside her go wrong.

"You must let this go EZ. You cannot change this within her."

EZ felt overwhelming anger and refused to be shown anything else unless the Mother promised to protect her. He was willing to fight this to the death. He was unwilling to be shown anything else in the Universe unless her protection was promised. With reluctance, she agreed to EZ's demands, but EZ wasn't so sure. The green light faded quickly. Maybe she was punishing him. After all, it was up to her what was to be determined in the Universe.

He had to relax. Match the two Icaros again in his mind. Align the left with the right, before the green light would take him away again. He wasn't sure if she agreed to his arrangement, but since he was allowed to go forward, he hoped it was so. The light was warm, bright, truthful. Mother Ayahuasca showed him his future wife. She was having an affair. He tried to call out to her. To tell her he loved her, and that he was sorry for whatever he had done wrong. He could not connect to her as he had with the people within the room. He could not travel closer, and it felt as if someone would not allow it even if it were possible. He was supposed to learn something from seeing this, but he couldn't understand the lesson.

"Ignore the voices. Women have burdens to void. Help your brother through his pain. Comfort your Father."

EZ heard a voice next to him. It sounded miles away. The voice told him to open his eyes.

"EZ, this is Daniel. You are safe. It's OK . Open your

eyes. Are you OK? Tell me that you are OK?"

EZ opened his eyes and realized he was still in the ceremony. Daniel had stopped by to check on his journey. He had taken EZ off of the bad path he had started down. Coaching him to slow his breathing.

"We are giving out second cups. Would you like a second dose?" Daniel asked.

He felt a flash of the warm green light pass across his brow. *Of course he did.*

EZ proceeded to the center of the maloca for his second dose. Eager to see where he would travel in the green light. He only hoped he could remember how to align the Icaros up perfectly to allow his brain to sync so the light would enter again. He swallowed down another half cup of the chalky, earthy brew, and returned to his mattress. He laid down as fast as his intoxicated body would allow, hugged the ground, and tuned his brain to the songs.

As he did, the light appeared, faster this time than the last, and he was surprised to see who his guide was for this journey. He had just met her. She had been his yoga instructor prior to the ceremony. Tina was her name.

She was beautiful. Her voice soft, calm, reassuring. A list of principals appeared in his head, they were things she promised to show him if he agreed to let the Father's voice in his right ear stay matched to the Mother in his left. He willfully agreed. She only required that he *"Make the best choice along the journey. The honest choice, The best human choice." "I want to show you what is possible EZ if you trust our Mother Ayahuasca, but first, you have some injuries to your body. Your foot, your back, and in your stomach. I'm going to fix those now."*

She placed her hands across and down the injuries he had suffered in combat, and he felt a tingling sensation turn into the absence of pain. She had now earned his trust.

"Remember to do good EZ, and you will see good. You now feel good."

The green light had become warmer now, brighter, and was filled with absolute truth and goodness. It was filled with all things good. The entire Universe of good. Purer than good. Perhaps what true devotion and love was meant to be.

"This is God." EZ whispered.

"This is what heaven IS."

For the first time in his life, EZ had met God.

There would no longer be doubts in any conversations. God was real. God was good. It took all that he could do to stay in that connection. Ground, breathe with the Icaro, listen to the Mother as much as the Father, the left as much as the right brain, allow the vibrations to connect, and he would receive the miracles of the Universe.

EZ was brought into the celestial heavens. Hundreds of pathways revealed themselves. His old pets were there, now hanging with their wolf ancestors. His grandfather was there, proud of his journey and efforts on earth.

Tina had promised to teach him life lessons as long as he agreed to only make the best choices, and the journey began.

Past life lessons, future life lessons. Two choices were always given, and as promised EZ always made the best moral, Godly, choice, and once he did, he was revealed as why that was the correct decision, and with that choice, the power of God only became stronger.

He suffered humility for his choices, but was immediately granted more access, more light after making the correct choices. More of the people that he loved from his past, more lost souls, friends, all came to join the lesson and to let EZ know he would be with them one day. The more humility shown, the greater the divinity revealed.

The light took him into the jungle, revealing how the leaves, trees, animals, and the soil were all part of one bigger being. A bigger world was revealed to him, through the voice of Tina, by God. The absolute ending message was that if and only if the *"entire world agrees to listen, on the same green channel, can we help each other."*

His eyes opened. The light began to fade away. His body felt numb, barely able to move. The Icaros had stopped, but no one had left the room. The staff were back on their pillows. He slowly raised his body up and braced it against the wall of the maloca. Nothing but silence existed in the room, spare a few individuals weeping uncontrollably. The moon's light beamed now across the maloca. The maestros were quiet. Daniel smoked his mapacho.

As he reached to grab his own nicotine, EZ was startled as the jungle bird of the night came to life behind him again. His ability to hear the voice of the forest was in perfect tune, hypnotic. The bird stayed, and he was disappointed when it finally made its way further into the jungle. Closer now to the ATV again in the distance.

A period of what seemed like fifteen minutes passed, and EZ listened as the ATV made its way further and further away from the camp before the engine finally died. The Peruvian's were likely out gathering food for the next day. The jungle needed constant labor.

With one last call, his new favorite bird bid farewell.

Kristin stood and spoke.

"That concludes tonight's ceremony. You may all stay as long as you wish, or go back to your huts. Take as much time as you need. If you need help, or need to discuss any of tonight's activities, just find one of us. Please do not disturb your maestros as they exit."

EZ made his way back to his hut. There was no way he could sleep, so he did as the teachers suggested, and captured all of his thoughts in his journal while they were fresh in his mind. The jungle was quiet. No sounds of insects or the monkeys he had heard before the ceremony. Odd he thought. He could understand the monkeys sleeping, but he could not understand why there were no insects chirping near his hut. Perhaps they are all tired from the ceremonial music.

He went to bed. Hoping the green light would reemerge.

At exactly two AM, and four AM, EZ awoke. He could still tell that the medicine was in his system. He was now sweating in the humid jungle air. He thought he might be able to ground himself more and sleep better if he were to go and touch the earth's soil outside his hut as his instructors had taught him.

He opened the huts door to the lack of jungle sounds, and placed his feet on the warm moist Earth. The contact seemed to immediately relax him. Leaving the confines of the hut and its stale jungle air.

As his sweat cooled, he glanced down under his hut as the moon illuminated the out of place PVC plastic pipe that carried the electricity into his hut to the one and only outlet. He was tired, still feeling sedated, but something felt strange to him.

Why would one tiny outlet need such a big electrical wire? He had worked with generators before, and he knew running wires at distance was quite expensive. And why was a 6 gauge wire necessary for one outlet?

He made a note about the outlet in his journal, and when more light was available, promised himself he would examine underneath the hut. For now, he brushed the thought out of his mind. Returning to his bed, he was able to sleep until around 5 AM, waking to the sounds of the monkeys, insects, and the forest's leaves.

He was glad that they had all made it back. He now understood that they were all connected.

<u>Day Two's Discoveries</u>

EZ went to grab a quick shower before his busy retreat day started. The day's plans included circle table discussions after breakfast, a lunch that followed the dieta principles of the maestros, journaling time, yoga, and the second ceremony that evening. He lingered in the shower's hot water until it turned cold, pondering his experience, trying not to put too much weight into it as the instructors had told them. It may take months to process all of the information.

Breakfast was some time away, so he decided to walk the grounds. The participants were highly restricted by the retreat's boundaries and had signed a form that stated if caught outside of the restricted zones, they would be forced to leave. They were told the ayahuasca might enable emotions not normally acted upon, so it was best to stay within the safety of the retreat. He passed the maloca, the other's huts, and proceeded down a trail that turned into a narrow graveled road. He passed the kitchen and conference rooms and noted a trail on his left. They had been encouraged to walk on the labeled trails that connect with the jungle, to be out in nature as much as possible between ceremonies. This trail however was unlabeled, but he decided to take it anyway.

It was well worn with gravel recently placed. After about a hundred yards, he came to an area with four buildings. In front of one, he saw Aruma and Luis there doing laundry. It had been stressed not to talk to the maestros, so he quickly passed them unnoticed. The other buildings were supplied by a generator and what looked to be a security building as it had a radio antennae, satellite dish, and WiFi dish on its exterior. He made his best guess that this was the facilitator's housing. Since it was so early in the morning, they would likely still be sleeping. Stepping around the edge of the security building, he came across an ATV. This must be where the ATV sounds he heard during the ceremony originated, perhaps to insure their security while at the ceremony. A separate trail presented ATV tracks. EZ decided to explore exactly how much of a perimeter they had to patrol.

Moving along a rutted trail, he followed a circuitous leftward route, eventually finding himself where he directionally guessed would be a straight shot from the maloca, about three hundred yards away. The trail emerged into a flat clearing beneath the jungle canopy. The clearing contained fuel tanks, propane tanks, and an ATV trailer. Opposite this equipment was a concrete blocked building. So far, this had been the only building he saw on the property that was of western construction, even having a metal roof. The building had two garage doors and one man door. He decided to enter and see what the building contained since the camp was still asleep.

The inside of the structure had been framed and sound proof foam lined walls, ceiling, and all three doors. Four generators were inside, and all were connected to a central panel. None were currently in use. In front of the last garage door was an ATV trailer, the mud on its tires fresh. He couldn't identify the device that was on the trailer. It looked like an inverter of some type. The words oscillator/inverter and DANGER: High Voltage Frequency were labeled on its exterior. There was a ten foot heavy duty electrical cord, and at its end held a large adapter. There was a panel door that folded down, revealing plugs for computers, WiFi, USB, and various other electronics. He closed the inverters door, and studied the room once more, noting that most of the sound would be directed away from the maloca, The bulk of the sound, if any, directed towards the garage doors. He wondered if this was the humming that he had heard the night before. He checked to see if he left any tracks and closed the door behind him.

He continued on the slightly wider trail where the ATV tracks led. He soon came across a traditional telephone pole cemented into the ground. An overgrown clearing snaked back to the concrete building. Although there were no telephone wires, he did note coming from the ground, multiple inputs of larger gauge wire. Totaling around fifteen different cables, they merged into a central voltage meter. Above this was another metal electrical box. Its door half shut. Opening the door, he realized that the plug matched the plug on the inverter "mystery" ATV trailer inside the concrete building. He returned the door to its half closed position, deciding he had been gone long enough.

The road formed a straight line back to the maloca, but he had crossed over one gate that held a sign, "NO ONE PAST THIS POINT", in three languages. EZ had stepped out of bounds. Good thing it was early in the morning, or he may have been kicked out of the retreat.

He made his way back to get breakfast. Although he had not attempted to use his phone since there was no obvious cell service in the Amazon, he noted with interest that there were some sort of white WiFi devices close to most of the huts. The retreat had done their best to mask the thin wires behind the trees, but he wondered now if he could actually log in to his phone by WiFi. He would try after breakfast.

His other classmates were in huddled discussions. Girls with girls, boys with boys. Some discussing their lack of an experience, others describing the magic of their prior night's journey. He listened more than he talked, not wanting to brag

about how rich his prior night's experience had been. The
facilitators soon showed up, reminding those who had no
journey, that ayahuasca worked in mysterious ways, and that this
was a process. The medicine worked at its own pace. She would
decide when she was to reveal herself. They could guarantee
that the medicine was doing its work and changes were
occurring, whether they felt them or not.

EZ finished breakfast and took a hike down one of the
labeled trails. He felt as if he could hear nature around him and
that he was more aware of the trees and plants. He wondered if it
was just escaping the city that had attuned his awareness.
Returning to his humid hut, he took a nap. There would be no
food allowed after the maestro's dieta lunch in order to have an
empty stomach for the ayahuasca. EZ thought it was likely to
prevent aspiration from all of the purging which was said to be
bad spirits leaving the body.

Waking from his nap, he realized he had forgotten to check
on his grounding session from the night before. Looking around
at the other huts, everyone seemed to still be attempting naps.
He walked to the rear of his hut, laid himself on the ground and
looked underneath the wooden floor. What he saw surprised
him.

Directly beneath his bed was thick wiring, copper in
appearance with no insulation. The wire was about three to four
inches in diameter and was composed of about ten individual
half inch copper wires twisted upon themselves, braided
continuously like a pretzel. More surprising to EZ was that the
only place the wires were located was directly beneath his bed.
The wires were connected to the hut floor beams in a swastika
shape as they extended back to the underground outlet he had
first noted.

No wonder there needed to be such a large power supply to

this simple hut EZ thought. Exactly what was this bundled wiring for? Insects? Rodents? Why was it just underneath his bed? Was it a grounding device of some sort? Pocketing this information along with that of his morning walk, he changed clothes in preparation for the pre ceremony yoga.

He had seen Tina, the yoga instructor, at the morning breakfast, quietly telling her about his Godlike experience and how she had led part of his journey. He described to her how beautiful the jungle bird was, and how its call had tuned him into the Icharos, enabling him to connect quickly. She told him the bird was called a Common Pauraque, and that her parents let her keep one as a child. She was honored by my stories involving her, and thanked me for allowing her to hear them.

Arriving at the evening yoga session, Tina pulled EZ to the side.

"I wanted you to have this for tonight's ceremony. It is a Pauraque feather from my bird. I felt it may connect you to your journey for tonight." EZ thanked her profusely, offering to give it back since the item was so special to her childhood. She adamantly declined. It was his to keep. "There is a reason you heard the Pauraque. Perhaps you will hear him again. It is a sign of good luck. He may guide you through the jungle and to Mother's message."

The group finished the one hour yoga session and proceeded to their respective mattresses. Dusk was well on its way. Those in attendance were tidying their nests for the evening. Pillows arranged, water bottles filled, red lights within reach, toilet paper checked, and ashtrays emptied. These were now veteran ceremony attendees. They knew what to expect now. The facilitators arrived and took their places. Daniel arrived smoking his mapacho as usual. Something EZ was growing used to seeing, almost like seeing Winston Churchill with his cigar.

Quietness soon consumed the building as the moon and candles became the only light.

Luis and Aruma entered the screened door, shutting it without sound. "Let the ceremony begin." EZ said to himself.

<u>Bentov</u>

Prague had been a human's worst nightmare. The Nazi's had killed both of his parents, his brother, and his sister at the concentration camps; however, he had been under God's watch, making it to the British managed nation now called Palestine. Although a Czech by birth, Itzhak was now amongst his Jewish brethren in the Negev desert. Aliyah had not been easy, but he no longer had any reason to stay in Eastern Europe. His family was gone. This was his new home. The Shoval kibbutz might not be glamorous for a person of his intellect, but the new Jewish state of Israel had provided him with opportunities to explore science, his passion, without a college degree.

The pipes he had used on the kibbutz irrigation system had given him the idea of repurposing them into tank destroying rocket tubes. His invention was quickly adapted. After joining the Israeli Science Corps, his new position was absorbed into a new military branch labeled HEMED. Because of a worldwide embargo against selling weapons to the new state, his ingenuity was a necessity for the survival of Israel.

With his fellow scientists, Itzhak had diligently researched new weapons for the IDF, and because of his ability to invent thoughtful, economically resourceful techniques and products, it was encouraged upon him to make a new home in the United States, which was experiencing its post World War Two scientific boom.

Only one thing bothered Itzhak. The rumor was that many

of the former Nazi scientists now held prominent positions within the research community. Could he work alongside the same ideologues who had murdered his family? The same Nazi's who had forced him to flee to the Negev? Perhaps, the IDF nudged, he could steal some of the experimental breakthroughs and further the expansion of Israel. Was Israel really hoping that he would become a spy, or did they wish for his personal success as one of their brightest, hoping that one day he would return to work for HEMED. It was a careful decision to make. With two options, he chose to cross the Atlantic in 1954, and decide how to help Israel when the time was appropriate.

Citizenship would have to wait. He had made his new home in Bel Mont, Massachusetts, which he had chosen for its high concentration of Jews as well as scientific opportunities. Cambridge, Harvard, MIT, Tufts, Boston University, Boston College, and the University system of Massachusetts were concentrated there. Not only would these Universities need knowledgeable scientists, but his hope was to start his own research, seeking out projects involving For Profit entities.

He was also aware through his work with the Israeli military, that the United States government would not only be working hand in hand with the University's , but also with private and publicly traded corporations on their own weapons and technology. He was a non credentialed Jewish scientist, so the private route would likely be his best path forward, not the Universities. He first had to find a location to begin his private experiments, and he found this at a Catholic church's basement in Belmont. He had no initial contracts, so his experiments ranged from chemicals, to plastics, to physics, or chemistry. If an idea came to him, he had to seek no committee or board approval. It was a dream come true. America was definitely the land of opportunity. In 1962, to his surprise, he was quickly granted his U.S. citizenship. His fears of Israel seeking secrets, or the Americans not recognizing his talents were of no concern now. He trusted in his own prowess.

During this time researching traditional sciences, Bentov became more curious about the human mind, particularly in consciousness. He had explained many of his ideas to other professors in the area who were doing research in the field and had also developed an interest in the traditional practices of Kundalini Yoga, Southeast Asian medicine, and all other ancient cultures that explored altered states of the mind. Because he was successful in his private laboratory, he was being noticed increasingly more around the University landscape. He had developed products such as diet spaghetti, brake shoes for cars, and had even created a technique to monitor the electrical output of the heart.

But it was the year 1967 that he invented his first marketable invention. Through listening to the tribulations of physicians in the area, he realized there was a need to enable a doctor to drive a catheter through scopes and blood vessels. Once he invented this steerable catheter, he realized the importance of finding a business savvy marketer, and he had found this in John Abele. Together, Medi-Tech was born.

The financial freedom to pursue his wildest inventions was taking shape. From the desert of Israel, to now selling a patentable steerable catheter, Bentov could finally claim success. If Medi-Tech could become what Abele eventually named Boston Scientific, then possibly his true fascination with the human mind, remote viewing, and kundalini out of body experiences could be explored, and he felt he was the right person to begin this controversial topic of the soul. This was his love. To finally not worry about the bills, or even a University review board, his dream came true.

From this love, he was scheduled to fly to California to give a presentation on the book he had written in 1977, *Stalking the Wild Pendulum*. He had been working on a way to fast track the Kundalini out of body experience. With others at the Esalen Institute in California, the quest for a breakthrough in spirituality and out of body experiences were now headed in a theoretical science based direction. Bentov knew he was close to finding a pathway through physiology to leave one's mind. He knew many who had achieved the experience, and often with delirious results. However, this he hoped to change.

Some had seen God, other worlds, and held direct communications with the Universe. He knew his theories were correct, but he needed more time. Now with his patents, he now had the finances. Being one of only a handful in the field of human consciousness, his expertise was also in strong demand. It was with this new found freedom that he was excitedly packing his bag for the flight when he heard a knock at his humble home.

Opening the door, Bentov stood before two intimidating men. One in a suit that looked new, but cheap. Perhaps a government worker he thought. The other wore a Yarmulke and a modest black suit, obviously Jewish.

"Good evening Itzhak. My name is Isacc Berg. I'm here to urgently discuss your research. May we come in?".

In thick Hebrew, the Israeli held a serious but polite tone hinted with a rushed sense of purpose.

"I come in good faith as well Mr. Bentov. My name is Sidney Gottlieb. I am a scientist just like you. We are quite interested in your projects, and we would like to discuss them urgently. May we say it's a matter of national security."

The rather large man leaned to one side, as if he had

difficulties with his posture, or perhaps a disability.

Bentov had been waiting for this day. Perhaps another Aliyah was at hand. He hoped he would have the final say as he had on his first journey. His packing would have to wait.

With a bit of fear, mixed with curiosity, Bentov replied in Hebrew, motioning the two men into his foyer.

"Welcome to my home. How can I be of assistance?".

The Offer

Bentov motioned Isaac Berg and Sidney Gottlieb from his foyer into his living area. He was a man of simplicity, and only had an older couch and two well worn chairs.

"Would either of you like some tea or coffee?" Itzhak offered the two guests, attempting to remember his breathing techniques learned from his yoga practice, to give himself time to read this unannounced visit. They had obviously known when he would be home.

"No thank you Mr. Bentov. We know you are packing for a flight and must have many things to prepare for before your departure."

Isaac revealed Bentov's itinerary which further confirmed to Itzhak that they were far more knowledgeable about him than he had initially thought.

Sidney and Isaac had taken up both chairs, so Itzhak placed himself in the middle of the couch, feeling almost childlike, sitting between two parents who were about to instill some form of punishment. He decided to make a go of who these two might be and regain some leverage in the conversation.

"I understand that the work I'm doing may be valuable to the CIA and the Mossad, but I didn't think either of you could operate on U.S. soil."

Bentov said matter of factly, actually not knowing if this to be true. He was aware though that the Mossad would operate on any soil of its choosing.

"Mr. Bentov, you are correct in assuming we are with those agencies. But we come seeking your expertise. We both see it as a matter of national security, and in the best interests of the entire peaceful future of the West. We have been doing quite a few experiments of our own, and we hope that you may wish to join us in our pursuits. Just so you understand, we feel that your work is on the level of a Manhattan Project in magnitude".

Gottlieb stated this as if he knew what Itzhak's answer was going to be.

Itzhak considered himself a peaceful man-scientist, Kundalini yogi, medical device inventor. He had served his homeland when it was required, but to be an agent of either spy service didn't seem to sit well with him. After all, he was financially independent going forward. Why would he ever feel the need to serve at the bequest of either agency?

"Itzhak, you came to the rescue of the state of Israel when we were achieving our Independence. We took note of your intelligence at that time, but our country still needs your help. The encouragement of allowing you to pursue your dreams in the land of the free doesn't mean that you should abandon your Jewish brothers and sisters. We know quite well what you have invented, and that future company, Boston Scientific, will undoubtedly do quite well. You stand to make more money than you could ever have imagined. But it is not these inventions we seek." Isaac continued.

"Israel will continue to be the world's evil stepchild. We will need a way to deter future conflicts that may interfere in us maintaining our capital for growth, and our young men to build a strong society. It is through scientists such as yourself that

Zionism shall prevail when our young state is surrounded by Islam and those who seek the destruction of our homes. As you can see before you, we also have many friends in the United States that share similar interests."

"If not these scientific inventions, then what could I possibly have to offer either of your agencies?". Bentov inquired.

"Itzhak," Gottlieb answered, "I have been, and when I say "I", I mean the entire CIA, following with great interest your thoughts and publications related to the mechanics of consciousness. As you have already written, you believe that you may be able to unlock realities that are not aware to us. It is through these principals, with you being the best on the topic, that we are here to offer you a job. We have already offered many of your fellow aficionados research positions. In fact, without your knowledge, you have already been working with many of our scientists, and they have recognized that your work is superior to their own."

Bentov began to guess which of his colleagues had made this transition. To whom had he stated his theories? People that he had been quite open with regarding what he thought was his hobby of passion were now somehow gathering data to be used against others. He now realized how Einstein's last statements about the atomic bomb made more sense. He remembered Einstein's statement.

"Had I known that the Germans would not succeed in developing an atomic bomb, I would have done nothing."

Itzhak also knew that Einstein had addressed the dangers of nuclear weapons after their use and had actively tried to persuade future scientists from helping develop nuclear technology. How possibly did they think that his work on mental holograms or new levels of consciousness could be on the level of a Manhattan Project? He had not been able to repeatedly get any person to that level of altered state consistently. Could it be that these agencies had discovered knowledge that may enable a participant to achieve what he thought could be achieved?

"Itzhak, you don't even understand how far you have come along on your own. We have been studying out of body experiences and mind travel for years. It's with some of your own knowledge that we have even gotten this far. You are what we need to get this project completed. You are the Oppenheimer for the development of the next defense against our enemies. Think about this? You, Mr. Bentov, are in a position to change the world, to insure the safety of future generations of Israelis. You, yourself, know what it was like to grow up without parents and siblings. How could we not come here today without humbly asking you to help out not only Israel, but our biggest world ally, the United States, just as many Jews have done in the past?".

Isaac was speaking with the passion of a Rabbi. This was more than science. This was the fate of an entire nation. The success of Israel might be what Itzhak held in his mind, and with the financial backing of the United States, his theories could be tested. Sidney continued.

"Itzhak, you may be quite interested in knowing that you will be working at the highest levels within our government. Access to the top University labs and studies. Scientists performing experiments under your design. With an unlimited budget, your dreams of proving to the world that you are correct on the human mind, and not just some peace loving Yogi who puts all of his beliefs into ancient philosophies that have never played out. You are being offered a chance to do your work, without red tape. To reach the boundaries of what we know is humanly possible, at the same time you are helping out the world against Communism's threats. I can tell you at this time, and with great reluctance, that the Russians are far ahead of us in this field. Even with the data we obtained from Germany years ago, they have not been encumbered by human rights or animal experimentation limits. With my program, you won't be encumbered any further. The CIA, the President, and the Joint Chiefs have determined that this is the number one issue at stake for our national security. And you Itzhak, your ideas, just like the greatest scientists of the 1940's, are considered the missing link to protect the world."

Bentov didn't know how to take the offer. How could he be an Einstein? He was a simple immigrant from Israel without a college degree. How could he stand with the greatest minds of a generation, and what was expected of him? There had to be more to this offer. He did not have to wait long for his answer, as if they knew what he was considering.

"Mr. Bentov, you have had difficulties in relationships. We have followed your marriages and interactions with your children. We know how much time and love you put into your work, and that has impacted your family life. We are offering something for you to give back to the world, to give back to those who may not have gotten the love or affection that your studies took away. We are offering you a legacy, and with the sale of your new steerable catheter by Mr. Abele, we can assure you that we can secretly obtain stock options should that company become a success. Plans have already been made at the highest levels to ensure you are compensated fully, and that your family is well taken care of." Gottlieb added.

Isaac continued.

"You will only be offered this opportunity once. Today. Now. And once you have made the decision, you must, for the covert nature of our experiences, take on a new name, and we must enact a plan that looks as if you have disappeared to the world. You see Itzhak, it's not only the Mossad and CIA that have taken an interest in you, but through our contacts, we know that the KGB has developed quite a fondness for your books and inventive theories. They have also been following you, and the KGB has also placed spies within your fellow Kundalini fellows in California. Not everyone is as they seem. We have come to you with an offer that is every scientist's dream, with open arms, telling you who we are and why your work is so important to our countries."

"What would I do with my home? My basement laboratory? My Medi-Tech company holdings?" Bentov asked confusingly now.

"I am even scheduled to speak at a conference tomorrow in California. There are many people awaiting what I have spent so long developing. I have partners that depend on my knowledge to push our companies forward." Gottlieb interjected.

"Your partners will make a nice profit off of your inventions, as will you, just under a different name. I can assure you that we have reviewed your business agreements with Mr. Abele, and that within one month of your disappearance, he will be able to form Boston Scientific. Our ability to buy stock in the company before the public is aware of its future possible profits, will be unknown to Mr. Abele or any other entity affiliated with your catheter's success. I can assure you that the CIA will insure you become rich beyond your dreams, as well as any other inventions of yours that go public. We have put that in a contract form for you Mr. Bentov. Your family will also be taken care of from this stock. We will arrange for a fair offer on your home.

All that we ask is that you fly to Chicago tomorrow, but don't board your connecting flight to Los Angeles. It's really that simple. We will take care of the rest."

"There isn't much more we can offer you Mr. Bentov." Isaac

continued.

"We are offering you the chance to be a hero, for not one, but two nations. One of which you owe your allegiance to God. Unlimited wealth, access to the best labs and research, the ability to do your own studies in a field where you are the expert, and freedom for your family's future. What are we asking you to give up Itzhak? A basement laboratory? Low speaking fees? Trips paid for from your own wallet? Risks from a startup company that may or may not be successful? Being known as a kook to the scientific world? We are offering you everything you could possibly dream of and more. This is your path. This is your next Aliyah. God willing." Bentov stood.

"Let me get a cup of coffee as I think about what you are offering."

He headed past his guests into his kitchen, noticing the dollar store kitchen table, the cheap metal coffee pot he brewed every morning before work. He really had nothing to show for all of his hard work-all of the lost nights and suffering in the lab. No great successes with his family as these men had so accurately pointed out to him. Where was he going? What did money even mean if Boston Scientific was successful? Would money make him retire a happy man? These men were offering him a chance to study his real dream-the secrets of human consciousness.

Something no man has understood since the beginnings of time. They offered what could be the greatest scientific breakthrough of his generation, and they were offering this to *him*. No one had offered him a distinguished research position, and this could be his last chance at such an opportunity. He was not getting any younger either. If worse came to worse, and he failed with his concepts, he could rent out another basement at another Catholic Church. He had been through worse times after the war and in the Israeli desert.

Bentov walked back into the living room without his cup of coffee, having not remembered to even turn on the pot, and sat back down on his worn couch.

"Gentleman. I will board my plane to Chicago as you ask tomorrow, but I will not board the flight to Los Angeles. I only ask at that time to review the paperwork for which you guarantee me this future. I need to see you are, who you say you are, and where and what you have presented are real. I will also need to see a minimum payment offer for leaving my company behind, as well as a severance package should you decide I am no longer needed. I do this to honor my beliefs, my homeland of Israel, and to secure the country that let me thrive as an immigrant. I agree to join should you be able to do these things."

Bentov actually smiled at finally being able to express a decision. As a scientist, making a rational decision could take time, and these two had summed up his current situation faster than he could have himself. For once, Itzhak felt as if he was worthy of his ideas.

"Congratulations Mr. Bentov. You have made a wise decision. Both of our countries thank you ahead of time for the sacrifices you will be making, as well as to the progress your acquisition will attain. I look forward to working with you in my laboratories sir."

Gottlieb struggled to stand, then shook Bentov's hand. This had gone much better than expected. He thought Bentov may need to be pressured into the decision from the Agency and that would not have gone well for Mr. Bentov's morale. Forced recruitment resulted in poor outcomes. The two men returned to the door, and Isaac raised his hand to shake Bentov's. Before departing, Isaac offered one last comment.

"Itzhak, you have made our nation proud. All of the Jews

around the world thank you for the sacrifices you will undergo starting tomorrow. The others who have listened to this conversation have also thanked you." Isaac pointed to an older lamp in Bentov's living room.

"Make sure to call your bank to check your balance after we leave. You will be surprised at what rewards your new agreement provides to those who are believers in our cause. Oh, and before I forget Itzhak. The U.S. citizenship you easily obtained in 1962 did not occur by accident. Should you change your mind about helping us, or perhaps want to discuss your offer with someone else, it might be that we need to go review that initial application. Good luck Itzhak."

Bentov saw the men out and glanced at the lamp. He called his bank to access his balance. What was a meager $1500 was now $100,000. He had to have the bank representative repeat the number back to him twice, unable to believe how these men could achieve something so quickly and efficiently.

He placed the receiver back onto the phone's cradle and turned to stare at the lamp.

How long had they been listening? His moment of joy was replaced by fear as he realized he would no longer be a free man. His identity was about to vanish, but it would never vanish to those who listened from the lamp.

<u>Second Ceremony</u>

EZ placed his good luck pauraque feather from Tina next to his ashtray and flashlight. He wanted to be able to reach for it should the urge arise. Sliding himself upright against the rounded wall of the maloca, he found his lighter and lit his mapacho, drawing it slowly in and setting his intentions for the night. He had been shown God and wanted to get back to the green light and the encompassing warmth. EZ touched his flashlight in the darkness, ensuring himself that if a bathroom break was needed he could find it easily. The light was also to be used in an emergency to signal a facilitator. A three burst flash, directed into the chest meant you needed help right away. He didn't think that would be necessary after his first ceremony went so well.

The maestros sequence was exactly as the night before. EZ waited patiently for the return of the pauraque. As he focused on the sounds of the jungle, the familiar sound of the ATV some distance away began. Its operator at very low speed, *perhaps to decrease his noise exposure,* the soldier in EZ thought. Like clockwork, the pauraque arrived from the jungle. Odd EZ thought it was in the exact spot as the night before, presenting its calls at the exact same level and syncopation, *perhaps it had a nest near the bathrooms behind his spot in the maloca.* It continued its calls for about two to three minutes before the silence returned. EZ no longer heard the ATV, but the bird called again from what he envisioned being near the concrete structures he had found on his hike.

Likely a mate returning the first bird's advances, EZ thought. He could hear the hum of generators in the distance as well, likely needed for laundry or kitchen work since all the attendees were in for the night. He waited anxiously for his turn to drink the medicine. As the dosing went around the circle, EZ saw that it was now his turn to make his way to the dosing pillow. He took a seat next to Daniel and Aruma. Both studied his intent closely.

"Are you ready EZ?" Daniel said, quieter than a whisper.

"I think you discovered the perfect dose last night. We agree that you should take one and a half cups to start tonight. Your experience last night was profound."

EZ agreed to Daniel's expert advice, and he drank the dose quickly, not noticing the chalky taste as he had the night before, being more interested in where this new dose would take him. Returning to his mattress, he waited for the Icharos to begin, trying his hardest to connect through the music as he had done the night before.

Unable to see the green path, he forgot that this had only occurred when he had grounded himself deep into the mattress, so he closed his eyes, laid flat, and pushed all of his extremities towards the earth where an immediate connection came. The sound began and wouldn't stop. One sound turned into a million then next a billion. Unable to escape the awfulness of his inner ears, he stared into the back of his eyelids. That's when the trip began. This time, it was one hundred percent visual. The visions increased, and he began to sink into an uncontrollable hole. Billions of sounds with each breath. He could see and hear himself breathing. Wherever he was going, the rollercoaster had lost its brakes.

He reached for his flashlight and began turning the red LED on and off into his shirt. He turned his head quickly and beckoned the instructors for help, but they were across the maloca. He could form no words. The medicine had overpowered all of his senses. There would be no help coming to save him now. His visions were interrupted by another smaller, almost television like image to the bottom right side of his closed eyes. It was the familiar three skulls. The furthest to the right-upright. The second was a skull slightly tilted to the left highlighted by a red arrow indicating the need to turn his head towards his left shoulder. A last skull was laid completely on its side in a sleeping motion. His mind performed this tilting motion on command. His head tilted left, touching the mattress, and EZ's world no longer existed.

Before him were one of his most admired Israeli Special Forces heroes, Dan, whom he had met once. His Mother was present, as well as many ancient native Peruvians, dressed in colorful leather, resembling American Indians. His mother's voice alternated with Dan's, telling EZ's mind that he would be exposed to the true heritage of choice. He would be presented with different physical challenges, and if he passed these tests, would be allowed revelations about his past and future. EZ might even become one of God's chosen, something that only happened every million years in the Universe. Dan told him he had prayed for him, and he would allow EZ to feel all of the world's prayers for his success. As Dan said this, an immense warmth covered him like a blanket. His mother said it was time for the first challenge.

He must perform a series of abdominal contractions and kicks, almost like swimming, which would take him to the light above. If he failed, he would fall further into the darkness. Dan would be his coach. EZ felt himself start to fall, and instinctively tightened his entire body, contracting and moving his feet in a rapid sprint. Kicking faster and faster into the air as he lay on his back. Contracting tighter, legs moving and cramping as fast as he could go. He started to approach a hole into the light above. The hole reminded him of how it must feel to be trapped under ice , swimming as hard as one could to reach the opening for a breath. As he kicked, the ex-soldier coached him on, yelling and telling him to give more effort. He was almost to the light now. Kicking, contracting his upper body and arms. His entire body in spasm. He heard his mother next to the mattress.

"Breathe EZ. You are in a safe place. Quiet your mind. Breathe. *Shhhhhh. It' s OK EZ.* You are safe, breathe."

Dan added, "You got this soldier, Faster! You can give more than that! Do it for me. You are so close to the great reveal EZ. Move your feet. Do not give up. Give more!"

His father appeared above him now.

"Only if I die EZ will you be granted your reveal. Do you wish for my death? It's you EZ, you are the chosen one. The next God of Knowledge for Mother Ayahuasca. With my death, you will pass my knowledge upon the entire Universe."

His mother's voice returned.

"Breathe EZ. Calm down. If you don't calm down, I will make you leave this maloca. You will be an embarrassment to all. I must reveal the secrets to you. Try harder."

He had tried his best, but he was weakening. His efforts waned. The smell of tobacco engulfed him, impeding his ability to breathe. Failure was imminent, and he could feel himself sinking into a bottomless darkness.

He kicked again. Harder this time. Tightening his abdomen. Squeezing his biceps with all of his might. The hole was within inches. Dan's coaching was pushing him to new heights of ability, but soon, this time, complete failure. He fell into an endless hole. There was nothing left to give, mentally or physically. Mother Ayahuasca had made sure she would control his body and mind. She was in complete control, breaking his cgo and dctcrmination. A lcsson was to bc lcarncd.

His mother talked to him once again.

"EZ, this has all been fake. Together, we just wanted you to see how much of a failure you are to us all. Forever, you have let us down. What will be revealed to you is how worthless you are. I have a surprise for you EZ. THAT is the true reveal."

"You have let everyone in your life down EZ, not just us. I never wanted you. I have hated you my entire life. Sad state of a son. Worthless. It's time for you to suffer as much as me EZ, and just when you think you have suffered enough, then I will reveal something special to you." What was a deep hole became a black hole of eternal falling. A falling that would go on forever, and as he fell, he began to suffocate. His Mother coached his breathing, for with each breath taken, the speed and the depth of his soul grew deeper and darker.

"Breathe EZ. Slow your mind. You are safe. Relax into the darkness."

It was the voice from his childhood crib. His mother's coaxing.

EZ waited until he could wait no longer. His chest rose, sucking in as much air as he could possibly hold until the next, and with that breath, he was rewarded with an exponentiating black hole. He could not understand how darkness could get darker, how the hole could grow deeper. His mother was right there by his side, talking to him in the voice he had heard from her as a child. His mind in free fall, dropping through thousands of black holes.

"Good boy EZ. That's it. Now you understand the reward for disappointment. You feel the drop into nothingness, just as your life has been. You made my life miserable, and now you must understand that eternal pain. *Shhhhhh.* You can't hold your breath forever EZ. You are safe with me. Take another breath."

His brain was about to explode. He held on as long as he could. Praying it would not happen. Wishing for someone to help him escape the darkness. He took another breath and began to fall deeper and faster than before. His heart was broken. In his mind, he knew he was a failure, a fraud. He had let them all down, and this was now his life forever. He went from one drop to a thousand to a million to a billion. Each breath exponentiating his time in the abyss. His life was over. Just as he had been revealed to heaven, he had now been revealed to hell. A hell bigger than all the space of the Universe.

"EZ, now that you have realized your past mistakes, I will

now reveal to you what could have been your future."

A beautiful woman was now before him. She was full of love and happiness. She would be the mother of his children. She bathed EZ in love and light. The soulmate he had yet to find in his travels. Here she was before him. The great reveal his Mother had promised. Perhaps she had made him suffer enough. His Mother now wanted to educate him on some way to improve his remaining years. His Mother spoke again.

"Why do you think you are here EZ? I paid to have you brought here. Daniel was hired just to coach you and tell you to breathe. That wasn't your old friend Dan. Tina was here to coax you into this room. I paid all of them EZ. You are a failure to the world, the Universe. I never should have had you, and you do not deserve the light of a future wife. For if she were to marry you, she would end up killing you after she discovered how worthless you are. Remove yourself from this maloca."

This future wife now stood next to his mother, ecstatic at this reveal. Realizing his mother had saved her the time of falling in love and having her children with a man so unworthy. Together, they rejoiced as EZ fell further into an eternal blackness. Both were celebrating his demise. His future wife, and his mother, had cast him into eternal hell.

Daniel touched EZ's arm.

"It's time for a second dose EZ. Would you like another?".

 EZ laid dumbfounded on the mattress, slowly regaining his senses. *Hell was as real as heaven. He was sure of this now.*

"EZ, would you like another cup?".

"No Daniel. Not tonight."

EZ could hardly get the words out of his mouth. Fear, regret, and sadness surrounded his entire being. He no longer wished to be in the maloca. He wanted out. Up against the wall, he lit his ancient tobacco, hoping to calm his mind. Glancing around the room, he heard hiccups, vomiting, Icharos, and chanting. Everyone was on a different journey. He wished for no more journeys. Whatever this hell was, he never wanted to experience it again.

He observed the rest of the ceremony pinned against the wall on his mattress, being quiet so as not to disturb those on the mattresses next to him. He remembered a rectangular, spinning object taking him deep into the bottom of the Universe. He decided he would find Daniel after the ceremony ended. It was time to leave. He had failed his mission for UUONE.

The maestros returned to their spots. EZ figured the bird would chirp soon, and he would hear the ATV, and he was correct. *The bird must not like the Icharos as it always flies away when they start. It only comes near us when they are over.* The ATV sound evaporated into the night, and as expected, the return mating call of the pauraque in the distance called back to the maloca.

"That concludes tonight's ceremony. You may all stay and sleep here or return to your huts. We are here if you need guidance." Hanna announced.

It couldn't come fast enough. He had to talk to Daniel about how and when he would be forced to leave the next day. His visions had been made clear that the facilitators expected this. He looked for the cigar and found Daniel right away. *Of course he would still be smoking, he always was.*

"Daniel, what time do you want me to get on the boat tomorrow? I will pack tonight and be ready. I'm sorry for causing such an issue at the retreat. I've let everyone down." EZ turned away, fighting tears, unable to look Daniel in the eye.

"EZ, what are you talking about? I never said for you to leave. You went into your journey before we had even finished dosing the entire room. I had to call Luis over to you for him to perform an emergency Icharo. He felt the spirits of the jungle had overwhelmed you. He performed numerous spells over you to purge out the demons. Are you sore? You were contracting and kicking. I was reminding you to breathe for over fifteen minutes, trying to calm you down, and tell you that you were safe." Daniel informed him.

EZ looked up in disbelief. Nothing had been real, but he had never experienced anything with more truth. Surely Daniel wasn't lying.

"So, you didn't ask me to leave?."

"Not at all EZ. Mother Ayahuasca has revealed much to you tonight. Get a hot shower and sleep on all of this. Don't try to interpret it all right now. We would never ask you to leave EZ. This is all part of the process, and you have two more ceremonies to go. You must trust in the process." Daniel placed his hand on EZ's back.

"I'm here for you EZ. You are in a safe place."

Putting his cigar back into his mouth, Daniel walked on to consult the next person needing his expertise. EZ took a shower as instructed and walked back to his hut. He turned on his fan in the stuffy room and looked at his watch. One AM. He had been on a trip for over five hours. His body felt like it had been through a marathon. He tried to close his eyes and go to sleep, but laid awake in his bed, sweating profusely. He thought about getting some water. His watch now said two AM, and he was no sleepier than he had been an hour before.

As he was about to rise from his bed, EZ felt a strange sensation. It started with the hair on his arms, but then traveled to his legs. It felt like static electricity. Vibrant fast vibrations, or sound waves pulsating through his extremities. He froze in fear. It was likely the ayahuasca playing tricks with his senses. After about a minute, the feeling subsided.

Within seconds, it returned. This time the pulsations were alive in his chest. Another minute, his head. Another minute, his neck. The electrical waves were almost unnoticeable. He had to remain perfectly still in order to feel them affect his body, each time being what felt like a different area. Each pulsation lasted about a minute. The controlled buzzing eventually became too overwhelming. EZ stood next to his bed, and headed to the small back porch on his hut overlooking the jungle.

As soon as he arrived on the porch, about ten feet from his bed, the vibrations went away. EZ's mind raced, fearing another journey to the depths of hell.

Am I going crazy? Were these connected to the wires under the hut? Why are they at timed intervals?

This was all too overwhelming after the ceremony, but he had to prove to himself whether they were real, or was he starting to lose his mind. Inching his way towards his bed, the hair on his arms vibrated. He laid down in his bed, feeling the changing pulsations every one minute. They were on a timed cycle. He looked at his watch and began timing each length of their rotations just to be sure. The watch would not lie like his mind could. *One minute each.* He stood, and this time walked out the front of his hut. Once he was about four feet away from the front door, the feelings were lost.

He sat outside his hut pondering what was happening.

What caused these feelings? How were they being generated?

EZ returned to the safety of his back porch. He leaned over the porch's back rail, listening to the jungle, searching for clues. As his body crossed over the railing, he felt heat pierce his arm and chest. He jumped away from the railing, looking for what may have caused the intense heat. Moving slowly towards the rail, he looked to his right, above him, seeing the source of the heat. Near the maloca attached to a guard shack, was an intense blue light shining towards his movements. It turned in his direction, instantly heating his skin. When he was behind the corner of the hut's wall, the heat stopped. This maneuver achieved repeatable results.

Was this to keep the monkeys away from the tree tops during the ceremonies? Some type of directed energy weapon? But, for what reasons? Why would the camp want to keep him in his hut? It's almost as if they want me to suffer through the synchronized pulsations.

He stayed on his back porch, out of the blue light's heat waves, and tried to time when the sensations would end. There was a floating chair swing, and he sat, moving back towards the bed every one to two minutes, feeling the electricity return to his skin.

The jungle was quiet. As he grew tired, he laid his head back in the swing, the time was 2:45 AM. Just as he was about to fall asleep, he heard a "click" from under the hut. The sound that comes from an electrical timer or circuit breaker. Inching back in, he realized he was not crazy after all. The vibrations were completely gone. There was no way he would sleep now. Pulling out his journal, he documented the times and the blue lights. He lay in his bed, using his red LED flashlight to take notes, hoping none of the security would see that he had not gone to sleep. The retreat was not as it seemed. Remembering as much as he could about the day, before returning to the back porch swing. His head bobbed with sleepiness as he contemplated his options, his mind closer and closer towards sleep.

EZ had just reached the level of awareness just before sleep would arrive, and as he did so, the three skulls appeared in the bottom right side of his mind view, instructing him to tilt his head to the left. As he did so, the weight of his head smashed into the side of the swing, startling him back to his full awake state.

"What the fuck just happened to me? Who is controlling my mind?

"Click".

The breaker underneath his hut made the familiar noise, and the pulsations were back. Not wishing to endure the sensations in his bed, EZ decided to sleep in the safety of his porch swing. It was exactly 4 AM, and he predicted the vibrations would last for one hour. He understood why UUONE needed him there now. Something was going on. Some form of manipulation.

There was some way of instilling thoughts into his mind.

At 5:30 AM, like magic, the monkeys were back, waking EZ from the tree tops. He leaned forward in the swing, checking on the blue heat light. The fixture was there, but the light was now off. It was going to be an interesting retreat day.

AA Flight 191

Bentov finished packing his bag. What was left from his time in Massachusetts would be the information and experiments that he retained through memory.

"I'm sure they will be in to pack up my house anyhow," he thought.

The CIA and Mossad would not want to leave any evidence of his prior existence starting today. After placing his bags by the front door, he looked back one last time over his humble home before hearing the cab honk its arrival outside. May 25, 1979, a new birth date for whatever was to become his given name.

Bentov hadn't realized until his airport check-in that his bags would have a final destination of Los Angeles, but he decided it best not to change his ticket for a final arrival in Chicago. It was now on his mind that he needed to play a new role, and this would be expected of him by the Agencies. With his one carry-on briefcase, he dropped the bags off at the American Airlines counter and proceeded towards his gate. He grabbed a coffee, looked around to see if anyone was following him, and chose a seat near his gate. Without any fanfare in Boston, he arrived at Chicago's O'Hare Airport.

He noted his next flight was to depart Gate H6 at 14:59. Bentov stopped into one of the many restaurants to grab lunch. Sitting with his back to the wall, he still had not noticed anyone out of the ordinary-no familiar faces or repetitive passers by. His memory was excellent with faces, so he felt confident that he was not being tracked, or was it that these agencies were that good? He liked to think the latter as he was soon to be their new employee.

He arrived at Gate H6 about a half hour prior to boarding. He had not seen anyone to give him further instructions and was starting to question himself. *Didn't they tell me not to board the plane to Los Angeles?*

Surely, someone would guide him soon. His boarding section was called. He looked down, checking his flight number and seat-Flight 191, Seat 33A, to Los Angeles. Confused, he proceeded in line with the other passengers. When it was his turn, he handed his boarding pass to the gate agent.

"Mr. Bentov?," she asked.

"Yes, I'm Itzhak Bentov." He replied.

"Please proceed down the ramp. Thank you for flying with American today. We hope you have a good flight."

Proceeding down the ramp, he noticed a family of four in

front of him. The parents were overwhelmed with their stroller and bags for their kids. He slowly made his way to the aircraft door and was forced to a stop as the father broke the stroller down to pass to the line workers for storage under the plane. A young man in American Airlines coveralls was handed the stroller, passing it out an open door to his left. He then turned to Itzhak.

"Sir, your suitcases appear to have opened on your prior flight. Do you mind assisting us downstairs to verify everything is in order since Boston?".

Realizing that this was his clue, he replied.

"Of course. I hope nothing is lost." Stepping through the open door, he carefully stepped down the attached rolling steps, following the two workers under the belly of the aircraft.

"Mr. Bentov," the more senior airline attendant voiced, "your bags are just inside the door at the front of the aircraft. Please head that way to do your inspection."

Bentov shook his head in affirmation and walked without hurry to do as he was told. Upon opening the door, his luggage appeared alongside a familiar face.

"Good afternoon Itzhak."

Sidney Gottlieb greeted him and offered a warm handshake.

"Welcome to the CIA. Please leave your bags, we will take care of them. There is someone upstairs who would like to chat with you before we depart. Would you mind changing into these clothes?"

Gottlieb motioned to an adjacent room, and Itzhak changed into the provided blue button down shirt and pair of gray slacks. He was intrigued at the perfect fit. *Of course they would know his size.*

"Please leave your old clothes. We will take them as well. And for safe keeping, may I have your wallet, boarding pass, and identification?"

Itzhak held out his wallet. He realized he held in his other hand his license and boarding pass, still fresh from his check in. This would be the last time he would be Itzhak Bentov. Following the limping Gottlieb down the secured hallway, he was quite impressed by their actions. He had not thought of the oddity it would seem if he had suddenly vanished from his flights. The only people who had seen him go down the ramp to board were the family of four, and the gate agent, who would soon be on the aircraft.

They went to the first floor of steps and continued to a higher floor overlooking the boarding level. Gottlieb swiped his badge on a sensor outside an unlabeled door, and they entered into a deserted hallway which seemed to be a waiting areas for pilots and staff. Each room held a window facing the outer runway, so that staff could keep a timely watch on aircraft coming and going. Proceeding down the hallway, Gottlieb knocked on a door before he opened and entered.

Standing before Bentov was someone he had only seen on television.

"Pleasure to finally meet you Mr. Bentov." Stansfield Turner, Director of the CIA, reached forward to greet him.

"We have been waiting to finally bring you on board. I hope you understand there was a need to study your research for quite a number of years. Although Mr. Gottlieb had to shut down Operation MKUltra in 1973, he has been more than helpful in moving our efforts underground since his retirement. I would say taking him out of the public's eye actually let us expedite our progress. It's no fun being in the public's eye, let alone the eyes of Congress. Just so you know, we have tracked your studies through Director Dulles's days, through McCone, Raborn,

Helms, Schlesinger, Walters, Colby, Bush, Knoche, and now Mr. Turner. It seems that the issue of mind control is a little harder to crack than we initially thought, but all through that time, your name kept appearing as the expert. Have a seat."

Bentov took a seat and listened as the Director continued to speak.

"Mr. Bentov, have you ever heard of Operation Northwoods?" Itzhak shook his head no.

"Operation Northwoods was a CIA Project developed under the Kennedy administration that took a giant nose dive once the President declined to sign on to our long term goals. Within this Project, the takeover of Cuba had been planned, American civilian lives were offered in exchange for securing western freedoms, as well as many other secret objectives the country's finest had laid out after World War Two. Those that have the power over our long range goals did not take it lightly that their plans had been canceled, so it was decided to approach our objectives over a longer term. Placing those with our beliefs in positions of lesser power in order to secure positions in higher power down the road. This has led to the Agency being able to enact plans such as this one today as we have had a chance to monitor your knowledge in Massachusetts."

"Seeing also that we can now effectively have some say in Presidential elections, the days of idealistic Presidents like Kennedy are no longer a factor for American security. You see, Presidents come and go, but the CIA, and its secrets never do, regardless of politics. So in a way, the CIA runs this country, not the politicians. Being that we now have the complete idiot of Carter in office, my point is proven. Eisenhower knew this, and he even warned the country of the great power we would obtain over time. And now, we are happy to make you a part of our long term goals. Your future place with us will be for quite some time. I can't thank you enough for deciding to become a part of something bigger than yourself."

Bentov sat quietly listening to what was being presented-in awe at the man before him. Surprised at him revealing so much intimate detail and espionage to someone so new to the Agency. He had hardly left his home, and now he was being exposed to some of the biggest cover ups his country had ever committed.

Turner continued on, noting Bentov's silence.

"Anyway, back to Operation Northwoods. The Chairman of the Joint Chiefs at the time, Lemnitzer I believe his name was, presented several options to Kennedy that were flat out rejected. Those were different days, with different goals. Time was available to those men. Other methods could be enacted to meet CIA objectives. But today, going forward under Carter, and going into our soon to be hand chosen President and Vice President, the defeat of

Communism becomes the priority . The Soviets are at a tipping point, and that risks two things: the Agency not being needed as much in the future and former Soviet intelligence falling into the wrong hands. Being that they are far ahead of us in your field of expertise, we cannot allow that to happen.

"Sorry to rant, but it's needed to convey to you your importance. Something irreversible. Something the American people would see as traitorous, and that Kennedy stopped. You see, one of the ideas of Operation Northwoods was to take down one of our own jetliners, or at least make it appear that it had been taken down. What you are about to witness is what we hope to be the future of the CIA. So to secure your loyalty, to make our enemies regard you as deceased, and to further your theories on mind control, I want you to understand the gravity and necessity the absolute expediency-of what you are about to witness. The efforts to bring you into our Agency will come at a great cost should they ever be revealed. The reason for your disappearance will now make the utmost sense for the security and the safety of the entire free world. Sometimes it's difficult making a sacrifice to one's own personal goals, but it's even more difficult to make the decision on 270 others."

Not making a connection to this story of Operation Northwoods or the speech just given to him, Itzhak looked down at the table for answers. The room suddenly got quiet until Gottlieb's voice broke the silence.

"The plane is lined up for takeoff Director." Turner now spoke to both of them.

"Please gentleman, pray for us. God help all of us if you're both wrong."

Bentov, Gottlieb, and Turner looked through the window as American flight 191 sped down the runway, slowly lifting into the air before what looked like its left engine broke away. The plane dove quickly into the Earth and exploded into a ball of flames. Operation Northwoods had become a reality.

<u>Third Ceremony</u>

After the morning yoga and group meetings, EZ had developed a plan for the third ceremony.

He wanted to treat the ceremony with intent and focus. Focusing not on discovering Mother Ayahuasca's powers, but rather on observing the maestros, facilitators, sounds, participants, and the chain of events with a clear head. His lack of sleep was starting to take its toll, so an afternoon nap would also be required.

He realized that not drinking his dose might look suspicious to the staff, so he decided to limit his dose to one cup only. To not re-dose would allow him to stay alert during the second half of the ceremony and throughout the time back in his hut. After the initial cup, EZ made the decision to decrease all possible external stimuli. He would not sync to the music and maestros, and he would not entertain visualizations or move his body. The goal was to keep as still as possible to make it through the initial phase of the medicine's effects.

He was unsure he could do this, but UUONE had sent him here for a reason. It was time to go to work. His sixth sense was on full alert after discussions with the staff and participants. At this point, he didn't believe anything legitimate was occurring at the facility. Either this was an expensive scam to profit off the vulnerable, or some type of government controlled experiment with mind control.

He could not doubt the effects of the ayahuasca in the first two ceremonies. He was very certain of those experiences, but all the other activities of the staff, property, equipment, and his late evening vibrations were just too odd to discredit. The staff kept discussing the need to set intentions and goals. His just happened to be a little different for this third ceremony.

Waiting on his mattress with his back against the wall, he did his best to blend into the ceremony and not draw suspicions. As he lit his cigar, blowing the smoke over himself, he tried to recall the prior two ceremonial events, their sequences, and to keep a better eye on the staff. Prediction one. Would Daniel come in with his cigar in hand, smoking so all could see? There had to be something to this charade. No one smoked cigars that often. As if on que, the three facilitators arrived. Daniel with a cigar in his mouth. They quietly took their spots in the center of the maloca.

He had gotten to know the other attendees throughout the week. They were taught the strength of revealing past traumas and ceremony experiences in a group setting and when off the clock. EZ rationalized that if he was performing a government experiment, he would place undercover staff within the attendees to note any concerns not expressed to the staff. Perhaps, someone like himself might discuss that they were on to what they were up to there. The entire event was a perfect setup for mental manipulation from the start, so why not continue the data collection within the participants.

The experience of the retreat began with an initial interview, which required revelation of medications, life stories, current psychological issues, finances, money, and consent. The facility could determine who and who did not get to attend, and any reason could be provided without others knowing why the exclusion occurred. If one were to do the best of scientific studies, they could control for all outliers as well as select for those they wanted to test, manipulate, or blackmail. He thought back and only now realized how much they knew about him. All voluntarily released, and even worse, paid for by the attendees themselves. Further, in group talk or through reading journals when the participants weren't in their huts, the results of different medications or manipulations could be instantly self-reported for analysis. He could think of no better situation for a mind control experiment. EZ's sixth sense was almost to its seventh level.

Without a doubt, he knew something was amiss here.

The maestro's arrived. His next goal was to stay vigilant during the dosing phase and observe. He went for his dose, and told Daniel and Kristen that due to his previous night's dark journey, he wished to only take one cup. They both encouraged him once again, to not become disillusioned. He should *trust the process.*" At this point, he knew that would be their answer. He adamantly refused. The two looked at each other, the maestro, and then allowed him to take his one cup. Obviously, they weren't happy with someone refusing to trust *their* process.

He could sense he would now be on their radar. His level seven sense opened.

Returning to his mattress, he got as near to the wall as possible and sat upright, lighting his cigar.

Remembering the brew's timing from his second night, he needed to prepare himself quickly. He also noted that some of the attendees were starting with two, three, or more cups of the ayahuasca. He shuddered at the thought of how much misery that would cause if he took that much. Not only would they take that much now, but they would redose on their second opportunity. There had to be other factors involved than the medicine. How could it be that some in the crowd could take four times the dose of DMT than the person next to them? Perhaps, there was not even ayahuasca in some of the doses. He observed that two different pouring vessels were near Daniel. Another controlled experiment perhaps.

The maestros took their places and lit their cigars after their own dosing. He failed to see which vessel they drank from, but he could guess. *Was he being paranoid?* He didn't feel paranoid. He felt more right than at any time in his life. His street senses were on high alert. The smell of bullshit was beginning to increase every second.

"Next up, I will hear a pauraque bird sound behind me. It will be consistent in tone, pace, and volume. After the bird noise, or close to it, I will hear an ATV, constant humming, and then the pauraque's answer from the ATV's direction. Only then, would the maestros begin their Icaros." EZ thought and waited.

He didn't need to wait long. Bird, ATV, generator sounds, then bird again. It was obvious now that someone within the maloca was signaling with the bird that the doses were in place, and to initiate something EZ could only guess had to do with what he had found in the concrete building and within the electric box. Once whatever that generator powered, and whatever that oscillator affected was ready, the bird call was signaled back to someone in the maloca. The fact he had not heard this bird throughout any of his stay was even more suspicious. Jungle animals and jungle night sounds are usually consistently random. This reminded him of the fact that the monkeys seemed to disappear and return at the same time each day and night, except on his day of arrival. Insects, monkeys, and bird sounds had been present throughout the night when he had tried to sleep in his humid hut. He remembered this because they were almost so overwhelming in number and volume that he had trouble sleeping his first day. There was no way a pauroque would make this exact sound at this set time and place every single night for three days in a row, and then vanish for the other nights.

The bird noise was important, but more important would be to discover the purpose of the oscillation device and the coils under his hut that needed such giant copper wiring. He didn't know if he could sneak away to investigate now. In a way, he could tell they were treating him differently. He was altering their control-their experiment. If he was an agent with UUONE, and in the shoes of these facilitators, what would he be doing? He had to think like them. He had to focus on what was about to occur in the maloca, and that was going to be hard to do under ayahuasca's influence. Who knew what they had given him tonight? He must stay in the fight.

He could feel the medicine begin its ascent. Just as he had the first night, the tingling in his arms and legs first, followed by visual changes. EZ pinned his head against the wall and looked out across the room. He could focus for about a minute before his eyes lost control in the matrix. If he moved his head the slightest, the sounds would turn into echoes of auditory apocalypse. His body wanted to lay down, to ground to the floor, to let the medicine take over his soul and body. Moving his head was out of the question, he knew that the sense of balance was controlled by the vestibular system of his inner ear somehow. *Why had he not listened more in his biology classes?*

Locking his head against the wooden wall of the maloca, he struggled to remain focused. In an attempt to escape the optic changes, he looked up towards the maloca's roof. While he did see the firefly effect of prior nights, he regained control of his ability to rationalize. Perhaps from some leveling within his inner ear. Slowing his thoughts, he could return to his breathing. It had become sporadic and reactive to his inner ear's motion and his eye's inputs.

"Don't listen to the songs. Don't move your head. Remain still. Remain calm. Control your breathing. You can do this EZ. Stay in the fight. Don't let them win." He whispered to himself. His sense of time had vanished. He guessed he was at forty five minutes. The Icaros would start soon. How he would fight through that level of sensory overload, he did not know. The maestros rose from the center and took their positions opposite the room from each other. They each carried a small basket which he assumed had mapacho, an ashtray, a spit cup, and objects necessary for the ceremony. He had never actually made it to this part of the ceremony sober. *What may be in those baskets?*

"Ceiling. Focus on the ceiling. Don't move your head. Stay in the fight. This can't last much longer."

EZ knew that peak effects would hit soon. Once the trip starts, it may not end for hours. The goal was to fight off the initial surge. He just had to be patient. Once the medicine started, it would slowly fade, requiring that second dose to increase DMT to effective levels again. He phased out the Icaros the best his mind would allow. As long as his head and body did not move, he could manage the audio. Glance at the ceiling. Phase out the sound. Repeat. The medicine's ascension was starting to decrease. The ayahuasca's peak was starting to loosen its grips over reality. The matrix of the wall and of the ceiling's patterns were returning to normal. It was time to focus now. It was as if he had gone from one beer to twenty in forty five minutes and was now returning to the level of a six pack. He felt that he was now at a point he could listen and observe, and importantly, be able to recall the night's events with accuracy the next day.

"Fuck you assholes. I beat you. Game on." EZ began his mission.

The first thing he noticed was that the Icaros weren't as eloquent as he had remembered. In the first two ceremonies, they had been magical, enhancing every moment of the night. Currently, it sounded like pretty good karaoke. He would never be able to hit the notes the two maestros were achieving, definitely not in the biphasic harmony. Luis would sometimes perform a special ritual over individuals who seemed to be struggling. The ritual ended in a unique popping sound after his spell. Was there more to this? Where were the facilitators?

Looking across the room, he spotted Daniel with his cigar first. He was walking slowly around the room assisting those who may need guidance or were struggling with their thoughts. He would walk close to them, kneel, remove his cigar, chat, and move on. Kristen had taken up a position by the exit. Sometimes shining her red LED flashlight to direct those needing the bathroom, or lighting a path back to their mattress.

If at any point you became out of control, you were to shine your light three times quickly into your chest and help would be on the way. EZ had done this on his second night, but no one came. They either had not seen his mental emergency, or they had let the experiment on him run its course. He saw a three burst flash across from his mattress but could not make out who Daniel went to console.

Hanna was doing the same. Wondering the maloca, offering advice as necessary with the same red light. If needed, they would each walk close to the person in trouble, lean in with their light, before walking away. Exactly what were they doing? And why were some of the attendees never needing any help? It was almost as if they had not taken any medications at all? Even those who had taken six to eight cups were calmly sitting on their mattresses. How was it that DMT could have no effects on these individuals? Why had one to two cups demolished his soul? Were these people resistant to DMT? How could a person build up a tolerance to DMT? Was that even possible, or were they working with the experiment? EZ decided to go in for a closer look.

EZ slowly slid to the bottom of his mattress, making sure to trust his balance and feet before turning on his light to guide himself to the exit. With his light directed to the floor, he moved across the room, noting who looked sober, where the maestros were, and what the facilitators were doing. Not wanting to appear too sober, he paused often, offered a few moans, and shuffled to the bathroom.

Along the way, he observed the WiFi box situated next to the maloca now emitted a dim red light he had not noticed on his prior night's trips to the bathroom. He arrived at the bathrooms, locked the door, turned on the faucet, and sat on the toilet. Flushing frequently with appropriately timed groans, trying to settle his mind. There were too many things out of place.

How were the instructors and maestros so completely

sober? How had they eased through their dosing? Tolerance?
He watched as they had taken their doses from the same vessel as
others.

Or did he?

*"Breathe. Stay calm. Observe. If they are this sloppy with
their experiment, they will reveal more. Just wait."*

He turned the water off, opened the door, and was surprised
to see Kristen standing before him, waiting for him to exit. "Are
you okay EZ?", she asked.

"Uhhh, yeah. Sorry. I'm a little sick to my stomach. I felt
like I needed to purge. You said that means that Mother
Ayahuasca is ridding the bad spirits from my body, right?".

"Exactly EZ, and tonight is the Scorpion Moon. The fullest
moon-indicating a regrowth-the beginning of rain season and
your spiritual growth here in Peru. It is said the most powerful
journeys can occur with the Scorpion moon."

"OK Kristen. Thanks for checking on me. I'll go slow, but
I don't think I'll be able to do the second dose with this nausea.
I'm feeling so sick right now."

"No problem EZ. I think you will have your own
experiences without the need. Only She knows what you need.
Just listen to what She says. Trust the process."

EZ returned to his mattress feeling more awakened. Why
had she followed him? There was already a guard near the
bathroom to assist there, but she had made a line straight to him.
He was no longer paranoid. They *were* watching him for sure.
He would have to role play at certain parts of the ceremony to
take the eyes off of him and keep them guessing. As this thought
crossed his mind, Luis arrived at the foot of his mattress to sing
his individualized Icaro. EZ thought this would be a good time
to act. It was expected that you sit at the foot of your mattress to
show respect to the maestro and this personal Icaro, sung only to

you at that moment, which would happen to each attendee twice throughout the night.

EZ sat upright on his knees, and closely observed the maestro. Listening to the tranced hymn written specifically for him. As he watched, he heard a clicking sound. Was it a speaker? What was the click? He could not tell, but he had definitely heard the click. EZ raised his arms to the Scorpion moon, then touched his head to the mattress, paying respect to the maestro's offering.

Click.

There it was again. Something in his tray that he touched in front of him. Was it for him? Was it for someone next to EZ? Was it a directional device? He returned his attention back to the facilitators as the maestro moved on to the next person.

Once again, he put his back to the wall and remained motionless. If Kristen was watching him, he would need to keep playing out his sick role. He closed his eyes. The ayahuasca making it hard to piece things together. He had all the pieces he needed, but couldn't put them together.

What was he missing?

EZ began to feel the strange sensation that he had felt in his hut late at night. The tiny vibrations, a buzz, a warmth. Almost unnoticeable if he had not been paying attention. As the buzz continued, instead of fighting it off, he accepted it. Where would this take him? What did the vibrations do?

He felt the cycling of the vibrations. Around thirty seconds, pause. Repeat. But with each change, a different part of his body was affected, and slowly, with his mind sobering, he realized his emotions were affected as well. He had to tune in to his emotions, but there was zero mistake now. Warmth, chest, happiness. Pause. Warmth, neck, anxiety. Pause. Warmth, back, sadness. Pause. Warmth, stomach, regret.

Empathy, boredom, calmness, joy, excitement, adoration. With each change in frequency came a change in emotion. They were controlling his emotions, but how? It was man made. Add the medicine, and you wouldn't be able to differentiate. You would blame your change in emotions on the medicine. But, emotions, much like the bird, don't decide when they come and go. Sadness may last for minutes or hours. Joy may be fleeting. These were timed, predictably, and in someone else's control. He could not let them on to his discovery. Whatever he was to do at that point, don't move. Stay focused. Stay in the fight. If he had self control, he could wait until the next emotion. *Observe EZ. You are close.*

An emotion of sadness, pain, and regret swept over his body. As it did, the person to his left thrashed uncontrollably on their mattress, seemingly possessed. Moaning in pain, grabbing their bucket to purge. Looking up to Mother Ayahuasca and the Scorpion moon, thanking her for the purge in bad spirits from his body. These were truly sick fucks who were running this experiment EZ thought.

The emotion and pulse was stronger than the prior heat that he had felt before. Where was this coming from? A puff of a cigar caught EZ's eye. Daniel. He was looking straight at the guy to EZ's left. He was about ten yards away, and as he took the cigar away from his mouth, he placed it near his leg. When the cigar came back up, EZ happened to be looking directly at it. A red glow was emitted from the cigar's tip, but the cigar's tip, instead of being uniform in glow, was slotted and increased in its level of brightness. Pointed directly at himself and the mattress to his left, he could feel the pulses increase in magnitude. As Daniel took the cigar down to his leg, the waves stopped, and so did the contractions of the man to his left.

"Watch for smoke on the exhale? Watch EZ? Watch for the

smoke. You are not crazy EZ.

Watch for the smoke. "

Nothing. No smoke. EZ had it. He watched as the real cigar made its way back to Daniel's mouth. He inhaled, then exhaled a circle of smoke. *A directional electromagnetic pulse device of some type.*

EZ had seen larger units used in military crowd control, but whoever was part of this unit was next tier. He had to be careful now. How were they cycling the emotional pulsations?

Observe. You are almost there.

He changed his focus to Kristen, as Hanna was on the opposite side of the room. He watched as she approached a struggling participant. She knelt over, and he saw her turn and point her red LED flashlight onto the person, who immediately calmed themselves, almost seeming to be reset. She went to the next person who seemed to be resting peacefully, knelt down, initiated the device, and presto, they were reaching for their bucket to vomit.

The mandatory red LED flashlights.

The facilitators were in on the experiment. The maestros had made a full circle. Time for second doses if requested. EZ took note of who went and who did not. This pause in the Icaros would be a good time to explore.

Slowly, he took to the exit, heading to the bathroom as the instructors were occupied. He noted the WiFi light was off. Locking himself in the bathroom once more, he waited for the Icaros to begin. He left the bathroom noting that the WiFi light was back on.

They had control of the vibrations. This is where they were broadcasting the signals. From the generators, from the oscillator, from the concrete building and the electrical box.

He made his way to the grassy area in front of the maloca,

and like clockwork, Kristen appeared.

"How are you EZ? Feeling any better."

"A bit Kristen. The Icaros are helping, and this moon? It's so bright and full of magic. Mother Ayahuasca is teaching me valuable lessons this week." He reached his arms into the sky towards the moon, reveling in its power.

Keep up the act EZ. Complement them. Distract.

"Well done EZ. Don't stay out here long. The mosquitoes will eat you alive. Why don't you head back inside for the last circling of the maestros?" More of a demand than a question. EZ kept up his act, shuffling sideways and appearing to take the maloca's steps with caution. He had not noticed before, but the yoga instructor, Tina, was manning the door. She turned on her red LED, and guided him to his mattress.

Was she in on this too? The feather. She had given me the pauraque feather from her bird. It was all part of the show. He had not been the first to question the bird. They had come up with an excuse in case someone figured out the signals to turn on the oscillator. One with personalization and intimateness.

This time, he wasn't worried about the pulsations. They would cycle and cause no long term harm. As the maestro made his way closer to his mattress. EZ watched his hands.

Click. Click.

He was either changing the pulsations with the songs, or communicating with the other maestro.

Whatever was involved, it was artificial. He was instigating change of some sort, perhaps to the WiFi, in a pattern to their tones. *He has a directional device in the basket. They were syncing the left and right brain through tones. That's why they are one hundred eighty degrees apart.*

Within the maloca's circled roof, the brain would be able to hemi sync. They would have to be a half circle apart at all times. It was in Bentov's book I read on the plane.

EZ reflected back on the homework he had studied before the class. He had gone down a rabbit hole on brain hemi synchronization used by monks and yogis. He had also read about this technique being refined by a man named Robert Monroe for the CIA. This sync of the left and right brain was supposed to open up a third eye to the Universe.

Once the last Icaro was complete, EZ knew what to expect. He now watched the maestro's take their seats with the facilitators. Quietness took over the room. Hiccups could be heard. A few groans, tears, and mumblings.

Wait for it EZ. Wait for the bird. What happens before the bird?

Click.

Luis's direction.

Bird.

Thirty seconds of the bird, then ATV, then bird by the ATV.

Wait for it EZ. You are not paranoid. You are not crazy. You have won!

ATV. Muffled ATV. Pause. Bird.

"Alright everyone. That concludes tonight's ceremony. You are welcome to stay as long as you would like. We will be here to answer any concerning thoughts. Please let your maestros exit before yourselves. Thank you maestros for your beautiful ceremony." Hannah said.

EZ was almost laughing at this point. Someone else had to have listened and put all of this together. He knew what his next job was. Being sober, he had to prove a few more things to himself. He exited the hut and merged himself in the group. Some were joyful, others had tears. Hugs were given amongst the girls. Guys the same. They were sold on the process.

Perhaps he was the only one to understand what had just happened.

He locked the door on his hut and set the alarm on his phone for 12:55 AM. This would be about an hour after everyone had fallen asleep in the safety of their huts, too tired emotionally from the ceremony to care, or if awake, overwhelmed with their emotions, to notice subtle changes..

Perhaps they needed a little more reinforcement with some electromagnetic frequency.

EZ went to the rear porch of his hut. No insects. No monkeys.

The animals can sense the WiFi. The EMF frequencies. They don't want to be near them.

Easing his head around the hut, he looked for the blue light, seeing it, the unit arched itself towards his head's movements, and he felt the burning on his skin. He moved behind the safety of the hut's wall, and the burning went away.

Were the lights to keep the monkeys away from the WiFi boxes? Were they to keep people in the area away from the ceremony? They were motion activated, so unlikely to emit mind control waves.

The alarm buzzed at 12:55.

Listen for it EZ. Listen for the junction box. You are not crazy. You are not paranoid.

Click.

Arm sensations. Emotional, sequential patterns-turning off at 2 AM with another click at the junction box.

He set his next alarm for 3:55 AM.

Listen for it EZ. Listen for the junction box. You are not crazy. You are not paranoid.

Click.

Feeling accomplished, EZ headed to his bed knowing the

electromagnetic waves would be done for the night. The monkeys would be back to wake him around 5:30. Sunrise was pretty consistent near the equator.

191 Destruction

Landon Haus had worked for the agency for nearly twenty years. He knew the idea that the CIA operating only outside of the United States was humorous. A more accurate image would be that the CIA operated outside of the Federal Bureau of Investigation, and many times, outside of the National Security Agency. While the FBI may be tasked with homeland intelligence, the CIA was tasked with long term implementation of deep state goals-regardless of who may be President or in Congress. No one ever questioned his expenditures, and with how busy he was, there seemed to be an uptick in operations nationwide after the Kennedy assassination.

Absolute power corrupts absolutely. He thought.

After assuming his aircraft inspection attire, he easily picked out the target coming down the runway ramp. Bentov was his name. Doing as asked, he proceeded to ask Bentov to follow him down the adjoining step ladder to inspect his bags in another part of the airport. He did not know who or what was beyond the door, only that he was to insure Bentov made it there. He then proceeded about the rest of his mission.

The pilot of American Airlines 191 had brought down the day's flight logs, and he was to hand those over to be input into the American Airlines system. However, in violation of procedure, he placed them into his own personal duffel. Someone did not want this plane to have a record of its flights for that day. His research did note that the log books were recorded into American's system for flights the prior day. He then moved his inspection ladder over to the left wing pylons and inspected the aircraft. Although, this wasn't the first time he had done so to this particular aircraft.

During March, he had been sent as a representative of the NTSB to evaluate a new method of exchanging engines in Tulsa, Oklahoma. American Airlines was using a new technique to replace engines that would save the company over 200 hours during engine exchanges. By limiting the number of fuel, electrical, and hydraulic line removals during replacement, the process could be expedited. The Agency had learned of this procedure from one of its standard wire taps in a New York City phone office. Apparently, the agency saw an opportunity related to how American was performing the procedure. Rather than using an overhead crane to support this disassembly, American had chosen to use a forklift to brace the engine during the repairs. That's where he came in. His goal was to delay the plan until shift change at the repair facility. Once the shift change occurred, he walked past the forklift operator at just the moment he was leaving his station and turned the machine off. This caused the hydraulics to decrease enough on the forklift to jam the pylon onto the wing. It was now up to him to determine if the repair should go on. The Agency knew that damage to the pylon mounting brackets would continue over time, and thus provide a cover to why, at just the right needed time, an airliner would suddenly have an engine separation.

Once their mission had been accomplished, an immediate response would be necessary on all DC-10 aircraft. Upon his team's inspection of the forklift drop, employees had also been unaware of the pylon retainer bolts being swapped with nearly identical bolts. Had they inspected further, a difference in weight and strength may have been noted. The Agency's bolts had embedded thermite cores, connected to radio transmitters.

Once replaced, the Agency had plausible deniability through bad maintenance techniques as well as zero evidence of bolt failures, as thermite would erode the metal enough to look as if a few thousand gallons of jet fuel had caused the damage.

Seeing that the Agency's bolts had not been replaced since March, the operation was to be a go. He questioned whether the death of Americans from an intentional crash should bother him, and he shrugged it off.

"What were the deaths of a few hundred Americans compared to the thousands of deaths the Agency caused across the world?"

The long term mission of the United States didn't matter much to him, but the ability to retire in a few months with full benefits did, and he doubted the Agency would let him live to see retirement if he were to quit now. Only a few operators were tasked with continental operations such as this, and he could guess only a few at the Agency even knew of this mission's existence.

The Agency was compartmentalized for a reason.

Returning back to the door he had escorted Bentov through, he walked up the steps and placed himself in front of one of the large glass windows to observe takeoff. He had already activated the altimeter detonators on the bolts, and they would automatically activate with the preset elevation. He was unsure how long it would take for the engine to shear off. Landon knew that their research indicated the most important engine to blow up on a DC-10 was the first left engine as it powered the slat warning light as well as the pilot's low stall stick shaker. A backup stick shaker for the First Officer was not ordered by American Airlines during production, nor was it mandatory.

There would be no way for the pilot to use the two backup engines to recover if the slats on the left wing were retracted.

The plane would stall with no correction from the cockpit. At the same time the left wing was decreasing lift, the right engines would be going to full power per pilot protocol to stop the stall, and this would only expedite the airplane diving to the left. The cockpit's reaction would likely not be fast enough at that low of an altitude to use their prior flight experience to correct the dive and stall.

He watched the plane roll to runway 32R with what his duffel's flight log recorded was 271 occupants on board. Replacing Bentov on the flight had been easy. A prior informant, similar in size to Bentov, had been instructed to change into Bentov's clothes. He was a cocaine addict the Agency had busted with child pornography. He had been persuaded to do one mission in exchange for all charges being dropped. He had been told he would be meeting another agent in California. Landon figured his loss was doing the world another favor in the name of Democracy.

AA 191 reached takeoff speed, and just as it cleared the runway, Landon watched the left engine separate as expected, falling to the runway. Inverting nearly upside down, he thought he could see hydraulic fluid spraying into the air just before the plane impacted the ground. Mission complete.

He didn't know who this Bentov character was, and actually wished he did not know his name. This was the first time that he knew the Agency had blown up its own citizens to achieve whatever in God's name they felt was so urgent. He would now have to continue his nightmares wondering if the Agency would see him as a threat, knowing secrets of the operation. He was now a liability, as he was on so many missions before this one. He had been privy to meeting some of his coworkers who had planned Operation Northwoods so long ago, but now he would be the one who could tell them that on his retirement year, he had actually pulled off one last great achievement. It was all part of the bigger picture, outside of his compartment to ask. He stood and walked through the airport. Going unnoticed to the crowd around him, now all staring out at the crashed debris. The airport was in mass chaos with firetrucks, ambulances, and news crews rushing into the area. Airport police were too few in number to establish a perimeter, and he waved down the first cab that pulled through the departures lane, ducking his six foot one frame into the Yellow Cab.

"Hi sir, I'm Johnny. Where are you headed?" The driver seemed uninterested and bored with the day.

"Please take me to the Palmer House, corner of State and Monroe."

Landon closed his eyes and looked forward to the luxuries awaiting him at the Palmer-the longest continually operating hotel in America. He loved the French lobby, the murals on the ceilings, and the 24 karat Tiffany gold chandelier. Murals depicted his love of Greek mythology and featured Aphrodite, Pluto, and his favorite, Apollo-the god of the sun. Its geometric patterns around the Gods and Muses reminded him of some of the Mayan art he had seen on missions in South America-concentric, tight, repeating geometric shapes representing their own Gods and Goddesses. The success of a big mission required celebration, and he didn't think the Agency would mind him putting it on their standing expense account at the hotel. Presidents, politicians, Hollywood elites-he had followed them all to this historic venue before, so it's unlikely his expenses would even be noticed. He wasn't even sure the CIA's budget was tracked at all. The driver was an African American man in his late forties. He wore a blue Chicago Cubs hat, was chewing gum non stop, and drove way too fast for Landon's liking. Nearing the hotel, he also turned the wrong direction, placing them not at the front entrance, but near the transit authority station on Wabash.

"Sir, can you please take me to the front entrance. You are about one block off. Are you new to Chicago? I see you're a Cubs fan, so I would think you would know downtown," Landon said impatiently.

The driver turned to face Landon in the backseat.

"Actually I'm a Braves fan. I hate Chicago."

Turning quickly to his right, the driver flashed a suppressed pistol towards Landon's left chest. Landon recognized the Smith and Wesson MK22 "Hush Puppy". It had been his favorite for years, but he had never been on the receiving end of its quietness.

"Here's for all my Vietnam brothers, you long toothed bastard."

The driver emptied the pistol straight into Landon's chest until the magazine was empty, and he heard no breathing from the back seat.

Having used this same gun during Operation Plan 34A on the North Vietnamese coast, Johnny felt it appropriate since today's mission was keeping it "in the family". That operation, some argued, started the Vietnam War. He didn't know what this cat had been up to, but only that he matched the description of the man he had been sent to pick up and kill at the airport. Johnny was hired often by the Agency as a paid assassin. When they told him his target had helped in the espionage leading up to Vietnam, Johnny had taken it for free. Many of his brothers had died there.

He also could tell that the CIA was likely up to more dirty tricks. His radio was describing the deaths of over two hundred people from a plane crash at O'Hare. He now realized they had sent him there to take out their operative. Operatives could always talk. Closing his eyes, he reflected back to his meditation practices from Vietnam. His Thay, Monk, had always reminded him.

"There are no coincidences in this world. We are all connected to a greater spirit. A spirit that is invisible to most of us, but visible to many for centuries if you can open your inner eye and soul."

Johnny had always practiced meditating, hoping to see the spirits, to visualize Gods, to predict the future. Little did he know, his actions today would conceal and protect the CIA's mission to do what his Thay had been able to do through years of meditation.

Giving up on his spiritual intentions in the Chicago traffic, he focused on getting to the safe house. He was hoping to be done in time to listen to the baseball game that night. The Cubs were playing away in Philadelphia.

He started laughing and looked into the rearview mirror at the unknown dead agent. "I do have one prediction for my old Thay, I bet the Cubs beat the Phillies tonight by three runs."

Fourth Ceremony

How could he get out of taking the last night's dose? EZ had no idea what was in the drinks they were handing out in the maloca. He remembered, prior to attending the retreat, reading about hospital related admissions following ayahuasca ceremonies in the United States. There had been several research articles describing patients in a dissociated, almost schizophrenic, state for days after ceremonies. Individuals prone to bipolar disorder or schizophrenia, or with family histories of those diseases, were at a higher risk of possible side effects from ayahuasca. His mother had not been diagnosed in those years, but likely suffered from manic-depressive disorder, and possibly bipolar disorder. He had not told the health surveyor this on his pre retreat phone screening.

The staff would not have had time to evaluate this, and may have never let him attend had he mentioned it; however, it really had never been "diagnosed'. Technically, he had never lied on the screening. He had also already taken three doses and seemed to fall under the normal outcome of psychedelics.

EZ thought of different ways to skirt this issue. Perhaps take the dose, but not swallow, spitting it out in his purge bucket. Asking for a smaller dose was another option. He had already made it through his last ceremony with enough proof to know the experience wasn't as advertised. He also wanted to be away from the maloca. He wanted to reassess the timing of events, the ATV, the vibrations, and the heated energy device without being under any influence of the drug. He decided to approach Daniel at the communal lunch.

"Daniel, I had quite an experience last night. It was rather paranoid in nature. Being that my second experience was tragic, and last night's has led to a high level of paranoia today, I don't think I will be taking tonight's medicine."

"You must trust the process EZ. We would never force you to take the medication, but we do expect you to please attend the ceremony with us."

"Daniel, I need to tell you that my Mother suffered from paranoid-schizophrenic episodes when I was younger. I didn't think it was relevant until today. I've read prior to coming about the dangers for people with my family history. Even being in attendance, I fear may lead to an episode at this point. I hope you will understand that I will remain in my hut for the duration of the evening. I wish everyone the best."

"I'm sorry you feel that way. I do hope you change your

mind. We do expect you not to leave your hut. There will be a few facilitators to oversee your safety on the premises. We will make sure that you are there prior to the ceremony. I hope you understand."

"Not a problem. Thank you for understanding. I feel as if I'm really struggling right now. If I could guarantee my first night's experience, then I would love to attend. But to have three negative journeys in a row may lead to me taking time off work when I return home. I just need to protect my long term sanity at this point."

They could not argue his rationale, but he knew they had lost their control over him. They would be watching him now like a hawk. EZ wanted to take pictures of the concrete structures on the trail, the generators, the electrical components, and the WiFi before he left the retreat, but he also knew that they may search his phone at some point. From this moment forward, he just wanted to get out of the Amazon and make his report to UUONE. He also was quite sure retreat employees were evaluating their journals while they were in the ceremony. Taking notes on personal revelations would add more data for their experiment. No one expected their private thoughts to be read, but EZ felt that if he was running this chaos, he would have secretly done so. He had no internet or phone access, no friends or unit to call. It was on him to get out of this safely without causing further harm to himself mentally.

He desperately wanted to research current EMF technology, EMF pharmacology, directed EMF devices, and what other intelligence agencies were currently up to concerning mind control. It was better that he couldn't, as they would likely track internet searches and phone calls off of the local tower. Whomever had this level of money and technology would certainly have data capture ability as well.

As dusk settled over the camp, EZ noticed the monkeys that had been near his hut begin to travel further into the jungle. Many of the birds and jungle animals that had been present during the day also started a journey away from his hut. He noted the WiFi boxes had turned on as well. They were likely getting their computers online and testing the system prior to the ceremony. There were only a few things he wanted to confirm, just to triple cover his prior sedated brain.

EZ remembered an old proverb and added to it a bit.

Fool me once, shame on you. Fool me twice, shame on me. Fool me three times….not gonna happen.

He knew the sequence of events for the maloca. He peered towards it, only noting red LED flashlights occasionally piercing the darkness. He saw the maestros walk by his hut and began his countdown. He lay on his bed and knew he had a long night ahead of him. The conspiracy theories of who, why, and how entered his mind.

Was this a private experiment? Did the medicine have something that stayed in the system permanently? Who had developed the technology? Was this Russian, CIA, British, or even an Israeli secret project? Did the mind need the vibrations, psychedelic, and another molecule to work, or were the EMF waves enough on their own? He put these thoughts aside. It would soon be time, and he needed to focus. He turned on a small lamp in his hut. He wanted them to know he was present if he was being watched.

Pauraque, ATV, generators, humming, no animals in the jungle, pauraque return call. Silence. Icaros. Screams, moans, groans. Red lights. Everything was confirmed in the exact order he predicted, even the one and four o'clock EMF waves. The good news for EZ was that this was the last ceremony. He would get to depart in two days. The retreat felt that the students needed to be supervised one last day before returning down the river to civilization. He went to sleep happy that there would be no more yoga, no need to continue on with lies, and no more worry of mind control.

The next day's events were very routine. A return to normal diets, group photos, a last group share from the prior night's ceremonies, and packing. Apparently, EZ had missed quite the show. Almost the entire group had gone on profound journeys. He wasn't that surprised. The guests would be home soon, and those who questioned their trip would want to know if Mother Ayahuasca had spoken. He guessed they might have even backed off the negative emotions that night and focused the waves on happy, positive ones. Add the medicine with the ability to direct human emotion, and those in attendance would sell the retreat to others joyfully.

After all, he thought, the experiment needed to remain self funded as much as possible. Happy clients voluntarily passed along stellar reviews. The younger egos would want to post about their journeys of self awareness, bragging to the world where they had been and what they had done. It seemed as if these types of retreats were springing up all over the area. Were they legitimate or more places to experiment? The more conspiracy minded EZ became, the more possibilities were revealed to him of the possible use of this technique.

They boarded the boats the next morning. EZ had been the first to arrive at the dock. He could not wait to leave. Contact information and hugs were shared as some of the attendees were going on a tour of Peru, and some were headed back to Lima to catch returning flights back to their home countries. EZ fell into this last category. He listened on his bus trip to the stories the others told. There were some average experiences, but there were also some life changing ones as well. Perhaps he shouldn't judge the event so harshly. They seemed to be helping some of these people who had legitimate issues. But he could not bring himself to agree to this philosophy. They were manipulating people's minds without consent. Whatever devices and medications that were being used, were being used without knowledge of injury or long term side effects. He was happy he hadn't done the last ceremony.

EZ's cell service returned, and he booked a cheap hotel near the airport. He then booked a flight back to Montreal. Logging into a secure coded email with a VPN, he let UUONE know that he was "returning home soon." No other details were going to be provided until his flight landed in Canada. If these individuals could pull this operation off, then they could also make him disappear in downtown Peru.

He got the key card for his room and was looking forward to a hot shower, real food, and a good night's rest. Today, he would be drinking some wine to put him off to sleep. His mind was on a race track. He opened the hotel room door and discovered an older gentleman already occupying his room

"I'm sorry sir. I must have the wrong room. Odd that his key worked on your's."

"No need to be sorry EZ. Make yourself right at home. I won't be here long."

EZ stood in disbelief. How could they obtain this data so quickly? Who had followed him? The retreat was on to him. It was likely they would kill him tonight, in Peru. He had failed his mission. He had been so close to success.

"Don't worry EZ. I'm not here to hurt you. I am a fellow Jew like you EZ, also part of

UUONE."

The man appeared to be in his late seventies or early eighties. His hair was disheveled. His voice held a humorous tone. He seemed to be enjoying the moment. He spoke calmly, confidently. EZ listened as the man continued his surprise.

"EZ, I am Itzhak Bentov. Did you enjoy the retreat I designed? It seems you have figured out quite a large portion of it. Of course, that is why you were sent here by UUONE. If you weren't above average, you would not have been given the task. Many have come here and failed to the power of our suggestions. Could you or would you succumb to the process was why they sent you here. They also wanted you to have experienced the power of what you will soon be privy to. You, EZ, will soon be using this power throughout the world. We needed to test you. We also needed you to understand your future powers. Congratulations on reaching the next step. I have worked many years to refine our techniques, and certain agencies have gone to great lengths to protect our secrets in order to use them for our interests going forward. How do you feel after your week?" Bentov finished.

EZ had not moved since entering the room. It was true. They could affect the human mind. How far had they come? His conspiracy theories rushed back into his mind. He had not been wrong. Bentov read his mind through the lack of response.

"Come EZ. Take a seat. I will explain the whole process to you. You must understand its process and goals more than even myself. It will be upon you and a few others to introduce my theories to the world. I will answer all of your questions EZ. Remember your ceremonies and what your mother would have told you. *Relax. Take a deep breath. You're in a safe place*." The old man cackled at EZ's expense.

<u>Mekubals</u>

"EZ, I am what is termed a Mekubal, a Kabbalist. As you

have learned from your initiation with UUONE, I watch over all things. I am responsible for overseeing the walls surrounding

Jerusalem, our Holy Lands, and over the entire earth. You were given my book -*Stalking the Wild Pendulum.* It is through my theories in that book that I was able to open up my eyes to the heavens; however, it was only through combining ayahuasca, or like my colleagues at the CIA did with LSD, with my theories on consciousness that I was able to enter a constant state of dvekut, communion, with our Creator. As you experienced on your journeys, there is another world around us. Known for thousands of years before us, passed along in the oral traditions of Kabbalah. Only the most advanced Jews were privy to the true knowledge of the Universe.

"You will find that I died in a 1979 plane crash. You will also find my books a bit confusing. What is relevant for you to know, is that we were just beginning to understand the human mind in the Sixties and Seventies. My work opened new doors, and through those doors, Israel and the United States took a great interest in me. The United States government 's CIA works in the best interest of our country EZ. Some call it the Deep State. A realm that no politician shall threaten. Many of the secret projects surrounding mind control were starting to come to light from carelessness. Once the internet came about, there was too much revealed. The general public was never supposed to know what our two governments were up to. MK Ultra, Project Stargate, Montauk, and particularly my specialty, the Gateway Process. Once this became exposed to Congress, after this embarrassment, we decided to go underground.

"As many traces of the program as possible were destroyed, burned, or buried, including bodies of those who knew too much. To have the power to control minds and societies could not fall into the hands of the enemies of Zion. If things don't make sense in the world EZ, such as politicians making poor choices, or catastrophic events happening without reason, you now know that there is much more going on. Even more compartmentalized than mind control, is the next level. The level of true understanding regarding angels, demons, and all things gnostic.

"The CIA arranged for my disappearance in 1979 and moved me here, to Peru. Their prior studies with LSD, including those from the Nazi's at Dachau, indicated that the German invented substance would not be the miracle we needed to communicate with our third eye EZ. We allowed you to experience this during your first ceremony. Did you feel its power? It's truth?". "Yes. It was the most beautiful experience I have ever had. You are now saying that what I experienced was real? That you are able to communicate to enter dvekut?."

"Yes, EZ. The Kabbalah is real. Moses' visions were real. The angels are all real. There are many worlds EZ, but one must be able to open their minds to be able to communicate. The ancient tribes in this area did. How do you think the pyramids were built without modern equipment? Why do you think the same ancient architecture exists here as it does around the world? Being built long before modern historians place it, these pyramids had functions which you will learn about over time. It is not for me to tell you now. You will have many lessons now that you have experienced these abilities that so few have. Your Father, the Prime Minister, and many who contribute to our cause have been introduced. Celebrities. Men with power and money. Many of who we now call the Illuminati. God's molecule, DMT, found in the ayahuasca, should have been kept a secret."

"So Daniel, Hanna, and Kristen were all part of this experiment? They work for you Bentov?"

"Yes, EZ. Myself, the Americans, Israelis, and the British. We have developed our final product. It has taken us years, but with ayahuasca, hemi sync, and EMF, we have the ability to communicate and instill mind control. I knew that hemi sync would match up the brain's alpha waves and allow the chaos of both brain spheres to sync, but with ayahuasca, we were introduced to a more perfect synchronization. We determined that DMT suppressed the alpha waves leading to no sense of self. Ego is lost in an area we call the claustrum, and once it is lost, we can't relate to the past, only the present. We can no longer identify ourselves, and therefore, the brain does not know how to function. It recognizes only that we are living in a hallucination. The brain recognizes that everything is the hallucination at present. With this discovery, we could then instill what the future may be without being hindered by the past. The ability to program becomes much easier through radio frequency guidance as well.

"We can also determine who can sync and view with ease. You don't actually think that the CIA would give up on these ideas after Congressional exposure? Of course not. We just had to find a way to keep our own governments from finding out, as the politicians would want too much control. We, the Deep State if you wish, are the ones who have financed and developed this to protect our walls. Tell me, what did you think of the skulls you envisioned?"

EZ could now believe Bentov was telling the truth. He had told no one about the three skulls.

"So was I taking ayahuasca? Was the first night real? How are you able to control all of these emotions? How are you able to input thoughts?" EZ asked.

"It took the development of brand new technology EZ. We knew that my theories could be perfected, but this took much practice. Those who do something like Kundalini may take thirty years to become experts, but we wanted a way to expedite the process. This is why psychedelics were first being researched by the CIA. It was by accident, like many experiments, that the two came together. There have been many men over thousands of years who knew these secrets, able to become Prophets and wise above others.

"What we were missing was what I brought to the experiments. We were missing vibrations. These vibrations enable our minds to quickly sync with the third eye as you did. With ayahuasca's ability to open an almost hypnotic third eye, we could instill programming trials, but we still needed more for input and triggering when necessary. Sync the brain's hemispheres, suppress the alpha waves, instill a present and future self goal that overrides the ego when needed, and instill new thoughts using electromagnetic training.

"When I signed on with the CIA in 1979, extensive work was being performed on the Gateway Process. My techniques to disengage the left brain's control over incoming stimuli allowed the right brain to accept all new input as fact. All incoming brain activity was transmitted to the homunculus. We knew that meditation could open the Gateway, but we also discovered that acoustical vibrations would as well.

"That is why you heard the Icaros sung at the two frequencies you did, attempting to speed up the syncing of vibrations in your brain's ventricles, leading to the left and right brain pairing in hemi sync. The matched amplitudes could be induced for periods of fifteen minutes. During these fifteen minutes, restrictions on time and space were eliminated, opening universal thought, but also destroying all reference to the hallucinations of prior lived experiences that live in the mind as protective over chaos.

"We noticed that the energy field around the body in hemi sync would then match the electromagnetic fields relative to earth. Once paired, this energy could be used to communicate openly to the universe. Sounds and vibrations at near the 109 Hz range caused atoms and the body's cells to vibrate in tune to the energy around them. Our ancestors knew this years ago. Many of the ancient pyramids and ancient monoliths throughout Europe vibrate at this exact frequency level when sound is applied inside them.

"Add ayahuasca to those frequencies and you will expedite the communication with an entire new code of the Universe, but this kind of power is very dangerous. The CIA knew that LSD would open these universal windows through their MKUltra Project. That is why most of the original research was destroyed, and all further research went underground with black budgets and USAID funded projects. It is also why all hallucinogens were labeled schedule one drugs and illegal. My hemi sync, Monroe Institute proven Gateway Process, could open the mind to altered states of consciousness. Add hallucinogens, and one could speed up the process.

"But how could we create the hemi sync instantly with repeatable results while leaving out the necessity of the hallucinogens, meditation, or binaural frequencies? That was what I've been working on here for so long EZ. We wanted to create instant semi sync. Opening the brain's third eye, but not to the Universal code. We wanted the brain open to the codes we could instill. Vibrate the homunculus to the emotions and thoughts we choose. Was there a way to hemi sync and suppress alpha wave egos to get directly to encoding.

"What others see may be used against us, so it was in our best interest to manipulate these powers before others could invent it for themselves. Would you want the Chinese, Arabs, or other Gentiles to harness this power? Certainly not. But what we did want, was the ability to harness this new technology, to instill power over those who will not have our shared interests at heart. We needed to control their minds. This took money, time, and secrecy. Finally EZ, with our experiments here in Peru, we have something that you will be the first to impart on the world."

"What is this new technology? I understand the third eye, hemi sync, and communicating with other worlds. I just experienced this-electromagnetism of some sort, but what I experienced at the second and third ceremonies, was it manipulated?' EZ asked.

"That is a very wise question EZ. We gave you only ayahuasca the first night, combined with hemi synced Icaros. You had a true Ayahuasca journey.   What you so astutely found throughout our camp, the oscillators, generators, and WiFi amplifiers, guided your third eye. Your second ceremony was also ayahuasca, at a much higher dose, but we then wanted you to experience what we could do to your mind. Your third ceremony used no ayahuasca, just the EMF technology. It was important for you to see its effects on yourself as well as the other attendees. Since you figured out our experiments quickly, we allowed you to stay in your hut the final night to understand that you are not as crazy as you thought you may be, and after all, why manipulate one of our own."

"So the WiFi boxes, the oscillators, birds, heat rays, clicks, fake cigars, EMF coils. All of that I was correct on?" EZ inquired.

"Yes, EZ. But first, you needed to believe before you disbelieved. You had to know the greatnesses of what we have and why we must protect it. You must also know its power and understand how to use and not abuse it. Those that built pyramids understood its powers, and they developed a way to project the frequency around the world. I think that you are now more likely to believe that the ancient civilizations were far more knowledgeable to the universe than we are today. Their understanding of astrology, religion, and other life forms is now evident to you.

"There is a new technology EZ. Developed and implemented that will allow us to electromagnetically vibrate our messaging for control. We first had to run experiments across the world in order to see people's reactions. This has taken many years. It is much easier to give the ayahuasca to suppress the alpha waves and encode. I am now an old man, EZ. My ideas will protect our home land for now, but if rogue nations are allowed to develop and use these weapons, chaos within all of the Universe will begin here on Earth. It has happened once, around 12,000 years ago, and we cannot allow it to happen again. We must be wiser this time. With new technology comes new opportunities to protect all of us." Bentov continued.

"We first attempted our efforts with neuromodulation through cochlear implants, but this would have been too restrictive for large populations. We were trying to achieve something that could be placed in a targeted population, and for that we needed microscopic neuromodulation, an ability to modulate neural circuits or even individual neurons within the brain. Hidden as medical research, we had been able to do larger brain modulation such as holographic or optical changes, but we needed finer control. We also needed to refine a method to transmit our messaging. This required the use of spherical matrix arrayed ultrasounds which affected calcium at the level of the individual neurons. The use of the oscillator at scale required more energy, like the device you discovered here. But like cell phones, technology has allowed these items to become smaller.

"Focus was then placed on rTMS technologies. These are

repetitive transcranial magnetic stimulations that use a magnetic pulse to activate and direct neurons. This is why you saw the WiFi boxes, which were not for WiFi at all. We disguised these studies as therapies for depressed or psychotic individuals, just as the CIA had done at hospitals in Canada in the 1960's. Over time, we injected gold covered nanoparticles which could be magnetically vibrated at specific frequencies in order to achieve hemi sync instantly. Much like the cochlear devices, this would be hard to install, everyone would need an injection."

"Unless you told the entire world that an injection was necessary to save them. I think I know where we are in the time line now Bentov. Covid mRNA vaccines," EZ said.

"You are quite deductive EZ. Yes. Lead the world to think they will die, or worse, be responsible for their neighbor's deaths. With our political power all over the world, we directed a narrative, easily established through our controlled press, University experts, and multimedia.

"We quickly established the necessity of getting a Covid vaccine. Not everyone received the injectable nanoparticles, but let's just say that enough did to run our experiment. We could also show that our own country, Israel, was readily injecting the mRNA vaccines, but let's just say that our population was one of the controls. Controls are needed in all good experiments EZ. Over a period of five years, we easily proved the power of the directed nanoparticles for control of minds. Look no further than the division happening within the United States.

"But to sell injections a second time would be difficult. That's where more technology led us to aerosolized delivery of the iron oxide nanoparticles. A virus encodes mRNA into the brain's DNA coding, forcing the neurons to incorporate that gene into their own genomes. After the mRNA codes the relevant neurons, we can then vibrate for all human emotions. And as the virus can be introduced, so can the aerosolized nano particles that will respond to electromagnetic waves. These metal nanoparticles become permanently engulfed by the neurons in the brain.

"With the same Russian scientist who UUONE paid to develop this technology, she was able to also get the particles past the blood brain barrier, directly into the ventricles that contain CSF. This is what you felt in your hut EZ, and with the red lights. Those vibrations you felt were not from the ayahuasca, although the instructors would tell you that is a common side effect. Our scientist obtained new grants at her University and developed an oral pathway for the nanoparticles, easily absorbed through ingestion. This is the version we tested you with EZ. This week's experiment focused on the amounts ingested based on weights, gender, and magnetic abilities of those doses. We can now put this into pill form, or something as big as a city's water supply.

"Do you remember the instructions for a specific diet prior to your arrival? Necessity to stop all medications and alcohol or the ayahuasca would not work? We control everything here EZ. This is a giant science lab in the jungle. We controlled which mice would arrive, how they ate, what they were to believe, and we were able to obtain all of this with their free will. Do you remember your Vomitivo? You did not get breakfast or lunch that day, and you also voluntarily decided to empty any remaining stomach contents with the group. Then, you of free mind and spirit, ingested on your first night what we now call NanEmo, Nanomere Emotion particles. Ayahuasca was given to some of the participants, but not all. The NanEmo was given to some participants, but not all as well. There had to be a control. You will remember that some participants failed to ever have a journey, and some even were willingly consuming up to eight cups per ceremony. This was not a predisposition to the psychedelic. This was our scientists performing necessary objectives."

EZ was shaking his head. It all made more sense now. His UUONE team was far bigger, smarter, and placed all around the world. He wasn't a lone individual on a mission, but a cog in the wheel of a giant one.

"EZ, NanEmo will enable us to control the world. Create unity, or divide populations at will. The participants here, many with past traumas, could be manipulated through our literature and videos to believe what the medicine they were taking could do, so they did not question things on the property out of the ordinary. It is much the same way that NanEmo will work. We will buy social media companies like TikTok, Facebook, Instagram, and online news sources throughout every country in the world. However they are emotionally directed, our country will be involved. Either through our control on American politicians or with direct assistance of Israeli interests financially. The final product is now ready, and you will be the first to implement it. We have already been prepping for its debut. Creating division, angst, anger. Covid was just the beginning of this division EZ. It is about to get much worse. People will disown their own families and friends through the content we distribute. We have had fifty years of war to refine how to divide a populace, and now we have NanEmo to control what they will now do for our benefit. You will lead the biggest test of our product to date."

"Bentov, where will this occur? How could I, as one man, do this?" EZ asked.

"You will not be alone, but all parts are compartmentalized. We have established routes to get NanEmo into your area, patsies to blame if caught, and have also developed a plausible story for you to get others to distribute the aerosolized version. This will give us time to produce the oral version in large enough quantities which could be placed in water supplies or food. We have been spraying the aerosolized version over the United States for quite some time under the guise of climate change. Their government has been involved the entire time, just as they were aware of their Tuskegee, Covid, MKUltra, and other CIA experiments. The CIA is just as involved as UUONE. The Jewish state can infiltrate the best agencies around the world, and for whomever can't be infiltrated, we reveal our techniques. They then beg to become a part of it. We work as a team. It just so happens that since I'm Jewish, you got to meet me through the Israeli science side of the bigger plan. You are meeting the Mekubal of this process EZ, and one should always be humble in the presence of a Mekubal."

"Does Kabbalah have something to do with this mind control? With the Tree of Life? With the third eye?" EZ asked.

"Kabbalah seeks to understand the nature of God, the universe, and human's relationship to both. In biblical times EZ, Elijah and Ezekiel both experienced journeys of mysticism. The secrets of these journeys were so real and strong, that much like NanEmo, that needed to be hidden. The Sanhedrin made these ideas secret. Our souls will all be reincarnated after death. This you have seen in your first ceremony, just as Elijah. Oneiromancy, the interpretation of dreams for prophetic meanings, is quite real when your third eye can see out. Ezekiel's vision of the chariot throne and his ability to meditate into heaven's chambers were all true. Your second journey was to teach you about the writings and truths of Sepher ha-Mashiv, for where there are good gods to be summoned, one may also summon the demons. With NanEmo, we summoned those demons. If other countries were to summon our demons before we summon their's, then Israel may not be in a good place soon. Had you gone on to the fourth ceremony EZ, we would have shown you our real power of instilled thoughts. Many you have met here at this event will go on to perform actions against their own states if needed. They came here to improve themselves EZ. They will go back able to help our cause.

"The greater Jewish faith spent years discrediting Kabbalah. Rabbis promoted it as a hoax-intentionally. The masses are not intelligent enough to respect its abilities, and the greedy will be tempted through what the demons can offer. It was decided long ago that this sacred knowledge would be kept hidden, revealed only to a few, such as yourself, to preserve our religion and our people. We cannot assume that the Mekubals were the only believers to understand the mystic world EZ. It is obvious that prior to our people, there were cultures well versed in the powers of the Universe. The Incas, the Egyptians, the ancient prophets of the Far East. Even Jesus was aware of man's danger in knowing the truth. The Tree of Life must be protected for our own. Do you understand the importance of what we have done here? Of what you will be expected to do? Why now your father and the Prime Minister administered your oath to UUONE?"

"I do Bentov. I accept this responsibility. Had I not seen the power of the Universe through Mother Ayahuasca, I may never have believed it possible, but I now know that the holy books are true. You have made me a true believer." EZ humbly responded.

"Where is it that you wish for me to go now Bentov?"

"Back to Montreal EZ. The division has started, even between Canada and the United States. You will see our work already in play. We have created the messaging. Israel controls the United States through its CIA. Controlling their banks, defense budget, and laws allows the seven million Jews in Israel to achieve global dominance. We must keep their citizens divided and distracted. Once in Montreal, you will then head towards a place in Northern New Hampshire within the United States. It is a well known area for free thought, and its at the top of our lists to manipulate. The location is quite fitting actually. The Infidels call it The Notch. It's where you must achieve absolute division."

Part Two: No EZ Day

<u>The 1916 Fenian Proclamation</u>

The Irish People of the World
We have suffered centuries of outrage, enforced poverty, and bitter misery. Our rights and liberties have been trampled on by an alien aristocracy, who treating us as foes, usurped our lands, and drew away from our unfortunate country all material riches. The real owners of the soil were removed to make room for cattle, and driven across the ocean to seek the means of living, and the political rights denied to them at home, while our men of thought and action were condemned to loss of life and liberty. But we never lost the memory and hope of a national existence. We appealed in vain to the reason and sense of justice of the dominant powers. Our mildest remonstrance's were met with sneers and contempt. Our appeals to arms were always unsuccessful. Today, having no honourable alternative left, we again appeal to force as our last resource. We accept the conditions of appeal, manfully deeming it better to die in the struggle for freedom than to continue an existence of utter serfdom. All men are born with equal rights, and in associating to protect one another and share public burdens, justice demands

that such associations should rest upon a basis which maintains equality instead of destroying it. We therefore declare that, unable longer to endure the curse of Monarchical Government, we aim at founding a Republic based on universal suffrage, which shall secure to all the intrinsic value of their labour. The soil of Ireland, at present in the possession of an oligarchy, belongs to us, the Irish people, and to us it must be restored. We declare, also, in favour of absolute liberty of conscience, and complete separation of Church and State. We appeal to the Highest Tribunal for evidence of the justness of our cause. History bears testimony to the integrity of our sufferings, and we declare, in the face of our brethren, that we intend no war against the people of England – our war is against the aristocratic locusts, whether English or Irish, who have eaten the verdure of our fields – against the aristocratic leeches who drain alike our fields and theirs. Republicans of the entire world, our cause is your cause. Our enemy is your enemy. Let your hearts be with us. As for you, workmen of England, it is not only your hearts we wish, but your arms. Remember the starvation and degradation brought to your firesides by the oppression of labour. Remember the past, look well to the future, and avenge yourselves by giving liberty to your children in the coming struggle for human liberty. Herewith we proclaim the Irish Republic.

The Provisional Government.

-The Military Council of the Irish Brotherhood-

O'Reilly History

O'Reilly liked the subtle warmth of the Vermont summers. Not too hot, not too cold. But it only lasted three months at the longest, and summer often felt like three weeks. He had put his time in patrolling the Swanton Sector of Vermont as a member of the US Border Patrol for over twenty five frigid years. Northwestern Vermont winters lasted eight months, and his arthritis could predict snow storms better than Burlington's "Stormy" TV weather girl. What a job she had.

"This week's weather, snow followed by cold temperatures and more snow." Back to you Mr. Anchorman.

No one even watched the weather unless they were getting ready to pull their ice fishing shanties off of Fairfield Pond, where the goal was to catch a buzz quicker than a trout. Summer weather probably was the highlight of her year. Stormy at least got to mention rain and something other than freezing temperatures. He still tuned in to watch Stormy. Attractive women were far less abundant than snow in Northern Vermont.

O'Reilly was a proud fifth generation Irishman. His grandparents had come over from Enniscorthy ,Ireland shortly before the US Civil War in 1856. What little money was to be had in Ireland had all been spent to obtain fraudulent papers, indicating they were Northern British citizens. In reality, they were proud, influential members of the Irish Republican Brotherhood. John O'Mahoney himself, the Irish leader of the Brotherhood, had requested O'Reilly's Grandfather's services along the border in Vermont. So to Liverpool, England and aboard the ship Circassian, a large passenger transport, he went for his first and last Transatlantic journey, knowing he would never see his Irish homeland again.

The Irish fared well in New England with similar winters, so he wasn't gaining a weather improvement. What he was gaining was food and freedom. The Potato Famine was the entire fault of the British, and he couldn't wait to extract some revenge on those evil bastards. John O'Mahoney could see an opportunity in the future clouded to most men. An opportunity inspired from watching your family starving and weathered, your children becoming smaller from the famine. One's anger grows instead of being a productive citizen. An opportunity of patience awaited him to destroy his enemy. Those opportunities took time and manpower. The great Irish Immigration to the United States and Canada would provide that manpower, and soon, these men would find the time.

John even went so far as to book his grandparents one of the luxury berths midship on the Circassian, not only to avoid nausea on the large swaying iron boat as it made its Transatlantic crossing, but also to give the appearance of prominence. No real potato loving Irishman could afford midship luxury accommodations, but a British citizen with his wife in tow wouldn't draw a second glance. Docking and touching Canadian soil in Halifax, Nova Scotia, no one cared about another Brit heading to Montreal. Little did they know who they had allowed on their soil.

O'Reilly knew that soil took on new meaning with the arrival of the Brotherhood.

John knew O'Reilly's talents. They were the type of talents that kept people awake at night. Talents that got British soldiers to extinguish campfires early, and to stare into a black night, wondering what the night would bring. O'Reilly inherited those talents. They were in his DNA.

Canada at the time of his grandfather's arrival was entirely run by the British, except it was a bit too far away from Britain to be quickly defended by her vast Navy and Army. Irishmen had been leaving by the droves and quite a population had been established in the United States and Canada.

By 1865, the U.S. Civil War had reached an end. Throughout the conflict, the American South had partnered up with the British to assist in ship building and material support.

Confederate troops could seek refuge in Canada, and money was loaned directly to Richmond, Virginia, headquarters. Not only was Britain involved directly in attempting to beat the North, but indirectly, the Canadian British population did all they could to end the North's cause. Not so much from believing in the South's rejection of the Emancipation Proclamation, but mainly to overtake materials and see an end to the growing industrial world competitor, the United States, enabling a stronger world for Britain by means of Canada.

Canada deserved to be taken over, O'Reilly thought. Canadians deserved it during his Grandfather's Revolution, and they deserved it now. Canadians were filled with this overwhelming boastfulness and ability to brag about almost anything Canadian. This wildly superior arrogance was directly inherited. One could tell the country was wreaking British heritage with this attitude. Entitlement had reached epidemic proportions worldwide, especially in the United States and Canada, and what should be rightly the people's soil, would come back to them soon, another Fenian Revolution.

Labor should be valued, and no one had a "right" to another man's labor, but printing more money entitled the lazy politicians to entice more of their voters, making them richer in the process. It was as if the political figures were printing more money for themselves at the polls every election cycle. It just never made sense that these politicians went into a political race poor, and retired years later multimillionaires, and no one from the press seemed to understand how that could possibly happen. Politicians were the same then as they were today.

O'Reilly watched as a Quebec Bank commercial came on his old television set. The intolerant, insufferable people of Montreal. Speaking their French and elevating themselves upon a pedestal of judgement of what was best for the rest of Canada and even the United States. Nausea ensued after each viewing of the evening news highlights. Government propaganda at its best. Only surpassed by Canadian Public Radio, or even worse, NPR in his own country, which only seemed to discuss critical race theory, racism, feminism, or some other far left cause. The propaganda machine was in full force every night. Local headlines that were skewed, followed by weather reports, followed by three to four stories required to air from their national affiliated mothership. No matter the channel, the liberal propaganda all had similar themes.

Never were there counterpoints or chances to offer a different opinion. National Public Radio was even worse. One week, just to prove to a co-worker who doubted his statement, O'Reilly wrote down the title to every story on NPR in the order he heard them as he drove his car home from work. God what a painful week. Stories were always party based propaganda. Everything was always pending doom. No patriotism was ever spoken of, just stories about how terrible the country was. Once presented to his co worker, it mattered not, as these were the tribal messages he liked to echo. Propagated thought had overrun free thinking.

No matter how badly his country was portrayed on these liberal outlets, millions were fighting to enter his country. Who listened to this one sided propaganda? And how could they possibly not wonder what the counter opinion was? Storylines went something like this: What's Right About the South African Takeover, Wildfires Increase from Global Warming, Trans-cheerleaders Enter the NFL, Police Brutality Increases in Inner City, Why the National Anthem Isn't Necessary, White Entitlement on College Applications, An Interview with the State's Liberal Candidates, etc. Every trip to the car was no different. The stories were no different. And still, when

O'Reilly showed a seven day list of NPR show titles to his co worker, he denied that a bias existed for the channel. Flat out denied it. Was even angry that a government subsidized channel would be accused of such bias. It was as if O'Reilly showed him a dog, but he literally swore that there was a cat in front of him. Groupthink in action right before his very eyes. Online activity was no different. From Facebook and Instagram, to Twitter, and every other user content, advertised directive, came the same propaganda.

Country splitting rhetoric driven from who knows what algorithm. Friends he'd known for years hated the fact that he offered political counter arguments on these sites, and he was sure that half if not more of the replies to his content came from Russian or Chinese bots. He saw no other alternative other than to point out discrepancies in stories, to join political groups that helped with causes and stories that supported his cause, to make memes that destroyed the narrative. Other countries were even attempting to influence elections by creating online narratives. The United States had done it for years, why would his NPR friends be surprised? The more he presented facts, the more he was labeled a racist, and also he noticed, the more he diverted into his own tribe.

The liberals were clearly pissed that the Russians had hacked the Democratic National Parties' platform, and were incessant that then President Trump had colluded with the Russians to win the 2016 Presidential election. What they refused to look at was the mirror. They were doing everything they could to become Russia. To become China. What was also baffling was that if the Russians had affected the election, shouldn't the party that was rooting for Communism be jubilant? Wouldn't their cause be expedited by the Russians?

The hot word of the moment was Democratic Socialism,

and not one person could define what that meant. O'Reilly knew. That simply meant more entitlement from another person's labor. Entitlements had never worked in human history, other than to destroy hundreds of millions of lives. No one had a right to another person's labor. That was clearly defined in the Fenian Proclamation almost one hundred years ago. British rule then was no different than the global world elite's rule now.

He watched in disbelief as millions poured across the United States border from Mexico and Central Latin America. These poor people were leaving places much worse than the United States. O'Reilly had traveled extensively across the Mexican border during his training with the border patrol. He had done patrols on Mexican soil with the FBI, ICE, and the DEA, partnering with Mexican government agencies and police. His eyes had seen Columbia, Panama, Nicaragua, Costa Rica, and El Salvador. These weren't CNN reports. He had been on the front lines. His opinions were based on salt, not sugar, a flavor that had no sweetness. Truth often left a bitter taste as well, sometimes sour, but the masses would always flock to the sugary sweetness and feel good emotions of cable news.

What he couldn't understand was that as a nation of laws, laws that were to be enforced by agencies such as his, were just ignored. There were states like California and Oregon who flat out refused to enforce laws that were passed by their own legislative bodies and were to be enforced by appointed judges. These laws, now within state Constitutions, were laughed at with defiance.

Public empathy was advertised and reinforced nightly on the propaganda machines-evening news, social media, and other websites. People were thrown in jail or publicly shamed if they spoke out against this migrant invasion. His grandfather's Ireland and the entirety of Europe were in the same dystopia.

Sweden would be without Swedes in one generation. England, Ireland, Germany, and France were not far behind.

O'Reilly understood that these migrants were facing extremely poor conditions, wars, cartels, or political turmoil in their respective countries. It often reminded him of what the Irish had faced against the British in Ireland. But he remembered what his grandfather had done. Stay and fight the oppressors. With a vengeance, they fought and *"suffered centuries of outrage, enforced poverty, and bitter misery."* He could quote all the best lines from the Proclamation.

One thing that had achieved the Irish victory was clearly provided for in the United States Constitution. The second amendment was so important to the early American Constitution authors as they had just faced the global superpower of Britain. What had led them to that victory? What was the one peasant owned possession that the British tried to get relinquished or be executed? What was the one item that the British confiscated from the farmers if found? What was the one tool that could shut down an Empire? Privately owned firearms entrusted to the masses and perfected in the militias.

This American right's necessity was even mentioned in the Proclamation.

"Republicans of the entire world, our cause is your cause. Our enemy is your enemy. Let your hearts be with us. As for you, workmen of England, it is not only your hearts we wish, but your arms."

A well armed citizenry could defeat the best armies of the world, if they had time.

O'Reilly knew that the people from those Latin countries were loving, hard working families. People that had been lied to by socialist dictatorships. It was confusing that the Socialist Democrats who welcomed the people fleeing Socialist countries were fighting for the West to turn into a Socialist country. These Socialist countries maintained promises of entitlements that no citizen would ever collect, except in fantasy novels like the Communist Manifesto.

These countries had incredible wealth in the forms of oil, minerals, and other natural resources. Most of which were sold to the Chinese, Americans, and Russians who made the real money. What O'Reilly wished these poor people had in their own countries were firearms. Every single individual in a socialist country should own a firearm. All governments on earth fear an armed populace. Perhaps if they did, they could sell their goods with real profits.

The Russians and Chinese currently enforce gun bans, as do most Socialist Latin countries. The politicians controlled a feel good narrative in the media, and they all knew that ninety nine percent of the populace wouldn't go out and commit mass shootings, but that mass shooter narrative led to legislation. And according to their legislation, these bans would lead to a better world for society as a whole, meaning, the government would protect you.

With anti gun legislation, corruption would eventually come, and the everyday citizen would find themselves in a world with no voice. Locked into endless political instability, in a world of chaos. Out of this chaos came a world where people were running to America. A world where mothers were willing to be separated from their children. O'Reilly had seen these terrified faces first hand throughout Latin America. When there is no choice, there is no turning back. There is nothing to lose. There is nothing to fight for, and most importantly, if there is nothing to fight *with,* you will risk everything to escape.

O'Reilly knew of numerous stories throughout Mexico of the citizens taking their country back from the politically backed cartels. The most famous was Jose Manuel Mireles Valverde, or simply Dr. Mireles. On the Michoacan coast, Mireles formed a militia to fight against the Knights Templar Cartel who was terrorizing families and anyone that stood in their way. Often paying off local politicians and police, the cartel had no natural enemy, other than other cartels. Mireles and other town members knew what everyone knows in small communities-exactly where the bad apples lived. What often exists between getting rid of these bad people, are more bad people, mayors, police, or fear of imprisonment. The entire community suffers as the problem increases.

While it is legal to own a firearm in Mexico, there is only one gun store, and that gun store's location is Mexico City, controlled by the Mexican Army. So in reality, there is no way a common poor person who is affected by a corrupt government and cartel violence has a fair fight. It's impossible to obtain a firearm. The cartels know this, as do the Mexican politicians.

Keep the poor away from self defense, and they become slaves to violence.

Mireles armed his citizenry and took back their town. And then the next town. And then the next town. Slowly, the towns turned back into safe, child friendly places. People had their country back. Gangs were kicked out. Cartels disappeared, losing local support of the people. Wars were fought, people died, but the people had a way of fighting back. But one event happened to end this spread of peace.

The government stepped in. The monstrous, overwhelming, always smarter than the people government came in and arrested the good doctor for having illegal firearms. Cartel backed law enforcement basically arrested him for embarrassingly doing their jobs and inspiring the people. Local politicians were losing payments from the cartels, and in turn, the Knights Templar were unable to pay off the Federales in Mexico City, who insured safe distribution to the United States. Take the people's guns away, and you take away the freedom of the people. The second amendment was second for a reason, and no other amendment after it will be upheld without its existence.

O'Reilly wished he could give every man in Mexico an AR15. He wished those men had the desire to fight for a cause like most Irish.

"The real owners of the soil were removed to make room for cattle, and driven across the ocean to seek the means of living, and the political rights denied to them at home, while our men of thought and action were condemned to loss of life and liberty. But we never lost the memory and hope of a national existence."

He could see the plights of Ireland were no different for the people of Mexico. He understood why they were coming. But was it the likable passiveness of Latin Americans that kept them from fighting back for their homeland? Was it the laid back attitude of Mexicans, thinking they had no control over their government? Was it that they all thought that- "it's always been this way" -that kept them from instilling vinegar into a generation that would take its country back? A generation of kids who hated O'Reilly's American values, but didn't have the guts to take their country back from the cartels?

It was this lack of passion. This lack of ability to remember the losses of those who had fought for freedom which caused him to lose his respect for the Latin American fight. The people had no will to take back from the cartels what was rightfully theirs in the first place. No will, and no weapons. The easiest out was crossing a border which at worst might land you back across the border, in a comfortable jail, or at best in a great job with Uncle Sam's government benefits. It was through these eyes that O'Reilly began to feel disgruntled at the Entitlements.

Entitlements that his country was giving away. These were his fellow citizen's tax dollars that he may never see in his future or his kids' futures.

The United States now owed the greatest debt of any country in global history, and yet the Federal Reserve kept printing money and handing out cash to illegals and other countries across the globe, all while he saw veterans without homes and medical care. Veteran suicides were at a rate of twenty two per day, and it seemed as if the Veteran's Administration was happy that pay outs would be less. The coronavirus brought even more entitlements and more misery. The United States was collapsing, from political idiots and the Federal Reserve's decisions.

"Our rights and liberties have been trampled on by an alien aristocracy, who treating us as foes, usurped our lands, and drew away from our unfortunate country all material riches."

The Proclamation always held truths. Old Irishmen were far smarter than he would ever be. It was as if they knew what was going to happen in his future. These illegal immigrants were no different than the British anymore. Nothing he had worked for would be his. His kids would not have a better America. The dollar's value continued to drop as the Fed printed more money. Add inflation, and his retirement was worth thirty percent less than what he had budgeted. Soon, O'Reilly would need entitlements himself.

"We appealed in vain to the reason and sense of justice of the dominant powers."

Events were no different years ago, he thought. No guns would be given to the Mexicans to go back home and take back their country. Why leave this country that seemed to have everything? O'Reilly understood this. His gun club friends understood this. It was time for the world to understand this.

"Our appeals to arms were always unsuccessful. Today,

*having no honourable alternative left, we again appeal to force
as our last resource. We accept the conditions of appeal,
manfully deeming it better to die in the struggle for freedom than
to continue an existence of utter serfdom. "*

If only Mexico had the will of the Irish. His grandfather had
told him even one man could make a difference. He no longer
refused to sit and watch the destruction of what his family had
helped build. O'Reilly decided it was time to enter the division.

Georgia to Montreal

EZ remembered his big break. It was in 2007. After Putin
had won the 2000 election, the emphasis for regaining the old
Soviet states took on a new precedent. Materials, shipping lanes,
food, ports, and people were all going to be needed as Russia's
population was declining. The Eastern expansion of Pro Western
philosophies was gaining strength. Intelligence suggested that
the United States was pushing Georgia and Ukraine to become a
member of NATO. Troops, missiles, and biological weapons
labs were moving East towards Russia. Putin could play chess,
and he knew this was another castling by the Americans to put an
end to his country.

Flying into the airport in Vladikavkaz in North Ossetia-
Alania, he could see the Terek River's reflection. At the foothills
of the Caucasus mountains, the land was a crossroads of Russian
global history. It was surprising to see the old Mukhtarov Sunni
Mosque intact after all who had tried to occupy its wide beams
and steep walls. Named after an Azerbaijani millionaire, the
mosque was home to Ossetian Muslims who were the minority
religion in an area dominated by the Eastern Orthodox. Putin
knew how to use the Muslims to his advantage. The President,
being Orthodox, could care less about Mohammed. What he

wanted was a violent faction willing to protect, secure, and die protecting their disputed religious lands, and in turn, this would insure that Soviet troops would not be needed to defend these border zones.

Vladikavkaz had seen its share of conflicts in the 1900's. World War I, the Russian Civil War of 1923, and Word War II, where the Nazi's were repelled and forced to flee. Putin knew the history, and for EZ, this was to be his ascent out of the shadows of the Israeli intelligence agencies and into the forefront of this new aggressive President who had already begun his unique style in Chechnya.

Seeing each other at the gun ranges, judo training, parade assemblies, and military balls, a friendship developed over a similar interest in his country's future, and over a fascination with Steven Segal movies. They both had watched the country he had protected during the Cold War turn to a Pro Western failure with the collapse of the Berlin Wall under Mikhail Gorbachev. Those with money and industrial competence seized control of the country's wealth and future. What these overtakers didn't have were the force and intelligence necessary to maintain that competence. Putin and EZ realized their opportunity. Control the military and intelligence and control those in finance and industry. Like a giant winter snowfall upon Mt. Kazbek, they would carpet the influencers. Over time, with heat, the snow would begin its melt. Their thaw became a drip, until that drip rolled down the mountain, and merged with the Terek, ultimately reaching the Caspian Sea. Just as the Caspian was considered the world's largest inland body of water. Before they could recognize the dangers of avalanches and the accumulated potential of the snowfall, Russia's magnets would be tossed into the sea. Together they would make Russia the world's largest superpower once again.

EZ wasn't there to roll south across the border into South Ossetia. His chess game was intelligence and counter intelligence. His goal was to begin the counter narrative to what NATO had begun, and on a further scale, begin the long range narrative that would be needed as Putin slowly built back the USSR.

EZ was put in a position at the local newspaper, as well as bringing a new "reporter" who would be in charge of propaganda on the local television and radio stations. The mission for EZ would be to convert North Ossetia's citizens into volunteer fighters, recruit South Ossetians sympathetic to the communist cause, to dissuade South Ossetian resistance to the overwhelming upcoming invasion, and to create the need for increased Georgian military involvement away from the Roki Tunnel, the expected route upcoming in the march against the Georgians.

EZ had done well. Volunteer militia fighters assisted and only minor fighting occurred as the Russian troops and tanks steamrolled through the Roki Tunnel once fighting had begun in 2008. A deal had been made with Israel to bring EZ into aid Putin's plan. A promise of mind control over the local populace within both the home country and against its enemy. Israel viewed any fight against the spread of Islam a worthy one. It would also instill the possibility of blackmail over Putin if ever needed as well as keep the United States on its toes. There was more than one superpower that Israel could manipulate, and if Israel wanted to disrupt U.S. policy, it had ways to do it. Either do what we instruct you to do, or we will find ways to make you.

Putin rewarded the Israeli undercover operation with payment in gold and US dollars to a Cayman Island bank. It was unimportant that EZ wasn't exactly "with" the Israeli government. Putin would never know. UUONE securing continual funding and making connections with a known enemy was. He had met Russia's goals, Israel's goals, and UUONE's. It had also allowed UUONE to use for the first time Bentov's technology in an area with plausible deniability. Should it go wrong, Israel could always say to the American's, "Why would we ever want to help the Russian's? We are your strongest ally in the Middle East. We would never jeopardize our relationship."

His techniques had been recognized and his reward was a bigger canned fish to open. EZ was off to Canada, the quiet giant sitting north of Israel's "strongest ally." Just as he had arrived north of the target of Vladikavkaz, EZ began his descent into a city known for its Communist loving traditions. A town openly accepting, promoting, and even once electing Communists, Montreal.

Looking east out his cramped window seat, he could see downtown Montreal, his home since 2008. His Air Canada flight was as smooth and bland as always, with a mix of French and English speaking Canadians, full of long held French superiority complexes. Add money and power to those egos, and the Canadians were easily manipulated, pretty much by every country in the world.

Montreal-Trudeau International Airport's runway lights appeared below the wing and the plane slowed for landing. EZ thought of the naive, socialist Prime Minister Trudeau who unwittingly had already fallen for much of his own propaganda since his rise to power in 2015, becoming Canada's 23rd Prime Minister. Trudeau was following in the liberal footsteps of other Canadians who had been elected before him, instituting legislation to ban guns, ammunition, and forcibly locking people in their homes during the Covid epidemic. His latest objectives involved stifling free speech and opening its borders to mass immigration. UUONE had many players to influence in this rapidly divisive environment. Power for politicians, money for cartels, guns for loyalists. Division was key to influence.

Trudeau's youthful ego was easily played by his willingness to be like his father, Pierre Trudeau, for whom this airport was named. Trudeau would have been a great Soviet leader EZ thought, manipulating the masses by force in the name of socialism. Criminalize guns first, and by the time those willing to fight realized what was lost, Canada would become prominent in the New World government.

Retrieving his bag, EZ headed to his home southeast of Montreal. Opening his used Honda Civic, he stooped his tall Israeli frame into the Japanese car. Canadians were more like Europeans when it came to automobile practicality, favoring fuel efficiency due to high gas pricing. While he had wanted the top selling automobile in Canada, the Ford F150 pickup truck, he could not force himself to buy a vehicle prided by the rednecks of the United States, and his research told him that the Civic was the top selling car in Quebec. A fact that made him stand out less as with his slippery French and English accents.

He had tried to learn the native French that the Quebec people favored, despite most of the country refusing to speak it. The dialect and accent he struggled with, so English it was. Being only able to master one language, at least it was the language of his Southern rival, and would help as he began to cross the Vermont border over time. He turned southeast on Highway 104, reached the marked speed limit to avoid the ever present Canadian Mounties, and proceeded with caution.

Driving the 25 miles to Saint-Jean-sur-Richelieu, he cleared his mind with the sounds of his now favorite Canadian rock band Rush, whose drummer Neil Peart rattled off endless riffs. It baffled him that three musicians could pull off such a big sound.

His fondness for Peart had grown after reading his books that exhibited his love for motorcycling in the loss of his wife and daughter. EZ had suffered similar losses, and could hear the intensity of Peart's drumming increase after the losses.

The song Tom Sawyer blared through the Civic's last functioning speakers as he pulled into his home along the Rue Jean-Talon, staring out at the river before him. EZ sang along to the song. "Though his mind is not for rent. Don't put him down as arrogant. His reserve, a quiet defense. Riding out the day's events. The river." He slapped the obligatory drum solo across the steering wheel.

From the Terek River to the Richelieu River, about to ride out the day's events, EZ smiled. Being in UUONE might be the best thing that ever happened to him. Rush could pull off this power with three people, surely, he could manage the Notch with one.

<u>Trudeau Bans Guns</u>

"Canadians Outraged Over Trudeau's Gun Ban" read the newspaper headlines.

On April 18 and 19 of 2020, a crazed lunatic with no known motive, in Halifax, Nova Scotia, dressed up as a police officer illegally. As he didn't have the necessary paperwork, he illegally obtained firearms. Those firearms were also illegal in Canada. He then proceeded to murder twenty two innocent civilians. Murder is also illegal. Making this the largest mass shooting in Canadian history. As an added bonus, he set fires along his route, illegally.

Prime Minister Trudeau stated that these weapons were designed for one purpose only, "to kill the largest number of people in the shortest amount of time." Trudeau proceeded to ban over 1500 "assault" weapons, a term not defined by Canadian law. Canadians who already owned these weapons had a two year period in which to sell or have the Canadian government purchase the firearm back, at a "fair" price. Trudeau promised a similar fate to Canadian handgun owners, although most crimes committed with handguns were with illegally obtained handguns by people with gang or criminal backgrounds-rarely with the over 80,000 legally registered with the Canadian Mounted Police. Overall, in 2018, over two million guns were registered in Canada, with between 300,000-400,000 imported into the country each year.

Crime in Canada had decreased over 30% from 2003-2018, as gun sales increased dramatically. Knives made up 6% of violent crime, blunt instruments 3%, and guns were 2%. Canadians owned 34 guns for every 100 people, ranking fourth in the world. Canada ranked 33rd in the world for total firearm deaths globally, behind such behemoth countries like Slovenia, Estonia, Finland, Austria, and Croatia. Canada ranked 29th in homicide rankings, behind the violent areas of North Macedonia, Costa Rica, Barbados and Cyprus.

In 2016, 130 homicides were reported by firearms, and handguns were used in 58% of those deaths. 80% of all gun deaths were either from suicide or unintentional use, with homicides ranking in at 20% of all gun deaths-that number being 130. But keep in mind suicide statistics, 44% are from suffocation (hanging), poisoning 25%, and lastly firearms at 16%, so banning guns may increase these other methods. Violent crime makes up 20% of all crime in Canada, with 3% of all violent crimes involving a firearm. In other words, 97% of all violent crime in Canada involved *No gun.*

Trudeau was also dealing with the global Corona virus pandemic, so maybe he was distracted or confused by deaths from other causes. Most Canadians were probably aware of the number of mass killings between 1989-2020. Eight total. *Eight.* With a grand total of 78 deaths, an awful statistic. In a country of around 36 million, 78 deaths over a period of 31 years sounds awful?

Probably the same number of deaths by accidentally tripping over one's pet.

Bear attacks in Canada from the 1980s to the same time period accounted for 42 deaths, but Parliament probably wouldn't consider banning bears. How about cheerleading? Something easy to control since it's usually part of the public education realm. Most cheerleading stats in the United States point to around 3.6 catastrophic injuries per year, so let's say 108 total, that's almost three times the number of mass shootings. But those are U.S. Statistics, maybe the Canadian cheerleaders fall less.

Texting and driving in Canada? Trudeau could easily pass legislation to not text and drive, but it already existed. making millions of Canadians criminals. Over 310 drivers per year died, with 32,000 injured per year as a result of texting and driving. So, about 3,100 deaths over that same mass killing period. 96,000 permanent injuries. And still, Trudeau doesn't do more to register cell phone users yearly, track cell phone deaths for health statistics, enact tougher legislation, or flat out ban all cell phone use throughout the country. How about a buy back program for those iPhones? Trudeau didn't do that either.

How about motorcycles. 187 deaths per year on average in Canada. There is absolutely no reason anyone should own a motorcycle. They are an exotic form of transportation. One could use a bicycle or car to get to their destination just as easily, but the Canadian government did not deem them nonessential? Might they buy back motorcycles at a fair price? The statistics don't lie-around 5,610 deaths over the same period of 78 mass shooting deaths? Which is more dangerous, firearms or motorcycles? A true tragedy awaits each owner, but the government continues to profit off of the tax revenue.

How about something that is currently illegal? Trudeau surely knows that around 14,700 deaths occurred from opioids between 2016-2019 in his home country. That's around 3,675 deaths per year, or 36,750 deaths over the next ten years from a substance that's already illegal, and some of those deaths were prescribed, regulated, and taxed by the government. If overall deaths are important, shouldn't opioids be a main focus? Couldn't Trudeau legislate these deaths away? Or will criminals continue to perform acts of crime even when legislation exists, much as the Halifax shooter?

Surely Justin can work on limiting alcohol. The long winters in Canada lead to over 900 alcohol related deaths per year. 10,000 every ten years. And that's not counting all of the side effects such as diabetes, cancer, hypertension, and other related diseases linked to alcohol consumption. Wouldn't Canada's health benefit from banning alcohol? Has this been tried in the past? Yep, for about two years in 1918-1920, the Canadian Prohibition lasted. All those sneaking sips around their respective provinces, true felons. There was no telling of the death counts in 1920 involving drunk motorcyclists.

But, in the shadow of Covid-19 and a mysterious shooter with no known motive, Trudeau had passed an Assault Weapons ban. At a rate of 0.03% total deaths per year over the last 31 years, a Canadian gun owner might just wonder what the real reason would be, but after little thought, and a review of history, control is the only answer.

Bow before the new Canadian king, for the people of Canada will no longer have a way to dethrone him by 2023.

EZ took a sip of his tea as he entered the last sentence, the cherry on top gotcha moment of emotion for the reader. He would send this article to around 30 right wing sites in the morning, who would then publish to sites such as Facebook, Instagram, and various news sites and opinion blogs. He knew that Russian intelligence would also be reading his output and entering this into bot algorithms. They would republish in gun forums and right wing message boards, where he knew left wing "fake news" verifying companies, such as Snopes and the Southern Poverty Law Center, would be sure to mark its validity. True statistics, easily found on Google, with a harsh, down to earth rationale. The article had to be believable to be good. Knowing your reader was key. He closed his Windows laptop and turned on his MacBook.

All articles to the radical left went out in Apple format. All to the right in Windows. He preferred to keep his articles of disinformation in two different locations. Compartmentalizing his thoughts. When picking up the Apple, it was as if he was speaking a different language. More University professors and students used Apple. More liberals used Macbooks, and for the next article, he had to think and act like a liberal. He had to persuade a different listener, a different believer. For everyone believed they were correct about their beliefs, right or left, and everyone needed to feel that they could voice their message, but in reality, it never was really heard. They just had to feel as if they were heard, as if they were participating in the narrative.

They wanted to be part of an echoed tribe.

EZ could not relate to the radical left, but they were easily persuadable because emotions ran stronger than logic. He would focus on what the English language called adjectives and adverbs, and an article about *"Triggering Words of the Left"* he found to be particularly valuable when composing his fake content.

"Trudeau Ends Needless Bloodspill in Canada". It had to be fact based, believable, but most importantly emotional. Russia had learned from their Pravda mistakes. The disinformation campaign must split the United States equally. Canada had been easy. From one shooter came a ban. It was easy to win liberal hearts, but much more difficult for the right's minds. EZ's training was about to be trialed at a massive level. UUONE had a bigger plan for him in Canada, and it started with simple instructions.

Study your environment, blend in, learn how and what the people think. Figure out what makes them tic, and what values may be in conflict. Shouldn't be a problem he thought, everyone was upset, and everyone was voicing their own opinions as to why.

UUONE's directive-divide.

MAGA's Rise to EZ

MAGA. Make America Great Again. The 2016 election of Donald Trump's movement, marked the beginning of the great divide. An event where the other side could find an enemy. For every antagonist, you need another antagonist. Going a little against the old saying.

Barack Obama had solidified himself as the first Antagonist. Half a country battled against socialist policies being put into legislation. 197 high ranking military officers forced to resign. Pro liberal leaning ideology filled the FBI, CIA, military industrial complex, judgeships, clerkships, medical schools, universities, and cabinet positions. Enforcing targeted tax investigations upon political enemies through deep state operatives such as Lois Lerner, who never served any jail time for directed IRS targeting of political groups such as the Tea Party movement, using the state's own assets to monitor opposing political appointments. Chicago politics at its best, and really no different for any generation of politicians, just more effective in today's data driven, algorithm, bot driven society. News moved faster. Outrage today, forgotten tomorrow. Results were needed quicker for an impatient society that required constant satisfaction of its short attention span.

Obama's moves weren't discussed much in the media. After all, he could never do anything wrong in the media's eyes. How could he if he placed them there, or they supported his campaign? In fact, he never really did anything relevant in anyone's eyes if you put on your fact checking glasses. A Nobel prize winner that killed more kids with bombs than any mass school shooter. A man with a record likely to never be surpassed of approving drone strikes in non congressionally approved war zones with some even killing American citizens.

In comes Trump, firing many of the Obama appointees. Creating opposite but equal division.

Stirring the pot like no other President has ever stirred a pot. Multiple pots. Hundreds of pots. Pissing the globalists off like no other person has or will ever be able to do. A complete political outsider, not beholden to the rules that D.C. mandates. Disturbing their monopoly. Disrupting the plans set forth by the Bilderberg Group, Bohemian Grove, The World Economic Forum, and Skulls and Bones. While a billionaire himself, Trump was often excluded from these elite groups. No different than Henry Ford being rejected from the elite Huron Mountain Club in Michigan's Upper Peninsula back in the day. Being rejected likely for the attention and embarrassment his riches might bring, and being unable to employ the silence necessary to retain membership in the elite global club that determined the outcome of all other organizations. Trump's weakness was his delivery of the narrative, not the narrative itself, with his unpredictability and loyalty questionable to the world's elite.

Once Trump was elected, promises were to be fulfilled from the campaign, and just as Obama had done, he took action. Directors fired. Judges appointed. With former President Bill Clinton, Janet Reno had fired 93 of 94 U.S. District Attorney's, which was twice as many as Trump's Attorney General, Jeff Sessions. The story is no different. Each President wanted those enforcing policy to enforce what policy their campaign had promised. Obama nominated over four hundred for judge positions and got 329 confirmed during his Presidency. But the media, the Deep State supported media, including CNN, MSNBC, CBS, ABC, NPR, large newspapers, somehow always managed to get amnesia on what prior President's had done. They hated Trump, and hate isn't even a strong enough descriptor.

Under Obama, the United States had an overwhelming supporter of entitlements. Those entitlements required money. The United States didn't have much money floating around, especially after the Great Recession in 2008 under Obama's watch. The world was very reluctant to keep loaning money, while the United States kept printing dollars, at the same time having nothing to back the paper's value with such as gold. Chinese investors bought bonds, properties, businesses, largely within the United States. Russians interfered in politics and global oil flow, crashing websites, buying advertising, creating bots, and in 2020, departing from OPEC, causing the Saudi led organization to slash the price of oil to create another oil war with the Russians. Little did they know how much oil they would soon have on hand.

The Chinese had an idea of what was to come for about a

month. That idea was hidden in a little market in Wuhan where bats and rodents were considered standard food fare. The Middle East continued doing what they do best-pumping cheap oil from the earth. There was so much oil being pumped that countries couldn't find a place to store it. During this time, the United States was also the largest exporter of oil and natural gas in the world.

American debt became the largest in the history of the world. Growing daily with no end in sight. No way to pay the interest for generations to come, and yet, the entitlement programs kept flowing. Less people worked. More people went to college for free. Healthcare became free to those in need or crossed the borders illegally. Drug use increased to the point that Narcan was free. While Trump did increase jobs, and overall increased exports, he increased spending even more than his predecessor. As prior Presidents had done, Trump enacted tariffs as well. And this was all before the virus. *Before.* Things were about to get worse. Much worse.

The 2020 elections would foretell the Great Fall. All those brilliant University professors who touted socialism's benefits had forgotten a civilization called Rome. The collapse was inevitable for any President. If you aren't selling more than you're consuming, any businessman knows the outcome, as does any bank. And the banks would profit one way or another. Being run from a global perspective, money could shift from a bank in the United States to one in Germany or China. Tax laws favorable in one country could benefit yesterday's losses. Banks never lose.

They don't care what country they side with.

Look no further than J.P. Morgan, Kuhn, Loeb, Schroder, Warburg, Baruch, Guggenheim, and especially the Rothschild family during the two world wars. Wars were profitable. What country was destroyed would never affect their deposits. Two German Jewish brothers held large parts in developing both the U.S. Federal Reserve in 1913 and the German central bank, as well as establishing the globalization strategy used by all banks today. At the same time, these brothers helped on the boards of the IG Farben German Chemical corporation, which helped develop for the Nazi's tabun, sarin, and Zyklon A and B biological nerve agents which were used to gas the Jews during the Holocaust. IG Farben later was split into companies known to many of us such as BASF, Bayer, and Hoechst. Where there was a need to loan money, the banks with a familiar list of families were always near.

It was now chic for the biggest U.S. Corporations to be "Global", meaning they needed manufacturing to occur in different countries around the world. Marketing, development, sales, whatever be the department, were established globally thus enabling shifts in profits and losses to the greater parent corporation. Giant corporations such as Facebook, Apple, and Google paid zero federal taxes to a broken U.S. Government, but reaped all of the tax breaks and incentives driven by small local communities begging for local jobs. Industrial based companies in the

U.S., such as steel, automobile manufacturing, and military production all followed suit. Banks bought smaller banks in other countries, combined their influence, and could also show wins and losses on paper, no matter the location. Hedge funds were ten times worse than the banks. Politicians loved this because they got local votes for low paying jobs in environments of dissatisfaction. The companies loved paying zero taxes, and banks loved it all once again. After all, the banks had caused much of the 2008 Great Recession through lending to those who shouldn't be borrowing, letting appraisals go unchecked on real estate, and especially through the known corruptness of the Vegas like product that the general public would never understand, derivatives.

In 2020, because no one had ever been convicted in the banking industry, and the United State's inability to learn from its own mistakes, derivatives were back, and bigger than ever. Banks and financial gamblers loved them. The same people that told the little guy to save three to six months of income should they become unemployed, the people who never lost money in 2008 because they were given billions in tax payer funded bail outs, the same companies not paying any taxes, the people profiting by shifting income from country to country, were taking risks far greater than playing house roulette at the MGM casino. Their strategies were closer to Russian roulette. But if you can be hurt through losses in one country, you can quickly shift to profits in another. Globalist companies were killing the global working class. The income gap between the rich and poor was the largest the world had ever seen. Add in cheap labor through mass immigration, and more division developed.

But viruses don't distinguish the rich from the poor. Viruses make one deposit and no withdrawals. They are the ultimate derivative play, and banks were no longer safe.

Tariffs instilled by the last and next Trump elections hurt the bankers flow of cash overseas, and a rapid de-globalization began to occur. Tariffs disrupted a global balance of trade in China, Japan, Brazil, Russia, and Europe. What could easily be manipulated at the banks, became more difficult to manipulate. Too many moving parts with too many numbers to shift . It was like putting dams along a river. The water could still flow, but it took a lot of effort to harness the same amount of energy, and too many others could take some energy away from the river along the way, making those same banks less profitable. And profit versus loss is what led to viral creation.

Some thought it was Hollywood's constant grumbling. Some thought it was the press. Others the racial division, the class strife, the political opponents. What only a few would know, was that it was the bankers. Those who held the world's money could make money in any market as long as they could control another market. Newton's law of every action requiring an equal and opposite reaction worked just as well in economics as it did for physics. Donald Trump's undoing was his disruption of the global financial system in 2019. This all occurred during his reelection campaign. While there were many who wanted to assassinate Trump on the left, the banks had a far better way of achieving a more profound global impact.

The banks needed a way to stop the tariffs. Finally realizing their own actuaries and scientists, the increasing older population and expanding world population would only add to global warming. Any end to profits because of globally enacted climate change had to be stopped, oil to keep selling, loans to be signed, and defaults to be captured. A plan had to be created that was believable and would impact the population increases globally. It had to impact everyone around the globe to be believable and just. The banks were "here to help you" must seem factual, and that plan had to be put into effect quickly, and blamed on individuals who wouldn't be believable if questioned.

Controlling the press, controlling fear, creating a crisis, creating a solution. These ideas worked for centuries of communist and political tactics. What better way to release your solution, than to release it within a country that the press would never believe? Through decreased income, thoughts of bankruptcy, and stench of death, the banks wouldn't even have to try and make money.

The U.S. Government would readily hand them freshly

printed money. Beg them to take it. It mattered not if the interest rates turned negative in the United States, more debt to the people meant more interest captured. More citizens defaulting on credit cards, auto loans, and late mortgage payments. A deferral wouldn't matter. Fear would only increase over time as the bills appeared around the corner. The government would create the solution. This philosophy had always worked in Communist China, so what better place to start the solution. Wuhan.

Wuhan, China, was the home of the Wuhan Institute of Virology, an arm of the Chinese Academy of Sciences. What was made to appear as a well meaning organization for the protection of its citizens health was in actuality a necessary establishment to protect and develop both offensive and defensive uses of biological weapons. The Wuhan Institute was involved in clandestine projects all over the world, and since the United States could not perform weaponized genetic research on its own soil, it even helped fund the institute through USAID funding, developing its own biological weapons concealed as University research.

Certain events would need to happen at specific times to be effective. The conspiracy media would need to be used first to establish likely truths, but then the deep state media would need to step in to print and establish "real" scientifically proven narratives. Neither could be right, neither could be disproven. Fear needed to be controlled. Fear would lead to a solution. The plan was enacted perfectly. First, the Chinese link needed to be established beyond Wuhan. The bait had to be placed on the hook before the big fish could be caught. And the bait was perfect. Long a part of China's government investments, the development of scientists to infiltrate competitive government projects was developed over generations and continents. Work visas, university jobs, and research coops demanded top tier scientists in their respective fields. Placing Chinese scientists in American universities, British colleges, and Canadian medical schools was all part of a master plan. The Chinese never paid for copyrights. They simply copied or stole them. If you developed the latest and greatest computer software, Chinese coders simply stole the code. And what were your options as a software company? The company could file a lawsuit in China. The lawsuit would never come to fruition.

Companies eventually just accepted Chinese copyright theft as part of losses, much as Wal Mart writes off a certain portion of thefts in its stores. But the global companies knew how to work the system. Google, Apple, and Facebook agreed to rewrite codes to the rules of the Communist system. Apple, Samsung, and Android needed parts for their phones, so rules had to be broken, yet kept hidden as much as possible from the press.

The plan enacted by China's government was entitled the Thousand Talents Plan. At face value, the plan sounded legitimate. Recruit and cultivate the world's brightest to enhance China's science programs, create economic wealth, and increase national security. Scientists were often lured to different countries for a better life, more money, more prestige, and a chance of publication and grants. Initially, bribery and blackmail were used to persuade scientists to work with the Communist's, but the incentives became less over time, so a smarter way was initiated. Rather than have scientists invent a product, and China need to possibly pay for that technology or defeat the encrypted products, China decided to pay the top scientists handsomely.

Part of the agreement with the Thousand Talents Plan required the scientists and defectors to declare cooperation with China on all projects, grow new Chinese talent, and apply for patents. In the case of viral technology, under the auspices of the Wuhan Institute of Virology, China worked with the U.S. Universities like the University of North Carolina to develop gain of function research. Most of the research was being paid through CIA shell companies through USAID grants. The Chinese had found a way to self fund, through the U.S. taxpayer, illegal research without paying a dime. In the end, they would just steal the technology.

In 2019, the U.S. Government began to try and root out some of these Communist's and defectors. One of the most publicized was Professor Charles Lieber, Chair of the Department of Chemistry and Chemical Biology at Harvard University. Working under his guidance, Yanqing Ye, a Chinese national, and Zaosong Zheng. Ye was determined to be a lieutenant of the People's Liberation Army of China and had lied about his status in order to obtain a position at Boston University where he sent data about the U.S. Military back to China.

These students were working on molecular biology research with Lieber. The FBI arrested Lieber on January 28, 2020. The stooge of Lieber mattered not. Ye ran back to China. But Zheng was caught at Logan International Airport in Boston. In his possession were twenty one vials he was taking back to China to further his "research". It mattered not what was in the vials, but one could only guess the sensitivity. The U.S. Government would release that it was "cancer cells", creating misinformation to the Deep State media who would run with the story. But a deeper look at events might reveal a little more to the evolution of the story.

On February 7, 2018, President Trump enacted the first "global safeguard tariffs" against China and then on March 22 filed a World Trade Organization lawsuit on behalf of the U.S., against unfair business practices by the Chinese concerning licensing and manufacturing. The tariffs escalated on Chinese steel and aluminum on March 23, with China instilling their own tariffs beginning April 2. And so, the back and forth Trump tariff war began.

Every sector involved tariffs and banning of certain products or companies, particularly in the realm of communications and security. For every U.S. action, the Chinese had an equivalent counter action-Newton's law. For over a year, this occurred, until on August 1, 2019, the U.S. declared China as a currency manipulator after the yuan sunk to its lowest level in 11 years. Finally, in October of 2019, on a fourteenth round of trade talks, the "Phase One" trade agreement was met. Through November 1, both countries agreed on the trading points in principle. On November 7, the countries began talk of tariff rollbacks, which were signed on January 15, 2020, just two days after the U.S. dropped China's currency as being manipulative. But all of this completely disrupted the banks. The dollar's manipulation occurred simultaneously with the yuan's manipulation-something the Globalist banks could not yin yang. The interdependence of disruption could not function with two yins or two yangs. Something had to be done as no end was in sight.

Banking leaders, government officials, the World Bank Group, the International Monetary Fund, and the U.S. Federal Reserve all met to discuss options at the International Monetary Fund Annual Meeting in Washington, D.C. Members of civil society groups were invited to the public meetings, but not those meetings held in private, where the real decisions were being made. Representatives from NGOs, religious organizations, labor unions, think tanks, charities, not-for-profits, indigenous peoples groups were all to be present to witness discussions about the world's finances.

Profits and interest rates were plunging around the world.

On October 19, 2020, the day after the public meetings were adjourned, the real meeting took place. The real bankers, politicians, and globalists met at an undisclosed location. To them, Trump was as unpredictable as the Chinese. He couldn't be controlled. He had won the election in a fluke. Hillary would have been their puppet. Hillary would have kept the banks on track all while acting as if she was for the little guy. The illusion of safety and solutions controlled the masses.

The decision was made by six people over cocktails at the most famous of controversial meeting spots in the world for deciding United States policy, the Hay-Adams Hotel, located directly across from 1600 Pennsylvania Avenue-The White House. Geographically iconic. Those cocktails were shared at the hotel's appropriately named bar-Off the Record. The virus was getting dropped. Late November would be the date.

Just as negotiations began to ease between Trump's White House and China in early November, an investigation was beginning on a Harvard chemist by the FBI. But before the Deep State triumphed in January with that victory, on December 10, 2020, Wei Guixian, a vendor at a wildlife market in China's Wuhan region, started to feel ill. On January 15, as China and the Trump administration came to their tariff ending agreement, the first confirmed U.S. case of Covid-19 virus left Wuhan and arrived in the state of Washington.

China, the U.S., the world-no one was prepared for what was eventually coined the Coronavirus. Only six people were aware of the plan. One, an Israeli, just happened to be a member of a gun club in Northern New Hampshire. EZ was his name, and this new virus, with the help of some divisive intelligence agencies around the world, would provide an opportunity like no other to run a test on society-mandatory vaccinations.

The ability to control the minds of the masses was his great power. It was UUONE's Excalibur. For those who held the money, the banks and the elite, this was a chance to unleash a tool that the world could not comprehend.

Division was necessary to print money, as well as to control societies, and EZ was the pebble being tossed onto the water's surface. Not only had EZ followed the shifts in history, he had helped steer their direction. The greatest world decisions were made usually by a handful of people.

"Keep dividing EZ," UUONE ordered.

The bigger mission will be revealed to you in time. We now have the emotional controls.

EZ's Plan

EZ's plan was simple. Create misinformation and disinformation for the purpose of division. What Pravda could not achieve for Mother Russia in the Eighties, EZ achieved ten fold in today's world. Pravda didn't have TikTok, Twitter, and Facebook. They also didn't have lipid nanoparticles and directed electromagnetics. Governments secretly watched all the data through Terrorism laws. The bots served up whatever flavor of truth needed to be told, and there was always someone willing to sell the secrets to the bots for the right price.

UUONE made sure to slip him out of the country early, going to the American south or the safety of Canada, where no one would ever suspect an Israeli operative. His goal was to educate himself on mass distribution of divisive information. The invention of Meta, TikTok, porn, and dating applications as data collection devices for UUONE could not have been invented by Russian intelligence on the best of days. Entire masses of people voluntarily posted face images, friends, locations, likes, and dislikes. Add a cell phone, essentially a tracking device that the world could not un grasp, and with which UUONE could create an addictive, manipulative environment. It also helped that the owners of most of these mass addiction platforms were supportive of Zionism. Giving UUONE access to backdoors and instilling what Israeli intelligence recommended into their algorithms. Should they deny access, blackmail or extermination were effective tools for cooperation. Cutouts like Jeffery Epstein types gathered those necessary tools for years and were paid handsomely, but with today's cell phone technology, blackmail was even easier. Even most of the VPN (Virtual Private Networks), where people went in hope of privacy, were all owned by Israelis.

One thing had been learned as Russia went to war in the Eastern block with the former Yugoslavia, information was not being intercepted or interpreted as it was in the past. Teams were assembled in Romania and Czechoslovakia to begin initial stages of implanting disinformation on popular technology. Chat rooms were hacked. Cellular technology breached.

Weaknesses were found on popular software platforms. The best hackers throughout the world were hired and paid handsomely. Chinese and Russian students spread throughout Universities around the world. One such creation was Pegasus, invented in Israel, currently the best spyware to breach Apple iPhones. Experiments revealed what worked and what didn't when it came to confusing the truth. EZ's team in Israel refined daily messaging using real time statistics. When Trump ran against Hillary Clinton, Putin quickly saw that much like himself, Trump cared more about money than principles. A populist at heart, Trump cared about the public's opinion.

Trump would make an excellent tool in the war on dividing the free world into two camps. Eventually those two camps would turn on themselves, even within their own party. The ability to divide was the ability to conquer. To get America to fight and finance Israel's enemies was UUONE's primary task, and it required secrecy, funding, and the two camps to believe that they were under constant threat. The threat would cause disillusion to their own sinking economy and living conditions. UUONE created the division while the Politicians offered the solutions. Between the epidemic, disinformation, American political division, and planning the biggest terrorist attack in global history, EZ was receiving much praise back in his homeland. Although UUONE was extremely compartmentalized, he was allowed to hear from a small contingent of voices on his effectiveness. It seemed the more missions he accomplished, the more of the organization was revealed, and the more resources he was allocated. He was beginning to prove himself. Trust was earned, not deserved.

Success would be his soon. All that needed to happen was the fall of the American Revolutionary Right wing gun crowds putting up the last defense against the government backed Left wing. It was his plans, his data, his infiltrations that had worked. Disarm the American populace, and he would disarm the idea of liberty. It had been successful in Canada and Australia, but the country of America had been built on these second amendment rights. It's people educated on the importance of self preservation and individual liberty. Countries founded by the British never instilled these into their voters and had been quite easy to manipulate through the right politics.

America though could oftentimes be no different than its weak twin-Europe. Russia and China would be in control of America by proxy. Its politicians would follow those beliefs that paid well, just as Putin and Xi had proven around the world. The Idealists were soon to be defeated. They were his only roadblock. No Russian, Chinese, or Iranian's would die from this roadblock either. No shot heard around the world. A new Civil War of Americans fighting each other online, in public forums, and in propaganda He knew the United States was capable of infighting of its own citizens. They had fought one Civil War already. History could be manipulated to repeat itself.

He was ready for the final phase to begin.

Why would Israel want to destroy America? It wasn't about the destruction. It was about the control, the distraction, the solutions. The more Congressional members could be blackmailed, the more Israelis could be placed in positions of power as money was divided to other problems. Controlling the hearts and minds, *literally*, was to be a game changer though. Hollywood propaganda and press control had been one thing, but in today's world, there were too many independent voices online and on podcasts. Israel didn't have the population to fight its enemies, and so far, they had spent little of their own money to combat its enemies. An ability to overcome the narrative was what was needed. Never before had a nation had the technology he was about to unleash.

UUONE had only told EZ one goal recently. Create as much division as possible between all political groups through any means necessary. Divide and conquer. He opened his flip phone to read a text he had been waiting for.

Liquid shipments incoming. WiFi, ELF, ULF, HAARP towers programmed. Proceed with Phase Two.

<u>Bovines to the Gun Club</u>

Cows. Cattle. Bovines. It all started with those damn monstrosities O'Reilly thought. The Bundy family controversy was making huge headlines. Militias, the Oathkeepers, and everyone else with an agenda were making a stink over those fucking cows.

Media trucks, media scum, political pundits, trashy reporters, come one, come all to the Bundy Ranch.

One could make an argument that somehow whales in New Zealand were being affected by the Bundy Ranch, global warming from the Bundy family's cow's asses, and global destruction from the hoofed outlaws. The likely next news headline from CNN: *Bundy Cows Cause Increase in Global Warming.* CNN was the epicenter of globalist agenda clickbait.

The Democratic socialists said Bundy needed to pay his fair share of taxes, he was breaking the law. Meanwhile, liberal heroes forgot about their own. Treasury Secretary Timothy Geithner, New York Representative Charlie Rangel-former head of the tax writing Ways and Means Committee, Tom Daschle-Senate Majority and Minority leader, Claire McCaskill-former auditor, congresswoman, and senator, from Missouri, Al Sharpton-notorious Civil Rights frontman, were all known for not paying their taxes. And now, they were considered heroes to the left. Why was it that a couple of cattle ranchers refusing to pay their taxes was somehow big news to the left?

Liberal companies that supported Obama were openly shifting taxes within international corporate shells to avoid taxes in the US. Google, Facebook, Costco, and Apple were all examples of international shifts. Companies that the leftist Occupy movement stupidly supported, when they should have been at the top of their protest list, at least if compared to Bundy's tax payment plan. A farmer trying to feed his cattle was considered a goddamn criminal to these liberal whack jobs. What should be a state issue in Nevada was now a Federal issue. Reminding many ranchers of the famous War of Northern Aggression which many thought was fought over slavery, and not what really occurred-a slashing of state's rights.

When the Federal government continued to buy up every piece of land in the United States, *despite being bankrupt*, everything became a Federal issue. The Federal government, through the Federal Reserve Bank, printed as much money as it wanted, never paying back what would be lost through inflation. The Fed, being a private bank, didn't follow normal banking laws. The Fed didn't pay taxes, but the Bundy's did, and would be put in jail if they didn't. The Fed had no accountability for success, other than politicians, which was laughable. The Bundy's had a farm to run, bills to pay, and mouths to feed.

Could a bankrupt business buy a bigger factory down the road? No way. The banks would never allow that. But when the government could endlessly print cash, and the Federal Reserve invented their own rules, you could buy whatever you wanted without repercussion. You could buy several bigger factories down the road, and you could hire the attorneys to make it happen.   It appeared as if the Federal government would rather buy more land than help those who currently couldn't pay for their own.

The Bureau of Land Management claimed that Bundy owed over $1 million in back fees for grazing his cattle on federal lands. Bundy's family had used the lands for grazing since the 1870s, but the Feds started to restrict his herd from roaming in an attempt to protect a rare desert tortoise. A fucking tortoise was at the heart of this tax debate. Could cows not coexist with a tortoise? Were cows really that big of a threat to a tortoise's existence? Turtles had existed since the time of the dinosaurs. Surely, they could withstand a few cattle grazing in their environment. With the Feds owning over 85% of all land in Nevada, the cattle farmers were faced with paying huge fees to a government that never helped their cause, or they could finally make a stand against the tyrannical spying, overbearing, overtaxing United States Government. These happenings in the Gold Butte area were a foreshadow of many things to come from a corrupt and dishonest Obama Administration whose shifty legal powers spewed like a sewage pipe from Attorney General Eric Holder.

O'Reilly had taken notes from a statement by Daniel Greenfield in frontpagemag.com in April, 2013.

"....finally we know that we are no longer a nation of laws, but a nation of whims, where politically correct victimization trumps every sense of right and wrong and the outrage machine grinds night and day finding more victims for the establishment to turn into heroes and more villains who still believe that rights are forms of immunity from government coercion, rather than forms of government coercion, to ritually destroy."

What was always interesting to O'Reilly was the counter arguments made against this farmer. His own State Senator, Harry Reid, labeled Bundy and his supporters "domestic terrorists'". Reid was an established long term politician, known for shady backroom deals and recent energy developments on federal Nevada soil involving elite, super wealthy Chinese companies. It seemed that Reid may be at the whims of an enemy nation.

Meanwhile, Eric Holder and the Obama Administration instructed O'Reilly's own United States Border Patrol to not detain illegal immigrants at certain border crossings, a blatant breach of the U.S. Constitution. Why were these politicians not punished for the rules they selectively enforced?

Fellow agents were told to stand down in prominent illegal border crossing areas. To not arrest, detain, report, or follow. Although Obama was deporting some migrants, he was selectively allowing others to stay, likely to the benefit of cheap labor, or worse, creating an increase in population in certain areas to generate House seats since immigrants could be counted in a new census.

Hadn't these US officials, from the White House, all the way down to the patrol agents working on the border, sworn the same oath to defend the U.S. Constitution?

While these events continued on, the most non compliant Attorney General in US history stated in a speech before the Mexican American Legal Defense and Education Fund, that illegal immigration was a civil right. *A civil fucking right? Illegally crossing a nation's border was a civil right?* So, to many who couldn't get jobs, whose kids went into life long debt, whose kid's college loans swelled with high interest rates, whose taxes continually increased to support those who weren't paying, this so called civil right was a slap in the face, especially to the working middle class and the poor. All while the rich politicians either didn't pay taxes or had the structures in place to hide their monies elsewhere. Global corporations and banks knew how to manipulate the system. A farmer does not.

The entire country knew the 30 million illegal immigrants were a real concern. This same progressive, liberal, political party stated now that *Amnesty was a civil right?* At what point does doing something illegal become a civil right? And who gets to choose which illegal activity becomes a civil right for their own purposes and choice? O'Reilly wondered if the Bundy's robbed a bank to pay their taxes and avoid jail, would that be their civil right? Did he have a right to not pay his electric bill because energy was a civil right? Laws were listed in one section of the U.S. codes, and he could not remember them in the Bill of Rights.

When Bill Ayers, an early Obama political adviser, college professor, and friend, bombed and committed acts of terrorism on U.S. soil with his Weather Underground organization, was that his civil right? Because now he is treated as a God in liberal circles. Is terrorism a civil right? O'Reilly guessed it depends on which side of the political spectrum one is on. Perhaps one day, all people could choose what they felt as their own civil rights. Civil rights violations were only somehow punished upon the lower and middle classes. It seemed that the political classes, even if in violation, never suffered any penalties, but rather seemed to only suffer higher deposits into their bank accounts.

When an illegal commits a crime on U.S. soil and simply gets deported, is that a civil right? If half the illegals in California don't pay taxes, is that a civil right or a right's violation? How is it OK that they don't pay taxes, but Rancher Bundy gets crucified for feeding his cows on traditional family land, refusing to pay a tax? Does the right to feed his family and support his business seem like a civil right? Does he have the right to the pursuit of happiness? Corrupt politicians not paying taxes, the Federal Reserve printing money, and Congress borrowing more money while the country is bankrupt is allowed, but cows sharing the soil with a turtle isn't?

How was it that the civil rights of one culture outweighs the civil rights of another?

If I, O'Reilly thought, murdered someone in the U.S. who was here illegally, would that be a crime, or my civil right? If I needed a car to drive to work, but didn't feel like making the payments, is that my right to steal it? If I can't seem to keep a girlfriend, and decide to rape my next door neighbor, is that a civil right? There were laws in place for all of these actions, but political judges selectively enforced political coercion.

When does written law become not a law? And is it only those in power who get to decide what's illegal and not? The same politicians becoming millionaires serving multiple terms while being their own judge and jury, is that their civil right?

O'Reilly was infuriated. The country was divided in two. He couldn't understand how this could happen in his beloved country. A country he had taken an oath to defend.

He guessed when the Executive branch decides not to enforce laws written by the people elected to Congress, that's when some decisions are made on civil rights. When only 20% of a population votes, that then decides what the other 80% should do, that's when it's a civil right. After all, rules were meant to be broken. You just want to be on the right side of civil when you appear in a courtroom, and with a judge that was appointed by your political party. Just ask any Jew from 1930's Germany. Those Jews will tell you the absolute power of the Socialist Nazi party, and the Communist party that followed in Russia. Those in power invented their own laws, installed their own politicians, and killed anyone in their way. Daring anyone to speak up. And if you did try to fight, doxxing, gaslighting, and revenge followed.

This whole Bundy fiasco represented much, much more to some individual freedom loving Americans. To someone like O'Reilly, it represented the need for a Constitutional convention. To the Obama Whitehouse, those cattle represented an opportunity to seize second amendment rights away from citizens exercising their first amendment. Where and who were these ideas coming from? It almost felt like to O'Reilly that an outside force or country was intentionally creating these endless theories and division. But why?

The story continued on and O'Reilly followed it with interest. Finally, the case must have fallen to someone sharing his view on rights.

After going to the judge, the Bundy case was declared a mistrial in 2017 because the judge discovered the government's "willful" failure to turn over multiple documents that could help the defense fight conspiracy and assault charges. The judge further identified 493 pages of internal affairs documents that said there were no documented injuries to endangered desert tortoises by cattle grazing on the federal land.

So it appears as stated, the government was lying. So, who would be held accountable for lying to "the people"? Which lawyer will be thrown in jail and pay millions of fines for their corruption? Which politician will be facing jail time for not overseeing that the District Attorney's case is held to a fair trial? The lawyers had all gotten paid again. The politicians had defamed with no consequence.

O'Reilly knew no one would be held accountable in politics. Some attorneys would meet over drinks and discuss who they could sue together for more billable hours. Luring clients into thinking a victory over the government was possible, or even luring some liberals into further suing the Bundy family hoping to bankrupt them and save the bovine eradication of the tortoise.

The Bundy's had slowed this process with arms.

Protesting with arms was what his country was founded upon, and something the Occupiers didn't bring to the table during their short lived hippy revolution. To take away more land from the states and give to the federal leviathan wasn't going to happen anymore. To O'Reilly, the Bundy fiasco represented a first step to what he had witnessed disappearing in his children's lifetime's, a Constitutional Republic. The government was intentionally lying to achieve a victory by using the internet, media, news outlets, and its never ending bank account to limit its own citizen's individual freedoms. Add to that the instilling of politically left deep state employees into the FBI under Biden, and the sickness was ready to spread.

The O'Reilly Proclamation was about to sprout its wings

and fly. Sometimes, it only takes one news story to change the world, and for O'Reilly, he had a "beef" to bring to the table. As he reflected on the need for change, a new story caught his eye. One that may reveal who may be behind much of the division he could not figure out.

Edward Snowden Releasing Government Prism Spying Program.

He had not been wrong.

EZ Recruits Canada

His route changed often, but the three cities were the same. Montreal, and then the Vermont towns of Burlington and Newport. All held vast numbers of conspiracy theorists and liberal sympathizers, praying to different Gods or what had become a new religion, The Far Left. EZ didn't have a religion other than division. His cause was that of a mountain range, dividing two areas in two, and if those mountains were tall enough, either side became too lazy to try and cross to the other. Staying on the left or right side of the mountain range, one could find comfort in the familiar, solace of the tribe. Facebook, Twitter, and Tik Tok would all ensure that they spoon fed only your favorite flavor of ice cream. And slowly, without even noticing, the mountains would grow even taller.

EZ found it very amusing to compare himself to the famous Canadian traitor Fred Rose. Rose descended from a Jewish European family in Lublin, Poland, an area once labeled as the "Jewish Oxford" for its concentration of Jewish settlers and scholars. Lublin was also known famously as the city that housed the headquarters for Operation Reinhardt during Nazi occupation. Reinhardt sought to eradicate all Jews from Poland. It had been involved in almost all European takeovers for centuries, belonging at times to the Russians, the Austrians, and now as part of Eastern Poland.

Fred Rose, known as Fishel Rosenberg in Lublin, took French in high school where it would eventually work well as a second language on his emigration to Montreal in 1920; however, because of his Judaism, Quebec did not allow this faith in the French Catholic school system, leading the young Rose to the majority Protestant and Jewish high school.

Rose became interested in Communism early in his life, probably as a result of being resented among the majority French speaking Catholics who looked down upon anyone who didn't resemble their side of the mountain. He joined various forms of Communist parties in the 1920's and vocally advocated for the Canadian government to become more like a Soviet platform. Eventually, Rose became a candidate for the Communist Party of Canada. Running, but losing for office several times before the start of World War II. After World War II, Canada saw to it that the Communist Party was banned, so Rose joined the relabeled party, now called the LaborProgressive Party. Same values, different name.

He won election in 1943 and again in 1945 with many Jews supporting his beliefs that only the Soviet Union would be the savior for Jews against Hitler. The Communist Jew from Lublin is the only Communist ever elected to the Canadian government. EZ wondered if Trudeau might secretly be the second.

What many who voted for Rose didn't know, was that he was secretly working with the Communist party. A Soviet spy after World War II, Igor Gouzenko, outed a large number of spies working within Canada and the United States. Rose was working with up to twenty Russian assets, all trying to further Russia's expediency in developing their own nuclear weapons. Working with an American scientist, Raymond Boyer, who was the expert on the explosive RDX, Rose had promised Russia to send the details on how to manufacture the chemical back to the Soviet Motherland. Gouzenko's list of spies helped the Canadians put a stop to a disaster. Rose's Canadian citizenship was stripped from him as he lay sick and banished in Poland where he later died.

Rose's ideas were still there in Montreal EZ knew. The foundations and rationale behind the Labor movement were present and only growing. EZ's ability to divide, and inflame each side of the movement, was no different than Rose had done in the 1920's. Abuse of the minority by the state, lack of workers rights, poor treatment of immigrants-the French Catholic Quebec of today was still holding onto these beliefs. Perhaps even more so since their young hero Trudeau was there to keep them safe against the Fascist ideas of the world and to the inferior American ideology south of Canada.

American types who would think voting for a President like Trump would be a good idea. America was younger than Canada, not only in years, but in maturity. Overconfidence in one's beliefs was a weakness, whether it be religion, politics, or world views. Build the overconfidence, and there was no way to see the other side. Overconfidence made the mountains taller because the other side was always wrong, and thus, always inferior. EZ had seen this in the United States, Ukraine, Israel, and the Middle East. Rich versus poor. Educated versus uneducated. Instill division and victory awaits.

EZ saw himself as the next Fred Rose, but he wouldn't get caught. He was too well trained. The media and message was much easier to spread than in Rose's day where he depended on writings in newspapers and radio broadcasts. And EZ's message could be distributed around the world, to both sides, every day all day thanks to cell phones and the internet. People as a whole knew they were being manipulated; and yet, didn't care as long as the manipulation strengthened the ultimate destruction of the other tribe.

Communism from 1920's Canada never left. Communism always has time. And much like UUONE, his actions were not for even his generation, but for generations to come.

EZ pulled into the parking garage just east of Howe Library. He could see students with hijabs and thobes exiting their cars with poster board protest signs.

"Islam Doesn't Silence Me. It empowers me", "Muslims Matter", "Hijabs for Hope". The basic signs he had seen at so many of the same protests across Canada and the United States. It was as if no one could be original, or was it that someone, like a George Soros type left wing non for profit, had already made the signs for the protestors. Soros thrived off division, *just as I do* EZ thought. The Hungarian Jew Soros was probably a huge Rose fan, having worked with the Nazi's in his youth and pursuing Western capitalist ideas as a profession.

Burlington, Vermont, was known as the San Francisco of the East Coast, perhaps being the most liberal city east of the Mississippi. Its former mayor, Bernie Sanders, was a well known Leftist. And what do all liberal towns need? An extremely left wing college. The University of Vermont fits that need with perfection. Tolerant of left wing ideology, but extremely non tolerant of any right wing group or message that group may seek to promote.

The University had a job-to instill the message of liberalism to the country's future leadership and educators: to educate these youth before the real world might get into their minds and instill white guilt and the message of equity over equality. EZ had seen Fox News that morning, as they were to cover the event live. CNN the Leftist view, and Fox News the Right's. Perfect division. These media conglomerates could make money off idealistic advertisers and existed much better in a world together. One channel could not do as well if the other were to not exist.

It was genius level societal notch. God he loved American politics.

EZ had seen online that the Christian's For a Cause Club was having Jordan Peterson as a guest speaker on the commons near the center of campus. "Why Should Young Men Value Christianity?" was the theme of Jordan's speech. What more could a divisionist ask for? Left versus right. Muslims versus Christians. Kids with zero experience in the world, no jobs, no struggles, somehow able to judge the entire world around them based off of TikTok shorts and Instagram Reels. Young idealized, testosterone primed males needed outlets for their boredom, and justification for their existence on both political sides. Young women, unsure of their place in society since the Feminist movement, could display epic levels of discontent and anger, particularly at the ballot box. It was uncool to not have one's latest political stance broadcasted on all social media or clothing. Pick a flag, a religion, a country to side with, and automatically, an enemy, a division, would exist to cheer against. To radicalize young adults was standard issue Communism. Carl Marx's Manifesto taught them how to do it. It was even being proven at the voting polls as effective, with almost all single, progressive, white females voting for the left.

The brainwashing had worked. It just took getting them out of the home to accomplish. EZ pulled his own sign from his trunk. "Islam is NOT Terrorism". Not that he cared what his sign said. It could have supported the other side just as easily, but today's division goal required this message, plus he had used it at three other rallies. His trunk was filled with signs that could be displayed at either left or right protests. It was time to go to work. He placed his shemagh on his head and looked down at his tan colored thobe. Not perfect, but the crowd of teenagers wouldn't be looking at him, but rather at the speaker.

Much as Rose had done, EZ had to change some hearts and minds for the Motherland. Just another day to create division and recruit.

His goal was to find two true Islamic believers. Two individuals idealized enough to make a trip across the Vermont border on a special mission. He had found his two Americans at their gun club, and now he would find his next co-conspirators. The overall accountability of the mission would need evidence and motif.

UUONE would create that for those who chose to do the deep dive later. CNN and Fox would need content. It was hard to makeup bullshit 24 hours a day.

O'Reilly's Thoughts

We were all used to the cold. Highly entrenched, starving, and ready for our cause. Without much of a cause to believe in, the entitled Sheep were "out to pasture". Many had run to Mexico, New Zealand, Costa Rica, or Western Canada, away from the fighting, taking their children in tow. Hoping that the government would take care of the problem. Hoping that the government had a solution. There would forever be a problem now though. Once you had nothing left to lose, you had much to gain.

O'Reilly had his own thoughts and theories on the current state of the world.

The big talkers online weren't much for actual fighting. They were an entire generation who had spent their younger years on a computer, being reinforced at state schools and Universities which no longer promoted trades, outdoor activities, or exercise. The only running that was occurring was to other countries. It was easy to talk shit in the comments section, but it was not so easy to talk shit in person. To take that talk into action was the next level.

Many felt it crazy that Mexicans were coming in to harness US entitlements, at the same time hard core Socialist's and Antifa members were going to Mexico to embrace this so called utopian form of government that these Mexicans were abandoning. You would think they would have traded notes at the border.

O'Reilly remembered asking the richest doctors he had worked with before the war what would it take for them to quit work and come to arms against a tyrannical government. Tax rate of fifty percent? Sixty? Ninety? One hundred? None would ever answer. Comfort is the enemy of progress, of necessary change and revolt.

But one's labor isn't free, and at some point, enough entitlements make everyone's labor free and without freedom. The farmer who gives his sheep away soon has no sheep to sell. The government had released its sheep. It could no longer protect the flock, nor could it feed, medicate, or keep them from the cold. The barns were full, and predators knew where the barns were. Once starvation sets in, only the hardiest of the flock will survive against all odds. Sheep dogs were long gone as they had seen what was about to occur.

These were the Sheep he was up against. True believers in the Socialist movement. Progressivism. Communism hidden over time. Hidden in false accusations of racism and the promises of handouts. Brainwash the laziest and soon everyone believed they were entitled to more. Control the people's information and disinformation through the global takeover of all information-Google, Palantir, Oracle, Tik Tok, and Meta. There no longer existed a need for gun registries, Jewish address books, or disbelievers. All personal information was on display after accepting the terms and conditions of a platform, only learning those were passed along to the National Security Administration. With servers around the world, private data was saved in real time. The NSA, CIA, and Palantir types now accumulated, shared, and processed all data about every human on earth. Facial recognition was often not needed since photos were posted freely.

Simply add a face to a name and a bank account. Universal ID was already in effect.

From birth, parents posted their children's pictures online. Facial recognition software uplinked these years of images across the globe. Fingerprint access to an iPhone or Android lock screen was acceptable. Even when visiting Disney World, a fingerprint was required at entry. With over nineteen million visitors from around the world visiting every day, a lot of data was being collected.

Every phone call was taped. Every email is saved. Every Facebook, TikTok, Twitter, Reddit post recorded into the cloud, and even each word and phrase typed into a search engine could be saved unless you knew how to delete your search profile, which in reality was a joke, because once you deleted your search profile, it went into a trash bin on the company's servers that could only be truly deleted by the companies themselves. Some web engines only allowed searches if linked to a pre-existing IP address and verified name, and anyone deleting their search history was immediately researched, because of what might they be hiding. To delete meant there was something to hide. No one was allowed to hide. George Orwell's 1984 was becoming more relevant by the day.

A fallacy existed in deleting a Facebook account. A process which took thirty days, according to the web giant-just in case you changed your mind. All of those cute moments on file of your memories conveniently saved, sent to you daily. Incriminating photos from college or high school friends. Friend lists and political beliefs, all readily available. Viewpoints you quickly clicked and accepted, or shared to others within your friend groups. All of the photos provided locations and times. Guilt through association of extremists might affect social credit scoring.

Big Brother didn't have to dig, it was all voluntarily uploaded.

To display opinions openly and be accepted within the flock was of great importance in the later stages of decline. If an opinion was different from the generated greater opinion, your account could be suspended, terminated, or worse, singled out by the in-house thought police to pursue destruction of the individual through loss of employment or better yet, through lawsuits which would destroy anyone's finances and mental strength over time. .

Only the multimedia corporation determined who was on the correct team, and their in-house department decided what was offensive, and that was determined by whomever had political power. Since these companies all shared access to their databases with the NSA and CIA, then those in political power could decide who might be a problem against the current agenda's goals. The FBI started to become the Stasi but with better intelligence tools. Artificial intelligence would finally add enough power to institute Universal ID and a global social credit scoring system.

It's like Marx hiring Lenin to grade his homework. Don't

dare be the black sheep in the field, for you'll stand out from the rest of the flock, being noticed by the farmer. Impure in image, even if genetically superior to the other sheep. Never stand out, never beg for attention. The best defense was to always agree. That is what was best for the greater good of the flock. The current populace was being trained to go along with the flock or become a lemming.

One world revolved around one master identification card, one form of payment, one league of ideas. All controlled by the hands of people one would never meet. Mental control, without knowing one was controlled or why, was the ultimate mastery of a society, of a global economy directing its workers for its goals. Removal of self defense taken away without firing a shot. The one world order needed compliance in its workers. Compliance in its slaves is necessary for growth.

Doxxing became standard practice. Black sheep were found easily in online forums and exposed to the wolves. Opinions of dissent were there for the farmer to read and evaluate. Real time conversations recorded through bluetooth devices willingly placed throughout the home. Cameras recorded every move. Wifi could sense shapes and people within the home. The police could be called if violence was detected by AI. Vibrations from voice could now be picked up with basic electrical outlets.

The Amazon Echo, Siri, Google Home, Smart TVs, all provided real time microphones to listen in on black sheep. Tracking phone signals was cemented during the Coronavirus, and afterward phones became free to all citizens. All bills, bank accounts, and disbursement of free services were through the government issued cell phones. All made in China and running on Chinese 5G networks. Traded on the global stock exchange with Yeuros. Financed through banks located in any country.

Children were required to start free Google email accounts

which tracked all ideas and conversations for life. Schools signed contracts with Microsoft and used taxpayer dollars to pay for the contract fees and virus updates. The Chinese never paid, saving even more money in their schools. A U.S. or European child was required to have a cell phone for school assignments, a school email, and a school issued computer accessible at any time by any teacher. All teacher's unions approved, stating progress. Salaries and benefits became lower over time, with the union blaming political rivals and never themselves. AI and online teachers soon replaced in person teaching enabling more global mind control. Instead of U.S. history, a politically correct version of global history emerged, heavily catering to left wing messaging.   Video messages logged facial recognition through FaceTime, Youtube, Kik, Reels, Telegram, Groupme, WhatsApp, Bumble, Tinder, Grinder, Microsoft apps, Skype and many others, where all agreed to the end user agreements that were never read. If one didn't sign the user agreement, you couldn't use the app. Many of the apps were necessary for an occupation that also followed their online content. Others didn't want to feel excluded from dating or friendship groups. People were willingly allowing these companies to follow, study, evaluate, track, and directly advertise to them. Even important documents: taxes, wills, school papers, diaries, etc. These were all stored for "free" in the cloud from the very first days of school, marriage, divorce, or necessity, or they were used in scan, fax, or document signed apps.

Political activism, voter registration, bank accounts, porn site visits, all matters of thought-stored on hard drives across the United States. Many thought they were safe with VPNs and third party log-ins, but what they didn't know was that these companies were all started by the NSA, CIA, GRU, Mossad, or similar. Driving apps like Google maps, Waze, Life360, were all recording locations, speed and being saved. Waze was developed by the Israeli military and sold to Google with no one batting an eye. Phones could be tracked even when turned off. The ability to black mail and control another's future was now in someone else's hands, or maybe even another country's hands if they hacked the servers. Routine blackmail was the strongest way to bring spies into use by the Chinese, Israelis, and the Russians. Drug use, sex habits, addictions, and kinks were all logged under the one world ID. Agree to the user agreements, and you have agreed to the end of the user's freedom. Blackmail, extortion, jail or cooperation were the only choices if needed by the government. Find the person, and they would find the crime. Lawsuits could easily grind a citizen into non-existence and forced cooperation.

When it came to population control, the cellular phone was the best invention of all time.

To control all forms of thought. To hold all former thoughts. To understand what motivates. That's the ultimate power. But who holds it? Who decides which direction the wind blows at the NSA? As in Germany, it's all about the timing. As one dictator was defeated, another was being formed. The goals could be for a fascist or an antifascist, but the ability was there. It was just who was at the right place at the right time when someone chose to abuse your beliefs. Don't be on the wrong side of history. The companies that developed and implemented the technology didn't care who it was used for or against. They cared about the next stock price and government contract. They cared about the politicians creating crises and solutions, and since the ego would always control a politician, the stock prices would continue to soar. Banks could generate more money from chaos than in a peaceful society.

O'Reilly was fucked from the beginning. He had been

posting, reading, commenting, and watching Pro Militia content and illegal gun chats. The ATF and NSA picked up on the feeds.

Was he considered a terrorist? Or could he be used to achieve a desired outcome or crisis? Show the agencies the crisis, and they will show you the people to instigate it. Create the crisis, and they could direct the solution through politics. Create more crises and solutions, and create more need for funding. But to control all the minds, and all the crises, that was the next step. It was with this over reach that O'Reilly was placed on a watch list for possible militia activity.

Using AI, the NSA had started searching private message boards of gun groups and Libertarian Reddit forums. AI was able to associate email addresses, IP addresses, and identify likely content contributors across multiple platforms. O'Reilly's name appeared, one of their own, a border patrol agent. The NSA passed this evidence to the FBI. Also privy to possible hate crime activity was Israeli intelligence, who just happened to be looking for the perfect individual to complete a task.

To stay off the grid, UUONE was assigned the task of operating a shady mission on their "closest " ally's soil. This required a certain type of extremist. O'Reilly's entire online history was psychologically processed. With his position near Montreal, and his border patrol occupation, they elected to distribute the candidate's name up the chain of command.

EZ's job would now be to flame the extremist beliefs in the American. Create the foundation of a plan into O'Reilly, fund him, direct him, and instill the need for control of the flock. O'Reilly and his associates would be molded into the urgent need of committing a terrorist act in order to save the morals and beliefs that he felt sacred. The FBI had become quite good at this technique, but EZ knew he had something they didn't. He may be able to do something mass media and data algorithms had been unable to do-instill the thoughts and emotions before bots or agencies could. O'Reilly's thoughts revealed his desire to divide.

<u>EZ Goes Viral</u>

EZ looked across the brisk St. Lawrence river, trying to identify the name on the Chinese container ship. Traveling to Quebec City from Montreal wasn't a bad three hour drive, unless it was snowing, and today his Honda Civic's front wheel drive struggled through the March snow. The scent of the gray water, diesel fuel, containers, rail cars, and tractor trailers, lay trapped under the weight of the falling snow. His shipment would be arriving soon into its Communist friendly host port.

Canada had always had a great partnership with Communist countries. From Prime Minister Trudeau's bond with Castro's Cuba and China's Mao in the Sixties, to the formation of the Canada China Business Council, that included ventures with three local Montreal based businesses that EZ knew about-Power Corporation, Bombardier, and SND Lavalin. Most concerning, if you followed Canadian politics, was the extremely close relationship of Power Corporation's Montreal headquarters to Canadian and world politics. Four Canadian Prime Ministers-Trudeau, Mulroney, Chretien, and Martin had all either served or had connections with the Power Corporation, including many of their former staff members. People privy to the inner workings and funding available at the Canadian capital. People that understood how the world worked.

From former German Chancellors, Saudi Sheikhs, and even the former head of the US Federal Reserve, Paul Volcker. The Power Corporation was exactly that, a power corporation.

Further linkages existed between the family that ran Power Corporation and the members of the Canada Chinese Business Council. Marriages between business and council members were on record. Relationships went all the way back to 19th century Canadian Methodist missionary trips into Western China, EZ wondered why on earth all of these Prime Ministers openly served or worked proudly with Power Corp, and how the Canadian people didn't bat an eye at the possible corruption. It was as open as Hunter and Joe Biden's transactions with Ukraine's Burisma. Through one global wealth management company, holding $629 billion in assets, Canada and China could form partnerships few could understand. One such project could benefit both companies, as well as the Canadian government's standings with China.

Although the construction project, named Laurentia, to build the largest container terminal ever in Quebec City fell apart, Chinese owned Hutchison Ports continued negotiations with the Canadian parliament and Canadian National Railway. This would have increased the Chinese company's global port ownership to 52 ports in 27 countries. It was clear that the Chinese wanted to influence global sea trade, already able to control 11% of all container cargo worldwide. With decreased water levels in 2022, the need to deepen the canal and increase flows out of Lake Ontario were environmental disasters and hurdles the Hong Kong based Hutchison could achieve at some point.

EZ had been following the progress of the deep water port closely since Laurentia had initially passed in 2019, ecstatic to think a Chinese owned company would be right in America's back yard. And who would the Chinese help in their fight with the American's? Russia. And who saw a vested interest in China doing well? None other than the Canada China Business

Council. Despite the fact the deal fell through, Hutchison or subsidiaries still held influence over the Quebec port, expansion or not, they were the world's leader on ocean shipping. Somehow, some way, they would have a say. Whether it be container delays from other ports, crane parts, or labor supply. The power lay in China, and China had a great friend in Canada.

The CIA and Mossad had its eyes on these businesses affiliated with the Council for years EZ knew, but if you were able to persuade enough high ranking board members and past Prime Ministers, the companies such as Power Corp had little to fear. It was worth the risk to garner more assets. The global level of corruption was something those less powerful feared. This was basically a Chinese owned port.

To add icing on the cake, the Americans were being devastated by the fentanyl crisis. Almost 70,000 Americans overdosed on the opioid yearly. Fentanyl was in every drug sold on the streets: cocaine, heroin, and pills. The Americans knew who was responsible for its synthesis and its distribution. The chemical precursors could only be manufactured in China, and the distribution was primarily by Mexican and Canadian cartels across the U.S. Border. While the Border patrol was too weak and understaffed to enforce drug busts under the ever increasing weak Biden and Democratic administrations, it rarely batted an eye towards its northern neighbor.

The Canadian Royal Mounted Police were extremely vigilant in bringing narcotics into Canada. Drug searches going the opposite direction, into the U.S., were of little concern. If the Americans wanted to poison themselves, knowing the consequences, then so be it. It was much the same attitude with Mexican law enforcement, especially with the notorious corruption and bribery in Mexico City.

Quebec's port provided a friendly place to deposit fentanyl

precursors or already synthesized fentanyl. As many U.S. officials scoured the Mexican border looking for the cheap fentanyl importers, it was actually the Canadian port system responsible for the bulk of fentanyl's arrival. Companies kept quiet. Companies that ignored the Chinese bad stuff in order to get the Chinese good stuff. Upping profits at the expense of the American taxpayer. And all of that cash needed to be invested and laundered somewhere. EZ couldn't fathom the billions changing hands, and the number of eyes looking the other way. The Albanian, Italian, and Russian mafias controlled this drug trade once unloaded, and the Canadian Police were too small in number to make a dent in the flow.

Canada could do much better if the American dollar was low. As he saw with the UkraineRussian conflict affecting global oil production, EZ knew that to make money, you must export more than you import. He had exported his share of fentanyl across the border. Selling to his biker gang connections in Montreal who further transported the product to their Mexican cartel counterparts in the U.S. The bikers were by far the best method of distributing drugs in Canada.

The police had infiltrated the gangs once, but never again. It took time, money, and bravery to infiltrate even one small sector of a gang, and even if successful with prosecution, another sector would take its place immediately. Many biker gangs in the US. had been smart enough to label themselves as "churches" in order to avoid IRS investigation. Technically they fit the same tax codes as a Not For Profit, and no longer had to turn over their financial records for evaluation by the government. The U.S. legal system was a joke.

As part of the Chinese maritime silk road, Yangshan Port was just south of Shanghai. EZ knew this was the shipping container's origins, sailing aboard the Chinese made container vessel, Ever Atlast, under a Panamanian flag, a benefit when using the Panama Canal.   The Americans had stupidly handed over the canal's lease. Ever since World War Two, the Latin American countries had been a home base for CIA and Israeli influence and control. To lose the port would make life a lot harder to operate undercover missions there.

He could just make out the ship's bow through the distant snow. It wouldn't be long. The ship's tracking systems could be watched by everyone involved, corrupt or not. His phone app gave him minute to minute progress on its journey.

There were certain benefits of dealing with the Chinese. Access and control over global ports was certainly beneficial in this case. As the Chinese upper class greed grew, the ability to persuade or bribe shipping companies for the Communist cause against the United States became easier each and every year. It was now apparent that the Chinese upper class could get the middle class, which was new, to work in their favor in order to move up the ladder.

The fact that the ship's Captain wouldn't have to enter the United States also came into the play. The American Navy and Coast Guard were far more likely to search boats than the Canadians, who loved the free military presence to their South, and the benefits of free trade with the Chinese shipping container vessels. It helped to have prominent politicians on companies controlling the money, as they knew who to pay to keep quiet in the Provinces. The politicians knew who would pay to play, and who would keep silent.   Just like the Chinese, Canada was not a capitalist society, so the ability to increase societal rank required a degree of corruptness. It also helped that the Chinese owned all three of the companies that manufactured steel shipping containers. China had cheaper steel production, cheaper labor, access to the refrigerator and cooling manufacturers, and there was no need to deliver the containers somewhere else in the world once manufactured. The finished container would just go off on another Chinese container vessel, joining the other 65 million containers globally on one of the 5,500 container ships. A needle in a haystack was EZ's package to anyone searching. Being delivered to a traditionally

Communist sympathizing country, directly next door to the American's, using corporate Capitalism. The longer he traveled around the world, the longer he could not envision an honest global trade. Since the Chinese owned the ships, affected timing and labor, managed most of the ports, built most of the cranes and hardware, affected the local politics, and could build hidden compartments into their own steel containers, EZ wasn't worried about his container even if it were off loaded and searched.

Chinese owned companies like Hutchison were bound to grow in locations around the world as China looked to dominate the world's oceans-holding the ports necessary for that trade was icing on the cake. State owned companies like Hutchison would always do what the State forced them to, as long as they deposited their wealth with Chinese friendly investment companies. His mission had finally been sent from UUONE. Now, EZ was able to change from division to deployment.

He knew it would take around a day to unload the container ship, so he took a deep breath, reached into his pocket, and dialed a preset number on the burner phone. A Burlington, Vermont, number appeared on the outgoing screen.

"It's pulling in now Jamal, God willing."

"Thank you brother. We won't let you down. We will be up to Montreal in three days. Ma'a salama."

His Islamic recruitment in Vermont had gone as planned.

EZ closed the burner as Ever Atlast slowly plowed up the colorless river. Only Chinese eyes witnessed what had been loaded, and now only Canadian Communist sympathizers would see what was off loaded. All protected through shipping lanes manned by Americans and paid for by the American middle class drug user.

Thank God for fentanyl EZ sighed.

Israel's product had arrived. Allah would provide the delivery into the States. He just had to find the right people to put the product in action. Islamic extremists wouldn't be enough to create the division UUONE wanted. For this, they wanted home grown extremists.

Pulling out his GPS, he put in an address for Franconia, New Hampshire. The mountains would be a great place to hike and keep his physique up as he recruited the American. Every good conspiracy needed a patsy, and Israeli intelligence had provided him with a good place to start. He had never been to an American gun club, but he would be tomorrow. Hopefully, their profiling would pay off.

<u>Joining the Gun Club</u>

The Libtards had made it almost impossible to get out and go target shooting. People who owned guns were racist, evil, and responsible for all ills in the world according to the left. Lead bullet bans were instituted on environmental grounds, and ammunition faced 50% tax increases. Public lands were banned from target shooting or risk losing federal funding. State game lands were banned due to disrupting migratory birds and mating seasons, or so they claimed.

Some gun clubs instituted all out bans on AR rifles, stating that the guns caused fear in the other club members, even though it was explained to them that they shoot the same size bullet as Little Sally's .22 target rifle. All conversations with these Elmer

Fudds to convince them otherwise was a waste of time. Even the mention of making silencers available without a Federal tax stamp was dismissed after another round of pill-induced teenage angst or pill induced activist school shootings. The National Rifle Association was starting to cave on issues as well. Actually backing an age increase to buy a gun to 21 instead of 18, and making bump stocks illegal, giving these worthless AR add ons the same classification that applied to machine guns.

If bump stocks were so great, why weren't they arming militaries around the world with them? Every police department in the country should just buy bump stocks to save money over fully automatic rifles. The NRA had fought to make a National Reciprocity Concealed Carry Act possible for Interstate travel, but ended up instead creating a back door loophole which essentially created a gun registry. Local officials were hard at work taking away the tools that make the Second Amendment work.

Soon came the 50% tax on ammunition which had already happened in liberal cities such as Seattle, Washington. Statistics easily proved that these meaningless feel good laws had nothing to do with gun crime. Almost every mass shooter was far over the age of 21. Those who weren't usually had just stolen a gun from a relative or a friend.

If they ever made primers illegal, that would be a line in the sand. Reloading should never be infringed.

EZ was impressed by all of this rhetoric. He had studied this narrative online, and he felt he could pull off expressing the sentiment. He had to express the lingo and also sell and escalate the feelings presented by the pro gun Right wing and Libertarian groups. He also had to know the Left's anti gun arguments. His job was to continue creating division, and he enjoyed gaining the knowledge to do so. They must invite him into their tribe, and to do so mandated his understanding of their dialect.

The gun club was about two hours away from his house. A bit of a drive, but the intelligence he had been provided indicated a gun club where a member was likely to be easily influenced. He had moved into the area around Franconia Notch in New Hampshire. He hoped the Live Free or Die motto would hold up on his patsy search.

Driving down a narrow, poorly plowed road, he arrived at a parking lot bordered with large granite stones. He stopped into the office, signed a release form, and proceeded to the range. There were dozens of people in the different shooting bays, but one pair of shooters drew his attention. He caught the name Willis, but not the other taller gentleman. The two were shooting a custom built AR15. And on it, he heard the distinct sound of a bump stock.

No one at the range even glanced at the sound of the controlled bursts. He knew if an ATF agent were to arrive, mandatory arrests would occur, yet no one seemed to care. These were the type of people who may fit his profile.

The man, Willis, even appeared a little intoxicated. Alcohol and firearms never mix he knew, but this guy seemed to be in control and enjoying his best life-smiling a little too much, talking to himself, as he changed magazines. An internal dialogue probably more interesting than he found elsewhere.

Willis seemed to enjoy the fact that he was committing a felony. Essentially daring the Feds to drive up, or telling the ATF to go fuck itself. Willis seemed to bleed a degree of freedom not often seen in these Gestapoesque years. A flash of the American war hero Sam Adams telling the British to fuck off went through EZ's mind.

EZ understood that feeling. That feeling of telling authority, or Anti Zionists to fuck off. It was the same feeling that inspired him from talks with his father about the old days when Israel had been founded and wars were needed. When the country had told Egypt or the Palestinians to fuck off. He'd never felt that camaraderie with his UUONE job. He mainly worked alone. No one got to hear him say it.

Most of these gun nut guys were straight up, play it by the book type block heads. To even mention the words bump stock might have gotten them investigated. Discussing government overreach was a huge green light for what he was looking for, gun nuts who hated the FBI and ATF. Those that hated big government.

EZ had heard that the FBI hadn't always been so one sided. During the initial years of the FBI, neutral control was placed on staff placement, but under the direction of McCarthy, the FBI's head offices had been filled with Party loyalists, and the old school crew was forced to either retire or move on. From then on, investigations focused conveniently on anyone whose ideas ran contrary to the current party's narrative.

The press liked to call it the Deep State. A secretive but omnipresent group well placed in powerful decision making positions. Anywhere from the government, to the press, to city and county officials, one could find people who were part of the Deep State. Everyday Soviet citizens used to fear the KGB. Conservative Americans now feared the FBI. And you never knew who was part of the Deep State. Paranoia was the fashion of the day. Voice a different party opinion and get ready for your business to be investigated by the IRS. Post a comment online that a party member considers offensive, and get a visit from the FBI's new Cultural Appropriateness Division. Obtain a Concealed Carry Handgun permit, then you must have guns at home.

Every President elected since the Twin Towers collapse had

all signed off on the Foreign Intelligence Surveillance Act (FISA). FISA supposedly only allowed the government to investigate foreigners, not US citizens. But it allowed intelligence officials to collect and keep all information, regardless of citizenship or cause. All it took was the new Party to have an excuse to start a search on this saved data under the guise of an enemy against the state or terrorism. So basically, "don't give them an excuse" was what most people did to stay out of the Party's spotlight.

Even Facebook was now banning conservative political commentary and gun videos. The popular site Youtube wouldn't even allow videos on gun instruction or gun maintenance. The U.S. was literally 1930's Germany happening under the name of inclusion, equity, discrimination, or offensiveness, all while liberals used the emotions of gun violence as a tool to instill destruction of the Second Amendment.

Willis clearly didn't care about FISA or offensiveness. EZ sat back and watched him go through nearly an ammo can full of 5.56mm. Letting freedom ring.

EZ intentionally picked the shooting bay next to the two gentlemen, hoping to overhear what was being said. Careful not to look too interested, but with the range being busy, he didn't come off as being too suspicious. He opened his 5.11 double rifle case.

First, he pulled out his favorite. A custom built Wilson Combat Short Barrel Rifle in .300 Blackout, sporting a Silencerco Omega Suppressor. He had picked a Trijicon MRO optic because he hated the stories that went along with the Eotech optics failures in extreme heat and cold. The company had known about such failures and didn't let guys down range in Iraq and Afghanistan know as soon as the discovery was made. The grunts in the field had complained for years about aiming directly at the enemy in combat but bullets not hitting their target.

"Fuck Eotech", he thought.

Meanwhile,Trijicon had hidden a Biblical verse on one of their scopes, and although he wasn't a Christian, that was a direct Fuck You to the Party's anti religious platform. Being the Israeli he was, he would take bible verses over the Party platform. He was for sure a Nonbeliever when it came to the Party. EZ's lingo, his dialect, had to be perfect.

Think and say what they would say.

He then took out his home defense weapon of choice. The voice of darkness should a home intruder decide to meet his fate. EZ's choice was a FN Herstal P90, cut down to a ten inch barrel. He had loved the gun since it had come out in 1990. Attached to the end was his Silencerco Octane 45K Suppressor, and on top, a fifty round mag of the deadly 5.7 mm rounds sporting their blue tips. He then laid out his Halfface Blades Tomahawk as an additional conversation starter.

He hated to think about the fact that the Israeli government had paid the ATF $800 worth of tax stamps on items that should be legal in the first place. The documents were needed to sell his story. They would all be registered in his "brother's" name, who lived in Arizona, according to the paperwork.

The P90 also sported a Steiner Night Vision laser on the left side's Picatinny rail, a Surefire flashlight on the right rail, and another Trijicon MRO on the top. In the event someone did break into his home, he would be at a distinct advantage leaving the lights off and using his night vision monocle. He knew his home far better than the thief would. And much to the same reason the U.S. Secret Service used the P90, the recoil was zero, the round was super fast and lethal. The 5.7mm round was also super light weight, and he could carry tons of it in his "Go

Bag". His equipment would need to draw some attention, and the methodology of their purchase accurate. *Know the lingo EZ.*

Thinking of his choice on the P90 led him to his pistol choice. Opening his grey, Vertx Range Bag, he pulled out his pistol of choice, the FNH Five-Seven. Also chambered in 5.7x 28mm, he could now carry only one ammo load. He had made this decision right away after first seeing it at a police range eight years after he had acquired his P90. Magazines held twenty rounds, and the gun was light weight, even fully loaded. All of this information he had memorized from gun forums. All of his facts had to be accurate.

The 5.7mm round was the equivalent diameter as the everyday .22LR which most were familiar, except it had behind it a little more powder in the cartridge, leaving the barrel at speeds of 2,500 m/s with the military grade cartridges he could purchase with his Canadian law enforcement connections. Militias loved to know those in authority.

Although this Black tip, military grade ammunition was illegal for civilians to own, it was one perk of having his badge. At those speeds, the cartridge would go through a Level one bullet proof vest. For these reasons, the gun had a bad reputation with the ATF as it was the gun of choice with drug cartels throughout Mexico, going for five to six times its price on the black market. Mexican cartels were infatuated with the Five-Seven, as were American celebrities. EZ had read where one NFL football player, Plaxico Burress, accidentally shot himself in a club in New York City with a 5.7mm. It was important to know random facts EZ presumed.

On his belt, he had placed a Tepfer Armory Persian belt knife, just to draw more conversations. *"How was it he could own a gun in that city where guns are illegal?"* A passing thought as he pulled a thirty round extended magazine out for the pistol.

"Hey O'Reilly, get me that SBR from the truck," he heard the shorter, rounder of the two say to the other. The taller gentleman finally spoke, with a rather undeterminable accent.

"No problem Willis. Let's see how these new 3D printed versions run."

Now these two were speaking EZ's language with a tone of abrasive shadiness. Low key illegal fun guns. Time for an introduction.

"Excuse me, I was just admiring your SBR. Is that a Daniel Defense?" EZ asked who he assumed to be Willis.

"Yes. Binary trigger, drum magazine, and suppressor aren't, but I put those on aftermarket. I saw you shooting a short barrel P90. Since I'm one of the range safety officers and a club board member, I'm going to need to see your tax stamp from the ATF."

"I have it in my range bag. Don't leave home without it." EZ said.

The other man, O'Reilly, was returning with another firearm and overheard the conversation. "Shut the fuck up Willis. No one out here gives a shit. I'm sorry my friend is an asshole. He's just trying to see if you are ATF before he gets caught for some shit. I'm O'Reilly. What's your name?"

"I go by EZ. Pleased to meet the two of you."

O'Reilly looked EZ in the eyes with a bit of leeriness.

"What is that accent you have? Is that Canadian?"

EZ laughed, "Yes. Being that you are so close to the border, I'm sure you are sick of hearing them. I came down with some of my brother's guns that he lets me borrow. You know, in Canada, we can't have these."

Willis chimed in.

"Well technically, since you are Canadian, you can't own

them here either. Even if they are your brother's, I'm not sure a Canadian can be on a gun trust, and that's about the only way you could share all of the Class 3 stuff I see. And don't even tell me you have black tipped 5.7mm rounds out here. Those are highly illegal."

EZ looked down at his P90 and smiled. It was time to test his hypothesis.

"She's a beauty isn't she. Would you like to shoot her?" EZ extended the rifle towards Willis.

"Wouldn't turn it down to save my life. Fuck the ATF," Willis said.

"I'm up next, and I second that emotion," O'Reilly added.

EZ handed the gun over to Willis.

This was exactly who he was looking for, already willing to break the laws established by what they viewed as a tyrannical over reaching government. With a little help, he was sure he could lead their minds into the mission, and here he was, the one hand picked by UUONE, O'Reilly. *Damn I love cell phone tracking and Pegasus software.* EZ thought.

"I'll be right back, I have to take this call. Shoot as many rounds as you want of the black tip, I can get more where that came from."

EZ stepped away from the pair. Pulling out his cell phone, he called the command center of

UUONE.

"Tell the FBI and NSA to take these two off of their radar, and that if they pursue, they will be interrupting an active investigation involving Israeli intelligence that may compromise global security. These two are mine for the time being."

EZ listened as the message was repeated back to him, and he ended the call. Walking back to Willis and O'Reilly burning through his ammunition as they tried to shoot through steel plates. "You guys wouldn't know where I can find an auto sear pin for a B&T APC223-PDW would you?" EZ asked.

O'Reilly looked up from loading yet another magazine full of the 5.7mm.

"Find one? We make our own. Just come to the next club meeting."

EZ's first day had gone better than expected. Finding not only one patsy, but possibly two. His next job would be to sell the American's on losing their values and rights. Instill the foundation of his plan into O'Reilly and Willis. Fund, scare, direct, and instill the desire to defend their way of life, or risk losing their country to the Left wingers and government that they so despised. A half century's worth of mind control research was about to be revealed.

O'Reilly's Online World

O'Reilly knew that in order to really rile up his base, his tactics wouldn't be by showing support for his cause. His main goal was to create what Thomas Sowell had so eloquently spoken about in his book *The Vision of the Anointed,* a book he had read on some of his more boring shifts.

The first step according to Sowell was to establish the "Crisis". With the current state of political, military, and global unrest, another crisis of significant proportions would add significant weight to the news pundits selling step two, the "Solution" around Capital Hill. The "Results" would lead to new policies discussed in the "Solution". Often, ending a "Crisis" that was never a crisis in the first place. He just hoped that this time, the "Response", was to be issued forth by the Militias, requiring a burden of proof to its actions instead of never calling out a quantifiable measurement on the success of said

"Solutions".

The politicians were never held accountable for their actions. They never suffered public hangings or criticism. Elections continued on with the voter's always suffering amnesia. It was no different than the infamous Rubber Room in New York City O'Reilly thought. A building where unionized teachers, who couldn't or wouldn't be fired from the New York education system because of corrupt Union laws, sat all day taking language classes, playing poker, sleeping, and basically getting a paycheck, benefits, and a guaranteed retirement. All because the state deemed it more expensive to take these teachers and their Union to court than to fire them. These teachers were never held accountable for such things as rape and assault, underperforming in the classroom, or even stealing from fellow teachers or students within their districts.

How on God's green earth could our country become so corrupt that it tolerated these politicians and Rubber Rooms? O'Reilly visibly shook his head, as it was only a matter of time before the sheep would wake up.

Shouldn't one be judged by the quality of their work or be dismissed? Shouldn't you be held to the state's standards, or the employer's standards, and having not been able to meet those standards, be fired? Any private employer in the world couldn't survive with such a burdensome employee. No business could grow with dead wood sitting on the job site, taking up profits that go towards a non-working employee receiving the same income and benefits as an employee who gave it their best.

No country could be in the largest debt in world history and continue to fund such an institution that rewarded such union employees. And yet, this was just another day in the NYC School teacher's union. Another day in the politically rat infested, corrupt city and county government. Another day without any shame. Another day with no accountability for individual choices. Again, not reported by the news pundits as odd business practices. O'Reilly's anger seemed to be at an all time high. His tribal division peaking.

Politicians were no different. Multiple reelections led to massive income despite being paid paltry salaries during their political careers. Everyone in the political scene somehow became millionaires. Millionaires became billionaires. Bills favored relatives or supporters. Stocks of no name companies somehow made profits months after being discussed behind closed doors. It mattered not if they passed a bill, wrote a bill, or never showed up for a vote.

No one looked back on the bills that were passed and measured success. If a senator wrote a bill that led to massive tax increases with little returns, there was no system in place to remove the bill or penalize and judge the legislator for their ineptitude. Congress *was* a Rubber Room. There needed to be a system in place to evaluate politicians-just like teachers. Something besides the "Check a Party" ticket that enabled this scum to repetitively be in office for thirty to forty years without one ounce of liability for their actions. The people should be able to sue the politician, and maybe that would end the endless supply of bullshit bills coming about to "better" their districts. But the federal government and the political parties were the biggest Unions on earth. Just do what you are told, and you will be rewarded. Reelection was that reward. Keeping your mouth shut on legislation buried deep into page one thousand of a bill might enable your bill to be passed later. Track records were never kept, just more "solutions" to offer to the always present crises.

Attorneys were in the middle of it all, and thus great politicians, and when not politicians themselves, lawyers were guiding incumbents or sitting members on policies, i.e. solutions. To them, it was all about billable hours. If you could pass along a tip to a rival law office that might keep the case going for another year, and thus, more billable hours, then who was to know? O'Reilly had never really heard of an attorney being sued for malpractice like a physician. If one attorney got you out of a speeding ticket, or even worse an offense like murder, and another attorney failed, and both had the same evidence and similar juries, then how is that not malpractice? More crises demanded more solutions that led to more billable hours. If not solved with one law office, seek out another with the same results and a lighter pocketbook. Like the New York teachers in the rubber room, like life long politicians, like attorneys, it seemed more and more people were not being held accountable for being mediocre or incompetent. It was as if the reality of incompetence was built into the management of new systems rather than dealing with it at face value.

O'Reilly knew that on highly skilled military teams, like SEALs and CAG units, mediocrity would get people killed, and so these units did not accept failures, incompetence, or excuses. A union mentality within a system demanding the absolute best could not by definition make the unit the best. New innovations and the betterment of the unit came from competence and the desire to improve all processes involved-from employee to workplace. Surround yourself with no one who takes accountability, and soon you have no need for an accountant.

O'Reilly needed a crisis so big that it would demand action from the politicians. Something so sinister that the liberal electorate would go overboard selling their "solution". The liberals wouldn't be held accountable either. He knew this. He had watched their Communist Manifesto tactics play out all over the world with these same "crisis" tactics. Race, gender, salary gaps, wars, drugs-all immediate crises.

"Fix this today, or we will sue. Fix it today, or we will boycott! Fix it today, or your kids will suffer! Apologize now, or your career is over. Take this vaccine, or you will die. If your neighbor refuses the vaccine, you will die."

Anywhere lefties could create a crisis was a golden party rule, and everything related to that crisis was an emergency that had to be acted upon at that very instant. Politicians were at the heart of not only creating problems, but creating problems from their offered solutions, which then need more solutions. Something straight out of the Lenin textbook.

Edison invented the lightbulb. Lenin invented gaslighting.

This time, the "Response" would be different. He was counting on the average American citizen. One thing that separated all Marxist based countries from the United States was the heritage of disobedience. When the government instituted their elected officials "Response", chaos would follow quickly throughout the country. The common citizen would say no. Ordinary citizenry would then become felons—*willingly*.

The only class of people with firm Constitutional Republic beliefs left in this country would never stand for this action. The government would have overstepped everything they held dear: religion, schools, immigration, elections, treasury, banking, agriculture, entitlements, land ownership. Freedom for the individual would be lost. To "promote the safety" of the greater society, the Dems would try to establish total control, as they did during Covid.

In truth, it was the only thing they had never been able to succeed in doing, but the biggest part in the overall conversion of the United States in becoming a global partner with the United Nations, the European Union, China, and Russia. Marxism demanded a one world global government. There was to be no individual. Your labor was not yours anymore. You will own nothing and like it was the saying of the day.

The Marxist, "Socialist Democrats", strategy was out in the open. It wasn't hidden, and yet no one even witnessed its implementation on a daily basis. When the media was controlled, and online forums controlled counter arguments and user accounts, freedom of speech was immediately restricted. Not only was it restricted, but it was also recorded, allowing the government to know who the dissenters were. *Data was now the gun registry of thought.* Many sheep just couldn't come up with their own train of thought, and would instead regurgitate what was provided for them in the form of internet posts, bots, internet newspapers, media sites, and even the antiquated evening news. NPR and PBS dominated the extremely poor outlets who were already willing recipients to class warfare propaganda. Without the Freedom of Press, which was now basically the internet for the middle class, there was no informative knowledge outlet for one to make up their own decisions, but there was the illusion of choice.

Comcast owns NBC, (by buying out GE's shares) who owns Universal. With ownership in USA Network, Bravo, Telemundo, Peacock, and Universal Parks. Or, Disney owning not just its parks, but 20th Century Television, Hulu, ESPN, ABC and ABC News, Pixar, and Hotstar. What you thought might be an independent news source would always be loyal to the parent companies views and share holders, not necessarily to the truth. With the right amount of investments in advertising, the truth could be whatever the company, or government, decided it should be, and the mass marketing of said truth would be propagated across all corporate content and websites. Many companies existed to solely generate misinformation and chaos. Most led or owned by one religion as well, who seemed to vote

Liberal 70-80% of the time. The only Freedom of the Press was Freedom From the Press.

European companies owned American news channels. Latin countries blasted their own propaganda to the United States, despite every single country failing at the same policies and corruption decade after decade. Sites such as Facebook booted off controversial figures such as Alex Jones but kept ISIS terrorist sites up and going. Facebook, Instagram, as well as Disney and the movie studios from Los Angeles kneeled to the Chinese government's demands for censorship in order to build parks and sell ads, despite these companies knowing of the Communist atrocities taking place within that country's borders. Zionists propagated rhetoric daily.

O'Reilly's temper flared.

Before long, a plethora of websites just disappeared, but oftentimes these departures never got reported about in the news. The dominant sites regulated themselves, garnered American government server contracts, or were owned by a single party or individual; and therefore, the sites would truly promote only one agenda. A true global newspaper of no counter arguments, promoting George Soros's Marxist dream-the destruction of the American.

Control the companies that control the controllers, and win over the middle class. Lower class individuals knew they were slaves to the system, but it was the middle class that had to believe they were not. It was the middle class that were the true slaves to the system by enabling the solutions to fund the class beneath them in order to keep the goods coming at lower costs. Banks, attorneys, corporations, and governments could then turn created solutions into a revolving door of income primarily going to the top one percent.

Two things were needed, for Marxist's success, to be

destroyed in order to institute what was left of the United States non-conversion to communism. Two things held America together and kept it from converting the masses. One was Western culture itself, and the other was the Christian religion. O'Reilly had learned about this from Gramsci and Lukacs theories, both leading Marxist scholars, that had agreed independently that those two issues must be split in order to form a Communist America.

How could a dumb border agent be able to comprehend this but not the rest of the sheep? He steamed. *Was I this upset a year ago? Why have I become so passionate about this?*

In 1934, the Institute for Social Research moved to the United States from Germany. It had been founded by a Marxist, Felix Weil. A "Critical Theory" was introduced to destroy Western culture. The tactic was to attack every element of traditional culture to un dying criticism. Once the press was fully controlled, the attacks reached full effect. The traditional family, public schools, police, judges, jails, media, politics, churches all collapsed from the constant criticism and bombardment. Legislation was enacted regardless of proven crises or weighted with established outcomes. Politicians did what they were best at-promote "solutions" in places where there weren't even crises to be found.

Universities were infiltrated with Marxist professors to sell and promote the ideas to incoming generations of our smartest youth that communist ideas were the only way to a better society. The youth were resigned to such high college debt, and submission to the system, that they were scared to question the professors. Once again-freedom of speech in full remission at what was once the only place to question society-the Universities. Kids who had held on to what the church had taught or perhaps what individual freedom their traditional families had ingrained in them, were all mocked by people they were forced to believe were more intelligent than their own parents or church leaders-the college professor.

Those same professors lived in a fictional world O'Reilly knew. Worshipped and pedestaled by teenage students who depended on their grade, existing in a world of tenure that held no one accountable for mediocrity, surrounded by people with the same beliefs and values of Leninism and socialism. Year after year these professors faced no challenges or differing opinions. The success or evidenced based outcomes of their teachings were not held to outcome, but rather to evaluate further solutions of the spinning cycle of societal values. Simply marinating in their own opinions and the opinions of those around them on campuses, rather than getting out in the world to attain a bigger picture of what it was really like making it in the modern world. These professors also forged government funded studies and data to generate politically created solutions, reinforcing their own existence.

The best singer in Des Moines, Iowa, is the best singer in their own mind. Unplug all sources and feed all news outlets to agree. But take that singer to New York City for some different songs to sing in front of a new audience, and that mediocre singer can either excel, or realize that they were very average in the first place.

That was college professors. They were the new faces for the second fall of Rome. Exist in the comfort of the tribe that agrees with the rationale created by the tribe itself, but never understanding the wants and needs of the tribe suffering down the street. Sell those ideas to the tribal chief to enforce those solutions through war or legislation, and the professor, the chief, guarantees more buffalo meat-funding-back to the tribe, through the form of federally guaranteed student loans.

O'Reilly knew a gun registry debate in the Super Majority Democratic Congress would soon lead to discussions of a Gun Ban. Mass shootings, trans shootings, over medicated shooters, and school shootings all outweighed the actual true data on gun violence. In times of crisis though, politicians act quickly. Act completely. A good crisis is not to be wasted was the traditional Democratic way.

Good old Marxism saddened O'Reilly's thoughts. No good Democratic at this opportunity would be satisfied with a registry. Only a complete Gun Ban with Confiscation would satisfy this solution, and every American who fell victim to big city population voting and problems would be stripped of their Second Amendment. Shoot for the entire ban, and maybe we settle at a registry, or just maybe, get the entire ban. What could happen in Australia could easily happen in the United States with the right sentiment.

O'Reilly truly believed that this would be the only way the America of the past could be saved. Combined with the current crises going on throughout the United States, and the complete victory of the Communist Socialist Party during the last election, the confiscation and house to house searches would be the last dying inspiration to fight and take up arms against one's own country.

Youth that were hardly taught the tough lessons of World War Two, and the deaths that followed its tragic beginnings, would have a tough time abandoning entitlements for freedom *from* entitlements. The government had done a good job in placating the populace.

Little of society remembered how that war could have been prevented. O'Reilly had studied. He had watched from his border patrol job. He had read the internet forums. He had his fake Facebook accounts. His "fake news" posts. His anonymous servers and VPN logins. His balloons he hoped might just prevent the ultimate unarmed takeover of his country. It was time for the common man to take up arms.

The balloons were to be the solution. EZ had promised him. EZ seemed to know exactly what needed to be said. He wished that EZ would do the recruiting for the mission, but understood that he was just too busy behind the scenes to do so. To force EZ to recruit would mean the loss of their financial backer. EZ was never out of money for their cause. He seemed more concerned about the country than even O'Reilly-nothing moving fast enough to secure the victory. The mission was always being pushed, as if his life depended on it. His spirit seemed determined to destroy a way of life. O'Reilly respected that spirit. Between the two of them, this brand of energy was what would instill the spirit of a revolution.

The balloons would be O'Reilly's "solution". EZ agreed with the genius of his plan.

With EZ's help, he could now attempt to save his country from what only a few Americans were witnessing. He wasn't dumb enough to fall for what the sheep were grazing on, so sometimes it would be up to the sheep dog to bring the flock out of harm's way, and now that he had access to the means to achieve his ideas, perhaps only a few sheep would need to be lost to protect the herd.

Finally, someone had shown up at the gun club that believed in the same values that he and Willis did. Someone who was actually willing to act, not just talk. O'Reilly had finally been divided enough, angry enough, to lose everything. It just took EZ to convince him he could make a difference.

Balloon History

O'Reilly had first come up with the idea after reading about the Japanese use of balloons in World War Two. What can be described as the first intercontinental weapon system, the balloons were Japan's attempt to induce panic and fear into the American homeland. General Reichichi Tada with the Japanese Military Scientific Project was placed in charge of the Proposed Airborne Carrier Research and Development Program. Of the weapons investigated for use against the Allies, the Fu-Go Weapon was considered the most promising. Tada's name for the project was attributed to the Japanese language's use of syllabary. "Go" in Japanese is interpreted as the word weapon, and "Fu" is the first symbol in the word Fusen, meaning balloon. Put together, Tada had his Fu-Go Project. In 1944, the Fu-Go Project was on track to produce 10,000 balloons for release into the Transpacific jet stream. Balloons were to travel between 10,000 feet and 30,000 feet on their path to the United States and Canada. Engineers had learned through practice deployments that the best time to deploy the balloons was just after a high pressure weather pattern, but prior to a low pressure pattern emerging. Many engineering obstacles were overcome in the design of the weapons: weather, altitude, heat expansion, fuel, wind, weight, batteries, electronics.

O'Reilly could appreciate these obstacles. His own balloons had to overcome them as well, and his team was no less diverse and resourceful. Plus, they had a stronger cause than the land of the Rising Sun.

Not having the resources during the war for latex and other more practical components, the

Japanese used tissue paper produced from the kozo bush, similar in nature to the sumac tree O'Reilly was familiar with in the U.S. A special layering process was invented to strengthen the fabric into lightweight layers needed for the increase in weight. In order to seal the paper into layers and provide patches for leaks, a sealant, konnyaku-nori, was resourcefully produced from Japanese potatoes. O'Reilly knew that the paste of the potatoes had been stolen by the Japanese factory workers and eaten during food shortages throughout the war. Six hundred compacted kozo tissues would be sealed with konnyaku to form thirty-three foot diameter balloons. Japanese theaters and sumo arenas were taken over to test the balloon's pressures, being the only spaces large enough to keep the process secret from not only the Americans, but Japanese citizens.

The balloons had several components besides the main balloon fabric, or envelope as it was called. An altitude control box, bungee cords, detonator cords, barometers, sandbag ballasts, and different weapon payloads encompassed each balloon's load. Secretive radio techniques that were invented to track balloon paths in the jet stream were revolutionary, as well as batteries that would make the 6,200 mile distance across the Pacific, which on average took about three days. Balloons also would rise in the sun's heat and inflate while shrinking and deflating on cool nights. The altitude control box was wired to detonate and drop sandbag ballasts at low altitudes in order for the balloon to keep on track. Weapons usually were limited to stock Japanese ordinance such as thermite incendiary bombs or traditional explosive shrapnel bombs. Such an intercontinental device was revolutionary in design, science, and technique.

Next came the problem of deployments for the Japanese.

Hydrogen gas was necessary to inflate the balloons, and a necessary means of its production was achieved and delivered. Without hydrogen gas, there is no balloon flight, and the secrecy of hydrogen factories was necessary to prevent Allied bombings of hydrogen facilities. Teams of thirty men were needed to launch one balloon, and the ever present risk of fire challenged each team as the hydrogen was added at the launch site.

Fu-Go was to destroy American West Coast forests and farms, mainly by starting fires, while putting fear into the hearts and minds.

O'Reilly's hot air balloon was much better than what the Japanese had. The balloon spoke all languages, and it was able to instill in its passengers a message that all would understand. O'Reilly got the idea a short time ago after talking with Willis and EZ, and he had been saving up for supplies. Now with EZ's pocketbook, he knew just the right day to deploy for just the right change in events. He also knew that once those events happened, he'd get only one chance for perfect weather. He needed a tropical storm pattern that reached Quebec, and that only happened about every six or seven years. These opportunities took time. O'Reilly had time. His grandfather had insured him there would be time.

"Remember the past. Look well to the future." He could hear his grandfather say.

He could recite every word. Every sentence in the Proclamation, and somehow the writings rang truer today than during those times of famine that his relatives had suffered through to cross the Atlantic.

His plan needed to instill fear into the hearts and minds. His plan needed people to feel vulnerable no matter their location. EZ had agreed to his ideas and promised the perfect products for the event. O'Reilly's ideas were needed back at home where people appreciated his family's legacy to fulfill a cause.

The folks at the balloon festival knew his passion for hot air balloons, but he kept his true reason for this passion to himself. It was a passion he had been forced to adopt years before, requiring patience for the mission ahead, and fortitude to continue on his grandfather's path.

Acquiring the Product

O'Reilly's border patrol job was not how he thought his opportunity to join the Brotherhood's cause would show itself, but with America being in a global war with Jihadists around the world, his chance appeared out of nowhere, and in a place close to nowhere, his Swanton district in Vermont.

He had been working that Monday when his co-worker brought him over to the Honda Accord. An older model in the common gray he was used to seeing on Hondas. A little rusty around the lower portions of the car, as most were in that part of the north country. Most of the citizens in Northern Vermont had below average jobs, older cars, and were used to seeing the side effects of snow and salt on metal throughout the long winters, followed by mud seasons in the thaw of spring. EZ had given O'Reilly one head's up-watch all Honda's coming across his sector. EZ had given him a heads up to days when he thought his mafia contacts might be bringing cocaine across the border at O'Reilly's location. O'Reilly would conveniently find the drugs, but leave them out of the reports. Hand them over to EZ, where they would be sold to further support the Brotherhood's cause. Most criminals were happy to keep their mouths shut and drive away, likely knowing that the corrupt agents were keeping their product. O'Reilly didn't view it as stealing, but rather as being righteous. Taking drugs off the streets and providing funding for his future efforts to change the country.

Inside the Honda were two men with middle eastern accents, using broken English. Both were dressed in button down shirts and casual dress slacks with brown shoes not matching their black belts. Pastel shirt colors with brown pants. It was as if someone who was color blind had picked out their outfits, likely buying from a discount or salvation clothing store to leave no records. This had to be the target. No way would normal middle easterners dress this way. In fact, they usually wore high end clothing to almost brag of their land's oil wealth.

"Where are you headed?" O'Reilly asked the pair.

"Business in Newport," the driver sputtered in Arabic laced English, pointing the wrong direction to Newport.

Since one of the 9/11 hijackers had entered through his port of entry in Swanton, O'Reilly took his job very seriously when he saw Arabs stopping at his checkpoint. He didn't want to be responsible for another catastrophe like the Twin Towers on his watch.

"What type of business?".

O'Reilly was familiar with the dirty corporate programs that were occurring in Vermont. If someone wanted to apply for U.S. Citizenship, all that was needed was to fork over $500,000 for a rural improvement, or $1,000,000 for a city development. These programs were part of the EB-5 investor partnership with the United States government in order to garner foreign investments in larger development projects. If the investor met job creation numbers, he or she would be eligible for a green card and U.S. Citizenship.

We only wanted rich people crossing the border O'Reilly believed. Lower and middle classes would never make this journey. They were slaves to the grind of life, wherever that life may be. Jay Peak, the northern Vermont ski resort, was one of the hottest investor properties. Over 200 foreigners had shelled out more than $500,000 to an EB-5 program run by New Yorker Ariel Quiros and his son Ary Quiros. Involved in the development as huge promoters of its transparency and legitimacy for investment, were the Vermont Governors Peter

Shumlin and Jim Douglas, U.S. Representative Peter Welch, and U.S. Senator Patrick Leahy. Over 10,000 new jobs were to be created in Northern Vermont. A $110 million dollar biomedical research facility was also in the works, AnC Bio Vermont, near Newport, next to the Canadian border. $450 million had been swindled from foreign investors for Jay Peak. A new conference center, water park, hotels, and renovated ski mountain attractions were used for the promise of future green cards. Except it hadn't exactly ended as promised.

Quiros had a townhome in New York City, in the same building as Donald Trump. Large sums of money had been spent and displayed. The money was laundered, and green cards failed to go out. Financials were never audited. Much of the money was dispersed with relatives and staff of those involved in receiving the money. Because so many high ranking politicians and legal counsels were involved, investigating the entire affair had taken a backseat in Vermont.

Criminals and politicians often worked in the same circles.

The state's citizens were quite proud of being known for their hard working, honest demeanors, but since no citizen of Vermont had actually lost money, only foreign EB-5 investors, now without any return on their investments and no green card to match, were the losers. Every politician moved the case off their District Attorney's shelf, and the case went without investigation for years. Ultimately, Quiros and several others paid small fines, even having their legal expenses paid for by their insurance. The rich kept getting richer. Criminals needed politicians, and politicians needed criminals.

"We both do biochemistry research for AnC Bio in Newport. We are on our way from University in Montreal." The driver stated.

O'Reilly's thoughts were interrupted. He had to focus on

the task at hand, but he just couldn't quit thinking about the dirty politicians and what had happened to the middle class workers in Northern Vermont.

Once again, O'Reilly took a deep breath as he pondered the scheme, because he knew who kept making money as always. Banks. From New York to Florida, deposits came and went. Huge sums of money across the country changed hands. Commercial contracts for the renovations of the ski area and biomedical center were signed with interest. Politicians, attorneys, and insurance companies all covered their bases from the fraud. They had to know it was occurring.

Banks knew to ride along with the corruptness until it played out. With this many politicians involved, they couldn't prosecute everyone.

Banks just kept playing along. Knowing that there was no way the investments were legitimate. Seeing the money spent on Quiros's end was none of their business as long as he found a way to pay back the investors. All the money was coming as cash from other countries towards legal visa procurement, risks were low for the bank's shareholders. If bankruptcy was issued, those investors wouldn't be paid, but the money would be somewhere else in the bank's coffers-another investment, interest, or deposit. Once that money hit their system, they could make more money for themselves, and they could also shift those investments around their global system of banks, further confusing investigation should it ever occur.

"What time was your appointment at the Park?" O'Reilly asked.

If the driver looked at the Honda's clock he was creating his story. Neither wore a wrist watch. Both had darker skin in some areas than others, almost as if they had recently been out in too much sun.

AnC Biochemical Park continued on through contracts with companies from Montreal and the University of Vermont. Trying to play out as a legitimate facility helping Northern Vermonters find work. The scars caused to those without their green cards would be forgotten in a few years. And that's where these two claimed to be going. O'Reilly could have guessed before he even asked. Except something didn't make sense. He hardly ever saw the workers going to the Newport facility. They crossed near Derby Line and Stanstead, being the more direct route to the research park from Montreal's main highways. That crossing was accustomed to questioning more Middle Eastern, Chinese, Korean, Russian, and Europeans based in Montreal. Those professors making the journey to perform whatever experiments went on there at the Ponzi schemed AnC.

The driver glanced towards the console.

"10 AM. We are running late. We got lost along the way."

A hint of a British accent intrigued O'Reilly. He definitely didn't learn English in Canada or the United States. Most Indian and Middle Eastern professors usually started their careers with British or Canadian educations, and thus accents. London was full of Arab extremists, and Canada was starting to look more like London. O'Reilly knew without looking at his watch that it was somewhere around 9 AM. The morning rush of workers had subsided.

He was just about to grab his midmorning cup of Black Rifle Coffee. These guys had just ruined that morning cup of java, and he was aware that you can't be late when you are within an hour of the facility. They had no idea how far they were traveling, or the time it would take to get there. Every new car had GPS, but since this was an older model Honda, this wouldn't have been the case. O'Reilly needed to see their cell phones. He knew that if they were using a GPS service like Google Maps or Waze, then AnC would be pulled up on the screen, and by no means would either map service have brought them across at his border station this far east. He also had not seen either man with a cell phone on the dash or within reach as most people would do if driving to an unknown location. Not even a charging cable was visible along the car's dash, and he had legal authority to search cell phones at checkpoints.

"Thank you Patriot Act." O'Reilly thought.

"Please pull over to the side and place the car in park," O'Reilly advised the pair, directing them to an inspection point outlined with cones and railings under a shaded metal canopy.

He followed the Honda over to the side, trying to recall if he had chambered a round in his 9mm Glock 19 prior to his shift that morning. An un chambered gun might as well be a banana if these two tried to roll him. He had sent the Glock away to Cornbread Tactical in North Carolina so it would run flawlessly without being overly exotic with his border patrol uniform. He wanted the gun to function to his standards, not the border patrols. He also didn't want his boss to notice that he'd done anything to his service issued pistol. Cornbread had understood the assignment.

"Can I see your license and registration please?". Both reached for the glove compartment nervously.

"Slowly please. And keep your hands where they are visible at all times." O'Reilly said calmly to the driver as he noticed the two begin looking at each other.

"Off. They are both off," he thought.

He keyed the microphone hanging from his shirt five times in rapid succession knowing his partner would be coming to his aid quickly, approaching from the opposite side of the vehicle, providing cover fire as needed.

His partner, Kevin, had been with him for two years. They

shot together often at the gun club. Kevin was a prior Army Ranger with four tours under his belt. O'Reilly had caught him stashing marijuana and alcohol from border busts shortly after he first started. O'Reilly had taken that opportunity to befriend him. Jobs were scarce for Vets, not many companies needed the skills of a soldier, and since the US had been at war for so long, guys with a long military resume showed up each week asking how to apply to the border patrol.

Kevin had been selling the goods to support his family. He at least wasn't a user as so many of the other Vets had been. With a little guidance and direction, O'Reilly steered Kevin back on track, and shortly thereafter to the gun club where he excelled and had a new home with the other Veterans there. Angered at the V.A.'s treatment of his former injuries, Kevin was rather disheartened with the federal government. He'd given it his all, and for whatever reason, that same government he fought for would do little in return. Kevin's induction into the cause took little effort which was the case with most of the Veterans O'Reilly had recruited. Destroying your career, family, body, and future at the hands of mostly unjust causes determined by the CIA, oil companies, or Israel, the American veteran had been treated to a plateful of lies and deception by the very country they vowed to protect. He was now part of the Tribe.

The driver reached into his now open glove compartment, and pulled out three pieces of newly printed paper with his driver's license. O'Reilly didn't know a man alive who didn't own a wallet that held a driver's license, and that wallet was usually in a back pocket or resting near the center console. Another red flag was just raised on these two. They were up to no good for sure. Kevin was now in place behind the rear passenger window. His right hand on his Glock and ready to draw if needed. O'Reilly scanned beyond his targets to verify nothing would be in the path of his Sig Sauer V-Crown hollow points that he was issued. Fifteen shiny gold tipped rounds were rotated every Monday morning at the start of his shift to make those magazine springs happy and full of energy.

O'Reilly looked at the paperwork and ID. The ID was a Canadian driver's license. Pictured was a man with what must have been a four inch thick and foot long beard, eyeglasses, and long untrimmed hair. Maybe it was the driver, but the man in front of him had a three day stubble of beard and had glasses that were different in size and shape.

Jamal Talib was the driver's name, date of birth appeared similar to his appearance. The address was in the Cote-des-Neiges section of Montreal near the University, so that part fit the story; however, the Canadian mafia had excellent forgers.

On the first piece of paper was the driver's registration. Correct car, up to date, and had been recently renewed only a month ago. The second piece of paper was insurance with all the normal Canadian requirements. It too had been updated only a month ago on the same day. Leading O'Reilly to wonder if the car had just been purchased a month ago, or was it just coincidence on the dates. Addresses both matched. The third piece of paper was a passing certificate from a Montreal driving school indicating that the driver had met the requirements for safety. The last time he had seen one of these certificates was in the hands of a sixteen year old Vermont kid, driving his Dad's pickup truck to deliver syrup to the local grocer. He had been weaving because he was texting as most kids did these days.

He had never been given a safe driving certificate from anyone at a border checkpoint. He had seen $100 bills "accidentally" slipped in the paperwork. He had seen cell phones passed to him with political contacts at the ready, and of course he had seen his share of cleavage and hiked skirts. A safe driver certificate wasn't usually in a glove box. It may be something necessary to send to your insurance agent to decrease your rates, but not something necessary for showing at a traffic stop. It did provide something to further question the driver. "Says here you passed with flying colors. Are you new to driving?".

"I just moved to Montreal from Paris. We never had the chance to drive in Paris." Jamal responded.

"And may I see your friend's identification please." Kevin spoke up from behind the passenger, startling him in his seat.

"Yes sir. Yes." It was obvious the passenger spoke zero English.

"This is my research fellow Hadid Zaha. He just arrived from Paris to help me," interjected Jamal eagerly.

Kevin looked at the license that Hadid had passed to him from the down window on the Honda's passenger side.

"What's your date of birth Hadid?" Kevin asked him.

Hadid looked to Jamal in confusion, not understanding the officer's question. Jamal spoke to him in what Kevin recognized as Farsi. He had heard much of that same accent along Iraq's eastern borders with Iran.

Hadid stated, "12/08/74" and then smiled.

Kevin looked, and Hadid was correct.

"So you got to celebrate your birthdays in the summer heat?" Kevin looked to Jamal to send the interpretation to Hadid. Hadid laughed.

"Yes, yes, officer. Hot. Very hot birthday." He felt this was an honest answer as he looked into the skinny man's blank black eyes.

Only Canada, the United States, the Philippines, and Palau used month, date, year date stamps Kevin remembered from his intelligence training. Oftentimes, Iranian forged documents in Iraq were dated incorrectly, using the day, month, year format used throughout the rest of the world. Hadid hadn't been born in December as his license indicated. Kevin looked at O'Reilly laughing. Pulling out some good old boy dialect.

"Well, I'd be a Blue Falcon if I told you he wasn't telling the truth." O'Reilly knew what that meant.

It was time to get these guys out of the car.

"Mr. Talib, can I get you to step out of the car please?".

"Yes. Of course." Jamal said, appearing very cooperatively.

He opened the Honda's door and emerged from the vehicle.

"Please step to the guard rail opposite the car please, sir".

He was very wiry, thought O'Reilly. Strong and wiry. Reminding him of the meth heads that worked on the local farms in the brisk Vermont summers. He referred to them as Sinews at the station making his co workers laugh. A reference to the tough tissue that unites muscles to bones. They didn't really have muscles, but they weren't really ligaments either. Sinew had a nice ring to it. And Jamal was a Sinew.

"Just place your hands against the metal rail, and face towards the woods." The four were alone at the checkpoint.

Kevin next asked Hadid to exit the car. Hadid didn't need to hear a translation. He was looking at Kevin's right hand on the pistol's grip, and the other hand giving the universal "get the fuck out of the car" gesture.

As the door began to open, Kevin had gotten a little too close. He was trying to make sure he could see Hadid's hands.

"*Always watch the hands,*" he remembered from his training.

As Hadid's right hand was slowly going towards the door handle, his left was transitioning towards the floor board near the bottom of his seat. As he saw the hand sliding south, the familiar wood grain pattern of an AK-47 pistol was emerging. The barrel pointing towards the rear, having been stuffed between the door and the passenger seat.

Kevin reached quickly to grab Hadid's hand. His weight had gone forward towards the car as he was watching the situation unfold, and his pistol hand was now reaching towards Habib's left hand. O'Reilly, in front of the car door, was unaware as time seemed to come to a halt around the tiny gray Honda.

Holding the AK-47 against the crack of the seat, Kevin was doing his best to keep Hadid from raising the muzzle. He could tell Hadid was right handed, and that having reached for the gun with his left hand, was uncomfortable trying to manipulate and hold the weapon.

"Always train with both hands in case you are injured in a gun fight." Kevin could hear his old Master Sergeant in his head.

He reached to his duty belt's left side, and pulled out his Winkler Weapon Retention Tool. The serrated, sharp, triangular head slipped from its kydex sheath. Looking like a saw blade, it was designed to puncture and rip.

Kevin punched Hadid directly under his right eye. The tool not so much ripped into Hadid's flesh, but rather sank into the orbit of the eye. Piercing through the rear of the shallow orbit and furthering its tip into the brain cavity. Hadid was also Sinewy, and the teeth of the tool reminded Kevin of cutting up a steak with one of those wooden handled serrated knives popular at restaurants. Blood hadn't begun to spew until Kevin withdrew the tool. A few strong spurts came from the socket until Hadid's heart realized the brain's services were no longer needed. O'Reilly heard the punch but not the initial altercation. It sounded as if a rock had entered a pool of wet mud. *Smack.* Something soft slowing its acceleration. Turning in time to see Kevin retracting the Winkler tool from Hadid's skull. He immediately swiped Jamal's legs from underneath him before drawing his pistol.

"Don't move Mother Fucker!" O'Reilly screamed at Jamal who was now face first in the dirt. But something wasn't right. Jamal's body was starting to quiver. Small shakes from his extremities. He hadn't hit his head on the fall. O'Reilly turned the body over.

Froth and bits of Jamal's morning breakfast of hummus and pita were coming out of his mouth.

His black eyes rolled backwards. His arms began to clench towards his chest as the smell of urine and shit hit O'Reilly at the same time. O'Reilly looked closer at Jamal's mouth and noticed a tiny plastic capsule, now cracked and visible near his lips.

Jamal was on his way to see sixty nine virgins. His jihad had just been foiled at the Swanton Border checkpoint.

Border Crossers

O'Reilly stood in disbelief. What the fuck were these two up to that could possibly be worth even possessing a cyanide capsule, if that's what he actually swallowed. Who even had those anymore? That was lore from the Nazi era-not modern day Al Qaeda protocol. There had to be more to the story. He looked at Kevin whose left arm was coated in drying blood. The smell of Jamal's urine and shit filled the air. This didn't seem like something EZ would have set up. The two seemed to panic. Time to make some decisions.

"What the fuck just happened?" Kevin said, laughing nervously.

Shock filled his voice, but Kevin had been through much worse. He'd be fine. Not the first time he'd killed a man, and this guy deserved it. Killing for a just cause always made it easier to swallow the first drink at the end of the day.

"Think. Breathe. Slow down," O'Reilly said aloud, to himself as much as to Kevin.

Something still didn't make sense, and before he called his superiors and the FBI, he wanted to assess the situation a little more.

"OK Jamal. Let's see what's in the car. Had to be a bomb." O'Reilly said to the dead man before him.

He first moved to the main gate. Cars and trucks would be coming soon, and he didn't want to be interrupted. He told Kevin to clean himself up and put on a new uniform top. With the car pulled over to the inspection point, nothing looked too out of place to the average passerby. He jumped in his federally issued truck and pulled alongside Jamal's body, hiding it from the main throughway. He examined himself in his truck's mirror, making sure there was nothing too revealing about his appearance. People didn't want to have long conversations with border agents anyway. He saw Kevin coming out from the station house.

"Kevin, watch the gate. Check everyone coming through lightly. Let them pass easily, even if you suspect drugs. Only stop anyone who fits the bill of Jamal and Hadid. And draw early if you do. No exceptions. I'm going to inspect this Honda. Give me a few minutes."

O'Reilly got his mirror stick which was used to inspect underneath vehicles and walked to the drivers side first. Opening the door, nothing appeared unusual. Jamal had placed his papers back on the dashboard. The mirror revealed nothing as he circumferenced beneath the car. Nothing out of place. He started from the top down to the floor board. Nothing on the driver's side. The passenger side revealed some Coke cans, candy wrappers, and Hadid's AK-47. He did a quick peek at the gun, making sure it wasn't booby trapped. It appeared to be an older Polish model, in good shape, but it definitely had some range time, or more likely he thought, some combat in a different part of the world. Nothing was in the back seat.

There better be something in the trunk, or he was gonna have some explaining to do.

He walked over to Jamal before inspecting the trunk, patting his pockets. Nothing. Same with Hadid, who he had laid next to the passenger side of the vehicle, not wanting to disrupt anything the FBI would want to examine later. He hoped no lie detector test would be required, but it wouldn't be out of the question. At least he had Kevin as a witness. It would not be hard to dispute the need to kill Hadid as he had reached for a weapon. O'Reilly got the keys from the ignition and opened the trunk.

Two bags and a hard sided Pelican case were revealed. The duffel bags were of matching brand and black in color. He didn't like the bags as soon as he saw them. The Pelican case was tan in color. Probably used quite often when transporting materials in the biochemical industry. This would make sense for their cover stories. He had searched cars in the past and found these cases to be used by hunters, photographers, divers, reporters, and scientists-the latter transporting research equipment such as microscopes or slides.

He opened the first bag which had Jamal's name on a cheap airline provided cardboard tag. Nothing inside but toiletries and clothes. No different from Hadid's labeled bag. This in itself was unusual. People usually brought computer cords, books, electronics, and other items. Someone packed for these guys O'Reilly thought. Just as someone had likely bought their outfits.

He picked up the Pelican case. It had some weight to it. Lifting carefully to insure no wires or booby traps. He laid it on the ground at the back of the Honda. The case was locked with a cheap TSA lock. Four digit code, horseshoe loop. He twisted the lock, put the code in, and opened the latch. Slowly, he opened the case. Booby traps could be anywhere.

"Fuck".

He hated being disappointed. A tightly, plastic wrapped bundle of what appeared to be powder, likely drugs.

These two idiots would cost him a ton of time, resources, and man hours. All because they didn't want to get caught with about a kilo of heroin or hash. These guys were probably transporting a drug that had been originally made in Afghanistan, transported through Europe, and now crossing his checkpoint. It was triple bagged to thwart drug dogs, and packed in airtight vacuum sealed plastic. What a fucking disappointment.

He had been hoping for something he might be able to pawn off to EZ to obtain more dollars for his cause. Heroin would take too much time and risk to sell, and he would also need it to prove his and Kevin's innocence. He walked over to Kevin.

"Hey, go inspect the car. Make sure I didn't miss anything. We will need to do a quick test on those drugs, so take them into the shack and run our color tests. When you're done, we will make all the phone calls. This is going to ruin our week. Put some gloves on, and you might want a mask. It's starting to stink over there. Jamal shit himself."

Kevin walked into the guard house, grabbed a pair of rubber gloves and a N-95 mask. He spritzed the mask with some cinnamon spray and walked towards Jamal's body just as the first truck was pulling up to be inspected.

Kevin returned after about ten minutes. His face worried.

Which immediately concerned O'Reilly. He had done a detailed search and found nothing, almost disappointed that he might have out done the senior officer.

"Drug tests reveal nothing. The powder doesn't look like anything I've seen, even overseas. When I removed more foam from the case, I pulled this out." Kevin motioned to a folded paper. He held the paper up for O'Reilly to read. It contained writing on both sides. The paper appeared to contain drawings and instructions. All the writing was in Arabic, so O'Reilly was clueless as to its meaning. The pictures showed powder being placed into envelopes, and many different addresses were written to the side of the images. Addresses varied from Washington,

D.C., Atlanta, Los Angeles, military bases. No real pattern. Kevin flipped the paper over, and O'Reilly could only focus on two words that he recognized. It was two words he had hoped never to see at his border. It was also the word Kevin had recognized as well. *Bacillus anthracis.*

Jamal and Hadid weren't into biochemistry after all. The two brothers had come through for EZ. He had just not made the connection. EZ had just provided him the tool he needed for the balloon mission.

O'Reilly had originally planned to use his abundant supply of fentanyl from the border crossing to fuel his mission. Now, thanks to EZ, a much bigger statement could be made, and just maybe, blamed on Islam. EZ hadn't warned him because the risk had been too high. It needed to look natural if something happened. Compartmentalized.

<u>EZ's Powder</u>

O'Reilly's mind raced for a solution. He headed back to his guard shack. In the back, an evidence locker existed with a padlock on the front. Only he had the key. He grabbed a kilo of cocaine that he had planned on distributing to EZ for cash. He went to Jamal's body. Grabbing his hand, he placed his prints over the tight plastic wrap on the cocaine. He then locked up the anthrax Pelican case and put it in his personal vehicle.

Once he was satisfied with his story, he reviewed it with Kevin. He began to do the After Action Report that would eventually go to the FBI and his boss at the border patrol explaining why two Arabs with cocaine died on his shift. Once he returned to his home, he placed a call to EZ. "I think something special arrived today. Was that a gift from you?"

"Good job O'Reilly. I could not be sure if the two were trustworthy. I had them pick up the product in the port. I wanted nothing to do with them should they be tracked. The money was paid in cash at a separate location. We need to have the product inspected. I only wanted Chinese and Arabs involved in the shipment and deliveries into Canada and the United States. I will meet you tomorrow to give you more details." EZ ended the call.

Better to pay someone for the plausible deniability. No one would think twice about two middle eastern males trying to poison innocent Americans. And now, the product would get to the gun club with no connection to himself.

EZ had the product examined by a chemist in Mexico. The scientist had done work for the cartels and assumed it was another product either the Chinese or the Jihadist's were trying to get through to cause harm to the great northern evil across the border, the United States. 99% pure Bacillus anthracis.

Neither EZ nor O'Reilly had bothered to think if more of this product was out on the market, or who might be making it for distribution. The only thing that mattered was that it was now in the possession of the brotherhood, but how to use it was another matter entirely. His next step would be to instruct O'Reilly on how to turn the anthrax powder into an aerosolized mixture to be used on drone platforms. The drones were expected in the Port of Montreal within the week. He would bring an outside chemist from Israel. The next steps were far too important to involve cartels or mafia.

It would be necessary to set up a laboratory to prevent contact or inhalation of the spores, maintain secrecy, and test the final mixture's consistency with the farm drone. His contacts within the Canadian mafia hadn't batted an eye for his request of Ciprofloxacin for any emergency exposure treatment. STDs were rampant these days. He didn't press his luck on obtaining the Anthrax vaccine. There were too many doses over too long of a time, and the CDC monitored who requested Anthrax vaccines very closely.

Hopefully, he could manipulate O'Reilly into continuing on the righteous path he treasured. O'Reilly was an important tool for his own righteous path for UUONE. EZ's job was to manipulate the masses, and O'Reilly was the key player in making that happen.

What O'Reilly didn't need to know was what else was contained in the powder. EZ needed the entire Brotherhood to think it was solely anthrax, and its danger should be respected. Only he knew what the product actually contained-NanEmo. To kill a few thousand people would be a true terrorist act, but to control a few thousand minds-*that was power*.

<u>Douchey's Canada</u>

About forty minutes Southeast from Montreal, the Saint-Jean-sur-Richelieu was famous for its International Balloon Festival. At least 125 hot air balloons took off at once from the airport just outside of town. There were family events, food, beer tents, inflatable playhouses for the kids, music, and outdoor concerts for two weekends in late August. Over 500,000 people usually attend the festival each year.

Occurring towards the end of the brief Canadian summer, the weather was always pleasant. The festival would often precede the smaller Gatineau Hot Air Balloon Festival near Ottawa about two hours Southwest of Montreal. Gatineau Fest had a lot to offer as well: over 300 shows, more balloons, amusement park rides, craft fairs, fireworks, car shows, and even more food and beer tents. With over 1200 RVs pulling up, and over 200,000 attending, finding a hotel room was often the biggest challenge. Many preferred to camp and party away the holiday weekend at the campgrounds. Always occurring on the Canadian National Holiday of Labour Day, there were packed stands, hotels, and outdoor concert venues. The entire population of Canada was off and searching for that last bit of summer.

In recognition of the Fortieth Anniversary of the Gatineau Hot Air Festival, the Chamber of Commerce for Saint-Jean-sur-Richelieu offered to move their festival back two weeks so that Canada would experience an even greater tourism impact coming over from the United States for that Holiday weekend. Both festivals would occur at the same time. The Canadian dollar had taken a big hit due to the struggling oil and steel industry and the stronger US. Dollar, and politicians were being pushed to draw in as many people as possible to pour tax dollars into the local businesses.

Standing behind the plan, the Canadian Prime Minister, Douchey, was even scheduled to ride on a balloon from Gatineau to either Montreal or Saint-Jean-sur-Richelieu. Douchey had taken a lot of criticism after allowing some Middle Eastern

Canadians to fight for a foreign terrorist organization overseas, ISIS, and then allowing them to return as heroes to Canada, despite the fact that the terrorist groups were known enemies to the Maple leaf flag and to their southern neighbors. His handling of the coronavirus further decreased his popularity-locking up his citizens for months on end in their homes. His most recent action had been to keep Canadians out of their National and State Provincial Parks by stating there were risks for fires.

He was well known to support whatever might be asked of him on the European Globalist stage. Mass immigration, Arab rights, universal passports, antigun, vaccine protocols, and soft on crime policies fueled the downfall under his leadership. One returning Canadian grown ISIS terrorist had even committed a recent mass shooting in Canada, although the press buried it around day two of coverage. Douchey seemed to value the greater good of its immigrants more than it did of generational Canadians.

Douchey knew that the United States provided for the bulk of his country's defense budget. He could never afford over forty percent of his GDP to go to defense spending like the US did every year. He struggled just to maintain the below average benefits most Canadians would brag about over beers while spending winters in sunny Florida. Canadians always loved to mention their free healthcare, but never seemed to acknowledge their wait times to see a doctor. Canada was the land of Entitlements, and Douchey had to deliver on the undeliverable. He was a master of creating a crisis to offer his government's solutions. Mass immigration was a perfect crisis to distract from the average Canadian's miserable life, and he could then deliver statistics provided through University's to provide a solution. This revolving system of zero accountability seemed to exist in every progressive nation.

For this September Saturday, the weather conditions to deploy the hot air balloons were perfect. An ideal storm was brewing south of Canada and in the lower southern United States, what was termed a Colorado Low by the weather experts. Experienced ballooners knew that the best time to deploy the balloons would be just after a high pressure system had gone through the area, but prior to the low pressure system entering. A perfect, almost no wind, intermediate jet stream day was predicted.

Great weather for the balloons meant more people could buy beer, fill hotel rooms, attend concerts, and hear from the Prime Minister about what he was going to be able to give them for free if they would only reelect him. It was as always, "the most important election in their lifetimes." Douchey was quite happy to attend and hold babies for photographs.

O'Reilly pulled his RV camper into the same slot he had for the last four years. Everyone knew him at the campground as the American Border Patrol Agent sporting the big bright yellow hot air balloon. On the balloon's side was a giant Gadsden flag with the phrase "Don't Tread On Me" in large letters underneath.

"So obnoxious", he'd heard time and time again from his northern neighbors. Same thing they had told his grandfather years ago when O'Reilly had learned how to operate the giant balloons. It had been a special time as a child to learn this hobby with him.

The general public was always worrying about ICE and Border Patrol rights violations. Usually, the press aimed its complaints along the Southern U.S. border. That's where most of the illegals were coming into the US. What the press never ventured to think about was who might be allowed to cross illegally "intentionally" into the U.S.

Having a border patrol job was a very effective tool in the

development of a Revolution whose enemy was not only looking the wrong way, but failed to see the many enemies of the state had been placed throughout government agencies over the years, waiting for their turn at their own revolutions. Russia had placed female real estate brokers. China placed college scientists. The British had placed politicians, and the Israelis had placed someone everywhere. The Democrats had placed FBI agents. The Republicans had placed bankers. But without Revolution, the middle class would be at the bottom of it all.

The very class who had the most to lose. The ones who were being told what to do, as they watched everything around them fall to various people with no overall interest in the outcome of a once great country. The workers watched as they had been replaced with cheaper migrants. Their homes and businesses flooded with illegal immigrants. It was the working lower and middle class who bore the weight of Douchey's decisions and the one world government. It was no different in the United States. Climate policies, immigration policies, and the ever losing value of the Canadian dollar were never made for the common man's interests, but rather at the interest of who was in office.

As Sun Tzu discussed in his Art of War, "make your way by unexpected routes and attack unguarded spots." O'Reilly knew his spot, and Canada was only guarded by its ally to the south. As a US Border Patrol Agent, he could enter unguarded and attack unexpectedly. His cover had been solidified since his youth. He thought it was time to let the workers decide whether they wanted to live free or die.

Opening of the Balloon Festival

EZ pulled out his burner phone and dialed the prearranged

number, hoping he'd get the response he'd waited months to hear.

"Have you made it across?" O'Reilly recognized EZ's accent.

"We are both across with the balloons. We hope to enjoy perfect weather for the rest of the day.

I hope you can make it back to the club after the event." O'Reilly said into the burner phone. "Of course. I wouldn't miss it for the world." EZ pushed End Call on the flip phone, broke the device in half, and threw it into the garbage can beside him. He knew the "Alphabet Letter Bois", a term he learned at the gun club, would be monitoring all internet and phone traffic with the President in town.

O'Reilly was excited about the weather as he approached his Swanton crossing. He had been waiting patiently. He would have been happy to see the destruction of any city or any county, but was ecstatic at the possibility of a city plus a large public event. The more people that were affected, the more the cause would rush to donations and sympathy, the more rapidly blame and division would ensue.

Constantly living in fear of being monitored by the government, required destroying the cell phone. They were always tracked. The loss of freedoms after the Coronavirus had been overwhelming. "Necessary" the President had said, to make society "safe". A second constitutional convention was held, and immediately the second amendment was altered. That's when many decided that they were free men-from birth. Freedom wasn't determined by the New York governor and his armed guards, but rather from the Creator. For years, term limits had been sought after by the everyday common thinkers-the middle class for the most part. Everyday Joe Blow's who made the world function. The ones that no one acknowledged. Paying taxes as they went, with little in return, except to support the bottom twenty percent. Even petitions had gone forward to instill term limits, but for obvious reasons, politicians never want to lose power.

"Absolute power corrupts absolutely", he could hear Willis saying.

O'Reilly 's drive across the border was unchecked. His border coworkers knew his trailers and trucks. Why would you ever check your boss and fellow co-workers' equipment? For years, O'Reilly had come and gone across that border with the same equipment. Straight past the sniffer dogs that were drawn to explosives or seeking out drugs, and none of these dogs would pick up on the scent of what they were transporting today. Willis, his cohort, was following with truck and trailer number two, and since they were going to a prearranged event in Saint-Jeansur-Richelieu, where the Prime Minister was to attend, border agents needed to direct resources to credible terrorist threats in other places along the border. This little crossing in Northern Vermont wasn't a high priority, especially a familiar face coming through.

O'Reilly waved and shifted the truck into second gear.

As soon as the crossing was achieved, Willis split apart from O'Reilly. They had stored their balloons and UAVs unsuspiciously down the road from Swanton Station Headquarters at the Franklin County Airport near Highgate, Vermont, only about a mile from Interstate 89 a week prior. It was an easily accessible location to the balloon events and to work. They crossed the US Customs checkpoint in Highgate and proceeded directly through the Philipsburg Canadian checkpoint unencumbered, as the US officers called ahead for O'Reilly. Not a great idea to slow the boss down.

I-89 changed to Canada 133 North. O'Reilly followed 133

straight into Saint-Jean-surRichelieu. Willis continued through. Continuing north on Route 133 until heading west on Highway 10 towards Montreal. The last part of his drive split off onto Chemin des Moulins from the Bonaventure Expressway, pulling into the commercial parking areas for the Port of Montreal.

No one would think twice seeing an eighteen wheeler pulling into the busy port.

Willis pulled to the outer edge of the parking lot, further away from the building that housed the Maritime Employer's Association, parked the semi trailer and placed a sign in the front window.

"Afternoon Mandatory Meeting-Truck Will be Moved at 7pm, Call 802-999-7999 if Emergency." Willis had parked several times here during their practice runs and had never experienced a problem. He thought the phone number would add a layer of security should a guard come by to check the vehicle, although Willis had made sure to buy a similar brand and type of truck and trailer as those busy across the street at the Port.

He hopped out of the cab and called an Uber for his hotel a short mile away. Before the driver picked him up, a remote security motion activated cell phone tracking sensor was placed in the driver's seat. They had come this far, no need to fall victim to theft; although, Montreal was relatively safe for a big city. He looked Northwest and could make out St. Helen's Island. It will be a busy day there tomorrow.

"See you in the morning dear," Willis said out loud to his trailer as the Uber driver pulled up.

"To the Sandman Hotel sir?", asked the Uber driver.

"Thanks for the ride. It's been a long drive." Lied Willis.

Signs paved the way towards 5- Chemin de l'Aeroport, balloon festival home base. His lifelong balloon "bagger" friends were excited to see O'Reilly's new toy. The large helicopter device near his balloon could finally be unloaded. As well as all of the stored propane tanks O'Reilly kept under lock and key. Propane was used for all of the "hot" air. Many still thought helium was used, but helium's high flammability and shortage around the world made it a far distant choice. People were used to seeing propane tanks for grills and RVs, especially at border crossings in Swanton, and the border agents were forewarned about the necessity of tanks in large numbers needed for the balloon baggers weekend.

O'Reilly had secured a special rate from the Canadian LPG distributor which saved his fellow ballooners even more cash. He had ordered a far greater supply than even two balloon events could handle, but no one could judge how much a giant fleet of balloons would actually consume. His fellow ballooners thought he was buying extra supply for their summer tours from the airport but not all of the canisters contained propane. Some contained compressed air, disguised as propane.

O'Reilly removed his balloon from the trailer in the same way his grandfather had shown him in the past. The basket he had always stored on the rear. First to come off, and last to go on. His basket was the traditional wicker type. While not as light as the aluminum or fiberglass baskets, it better absorbed hard, fast impacts on descents. The traditional square basket was traded last year, at EZ's request, for an enclosed gondola type basket.

Unknown to the other ballooners, the extra space wasn't for passengers, but rather for the positive pressure air system. Tanks of compressed air were located under the large passenger seats normally reserved for extra electronics. EZ had considered the idea of poisoning his own ballooner undesirable. Unlike Middle Eastern terrorists who blew themselves up after terrorist activity, EZ had spent too much money and instilled too much knowledge into O'Reilly. Next out, the burner system, which attached to the top of the balloon in such a way that its fulcrum effect balanced the basket from tipping over upon impact. The pressure gauges on the burner adjusted through the coils delivering heat through the blast valve centered below the balloon's opening. O'Reilly's favorite sound was the eight foot flame's whoosh northward towards the sky. EZ had also requested a two burner redundant system. Two ten-gallon stainless steel propane tanks were stored inside the gondola, instead of one twenty-gallon tank. Following the old military rule- two is one, one is none. Altimeter, variometer, pyrometer, fuel gauge, sparkers, and a GPS topped off the gondola's inventory.

Last off the truck, the balloon itself. More appropriately called the envelope or bag. Woven from rip stop, fire resistant nylon into 24 panels which were held together by load-tape webbing, similar to seat belt fabric. Holding the bag to the gondola's frame were 24 stainless steel cables. O'Reilly's balloon color and logo? That had to be something perfect for the mission-a theme personal to O'Reilly. Something different than the traditional Gadsden flag.

One of the festival's biggest partnerships was Molson Coors Brewing Company. Molson

Brewery, founded in Montreal in 1786 along the Saint Lawrence River by the Englishman, John

Molson, was North America's oldest brewery. Molson noticed the influx of English and Irish working classes who couldn't afford the high price of rum and liquor. Molson's success included steam boats and even his own banking system, Molson Bank, which eventually became the Bank of Montreal. Over the course of generations, Molson owned hockey teams, what would become Home Depot stores, and stakes in Universities. The Molson name held a powerful history throughout Canada.

In 2005, Molson also acquired SABMiller's interests in MillerCoors, obtaining all the companies Miller and Coors portfolios of beer and beer distribution. One of these beers happened to be

O'Reilly's favorite, and also a favorite of his grandfather. Originally based on a recipe from Lett's Brewery in Enniscorthy, Ireland, Killian's Irish Red Ale was first brewed in 1864 at what was once called Mill Park Brewery. O'Reilly's grandfather had known Stephen and Edward Lett before sailing away in 1855. Henry's grandson, George Killian Lett, was for whom the beer inherited its name. Stephen Lett and John O'Mahony, the future leader of the Irish Brotherhood, had met in Dublin while O'Mahony had attended Trinity College. O'Reilly drank Killian's because everyone in his family had drunk Killian's, except for a time when it was bought by a

French company called Pelforth. O'Reilly couldn't force himself to support anything French. Regionally, you supported local beers in Ireland. Guinness and Murphy's brewing might be bigger and possibly better, but O'Reilly believed in tradition. His narrative couldn't work without tradition.

Eventually, in the 1980s, Coors bought the rights back to brew George Killian's, and the beer circle was complete. O'Reilly didn't care about the beer's circle in the industry. The giant, bright red balloon, with the logo Killian's Irish Red underneath a black Irish stallion, displayed its signature slogan, "Brewed in the Irish Tradition".

O'Reilly had talked the festival board into letting him use this on his balloon for this year's festival. Fussing over his Irish tradition, and how he and his father had done so much for the festival over the years. Not being their top selling beer in the area, Molson had initially not gone for the idea, but when he mentioned going with their competitor's Guinness Beer sponsorship on his balloon, Molson enthusiastically agreed.

The Irish Brotherhood would live on in Canada. He would make O'Mahoney proud. It would have been nice to pop a Killian's afterwards and trade stories with the legend. He also loved the fact that what he was doing was for the working class. The men who had made John Molson rich from drinking his beer would love to see payback to the company that had gone on to form banks that ruined their lives, and promote Universities professors that instilled into the youth the necessity of their destruction.

His Killian's balloon was a Proclamation for the Brotherhood, a symbol of payback to those who were ruining their way of life. Live free or die would take on brewed in the Irish tradition.

The End of the World

Sitting at the hotel bar, Willis saw the phone vibrate. From all the years of shooting, he sure as fuck knew he wouldn't hear it, so he always put his phones on the vibration setting. He glanced at the number and opened the flip phone.

"Hi there Big O," Willis said.

"Did you make it to your hotel without issues? I didn't hear back from you. You said you would call upon arrival." O'Reilly didn't seem too happy with the hard work he had gone through, Willis thought. He'd spent the last two years learning everything there was to know about hot air balloons. He hated the damn things, but he saw the genius in the plan.

"I'm here. I needed a couple of beers after getting the balloon trailer out to the airport. It's there and ready to go in the morning. I dropped off your second balloon where we planned as well," he said proudly.

Willis did have a passion and commitment that O'Reilly found inspiring. Those who could actually take initiative were difficult to find these days.

"OK. All is a go. Don't forget to charge all the batteries tonight. The UAVs will eat the life out of those batteries. We need them to fly as long as possible. The weather is going to be perfect.

I'll see you tonight at Berges de Saint-Jean. EZ is coming in by boat."

Willis heard the line click. He destroyed the SIM card on the phone and smashed the battery and cheap piece of plastic thinking about how these little devices had caused so much trouble in the years since their invention. From Edward Snowden's leak on the US government's snooping, he knew an agency of some type had likely recorded their call until the festival was long past. It was amazing the ease with which O'Reilly had gotten the big tanks across the border. He'd have to give it to him. It was one thing to have the advantage of being a border patrol agent, but it was an entirely different beast to dream up the idea of using hot air balloons to spread the anthrax. Agriculture crop helicopter UAVs, pure genius.

Farmers had been using them now for years to avoid crop dusting fees, and the terrain in the mountains of Northern New Hampshire was an even better reason to have the excuse to get the license to fly one. A venturi sprayer was attached to the bottom of the UAV. It could cover over thirty-three acres per trip before needing recharged. He knew that one safe fill of the tanks into the jet sprayers would be his only exposure. He would watch the rest from his balloon where a gas mask and positive pressured air would hopefully keep him safe from overspray. Although he would be quite some distance away, without prior vaccination, their likelihood of survival would be low if exposed.

As his balloon would get to a good height, he'd ensure the UAV followed its preset GPS coordinates all while he was in his lofty perch. The helicopter drone could carry a heavier load of chemicals than most of the recreational drones he was used to seeing. O'Reilly had talked the Balloon officials into letting him use his new aerial smoke writing helicopters to add to the effects of the balloon show. He'd also arranged for the same "smoke sprayers" to drop below his hot air balloon "for greater effect". O'Reilly and his grandfather had basically kept the entire festival alive during tough financial times, so they usually didn't question the Irishman. It was going to be a great day in Canada. For Willis. For O'Reilly. For the beginning of a Revolution they couldn't turn back from once it kicked off.

The Revolution of 1776 sparked the best country that had ever existed, but over the last thirty years, the entire world was becoming a slave to global corporate liberalism. The elites at the World Economic Forum, Bildeberg, and equity firms were attempting to turn the world into one universal system of slavery. The experiment that had been America was gone. In a global slavery system, the elite wouldn't allow a few countries to exist without their rules, or else the enslaved countries may revolt. Willis understood his mission. If the next Revolution did not start now. Win now. Then the former country he loved would never make a return. He no longer desired to live in a country that respected global investment banking returns over his right to pursue happiness.

He popped open his favorite Canadian beer he'd bought after the border crossing. A Unibroue Brewery Belgian triple. The bottle featured a beautiful label with a horseshoe curved title in French-*La Fin du Monde*.

"*The End of the World*". He could taste the irony.

* * *

<u>Berges de Saint-Jean</u>

EZ pulled his boat into his slip at the Restaurant Les Berges de Saint-Jean. It had become one of his favorite restaurants since moving outside of Montreal. He had purchased a boat as another resource to transport both people and equipment down the Richelieu River past Plattsburgh, New York, and onto Burlington, Vermont, under the cover of being just another wealthy Canadian who enjoyed dual citizenship privileges.

The restaurant welcomed him back, after all, his tips were always on the larger side. He held a fondness for their Steak de bison Canadian and their homemade Coupe gourmande dessert. Although he did his best to avoid alcohol when boating, their wine list persuaded a test each trip down the river, usually with his failure to abstain.

Night was setting over the river, and he wanted a last visit from his two operatives. He had one last thing to put into their minds before the mission tomorrow, something to insure their success. He had experienced operatives backing out at the last second, especially when it involved terrorism. Perhaps a nice steak, a pep talk, and a glass of wine would ensure a team victory. Tonight, he would not be drinking any wine. His mind would need to remain in the clear, and driving the boat would provide a perfect opportunity as to why he would not indulge.

He had called ahead, securing a table overlooking the river, and more importantly his boat.

Thieves, police, or out of place people were still a worry this close to the festival, and UUONE would not take his failure lightly. It had taken him a considerable amount of time and money to work his way into the gun club. He had guessed correctly in picking the club as a tool. The older white men in the U.S. could sense their time was almost up. They were being replaced around the globe with other skin colors and religions. The wonderment of their childhoods wouldn't be understood by the youth of today, so they were the last generation to have experienced the luxuries of a free society. Once they were gone, the path towards globalism would have no naysayers. Even the history of prior success would slowly disappear in online history. His country was largely responsible for what people were calling the Mandela Effect. Being labeled as racist, lacking equity, or inclusion. He knew this was one reason Israel was buying up media and publishing companies. They would rewrite history rather than acknowledge it.

Northern New Hampshire was known for its Libertarian movement. The annual Porcupine Festival, Porcfest, was held every June and sponsored by the Free State Project. It was the largest gathering of Libertarians in the world attracting most of the top Libertarian speakers and politicians. From this event, connections and platforms would be generated nationally for elections and debate. The event took place in Lancaster, New Hampshire, a town that would end up being only a short distance from the gun club.

He was not looking for far left or far right individuals to carry out his plan. He needed those who believed in the government's over reach. The Porcfest attendees would debate and promote crypto currencies, second amendment rights, gay rights, free speech rights, and overall, the government intrusion into personal freedoms. At any point of Porcfest, an attendee may be at a shooting event, a drug infused gay dance, marijuana production class, or a meeting to legalize off grid living restrictions. He had analyzed the Free State Project's web site, but those card holding members may be just a bit too smart to be convinced of his efforts, but he did guess correctly that there would be those in attendance who would consider a political revolt.

The Libertarians believed in being free from big government, and they had been very vocal about overreach from the Democrats and the Republicans. They were sick of endless wars. Being that the left and right were splitting further and further apart, the only way to correct the government might be a civil war. A need for the government to show its hand on massive surveillance programs, its lack of funding to infrastructure, and its overspending on foreign nation's problems instead of their own. True freedom comes at a cost.

They were small in number, but their rationale on the main stage was increasing, causing

UUONE's funding to decrease. The focus had to be on Zionism, and the US's spending on Israel. To validate legitimate problems in the United States would only divest from the money available to fight Israel's enemies. There was a fine line to US collapse and public support for foreign investment.

The goal of UUONE was to harvest Libertarian members into performing a terrorist act, supporting the action, and then turning over to the CIA all of the intelligence that the Mossad had conveniently collected. UUONE could cross the lines that Mossad could not. EZ knew of tools he had that they did not. Tools that should be limited to a few.

When a voice becomes too influential, as was the case with the American influencer Charlie Kirk, the leading of the sheep into the pasture may become distracted, not from the shepherd or the sheep dog, but from the wolves that could survive on their own. The wolves did not need wool, feed, or agriculture to survive. They could roam freely and decide on their own who they interacted with or what may be for dinner.

This could not be allowed in the minds of the sheep. For if one sheep were to see the world through the wolf's eyes, he may leave the flock, and that may mean others would follow. The shepherd could not allow that to happen. The shepherd would risk losing control over the flock. Even the sheep dog would be out of a job. It was the shepherd's job to insure what was presented to the sheep. What food they could eat, where they could go, with whom they could interact. The shepherd would allow some, like the sheep dog, to have more freedom on the farm, but the dog served a purpose, to instill further control over the sheep. For those who assisted in the regulation of control, they may be awarded more freedoms, such as staying in the warmth of the farmhouse at night, or being allowed to have a bone. Sheep were there to provide for the shepherd, and only the shepherd. Go outside the fence, and expect the dogs to wrangle you back into the yard. Escape the shepherd, escape the sheep dog, and you could join the wolves or be eaten by them.

"I'm here to protect from harm. Stay with the flock, and I will offer you safety. For if you head towards the wolves, you will be all alone. You will be devoured. Let me provide for you, so that you can provide for me," said the Shepherd.

The shepherd was UUONE. What the sheep could never know was that wolves were coming into extinction. There really was no danger beyond the fence, beyond the safety of the herd. The herd could likely all cross over to the fresh grass just beyond the fence and lead a free prosperous life, but to let them, meant that the Shepherd's farm may collapse. Those sheep that threatened this crossing were the Libertarians, and UUONE was not going to let them outside of the fence. The farmer screaming for them to cross, a Charlie Kirkish farmer, would not be tolerated. The sheep needed to live in a constant state of fear and division. Take out the farmer next door's invitation, take out the ideas of self thought, create the ideas of more wolves, and have the enforcer sheep dogs dare the sheep to leave without repercussions. Divide and conquer. EZ watched O'Reilly and Willis arrive at the restaurant. It was time for them to celebrate their perceived victory. It was time to manipulate their minds. He would turn them into obedient sheep dogs, but they would never be allowed to think they were the shepherds.

<u>Dinner at le Berges</u>

"You will be enacting a real change for your beliefs, for our beliefs. What will unfold may lead to the greatest changes in American history. Before me, I see Sam Adams and Paul Revere. At some point, all men must decide when enough is enough. Do not doubt your actions tomorrow, but understand their significance. This is only the first step in the change needed. More money and power will flow to our cause after tomorrow. The ability to lobby in Washington, to elect leaders who actually believe that Washington should never have become what it is today. To rid D.C. from the stranglehold of corruption. There is only one way to bond our country, and that is through tragedy." EZ continued.

"Look how the country responded to Pearl Harbor. Men were lining up to enlist and fight the Japanese and the Germans. Women were growing Victory gardens and working in the factories. This attack resulted in the United States becoming the greatest power on earth. Through the newspapers, and on their radios, Americans thought the attack was random and unprovoked, that no one in our government was aware of the ever present Japanese threat. They were told that the tragedy and loss of life in Hawaii was unavoidable.

"What they weren't told, until only recently, when it could not be hidden anymore with the power of today's internet and podcasts, was that our government was fully aware of the Japanese fleet. Fully aware of the dangers, but needed an event just like this to create a national mindset where people would voluntarily give up the comforts of home and willingly choose the possibility of death. Franklin Roosevelt needed a reason to enter the war in Europe, but Germany refused to declare war on the United States. Roosevelt provoked the Japanese by promoting the idea that they would be forced out of China. He knew the Japanese would not let this slide.

"Both of you clearly followed the history afterward. Do either of you actually believe that the United States just happened to have most of its destroyers at Pearl Harbor, but not its carriers? The intelligence had lost contact with the entire Japanese fleet. Do you think, as the broadcasters would sell, that Roosevelt felt they were heading to Midway and the Philippines ahead of the US fleet? Japanese codes were broken the day before the attack, and yet in Hawaii, no planes were in the air? Ammunition all stored in the same depot? Nothing makes sense about the possibility of so many Admirals failing at their jobs all at once. This is no longer a conspiracy theory gentleman."

"Just like tomorrow, the Brotherhood will no longer be a conspiracy theory. Your thoughts and goals will be forced into the spotlight. Your actions will cause the left and the right to finally battle against one another. Just like Roosevelt's inaction, your actions will create a response that would be too hard to achieve otherwise. Tomorrow is your Pearl Harbor."

"Let's toast to tomorrow." EZ raised his glass, touching Willis and O'Reilly's champagne glasses as they sat on his boat, the King Saul.

"Now let the three of us enjoy a great dinner. Excuse me for one second as I lock up the boat." EZ watched as the pair made their way past his boat down the dock towards le Berges.

Picking up the champagne glasses, he examined them to see if his addition was noticeable. With his pep talk, he had hoped the two's excitement would distract them from examining their champagne flutes. Only tiny remnants of the lipid covered flakes were noticeable at the bottom of the glass. He knew he only needed a small amount to make his plan work. Since they had empty stomachs, as their Russian scientist had developed, the lipids would be absorbed quickly in the stomach and transferred to the brain's ventricles.

Because he would be at such a close distance, he picked up his cigar shaped transmitter and placed it into his front coat pocket, next to the Cuban cigars he would offer to them later. With the alcohol on board, they wouldn't notice when he would swap out his real cigar for the fake one.

He would then see just what emotions these two had in them.

"What you don't know can, and will be used against you." He laughed and stepped to the dock. EZ let the dessert sink in before offering the two men cigars. O'Reilly at first said no, but Willis nudged him into it.

"You don't even have to inhale. It's just a relaxing experience." Willis told O'Reilly, doing EZ's convincing for him.

EZ pulled two cigars out along with his Zippo lighter, assisting the two in lighting their cigars at their dockside table. No one seemed to mind the three smoking outside.

They laughed and told stories. Taking turns exchanging ideas about the future. The two did not notice when EZ's cigar slid towards his thigh, being replaced by a glowing tipped Cuban look alike. He continued to hold it under the table. Neither two noticed the lack of smoke as night had taken over the day.

Pressing the EMF transmitter's buttons, EZ waited to see a

change in the men. He had only preprogrammed into the apparatus three emotions that would seem fitting to all men after dinner-sexual desire, satisfaction, and romance. The desired response was immediate from Willis. "I can't wait until this is over. I'm headed straight to Boston. Best strip clubs in the world. I can't wait to get laid." Willis smiled.

O'Reilly chimed in, "There is a new girl at the gun club I noticed without a wedding ring. Although, after tomorrow, I wouldn't care if she wore one or not." EZ laughed at his joke, changing to another button.

"I do feel great about all of this. We have worked hard. I have no regrets. What a great meal EZ. I've really enjoyed what you have done for us and the cause. We are doing the right thing." O'Reilly said as he sat back in his chair admiring the river. Fat and happy. Satisfied with his choices.

Returning the cigar to his jacket, EZ placed the real one into the ashtray. Mission accomplished.

Balloon Festival Day 2

Two balloon flights a day were permitted at the aeroport as long as no storms were within thirty miles, and winds were not above 7.5 mph. Morning flights started at 6 AM, and the evening flights were at 7 pm. O'Reilly was more than happy to find out that playing the main concert stage for the 7 pm evening launch was none other than Canada's own hippy spokesman, Neil

Young, who grew up in Northern Ontario. Young left for the U.S. in 1966, starting the band Buffalo Springfield, and never became an American citizen. Neil's father, Scott, was a sportswriter and quite well known throughout Canada. His Canadian heritage ran strong. The festival was paying top dollar to bring in one of Canada's own.

"I guess the free benefits were just too good. Another immigrant reaping the rewards of the American capitalist system, but ashamed to wave the flag," O'Reilly thought.

"Better to burn out, than to fade away." He hummed.

O'Reilly kind of liked Neil Young's music. Even the man himself. The struggles that Young and his family had been through, polio and cerebral palsy. But no matter, politically, Young was against almost everything the Brotherhood believed. Young would bring the crowd, and that's what was needed. It wouldn't be long before Young didn't play concerts anymore due to his age, and the hippy crowd coming to tonight's show would only do more to increase the message O'Reilly was after. Hippies hated violence, and loved to find a cause to bitch about- only garnering more attention over the next couple of days. The older crowd would also not recover as quickly from the spores either.

He skipped the 6 AM event, needing the day to set up his equipment. It was also a great time to have the other "baggers" up in the sky and not poking their noses into much of his "other" equipment. First up, was stocking the large gondola basket and double checking all supplies and that the electronics were up and running correctly. Two propane tanks were stocked, and two gas masks were stored out of view.

Gloves, goggles, and gowns were stored in duplicate numbers. The UAV controller was tethered and backup batteries times two placed in ziplock bags. All electronic safety systems checked their self start procedures without fail. The burner unit fired appropriately. All stainless cables were intact and without fray, and the bag had inflated perfectly on the prior night's ride. The crimson red balloon with black stallion sailing over the aeroport. Cameras recording the glorious sight. "Whooshes" of burners stirring up the evening sky at sunset. A truly beautiful sight. Last night was his only practice run. After the balloon setup was complete, it was on to the UAV. Since the ballooners were in the air, he was able to unchain the tarp and covers from the UAV which had been covered on the transport trailer.

EZ had done some research for O'Reilly since he had friends in the industrial agriculture industry in Mexico. The questions he posed were quite common and no one batted an eye. How much fertilizer spray could be flown on the helicopter drone at such and such weights? How long could the battery carry the drone at said weight? Is there mapping software available to insure efficient delivery of the fertilizer and avoid double spraying the same acreage? Of course cost really was of no concern for EZ. Neither were backup battery costs. More sophisticated software and guidance systems and obtaining the appropriate license to actually fly the drone were.

EZ's contact had recommended the Hercules 50 helicopter drone to achieve the large acreage demands that his client was planning on spraying. Payload for the Hercules was 50 kg with a twenty minute maximum flight time. EZ had some military contacts who could get him the Air Force grade, lighter weight batteries, and achieve a longer flight time of around thirty minutes, as well as increase the payload to 60 kg. Two batteries were obtained and tested delivering the expected results while flying the drone around his Swanton sector.

He had practiced take off from the northern Vermont airport, hovering over nearby forests so as not to raise concerns with the batshit crazy locals who feared anything artificial going on with agriculture and rednecks fearful of all drones. O'Reilly had told the airport manager it was a drone for use by the Border Patrol. No one questioned him since he had been in uniform and routinely came out to set up his balloon equipment.

Flight by remote camera would be unnecessary as well since O'Reilly would be assessing the drone's path from the safety of his balloon, high above where the helicopter drone was to spray. If needed, he could manually fly the device. A GPS mapping system was uploaded to the UAVs flight software. Topography of the Balloon Festival's exact dimensions including total acreage, elevation, temperature, wind speed, and humidity would all be calculated to determine the best pre determined flight path to fertilize the crop.

Today's crop was going to be a large one. O'Reilly attached the rotors which had been removed for transport. The sprayer reservoir had been filled at the Franklin County Airport. One slip up, and he would have been a goner. EZ had supervised that part of the mission. Although from a healthy distance and upwind. O'Reilly hadn't quite figured out a way to achieve mass chaos. Willis had suggested various terrorist activities: fires, bombs, aerosolized fentanyl like the Russians had loved and used on their own hostage rescues, but bomb making equipment in large quantities was heavily watched since the Oklahoma City bombings.

Chinese terrorists had successfully started large numbers of fires throughout California in 2019 but had not created a national sense of fear that EZ desired. California was still able to conduct most business as usual, only suffering heavy monetary and insurance losses. The only people making money during these crises in California were private equity companies and banks. O'Reilly frowned at the thought of the two financial systems. Fentanyl in large quantities was heavily regulated. Carfentanil, a more potent version of fentanyl used for large animals, was the rage in all the drug circles. Because the Americans had legalized marijuana in many states for recreational and medicinal use, the Mexican cartels were without a time honored income source.

The Estados Unidos was harvesting far more marijuana than anyone would ever need from Mexico. In order to make up for the loss, poppy seeds were brought in from Afghanistan, becoming a vast source of profit. The new crop was a little harder to manage compared to pot, so the decision was made to increase the price.

Many at first were unwilling to pay a higher price for a product that had disappeared since the 1980s and was usually associated with hippy rock star overdoses. That's where the fentanyl came into play. Not only did it give a far greater high, but it led to greater dependence on the product and forged lifetime customers. Carfentanil was so powerful that it was used to sedate elephants, so the production and dilution had to be perfect by the chemist, for if not, you would overdose the addicts, otherwise known as paying customers. Being 10,000 times more potent than Morphine, and 100 times more powerful than regular fentanyl used most commonly in anesthetics across the world, Carfentanil was no joke. First responders who came into skin contact stood the risk of overdosing. The "cutting" of product and bad chemists soon led to overdoses across the United States. Depending on what was available to do the mixture, some chemists diluted the Carfentanil incorrectly, or put too much regular fentanyl into the batches.

So numerous were the deaths, that Narcan, the reversal agent for narcotics usually reserved for respiratory distressed patients in hospital settings, was being given away for free at Narcan clinics or in America's Emergency Rooms. Narcan was even handed out by police officers to junkies on the street. Public cities had "safe" houses for junkies to shoot up, trying to quell the deaths, even with Narcan readily available. Police officers carried Narcan just as much for themselves as they did for the users in case they accidentally touched the drug during a search.

Not only did the cartels have the heroin competition, but they also were dealing with America's pill crisis. Pain pills such as Oxycontin were being abused by all ages. Rather than swallow the pill, which worked great as a time release medication for severe pain, the pill was crushed and snorted. Delivering the entire drug's effects at once. Once again, killing the cartel's potential future customers. The chemist backed off the fentanyl slightly, diluted the product, and continued shipping the product North. Not hard to do if one had the right talent.

Once again, much like with the Coronavirus's origination, China was much to blame. China's Ministry of State Security (MSS), the equivalent of the United State's CIA, was largely responsible for promoting the "illegal" distribution of fentanyl and Carfentanil, either in its synthesized form, or in the components necessary to produce it. The MSS turned the other cheek when it came to enforcing the US requested elimination of fentanyl shipments and production. The pharmaceutical companies worked closely with the Communist Party. Little concern was placed on what happened to the powder once in Mexico, or in the United States.

In a larger conspiracy, the MSS actually promoted the shipments to the United States and Central America. The US Government, state governments, and law enforcement would be so busy dealing with this problem that they couldn't allocate more resources against Chinese infiltrations and intelligence occurring in other sectors of the economy. More money would have to be directed to this epidemic of overdose, causing the United States to keep borrowing and increasing its deficit. The Chinese had zero interest in stopping shipments of fentanyl. It was a win-win situation the whole way around, even letting the Chinese mafia profit at party expense, as the Chinese controlled most of the world' ports with their mafia. With more US.

spending came more need to borrow money from China.

With so much effort focused on Mexico and Latin America's drug production, little effort was made to observe China's biggest aid to distribution and synthesis, Canada. With the longest continual border with the United States, trans country delivery was almost unstoppable, and with complete control of ports in Vancouver, Quebec, and Montreal, the Chinese were making as much money as the cartels to the south. The losses incurred for mafia delivery were worth every penny.

Another reason to keep up the shipments was historical. In the 19th century, the British and Americans fought to supply Turkish and Indian opium to China. Americans, even the grandfather of President Franklin Roosevelt, provided 25% of heroin supply to the continent. Americans preached that China needed to control its demand of opium, its law enforcement over the drug users, and the drug's use in China. It wasn't their fault it was being abused, claimed the profiteers-the greedy Americans. China had always had more patience than the United States, and now saw this as revenge against all the senseless deaths that the West had caused a century prior. The Chinese had long memories and were never in a hurry to establish strategies that may last generations. Fentanyl, Carfentanil, and pill production was an easy, nonviolent way to bankrupt the country that had killed so many of China's people. There was no remorse. Profiting universally from it all were the banks. Deposits came from cartels laundering drug money, and from Chinese loans to validate legitimate business ventures. Exotic car, yacht, and estate loans brought cash deposits, knowing full well the money deposited was dirty.

Establishing attorneys, the money would be deposited into the attorney's account, and then passed back to the Chinese in the form of a check. Effectively washing the dirty cash.

Deposits also benefited insurance companies, needed to protect all of these new investments. Within the United States, money was borrowed or printed at record rates for increased hospital admissions due to drugs. Health insurance claims, increased law enforcement staffing surveillance, decreased motivation by the work force, addiction clinics, were all new private equity opportunities to cash in for a solution.

The harder they worked to stop the inflow, the more money that the banks made. As production went up in China, the branches there took on more deposits and made more production loans. China was booming, and only China had the components and equipment necessary to produce fentanyl.

All they had to do was sell the precursors to the Mexican and Canadian laboratories who did the real dirty work. No deaths were in Chinese hands. This was retribution. It was the Americans who needed to stop putting the drug into their bodies. The exact phrases used by the Americans a century ago were mirrored back by the Chinese. 19th century politics was coming back to bite the United States in the ass.

O'Reilly was well versed in the flow of fentanyl across the Canadian border. Most of America thought that Mexico was the big player in fentanyl production, but he knew from his border patrol statistics that the Canadian mafia was the king. Much quieter and efficient than the Mexicans and Columbians, the Canadian mafia went back to the days of the early immigrants. French, Russian, Albanian, Italian, British, and Chinese mafia worked all across Canada, and often with transportation and distribution assistance by famous motorcycle gangs. It was likely the drug he was using today had been produced in Canada. Only right it should be consumed in Canada.

These mafias, Communists, illegals, and addicts were all responsible for the downfall in quality of life and politics in the

United States. What O'Reilly remembered as a quality childhood would be unachievable soon for his kids. Dirty politicians, many making money from the very problems they claimed to solve, were not going to make impactful change as they would lose illegal money and votes. The extreme rich and the extreme poor would always be the same.

It was O'Reilly's middle class, the working class like his grandfather, that were forced to pay higher taxes and suffer in a society that wasn't worth the return on investment. There was predicted to be a shortfall in social security. Artificial intelligence was to replace many middle income jobs. All of society was at a divide, a Notch, in what the solutions were to be and who was to blame. Something radical was necessary to rid society of these politicians. If they wouldn't take care of their own at state capitals or in Washington D.C., then it was up to the populace to take care of themselves.

"Let the people rise up like my balloon today. Let my Grandfather's mission finally come to light. Let the Irish brotherhood's ghosts guide me for this change we are about to impart." O'Reilly opened his eyes from this thought and prayed for clear skies. Let the Notch begin.

Stormy Weather

With the weather patterns changing yearly due to climate change and weather modification, Stormy's predictions always seemed a little off. O'Reilly had studied the weather his entire life.

With a hobby like ballooning, he had to be vigilant.

He remembered from his weather research that he needed Stormy to mention either a Great Lakes Low jet stream pattern, or a Colorado Low. Either would steer his balloons in the direction he needed them to go, more northwestern instead of directly northeast as most of the jet streams flowed. His balloon payload needed all the help he could give it. Payload was near its maximum, and his plan needed just a little luck.

All good plans involve a certain degree of risk.

"Luck really decreases risk," his old First Sergeant used to say.

He had prepared for all other mission critical elements, but he needed some lucky weather. Sexy couldn't always accurately predict the weather, but today, she did predict a little bit of luck. As was the case in 2017 with massive Hurricane Irma, the jet stream was experiencing what Stormy called "high amplitude waves". The picture on his TV screen looked just like a waveform he'd seen in high school physics class. It was as if you connected the letter W three times across all of the Canadian mainland.

He'd never seen Stormy this excited. She was running computer simulations, interviewing weathermen in the field, predicting electrical outages. This was her moment to shine. Almost the entire evening news was dedicated to this oncoming storm. Some type of polar warming effect was going to be his luck. Maybe the liberal goons were right about polar warming.

If they were right about science, it just added fuel to his reasons to educate them on his favorite subject-Irish history.

EZ at the Balloon Festival

EZ stood near the balloon's preparation area, there had been little to no security. It was Canada after all, and guns had been banned years ago. Terrorist events were rare here. Perhaps a lone wolf knife attack or a bolt action hunting rifle extremist; but overall, the Canadian's sense of safety was an overconfidence that worked in his favor. Canada was much like Pearl Harbor right now. Multiple targets all contained in one spot.

He had taken his anthrax vaccine series years ago while in the Israeli military. The vaccine's effectiveness was over 90%, and since many of Israel's neighbors would be happy to deploy anthrax against the Jewish state, it was a requirement of enlistees .

The series of injections were administered intramuscularly, occurring at 0, 1, and 6 months. Booster shots were given at one year and also at month eighteen. Booster shots were administered yearly thereafter. Because he would not be using a respirator as he didn't want to instill fear amongst the crowd, he would be taking a thirty day course of antibiotics. He had also taken an extra booster dose two weeks ago following protocol.

He would take Ciprofloxacin 500 mg twice a day for a period of 42 days after the festival in conjunction with a 0.5 mL subcutaneous injection of the anthrax vaccine today and two weeks from now. What a large dose of medications for such a tiny spore he thought. Thank God for modern medicine.

The key part of anthrax exposure is *actually knowing that* you *had been exposed*. Unlike him, the crowd today would have no clue for around seven to ten days. The government would be unaware until their hospitals started to fill, and some doctor thought correctly to test for anthrax. Unless someone was prior military, or worked on high risk farms, none of these people would have prior vaccinations. Try as they might, the impact at volume and the shortage of antibiotics by the socialized, ill prepared Canadian medical system would be unsurvivable. Another reason why this attack would be better in Canada than the United States. For some, a massive drop in citizens would enable them to get a doctor's appointment a few months ahead of schedule.

Canada was full of useful political idiots.

EZ watched as O'Reilly's balloon inflated. He wanted to make sure that O'Reilly didn't develop any fear and walk away from all the hard work that went into this attack. Suicide bombers were notorious for blowing themselves up too early, or simply not showing up to detonate their vests in the name of Allah.

In his backpack, he pulled out the transmitter. It resembled something that may be used with his digital camera. Nothing that would create suspicion. He was just another photographer here to capture the beauty of the balloons.

He aimed the antennae towards O'Reilly, who he could see next to his basket. He touched the button to cycle anger. He looked on as O'Reilly stopped what he was doing. His face had changed into a grimace. His shoulders developed an aggressive nature with his posture becoming defensive. The champagne's additions continued to work. The metal particles had remained within the cerebrospinal fluid of the brain's ventricles after crossing the blood brain barrier. Their lipid coatings, which enabled them to cross the lipophilic cell membranes, had now long ago dissolved, leaving only the flakes which responded to electromagnetic frequencies. Quickly, he turned the anger button off, and switched to a preset cycle of frequencies-admiration, appreciation, amusement, nostalgia, and joy. Cycling in thirty second periods, the transmitter would resonate the particles in the third and fourth ventricles of the brain, causing it to release neurotransmissions similar to endorphins or dopamine. The device would resonate the particles as they traveled not only through the brain, but continuously within the cerebrospinal fluid that makes a protective coating around the spinal cord as well. Every nerve in the body would trace itself back to the cord and ascend its electrical signal to the brain. All in a synchronized frequency determined by EZ.

There was no way O'Reilly would back out now. EZ stood back and watched O'Reilly happily go about his tasks, remembering his time in Peru, and how unaware he had been of mind control.

"Stalking the wild pendulum, indeed Mr. Bentov."

Liftoff

O'Reilly loved the color of his balloon. Crimson red. Killian's red.

Whoosh. Whoosh. Whoooooosh. He had never felt so accomplished, proud, joyful.

The burner expanded the balloon causing it to start a slow ascent into the sky. 10 mph winds. Colorado front. I love you Stormy, thought O'Reilly. He was by himself in his balloon. Many of the sponsors had tried to beg and plead their way onto his balloon's evening sunset flight, but he had used insurance coverage as the scape goat, blaming a last second glitch in paperwork for him not being able to carry passengers.

He had one of the security guards clear away a takeoff zone around his trailer for the drone copter below him. He reached over and got out the remote. Flipping the power to on, the familiar green "Go" light illuminated the cockpit in the growing sunset's darkness. If need be, he would manually take over the drone's flight pattern, but the preset GPS should work just fine.

He was primarily there to get the drone loaded, in flight, and supervise should the GPS fail. Gas masks were brought out from below. He had prepared everything and gone over the plan with Willis multiple times, trying to predict possible failures, but as anyone who's ever done any combat will tell you, once in play, there are always processes that could have been refined. He looked down at the basket. A normal balloon could carry around 1,000 lbs. His balloon carrying the redundant backups for the mission was pushing the limits of the precision stitching above him. The low thermal activity of dusk provided a steady, unwavering rise to the first 1,000 feet of his ascent.

The balloons took off in stages to give each other space for error and mistakes if winds shifted. A predetermined altitude was also rediscussed. Because he was in charge of these discussions, he had decided his Killian's balloon would go up to a height of 3,000 feet, representing the pinnacle of the display. Spreading the balloons out over the span of the grounds as well as differences in height would provide for the greatest performance as viewed from the parade grounds. More experienced baggers went to the higher elevations. More room for error at those heights, and as he had suggested. The town of course wanted no negative press from injuries. "The banks wouldn't loan out cash to finance the event if the insurance companies backed out" they said. Always these banks O'Reilly grimaced.

At a height of 2,000 feet, O'Reilly powered on the drone. He could mentally hear its rotors begin to swirl, but couldn't actually see their movement below. He would take the drone up to 500 feet initially and place it in a holding pattern. He radioed to his ground crew that all was clear, and the drone moved into position. Most balloon flights lasted 45 minutes to an hour unless there were cooler thermal patterns, such as those with a cooler sun in the winter. This was also around the same amount of time his drone batteries would last with the weight of the anthrax solution.

EZ had worked with an agricultural engineer, Calderon, from Mexico City who was used to doing crop work for the larger poppy, coca, and marijuana fields throughout Mexico and

Central America. He was an independent contractor and found work with all of the cartels from Mexico to Peru, even at one point providing instruction to Taliban owned poppies in Afghanistan. Russians, Columbians, Mexicans all protected the engineer. He was the best in his field-corrupt and silent. He was also reasonably priced considering what he was expected to do. Mistakes to any one of the crops he supervised would mean losses in the millions and almost sure death. There could be no mistakes when it came to spraying and dusting the income of future drug profits. It took a special man to work in such a stressful world.

EZ paid him handsomely, almost ten times his normal amount to calculate a dilution and distribution calculation for the drones "crop". A similar weighted product had been calculated and dissolved for three prior test runs without issue. Working under the auspices of his Russian contacts, the engineer was told the anthrax was to be used in an upcoming Syrian conflict. Calderon had no interest in what the Jihadi's and Russians were doing. They had fought for centuries and would continue to fight for centuries. His Cayman Island account spoke only one language, and he planned on retiring soon.

Knowing he'd have a tough time going completely underground, he had taken to teaching his two sons the trade. Once you started in the global underground, you retired in the global underground. A way out was nearly impossible. He would just have to appear that he was still working while at the same time reflecting on expanding. Cartels loved to see people doing well from their business. It gave them more power to negotiate should it be needed, and Calderon bringing family in was a sure way to insure he wasn't going to hide. This man could be trusted. EZ had agreed, and Calderon's solution worked flawlessly as well. If you need the best, pay the best.

O'Reilly leveled the balloon off at 3,000 feet. He let the other balloons get into position. This 15 minutes would give him time to finalize his drone approach. He reached over and placed the gas mask over his head, placed his hand over the inspiratory valve, and sucked in. The mask collapsed appropriately indicating a perfect seal. He gowned up in two disposable gowns, two pairs of shoe covers, and lastly, two pairs of surgical gloves. Redundancy. There was also the issue of blowback or thermal rise from the anthrax solution. This was the purpose of the compressed air tanks. Connected to a series of hoses, the air would create positive pressure outward from his basket.

Since he would be at a distance, and only drifting in the wind, he hoped that this imperfect solution to overspray would offer some protection. No need to add stress from accidental contact. He planned on making a quick escape after his mission was over. The helicopter drone had been presented to the Festival as a way to write beautiful smoke images below the balloons. Adding another dimension to the thousands of photos that would be posted on Instagram and Facebook, documenting the event so all the sheep could graze on each other's narcissism. He promised white smoke, and agreed to fly in a pattern to honor the Canadian maple leaf logo. Everyone thought it was a wonderful idea, especially O'Reilly.

Lights on the remote flashed, changed colors, and proceeded through a preset pattern. Instead of the 500 foot level that was planned for the event, the drone dropped down to a height of 100 feet above the flashing phones and cameras. He could hear the crowd cheer in response to the drone's rotors. The safety crews would start their bitching now, so he turned off his radio. The drone approached the north eastern side of the crowd, paused, and initiated its sprayer system. A sputter of liquid dripped on the crowd below, and soon turned into a fine mist. It reminded

O'Reilly of his backyard sauna in New Hampshire. Scooping a water filled ladle and pouring it over hot lava rocks. Steam projecting into the air. Cleansing the pores. Sweating.

Ridding the body of unneeded toxicities. The opposite of what was occurring below him. The people below watched the drone as it passed over their heads. Low and slow it progressed in a semicircle rectangular type pattern. After it passed, the music played on, and the balloon photos resumed. As far as they were concerned, the drone probably was recording video. Most had not read the literature leading up to the event about the maple leaf smoke designs to come from the drone, and those who did know likely assumed that the drone had malfunctioned. Some would assume a police or media drone.

O'Reilly watched the drone fly its route from high above in his cool perch, a bit of wind on his sleeves reminded him of the dangers. He checked the compressed air tank volumes out of paranoia. It was now on to phase two of the operation. No turning back. He wondered how Willis was doing with his mission.

He set the balloon on a course for 14,000 feet. Observing below, he could see the drone finishing its spray pattern then shifting its course to the GPS waypoint set as "Home". The waypoint was about two miles due south in the center of the Richelieu River. There could be some boaters out who might see the drone drop into the water, but he had tried to pick a spot that was both deep and away from public and private boat docks. It could be recovered with some time and effort, but that's even if it was seen. And if found, whomever came into contact with it, wet or not, stood the chance of touching some leftover anthrax in the sprayers. He felt pretty safe with the drones disappearance plan.

Once achieving distance and checking wind direction, he

took off his protective gear, and reached in for his parachute, recalling his jump school in the military, hoping his ankles did better this time around as he wasn't eighteen anymore. He tied a string from the burner to the wall of the gondola. Wrapping the string to tightness, the burner's "Whooshing" was constant.

The balloon was to continue upward until the propane fuel was gone. Hitting the jet stream at 24,000 feet into Stormy's Colorado front. It might even go higher, but at some point, the balloon's burner would freeze as temperatures reached to minus sixty degrees celsius. Once in the jet stream, the balloon would go hundreds of miles before its final descent in God knows where-perhaps the Atlantic. He approached the basket's gate. Opening it without looking down to the Earth, he looked at the altimeter on his wrist and jumped when it read 5,000 feet. Around sixty seconds later, O'Reilly was hitting the ground and packing his chute. He had jumped far from the balloon festival and at such elevation, he doubted anyone would have noticed another skydiver in the area. The airport was nearby, and residents were used to seeing parachutes in the skies. The festival was in town as well, so plenty of tourists would be taking to the skies.

"Jump of a lifetlme." He thought.

EZ would come shortly after he placed the call. He had no time to waste. Another balloon was waiting for him at the farm. They would drive it far away from prying eyes to a location that would make sense with prevailing winds. He would explain that he lost control of his burner and was at the mercy of prevailing winds. An unfortunate risk when one took up ballooning. All evidence from his prior balloon and drone would be long gone. What was left of the balloon would be hundreds of miles away, thanks to Stormy's weather. O'Reilly's balloon idea was just what the doctor had ordered as it also included cover to get all equipment into the location. O'Reilly had successfully performed his own Japanese Fu-Go Project. General Tada would have been proud.

<u>Operation Willis</u>

Willis had practiced with O'Reilly many times. His targets were a little different. More people over a less defined area, but his target would truly create fear in Canada. That's why he was proud O'Reilly had left him with the job of spraying his target-La Ronde amusement park, which was owned by Six Flags Amusement Parks. La Ronde sat on 146 acres of St. Helen's Island in the middle of the St. Lawrence River, directly west of the Molson Coors plant.

Willis had slept in that morning. He didn't want to arrive too early in the day, it would be hours before La Ronde opened, and he knew with nice weather, it would fill in the afternoon with kids being out of school and summer vacations in full swing. He finished an early dinner at his hotel, and headed out, having his Uber driver drop him back off at the truck he had parked the day before.

He removed his motion detector and took down the sign, throwing it onto the parking lot's hot summer concrete. Directing the truck out of the parking lot, he didn't have far to go, and being Saturday, commercial truck traffic was not up to its weekday volumes. He drove North, just past the Molson Coors facility on Notre-Dame Street, and into the large U-Haul parking area next to the train tracks, under the west end of the Jacques-Cartier Bridge. Looking due East, he could see the Le Monstre Coaster going through its loops and turns. He had heard that it was the highest double tracked wooden coaster in the world.

Willis walked inside to talk to the U-Haul manager, explaining that he needed a smaller truck to navigate tight roads for a delivery in Quebec City. He didn't want to draw attention to himself in the rear of the parking lot where some of the bigger trucks were parked. He explained he had a couple of items to unload, but would be out of the area by nightfall. The manager, being a former trucker himself, could relate to the difficulties of trying to make big city deliveries in the old town.

"Take your time. We close at 3 pm, so you won't be bothering us anyway." The manager said. Willis thanked him profusely, complaining about the poorly labeled road signs, pot holes, and turn arounds downtown. Looking at his watch, 2:45 pm, he knew they closed at 3 pm, but you could never know if they had set up after hours delivery or maintenance. He appeared to be the only one left in the parking lot shortly after 3 pm when he waved at the overweight, hunched over manager.

"Too many years in the driver's seat." He thought.

He opened the back of the rig, stared at his forklift, then quickly dropped down the elevator ramp on the rear of the trailer. The fork lift was in a well rehearsed pattern. Willis hopped into the trailer, using the jack to maneuver the pallet to the rear, hopping to the ground. Lifting the pallet up with the fork lift, he smoothly lowered it behind the trailer, hidden from the view of passing vehicles by the adjacent tractor trailers.

On the pallet was an exact replica of the helicopter drone O'Reilly used, same remote setup, same sprayers. He quickly attached the rotors, turned the drone on for a brief moment, and moved it off of the pallet. Addressing the fork lift once again, the pallet was returned to the truck, and the fork lift was elevated back into the trailer. No effort to secure the items for long transport were made. No intention was in mind for returning the trailer to New Hampshire. The fork lift and trailer had all been stolen in Mexico. He closed the doors and returned to the cab of the semi.

Starting the big rig up, he maneuvered it tightly in with the other trailers on the lot. He unhooked the trailer from the truck's hitch, drove the truck across the lot, and positioned the it so that its window was facing across the river, looking at the coasters and biosphere which was a little further south. Walking back to the drone, he did a quick check of the area to make sure nothing would be left to track him. Video would be gathered over the next few weeks. The police would find the trailer. The manager would remember a nondescript truck driver leaving the trailer, but they might, with some police stupidity and laziness, not even realize from where the drone had departed.

Unlike O'Reilly's fervor for symbolism and the dramatic, Willis was focused on accomplishing the mission-quickness, without interruption from the unexpected. The unexpected was always present, as Six Flags was about to find out. Lights appeared on the drone's remote, and in the correct sequence. Battery charges were at full capacity. The rotors whirled to life and were loud in the quiet parking lot.

Willis hit start on the drone's preprogrammed GPS delivery sequence and watched it elevate into the air and over the bridge, cruising at an altitude of 300 feet. After reaching the island, it came to a stop, almost appearing as if it had second thoughts, and the vaporizers steamed to life.

He couldn't see the spray, but the light on his remote indicated successful activation. The drone changed its elevation somewhat, adjusting to just above the Vampire coaster's height, and flew off on its mapping sequence. Once empty, it would fly to the predetermined drop zone in the river, sinking to the exact GPS coordinates as O'Reilly's drone.

Willis returned to the rig, cranked the truck's motor, shifted into gear, and headed back across the bridge and away from Montreal. Doing the exact posted speed limit, and nervously checking the rearview mirror. Mission accomplished. He wondered how O'Reilly had fared.

He had failed to notice the car that had pulled into the U Haul center's side lot. He also had failed to notice his brain resonating away his fears. EZ watched Willis drive away, packing up his EMF transmitter. He put the car in drive and headed out to pick up O'Reilly. He knew the call would come soon for extraction.

<u>Six Flags</u>

Jerry had worked at La Ronde for three years in the security department. He had retired with the Canadian postal service, but soon became bored. The park gave him some purpose in a dull retirement. His sector to monitor today was near the southwest parking area, directly south of the Vampire coaster. It wasn't his favorite area.

The guests were in a hurry to get into the park on arrival, and hot and tired when the park closed as they labored strollers and kids back to their cars. He much rather preferred to be staring at the wet moms coming off the Splash ride on the other side of the park.

Jerry heard the drone's whiny motor coming towards him. It stopped over his head as it passed the bridge, coming to a stop. Some sort of mist began to emerge from the canisters located underneath the helicopter rotors.

"Another stupid way to beat the heat, and another stupid video for Facebook I'm sure," Jerry said out loud to no one but himself.

Never a thought of giving anyone a pay raise like himself,

but the park could always find some new and cheap gimmick to try and advertise. Off the aircraft went, spraying away. He reached into the cheap plastic red Igloo cooler on the back of his golf cart and took a swig of his Kool Aid mix as he watched two kids try to hide as they smoked a joint.

"Guess I'm no better than the rest of em. Drinking the Kool Aid too."

He laughed at himself, thinking back to the Jim Jones incident from his youth. No need to complain about today's youth when his laziness was on the same scale.

Flying over the park, patrons and riders at the Six Flags could not understand the drone's purpose. It was going slowly, likely recording video for a future commercial or some other advertising venue. Out from its spouts came a mist, never quite getting close enough to cool them from the summer heat.

"Maybe a mosquito sprayer, some said, the mosquitos will be out tonight when the fireworks are displayed."

Strollers were parked outside the Splash ride. One new mother noticed a little bit of whitish powder on the stroller's dark blue fabric. *Probably from the baby powder she used earlier,* giving it no second thought as she snapped her baby's photo with her phone. This was a first birthday she never wanted to forget. *You only get one first birthday.* She didn't know how right that thought would be in her near future.

At the Camping Sogerive campground Northeast of Six Flags and along the St. Lawrence, only one man viewed the strange low flying drone enter the widest and deepest part of the river, and since an entire joint and bottle of wine had just been consumed, he could be seeing things. More than likely, he wouldn't even remember the drone in the morning over campfire eggs. He looked back to the river, seeing nothing in the water.

Yep, he was definitely seeing things. Nothing was there.

The Why

"China is neither an ally or a friend-they want to beat us and own our country."-Tweet, Donald Trump Pre presidency, Sept. 21, 2011.

Biden didn't seek to be President at first. But as he was forced into the spotlight, people were forced to hear what he had to say on the evening news. He was slow. Age has its weaknesses. His mind wasn't what it used to be. He was like an old dog that barks at everyone walking by for no necessary reason, your senile Grandpa present at the head chair for Thanksgiving dinner.

His mental errors and pauses, documented daily by the cameras and the opposing right. He was your Grandma's jello dessert, something relevant and average in the past, but now untouched at the new age annual family Holiday. Someone present recognized the jello's mystique and historical context, maybe even taking a scoop, with the stale, moist pretzel chips sprinkled on the outside, and then regretted the caloric decision as the Anthony Bourdain Chocolate cake stared longingly nearby. The new replacing the old. What was once considered great was being replaced with more dazzle and creativity. New traditions replacing the old. This was how the world viewed Biden.

Even before Biden, there was always a problem. Always a situation that needed to be solved. Always someone else's fault, something echoed by people such as Democratic Governor Cuomo of New York. Always something missing or needed that hadn't been provided to *his* people of New York, where over 25% of the initial US cases of Covid started to build up in the early bouts of the Coronavirus pandemic. *His* strategy should be *the* strategy. Soon, New Yorkers who didn't worship him realized there were no Jello desserts around the family get togethers anymore. There were also no Anthony Bourdain's willing to take his place either. Someone else, the government, would take control of the menu.

Cuomo's spotlight in the evening news was usually preceded by a statement from President Trump's Coronavirus council. There was nothing they could really do for the older sicker Americans facing the disease except slow its progress. Keep everyone inside, perhaps some N95 masks for hospital staff. Trump became increasingly agitated at his inability to control the virus. Passing more legislation. Printing more money. He had achieved historic low unemployment and historic high unemployment numbers all within the same month.

Who was President was obviously irrelevant. The virus was unstoppable, and on a path to spread around the globe as viruses have done since the dawn of time. And with the spread, the press's fear became unrelenting. Biden never stopped barking, an old dog seeing opportunities to bark, gaining the attention of the masters of the house, and yet after standing up and researching what the bark was all about, realizing you have been fooled once again by the rhetoric hee hawing of the new leftist cult leader, establishing a franchise established from the anxiety dispenser. His expert rhetoric seemed eerily similar to former President Obama's, likely because Obama was running the show from behind the curtain.

As the two bickered with each other, it became obvious to the press that a contest between Democratic front runner Joe Biden and Trump in the Fall of 2020 would achieve great advertising sales, reads, and clicks. In order to keep the American people consuming content, someone else needed to run

against Trump. Someone with similar vigor and fighting spirit.
Someone not afraid to go before the TV and written press and
say anything to achieve a goal. A person that could be
controlled, but liked by the little people of the world-like Bernie
Sanders in 2016. Someone to match Hillary's speeches but had
as much money to pull for the party to achieve a victory.
Someone who knew corruption. Family linked corruption.

The Biden family was heavily involved in possible schemes
around the world. Even his son Hunter was now an expert on
Ukrainian gas companies although having zero experience in
energy. Biden was to get the Democratic nomination. If not for
his disgrace over Covid deaths, Cuomo likely could have been
the candidate to sale more ads.

Tensions increased when Biden was campaigning. Elizabeth
Warren, a possible Vice Presidential candidate, had claimed
American Indian heritage, and this had clearly been disproven,
ruining her chances for victory. Because she would attract
negative press, Biden instead went with Kamala Harris as his VP
choice. Adding a female to the ballot as Vice President, along
with the Republican party's lack of preparedness, pushed Biden
over the top in electoral ballots on the Democratic National
Convention floor. The Senate, as well as the House, were
pushed into a Democrat Super Majority, not seen since Obama's
first two years in office. Instead of focusing all of his might on
free healthcare, he focused on democratic socialism, gender
identity, woke ideology, and revocation of freedoms. All under
the guise to "keep us safe".

Tensions were at an all time high. Jobs decreased. Investors
pulled out of the market. Tariffs were revoked, but to no benefit
to the American middle class workers. Corona virus's fear
created the opportunity to rape Constitutional freedoms. Social
media companies worked with the party of record for "truth and

safety." Companies such as Meta allowed the government to control algorithms, and seek out those the NSA and FBI presumed as threats, despite the Fourth Amendment. The government encouraged its citizens to turn in non compliant neighbors, and to "trust the science" which just so happened to be killing so many around them.

Who cared what science, independent physicians, and multiple global studies said. If not coming from the National Institutes for Health, then it was labeled false. Twitter banned free speech and committees of Ivy League, cultish left leaning philosophy was allowed to infiltrate algorithms of who was banned and what users were presented onto their feeds. The Biden administration realized it could not only control the corporate traditional media, but also the now relevant online news information.

Long ago, the Universities dominating the tech money infusions had been radicalized since the 1960s. These leftist professors had spread faster than Covid throughout the entire upper education system in the United States to become not a place of thoughts, debate, concepts, and free speech; but rather to what was referred to as a "safe space" for only left leaning thoughts on diversity and inclusion. Average Americans were too naive and comfortable to understand what they needed, so it was up to the 0.1% of the 1% of the Ivy League ideologically captured to save the country, according to them at least.

As if to further reinforce what wasn't done, a common theme was to state "follow the science" while at the same time shunning actual scientists offering alternate hypotheses. Hundreds of scientists and researchers presented counter evidence to the administration. Many of these being prominent award winning individuals, who invented the technology being used to diagnose and treat the tools of the epidemic.

Ignored. Threatened. Banned from peer journals. Banished from speaking at the cult of personality Ivies. Many would even lose their medical licenses. Those refusing the vaccine were fired from their jobs.

The NIH would never take on a political leaning would it? This was a globally respected organization after all. Countries with no research budgets looked to the NIH leadership decisions to make their own policy. Decisions like the food pyramid were up to date, right? Large corporations had no influence, right? Grants weren't distributed to the same companies doing the research that would become policy, right?

It appeared that what the NIH had once represented had now changed. But what caused that change? Was there a law that over a few years would affect University and science policy spending to that degree? In fact, there was such a change, and those Ivy League cult schools were right at the heart of that change.

In 1980, the Bayh-Dole Act revolutionized the National Institute of Health. Birch Bayh and Bob Dole's bill allowed for the first time Universities and Non Profit Organizations to own the patents and to develop commercialization of inventions. What was formerly a private business task, developing and patenting what University research might have developed with tax payer funding, could now be profited by the professors and Universities themselves. Instead of doing research on what may be necessary and relevant to the American society at large, something like the morbid obesity epidemic or diabetes, could now be shelved in favor of research that might generate income into the University. Professors, as well as Universities, needed grants and donations to keep growing, and to keep their endowments at all time levels. It only made sense to steer studies towards what would make profits.

Studies and professor tenure may now be determined not by nuance, but rather by new income. Those on research committees could be steered into directing votes, not into benevolence which might be quite expensive, but into the coffers enlarging the already fat subsidies of the upper education system. Places like Johns Hopkins University, which led all NIH funding, and Harvard University, could vector research to ideology and politics. Inventions and patents could generate up to $150,000 a year for a professor-*for life*.

Make the University happy. Make the director of the NIH happy. Make the corporations selling the inventions happy. Make the ideologues happy. It was profitable to sell the treatment, not the cure. The days of Saulk's life saving polio vaccine were over. One shot and cured. What was needed was something that could be given over and over again. Not a vaccine at all, but a mRNA gene therapy. Easily changeable to the latest released virus or cancer in the lab. Easily funded research, with easily deposited tax payer subsidized money. Patented, and sold to pharmaceutical companies which had little funding into the research itself for that was all through tax payer subsidized grants. These pharm companies could then make billions off a product they had paid pennies to have developed, published, and patented.

Along with these alterations in policy, Immigration Reform wasn't reformed at all under the Biden administration, it was eliminated. Amnesty was not immediately granted, but rather laws were just not enforced on immigration policy. The border door was opened wide. 25 million illegals who had never paid a dime to entitlement spending came across to enjoy tax payer funded housing, food, and healthcare. Which in turn, invited more and more illegals across the border, assisted by endless NGOs, funded once again, through US tax dollars.

Local judges, many of whom on border states elected with the help of left leaning globalists such as George Soros, refused to enforce federal immigration laws, thus supplying millions of new Democratic voters and immediately opening Medicaid and Social Security to another future bulk of the population, tearing dividends away from the established tax payers, who had their paychecks raided since their first jobs. To instill amnesty would be to put a sword into social security and Medicare benefits for those in the future.

The Republican corporations were equally as guilty and turned a blind eye to enforcement. Republicans needed the cheap labor force, Democrats needed the votes, and both parties needed the population to generate the social security benefits pyramid scheme infusion as the baby boomers began their decline. The theatrical party division was laughable on the news. Both parties were now the same-the corporate party.

Division increased. Hatred developed. Business further declined as taxes and employee FICA pay-ins doubled. Biden suggested the highest capital gains tax vote in United States history. Small businesses crumbled, unable to make money where none was to be made. Fast food restaurants were expected to pay employees $15/hour in already high interest and inflation markets. Inflation rocketed to 9% to start, and refused to go down with ever increasing interest rate hikes by the Federal Reserve. Hospitals took on more care with no reimbursement, despite a coronavirus increase of 20% to Medicare and Medicaid. New building construction came to a halt. Research grants ceased. Pharmaceutical costs increased, as the corporations still had to show growth to their investors. Banks were raking in record profits. Banks thrived off wars and chaos.

Bragging about job growth by Biden was laughable as most people took on multiple jobs per household in order to hang on to middle class status. The devaluation globally of the US dollar, inflation, illegal migration, illegal employment without social service tax deposits, increased defense spending on foreign wars in Ukraine and Israel, increased spending on baby boomer retirements, and most importantly, a decrease in American industrial technology and industrial production, led a slow decline in what once was the greatest civilization on earth.

Globally, the effect was eerily similar. Socialist, elitist, cultish capture ideology was on a roll, and its members did not care that it was all downhill. Rather oddly, they cheered for its expedience. Former powerhouses such as Britain, Germany, and France seemed to be a mirror of the United States: mass migration, deindustrialization, homelessness, drug abuse, inflation. Entire cultures were being replaced by weaponized migration and the need for entitlements to care for the masses.

Next came more gun control. While he had whined incessantly in Connecticut, and had been a part of the former Assault Weapons Ban, Biden now had full power to restrict the second amendment. Not risking a total chaos ban because of the economy, restrictive gun laws took over, usually enforced by Democratic Sheriffs in districts held by strong police unions and local leftist judges. The National Rifle Association and the Gun Owners of America could only handle so many Constitutional lawsuits. Leftist media narratives echoed relentlessly.

Those in the middle class kept their mouths shut in order to retain their jobs and comfortable lives as they had the most to lose. If one were to speak up in the public square of Twitter, Facebook, or Instagram, more than likely the FBI, controlled also by the Left, would come knocking on the door to investigate the posts. The ATF would raid small gun store owners, fining them on minuscule paperwork errors, despite asking the ATF for guidance on the registrations.

Free speech came with a cost. Anonymous internet defamation was a daily occurrence. Tribal voices rendered alternate opinions or religious preferences into silence, and the middle class had the most to lose. Living week to week, paying college loans, and unable to afford high interest rates. To lose a middle income job became a death sentence.

Mom and Pop gun shops, existing for years in small towns, would go bankrupt from one lawsuit filed with the ATF-even if they won the case, and would likely drag out over multiple administrations. Bans on private sale and transfers, magazine restrictions, definitions of assault weapons, etc., were the initial holes in the dam. Banks could not loan to the firearm industry. Government restrictions hidden within legislation to deter cartel and terrorist sales penalized legitimate gun stores. Credit card processing services and business insurance were then regulated out of existence. The ATF began to keep gun registries of small gun stores that closed down due to minor violations that weren't really violations at all. The stores just couldn't afford attorneys to fight the ATF.

Private records required to be destroyed by the ATF had illegally been recorded for years without anyone's knowledge. All background check information, especially if done online, was on a server available to the NSA, FBI, and ATF. Artificial Intelligence was also weaponized against small shops, detecting errors in certifications, paperwork, or even IRS filings. Political targeting now had ammunition.

Despite clear language in the Constitution, each head of the ATF would enact frivolous policies that sank firearm and ammunition ownership. All sold to the American populous under the guise of safety backed by the powers of the Patriot Act. School shootings, terrorist activities, synagogue attacks, gay bar attacks-they could all be prevented if only guns were banned. This was *the solution.*

With current cultish control of the NIH, the Left magnified firearm studies to their stances, refusing to identify true problematic cities skewing data, racial disparities affecting mass shootings, and ignoring gun related incidents that saved victims. The left leaning Universities, funded by the left leaning NIH, whose directors mainly came from left leaning Ivy League schools, developed studies to promote left leaning ideology.

While retaining more money, by way of the Bayh-Dole Act, these studies could be profiteered, by giant corporations and patent development, which would further make profits by massive private venture capital companies, such as BlackRock and Vanguard, whose higher management were trained and developed from, once again, left leaning Ivy League schools. The circle was complete. The sheep had officially taken over the pen. If you could control the shepherd and the sheep dogs, the sheep could become quite gluttonous without outside regulations, or easier yet, unenforced regulations.

The age of firearm ownership went up from 18 to 21 in some states, yet the right to vote dropped to 15 in others. All while the NIH acknowledged that the human brain wasn't capable of adult decisions until the ages of 21 to drink alcohol. New regulated categories emerged, such as Assault pistols. Bump stocks were banned, and even pistol braces. Although completely legal according to the ATF years earlier, the devices were deemed in violation, so register your arm brace or be a felon. Many people who had purchased were unaware of what was even going on in the news or what was somehow now illegal, thus making ordinary citizens felons. The assault weapons ban of the past would have restarted under executive order during the second two years of Biden's presidency had he not lost the house of representatives. Trump's second term helped, but he had angered the swing states on his ICE roundups of illegals. The Left's Presidential candidate, Dutaja, easily proclaimed victory in 2028. Congress also went back to a Democrat super majority due to the mass migration and illegal alteration of voting machines..

New rules were being put forth in the wake of school shootings, and what were called mass shootings, defined as when more than three people were shot. Weapons were allowed to be owned for the current generation only. No weapons could be handed down to the next generation, only turned into local police for destruction at time of death. Pistols required a permit and the purchaser had to show a need to own. Background checks took up to six months to complete, and a fifty state mental background application was needed, and that burden was placed upon the buyer. Red Flag laws became ideologically enforced and caused massive delays. Accusations could be taken as truth until the accused could prove otherwise. Guilty until proven innocent was a belief the founding fathers had never intended.

Costs of firearm applications, $500. The poor need not apply. It was the idea that Mexico had long held. Guns were legal in Mexico, but there was only one gun store in Mexico City; and, you must have a need and the money to travel there to buy one. Only the government, and the cartels, could own firearms. One legally, the other illegally. Or what some said, both the cartel and Mexican government were in fact the same. Pay off the right people, or hold the right ideology, were the only methods to rapid and legal ownership.

Taxes on firearms were placed at 25%. Taxes to gun trusts began as transferring guns to family members became ancient history. Taxes on ammunition were similar, and citizens were required to have passed the same background check and requirements. There was an immediate ammunition registry.

While the NRA and Gun Owners of America fought for there to be no gun registry, the liberals found back door loopholes.

The headquarters of the ATF in West Virginia began to copy all gun store logs, and no longer destroyed old ones. Long standing rules were now ignored. Why fear breaking Constitutional rules if they were not going to be enforced? Much like immigration non enforcement, left leaning state governors and judges selectively decided what was to be enforced. There were no problems at an open border if blinders were placed on existing laws.

If bullets were reloaded, the primers needed to assemble the cartridge were taxed and regulated by the federal government, and strict documentation on the number of rounds and primers distributed were recorded at the private factory level, where any discrepancy would result in closure until investigation.

If a neighbor questioned your intentions, firearms were immediately confiscated under Red Flag laws, without promise of a timely return or trial, or even questioning the accusation of the neighbor-without penalty to the accuser. This strategy worked out well in gang neighborhoods, where police faked phone calls and complaints in order to search homes illegally without following Constitutionally protected search and seizure law. It was essentially a slow death roll to complete confiscation and registration. All branches and services within the federal system had been subverted and indoctrinated to believe this was necessary, just like a covid vaccine.

Trust the science. Trust the Ivies. Trust the solutions.

Anyone unwilling to lose their government entitlements, their steady jobs, and big houses, had to forfeit their guns. Why lose everything when there was no reason to use them the leftists advocated? The government would protect you. The middle and upper classes were not about to risk never seeing their families and children just keep a rifle and bullets in the home. Pick your battles. After all, "they", the government, have my best interests at heart. All the data from the NIH and FBI showed that guns were a problem-everywhere-not just in those big cities. The University professors are way smarter than "I'll ever be" thought most, caught up in their jobs, taxes, bills, evaluations, and paying the water bill every two weeks. The rationale of a second amendment became increasingly burdensome.

Division was in its prime everywhere because of these policies. Baseball games, churches, schools, colleges. Everyone had openly picked a side. Everyone had picked their tribe. Death could occur from wearing the wrong party hat. Former Trump supporters dared wearing his distinctive Red "Make America Great Again" hats, which might lead to a beat down at some Universities, who would not penalize the students for the assault, but rather celebrate them. Physical violence was to be accepted if the tribe deemed it necessary, just as Hitler's Brown Shirts had done.

Free speech was an afterthought, but falsely celebrated. Everyone would have a voice. Those who had suffered in silence for so long, he said, could now come out and celebrate their freedoms once again. The citizens would no longer have to live in fear of mass shootings. In truth, only the left would retain free speech. Political targeting against those who spoke out increased. What Americans had seen happen in Europe was now acceptable here.

There was only one issue they had failed to consider. Criminals don't turn in or register guns. Crime ticked up in the blue states as criminals were no longer arrested, and citizens were not able to defend themselves. Liberal policies, like Diversity Equity and Inclusion, developed through the Ivy League Universities, were causing mass chaos in underprivileged areas. Political reform at all levels of the elections, benefited the rapists, thieves, and felons rather than the civilized law abiding citizens. Bail was not necessary in some states, and since criminals knew the low risks of committing crime, began to commit more crimes. The border was reopened. Border patrol ceased to exist.

Small businesses closures, tent encampments, rapes, assaults-all went uncharged or un prosecuted by Left leaning judges. It was almost as if there was a bigger plan, often disputed as a conspiracy theory, that the Left was attempting to cause a massive collapse through high crime, weaponized immigration, and judicial process. To venture a comment or voice an opinion otherwise was risking civil forfeiture. Some had mentioned the Podesta Plan from 2020 as the culprit.

What could be the motivation of such a plan? And who on earth would ever want to see policies such as these come to fruition? The press, government agencies, and world leaders laughed at such a delusional conception, calling any reference to combined events conspiracy theory. Of course, gaslighting was also clearly labeled in the plan's notes:

"All we want is what everyone in the world wants. Safety for our families. Shelter, food, and clean water for all. With the right of each citizen to pursue happiness in life and employment. To not want the same for another human is racist and xenophobic."

During all of the division, the climate continued its natural change. New York and New Jersey suffered the largest hurricane in their history. Pushing inland as far as Buffalo and the Great Lakes. Mt. Washington in Northern New Hampshire experienced a new record wind chill of -108 degrees in February of 2023. Hurricanes doubled in strength and number from 2023 to 2024. This has happened in Earth's history, but not at this pace. One could graphically show millions of years of climate change, but one could not argue the up slope of this century. Weather patterns affected U.S. farmers heavily over the next three years.

Fertilizer overuse and lack of crop diversity led to soil degradation and mineral depletion for most commercialized farms. Only those using regenerative soil techniques were unaffected. And yet, these small farms were constantly being sued by large seed companies like Monsanto, claiming that farmers had illegally used their seed or fertilizer technologies. Once these farmers went bankrupt from lawsuits, giant wealth companies like BlackRock and Vanguard, or even worse, foreign owned corporations, would swoop in to buy up the land. The two largest pork companies in the United States were now in the hands of Brazil and Chinese owned corporations. It was archaic and dangerous to be an American farmer. Americans could no longer guarantee the safety of their foods or where they were sourced.

Insurance payouts were far greater than expected due to weather damage, and insurance rates went too high for most small farms. No farmers had prepared for this type of damage, as most existed from year to year, and the United States failed to recognize the need for national food reliance. The war in Ukraine had also disrupted one of the largest producers of nitrogenous fertilizers for Europe's food supply. Fertilizer and grain prices surged, as Russia became the biggest supplier of fertilizer in the world, preferring to feed China over the West.

New York, already bankrupt from migrant entitlement programs and coronavirus payouts, suffered the worst. California, one of the largest suppliers of produce for the United States, and the world, was out of water. As were most of the Western states that depended on large, slow, snow melts to restock reservoirs in Arizona, Nevada, Arizona, and New Mexico. The large water pipes supplying Colorado's eastern farms were also at record lows due to limited snow melts. The fight for water was on and even being discussed as a globally taxed commodity on the world stage. Water would become the next currency.

Larger hurricanes hit Florida and the Louisiana coasts causing devastating damages. Home insurance companies that provided hurricane and wind mitigation insurance dissolved, putting the only available insurance on the back of the federal government. Be it farm regulations, lawsuits, soil, weather, insurance-one thing was evident-a greater need of the citizen on the federal government, and a penalty to those trying to maintain self-reliance. Division and chaos solutions could only be attained by accepting a new world order of compliance.

Many companies were unwilling to insure future construction without triple the prior insurance rates, particularly related to the Russian invasion of Ukraine. Tanker ships across the world's oceans were being required to pay double or triple on piracy insurance as the United States started stepping away from protecting the world's oceans, further adding to the inflationary costs of hard to get goods. Small regional terrorist groups, such as the Iranian backed Houthi rebels, exerted massive disruption over an area at very little cost, supported by regional politics of Leftist leaning Universities and politicians who loved another country over their own. Further thought was needed on shooting a one million dollar rocket at a terrorist carrying a one hundred dollar AK-47. No country could keep up that level of spending.

Businesses either failed, or began moving out of the states of California and New York, to avoid high taxes and employee wages, only further increasing entitlements to those out of work, or to those remaining, being taxed to pay for entitlements. Lack of fresh food, clean water, and affordable shelter only worsened the crime ridden areas, the largest in the United States, that were so ineffectively studied and managed by a continuous voter supply of their leftist cult tribe.

California's policy failures and overspending were a model for most countries around the world. California faced the worst drought in its history in 2021. Snowfall to the Sierra Nevada mountains was at a record low. Rivers in Northern California were closed. Irrigation channels locked. Farmers had no water to grow crops. In the year 2026, Los Angeles was hit with another earthquake. While long overdue, the bankrupt state was still ill prepared. No money was saved in emergency accounts as it had all been used up on immigrants or interest payments. Governor Gavin Newsom once had record savings in California's coffers, but only a year later was completely upside down financially.

One of the world's most important shipping lanes, the Panama Canal, had so little water in 2023 that it could only allow a limited number of boats to cross per day. So severe the time frame to crossing, ships were going completely around the tip of South America, or worse, not transporting at all. New routes across Nicaragua and trains through Mexico were being explored as future options as some deep water ports were no longer able to exist. Banks were licking their lips at the possibility of issuing bonds and private loans. The Rothschild lineage was making record deposits.

Technology and possible terroristic threats also endangered American ports. The Francis Scott Key Bridge collapsed in Baltimore in 2024 highlighting two key possibilities of failure: lack of care to aged American infrastructure and possible Russian linked ship navigation capture. Both of which a Left leaning government wished not to discuss, other than the need to tax more for aging infrastructure upkeep, and give more money to helping Ukraine defeat the Russians, or Israel to clear Palestine. How financing one helps the other was unexplained, but these were the offered solutions..

Insurance companies played the same games as had been done in New York. Raising rates, and dropping high risk clientele. California, much like New York, was already deep in bankruptcy because of its heavily entitled state programs for the growing immigrant population. Increase the immigration, increase the number of house seats, and increase the voting populous, as California was making it legal for illegal immigrants to vote. No identification necessary at the polls, and mail in ballots remaining an option. Even voting by phone was under discussion.

Many in California couldn't rebuild, couldn't borrow, and couldn't escape the state to where the jobs had gone. With no water sources behind dam walls, reliable electricity was stopped, unreliable, or too expensive at peak times for production. Then came the mysterious fires. Lack of clearing forest debris sped up the destruction caused by the raging infernos. The lack of clearing related to budgets or species protection. The rich and middle class suffered the most as they watched venture capital buy up destroyed land and homes to build affordable rental housing for the ever expanding homeless and immigrant population.

Suddenly, states were also fighting to end property taxes, such as Florida and Texas, so that large venture capital rental corporations could save on their long term investments. Not once prior had these companies cared about property tax. Environmentalists refused the best option-nuclear, as it would hurt oil sales. Water was at all time lows and hydroelectricity unreliable. Fires were at all time highs leading to further destruction of homes and businesses that could hardly afford even higher insurance rates. Every industry was facing a circle of crisis.

In 2024, State Farm, Allstate, Hartford, Merastar, Unitrin, and Kemper insurance companies announced they would not renew home owner's insurance policies for high fire risk areas in California. So where would these Californians turn? Much like their hurricane counterparts, the Federal government would soon be the only option. Big brother is there to help of course. To provide the solution. The only solution.

The only entity to benefit were banks. Banks won with more takes on defaulted property, and issuing more loans to rebuild and borrow. Gaining interest on bankrupt insurance companies or interest on holdings of bankrupt companies. Managing venture capital. Providing high interest loans to the poor. Like lawyers, as long as the bank was involved, no matter the beliefs of either side, it could make money. Money needed not exist to loan, as a bank could simply create dollars on paper. There was no gold backing to the paper printed. Governments of the world knew that banks were a Ponzi scheme, and yet, allowed them to carry on.

The Fed printed more and more money. And the new President increased interest rates. Another Great Recession took place, except way bigger than 2008. With all of the division occurring in the United States, the Chinese began to worry about their investments. Americans didn't have money to buy merchandise; and therefore, the Chinese had no market to sell their products. China depended on the Wal Marts of America as a place to distribute what they made for pennies. Americans were broke and not spending, most dependent on some form of government assistance. America was not in the manufacturing business, but the service industry business. China's new middle class was becoming used to life's conveniences, and the Chinese government had to make this new segment of its population happy. China did what the United States had never fathomed-called in its debts through gold. Russia had converted rubles to gold for years, and Germany had called in all of their US gold deposits prior to 2020. But China held a stake in almost all aspects of the US economy. The new BRIC countries of Brazil, Russia, India, and China were taking over most global consumption and were already responsible for the most global production. US dollars not backed by a gold standard, printed endlessly, would be worthless over time. There would never be an audit of Fort Knox's gold reserves as Trump had promised. The BRIC countries knew this.

China held over $2 trillion of US government debt, around 25% of total US debt. Calling out the President's administration, China sold off tons of US. treasury bonds. The supply of US bonds escalated exponentially as they had during the coronavirus bond reform. This led to an immediate increase in interest rates, on top of the already steady Biden increases.

Consumers were unable to borrow, and neither could struggling businesses. Equities crashed. Yields rose. An entire economy came to a standstill. This great sell off of bonds caused other countries to panic.

Japan was next in line to dump their bonds. The land of the rising sun owned about $1.25 trillion in treasury bonds. While they had wanted to keep the Yen low to help exports, the future investments for their country could no longer ride on the USD. With their nonexistent population replacement, their production was dependent on United States factories. Safety and the rule of law were fading within the US. The Chinese could sense a division occurring politically. A division that they had sponsored on many levels: research grants at Universities, corporate espionage, patent infringement, and corrupt bribery. Future securities markets might not be so stable with no rule of law. The Chinese held a long term view of supporting the New World Order in flooding the United States with immigrants, creating the new home of cheap labor.

Combined with the new Entitlement taxes from the Biden presidency, a new depression would finally hit the greedy Americans. With no currency worth value, no production capacity, and the only export being cheap energy, the United States would be forced to come to the global table as the world had been forced to do at Bretton Woods in July of 1944.

To make matters worse, China had prepared for the US dollar to decline in value even more after the pandemic hit the world. A drop in the dollar would have helped the US. become attractive in the export of goods, but this declining dollar fell to another move-the Chinese devalued their own currency intentionally. They had thought ahead.

While being accused of devaluation in 2019, it mattered not to a global economy ignoring anything China wanted to achieve. The American banks, with locations around the world, were very familiar with the Chinese devaluation of their own currencies, and knew that the American government would be forced into more loans and more debts, and thus more bank profits. Having locations around the world enabled banks to shift currencies and losses to other regions, hiding loss and taxes, all while profiting on both sides. The George Soros's of the world continued to short existing banks and currencies.

A chain of events occurred over a six month period. The predictable being first.

The Yuan was tied to the dollar's value, so the dollar's drop just decreased the Yuan. Exports still flowed cheaply out of China without any losses. Microchips became in short supply from the Taiwan-China conflict, as well as from the covid virus's impact. The South China Sea dominant Navy of the United States was non-existent due to Trump's policy decision to not patrol the world.

The war in Ukraine was also taking a toll on the minerals used to make micro chips as the region was ripe in rare earth minerals. Ukraine shortages of fertilizer and over farming caused food shortages. All costs went up for everyday living and survival, while supplies of expensive defense department needed items like microchips and rare earth minerals were depleted. The Earth had become smaller in terms of travel, but it had become a burden in single state manufacturing. To produce something as sophisticated as a car or rocket demanded goods from hundreds of areas. Most of which were now owned or managed by China.

Although the US had been China's biggest consumer, China now felt the increase in middle class purchases throughout Asia, and the regrowth of the Indian and African economies enough to balance out the loss of profits from the US At worst, they would break even, suffer some loss, but gain in being ahead in the global market emerging in their own neck of the woods. The exorbitant privilege some had made about the USD were now at the beckon call of the exorbitant burden crowd. Many investors were actually happy, thinking that maybe the US could compete globally again now that the dollar had taken a fall, and that fall would lead to a decrease in unemployment as labor prices in the US became globally competitive again.

The Chinese leveraged their losses, and what everyone had always feared became fact. The US dollar became no longer the world's major reserve currency. China declared the Yuan the new world currency, and that they would discount all initial trades, and cover all losses to countries willing to make the change immediately. Germany, Japan, Brazil, India, Russia, and pretty much any country with assets jumped on board to create a bond market those countries could use to exchange against US. treasuries. Much like the start of WWI, when the Austro-Hungarian Krong ruled the world, a shift in global finance occurred. Who was once dominant financially around the globe, was now replaced, primarily the United States.

Adding more to this issue, China had come up with its own digital crypto currency similar to Bitcoin and Dogecoin-the Digital Yuan. Even the risk averse chose to go with the Chinese crypto currency. Since the Chinese owned most of the mass manufacturing, this Chinese backed coin seemed to provide the most stability. The Chinese digital currency also voids the anonymity of user's, one of Bitcoin's biggest strengths. User's could now be identified, followed, or taxed, which also allowed China to continue its social credit scoring methods. If an individual or corporation was not in compliance, the coin or property of those in violation could be harvested.

This one privacy issue had prevented its creation in the United States.

China also detached the Digital Yuan from the global system, unlike the dollar. Making those who use it even more dependent on China's stability. And since the Chinese were the largest miners of Bitcoin, they no longer had to waste enormous amounts of time and raw energy mining Bitcoin. Long suspecting that Bitcoin had CIA involvement, the Chinese beat the US intelligence agencies at their own game, providing a controllable, identifiable crypto currency. 60% of all global reserves were held in the USD, with the Euro close behind with 35%. From 2002-2012, the US debt tripled from $6 trillion to $15 trillion. From 2012-2021, the debt quadrupled-from $15 trillion to $60 trillion dollars. Unsustainable, especially with the entitlements required across America from weaponized migration. When China's AI defeated

Bitcoin encryption, all was lost.

Instead of the broad entitlements going into effect, the policies started under Biden would lead the country into a divisive, civil war like depression. The dollar was worth less than a roll of toilet paper. 401k and 403b plans were worthless. Pensions worthless. Only those with gold and silver in large quantities, with a means of getting it out of the US, would be able to liquidate their assets. The new global currency, part Chinese, part European Union, part BRICS, was appropriately dubbed the Yeuro, and officially replaced the dollar in 2028. Followed close behind in the black markets, the collapse of Bitcoin and other anonymous global payment options, replaced by Chinese crypto.

The US central bank collapsed. A run on US banks occurred, but was way too late for any average middle class citizen. Only tangible assets and vocational skills were of any value.

Division increased, a notch was created.

Competition for food was existent. Violence increased in blue states where incivility reigned even before the collapse, and still the banks were calling in on nonpayment. Being that they were in multiple countries and could manipulate different currencies, the banks were making money and could care less what it was called or who backed it. Demands were made by banks to Americans to make their house payments despite unavailability of unemployment assistance. Miss the payment, and the bank took back the mortgage which was then sold to a foreign investment company, likely Chinese or Indian owned, or to BlackRock or Blackstone.   World banks easily converted currency for their own profits before normal citizens could understand what was happening to their bank account's value. The banks could shift a little Yin, a lotta Yang. One country's up is another's down. And why would any bank want to pay high taxes? The ability to convert currencies through other branch transfers insured the banks lost little, rolling money across digital assets and giving out cheap loans now to China instead of the United States.

Densely populated US cities were the first to revolt. Those used to free food, shelter, and just about any other necessity took to the streets. Richer nations revolting suffered more than the countries already used to doing without. The poorer countries of South America and Africa hardly noticed changes socially, other than more Chinese projects starting in their neighborhoods.

Obama. Trump. Biden. Trump. Dutaja. They were one and the same. Blue. Red. Blue. Red.

Blue. Purple was the official color of Washington D.C.

Until the virus came, the US did not have the perfect divisive reaction. Then with two established narratives, citizens were all divided. Blue narrative, red narrative. White, colored.

Left tribe, right tribe. Rich versus the poor. Haves and Have nots. America versus the World. Literally, no one could come within six feet of each other. Policy division became actual physical division. Mandatory stay at home orders issued. In the end of Obama's presidency, during the fear of the SARS pandemic, Obama had signed off on the ability of the President to better control US citizens should a health threat appear within the United States. What was usually the responsibility of the state governors was now within the hands of the Executive office.

Obama wrote the law, Trump flirted with it, Biden perfected it, Trump initiated it, and Dutaja made it permanent. Broke, divided, and simmering, order would be needed to stifle the growing masses of discontent, but humans really hate having their freedoms stifled. Only a few had ever fought to protect those freedoms, and it took only a few to try and take them all away. Bostonians had once fought over an increase of 2% on tea. What might they fight over for an increased tax of 70% that possibly would go to an illegal immigrant, a foreign industrial profited war, a homeless Mexican drug cartel policy, a Hamas supporting American hating University student, another NIH backed BlackRock pharmaceutical study?

EZ had witnessed these sequence of events, and yet the citizens had yet to fight in a Civil War. Whatever the case, division was decisive. EZ and UUONE were creating division outside the limitations of the Israeli government. Performing tasks that their country could not ever be caught doing. UUONE was the USAID version of the CIA, except through theft ignored by its own intelligence agencies. It did not need government funding. Nothing would ever show up in the accounting. What showed up was the growth of Israel's interests, and its power to influence around the world. Blackmail by the Mossad was one thing, but off the books, continual illegal actions with secret abilities was another gambit altogether. Israel did not care if their new alliances were not in America. What mattered was the homeland's existence.

UUONE could be selective. They could leave the propaganda to regular Israeli intelligence, state backed special missions to Mossad, and political discourse to groups like AIPAC in the United States. They did not exist in the public's eye, and if Mossad was thought to be the pinnacle of Israeli intelligence, deniability if ever caught would be labeled as an independent terrorist cell.

It was taking time, but expediency was now needed under the current US decline. With the help of some Israeli billionaires, this time was shortened as many US media companies were purchased in the year 2025. The Chinese platform TikTok would now be managed by a mostly Israeli board, and that board decided to change the algorithm to focus only on Israeli messaging, both positive and negative, depending on the consumer. With the approval of US. politicians, this deal would be labeled as a positive outcome for the children in the United States since the algorithm would no longer be under the objectives of Communist China. What EZ knew was that this was the largest online propaganda tool the world had ever seen.

The purchase in 2025 of one of the "big three" US media corporations, CBS, would help in the same way. Jewish and Israeli executives could now steer the narrative, legally and politically, over the US airwaves. The shift in Israeli public opinion had taken a decline after the Gaza invasion. All polls internationally were showing this sharp decrease, so a decision was made rapidly to purchase existing platforms, whatever the cost, to regain control. Cell phone video and social media's global availability had changed Israeli strategy exponentially.

For EZ, he knew the division would grow faster now. With it, Israel had been able to commit genocide in Gaza. Israel wanted, needed, increased hatred through its actions. The destabilization within the United States, complete division, would turn the focus away from Israel's next objectives. The Jewish state could partner with China as easily as it could the West. America needed to be torn down and rebuilt, just as Gaza had. The counter narratives were becoming too strong. The United States was there to serve the interests of Israel, not vice versa. Only through the creation of Israel did the United States witness its exponential growth. Those productive years had passed. It was time to source from elsewhere.

His anthrax attack was to be the fire starter of the next American revolution. He had helped direct Zionist objectives through six different Presidents. UUONE and the CIA did not care who was in power. Only the long term financial commitments mattered, and the US had run its course. It would be remodeled into a useful extension of Israel's needs. Laws would be passed to arrest those who spoke out against Judaism, just as they had done in Europe, under the guise of hate crimes, and he now had a special tool to instill hate. For those UUONE needed to be placed in jail, those that didn't support Israel, their new tool would be very effective. Soon, the voices of resistance would be locked up by their fellow citizens. Willingly. And all that would remain, would be a society of Zionist supporters, backed with nuclear weapons. Eager to vote in support of Israeli causes. The takeover of something as small as Gaza was irrelevant. The real goal had been the United States the entire time. NanEmo's power would influence the Chinese just as easily as the Americans. UUONE existed only for the Chosen. He knew what was about to occur in the world. It would take time. And like the Chinese, UUONE had patience. This was the bigger picture for creating division. This was the Why.

<u>Gun Club Meeting</u>

"How are we going to know if the people responsible for these balloon attacks are located in our area? How are we going to be able to tell if we have been infiltrated? Could they be members of our club?"

Kyle was always the paranoid one, but he was correct in being cautious. While serving in Vietnam, he had been exposed to Agent Orange multiple times, infiltrated Cambodia illegally, and witnessed the murder of an entire village. Of course, all his superiors denied any knowledge of said events, as did the United States government. No one could say he was ever wrong, but his facts were filled with a history of salty truths. Kyle was the paradigm of paranoia. He loved his country, but he knew his country could lie to achieve an objective.

He provided gun theory to those who cared to listen, and if you listened long enough, Kyle provided some extensive political theory. Living through the mistakes of the Tea Party, he had seen a plethora of right wing idiots. Full of nuts and vigor, extreme Righties were always showing up at rallies, but he always knew they would never last in a real end of the world scenario. Second amendment rally figures were important, so they tolerated their bullshit at the Gun Club. Everyone could be used for something.

Righty extremists were equally batty and as delusional as the Occupy movement or the latest hipster phase, Antifa, who didn't have shit on the hippies of the Sixties. The Tea Party was starting to suffer at the hands of the media who continued to spout racism at any given opportunity. Outlets like the Southern Poverty Law Center, whose job it was to tell people who to hate, had an agenda of its own, but rarely did people question their facts. The Tea Party could erase world poverty and still be labeled as racists by the Libmerica. It had easily been proven that the Obama administration, through Lois Lerner, targeted Conservative businesses through the IRS, many of which were affiliated with the Tea Party, and no one served an ounce of jail time. The press helped cover up the entire endeavor as well.

"As far as I know, you are the feds Fucknut, so settle down," I told him.

"We will never know if someone is a terrorist or not. Assume that I am. That your neighbor is, that your wife is, and especially that any new people at this club are. It's the same for any motorcycle gang. Except we can't make them snort meth or murder someone to earn a patch." I was not in the mood for

Kyle's paranoia.

He was becoming increasingly paranoid. Most gun clubs across the country and Canada were experiencing the same. Six months earlier, two terrorist attacks near Montreal, a short 2.5 hour drive away, had provoked a weak American President into enacting the old theory of the Democrats, "Never Let a Tragedy Go to Waste".

Much like the testing of Constitutional freedoms during the Covid 19 pandemic, a full Democratic Congress and Senate were eager to come to the aid of their Canadian neighbors in the search for "safety". Guns, search and seizure, red flag laws, freedom of speech, freedom of the press-any freedom was coming to the forefront of abandonment. *A new European style government was needed*, they said, *to protect the people.* Gun collectors, gun clubs, and Right leaning registered voters were high on the suspect list.

The La Ronde terrorist attack had occurred on a packed summer day with maximum attendance at the Six Flag's owned park. Deaths had occurred slowly over the next couple of days after the attack, and similarly, the nearby balloon festival in Saint-Jean-sur-Richelieu had produced similar illnesses. Anthrax had tested positive in all of the victims.

Hospitals had been overwhelmed and stood no chance of taking care of the thousands of people showing up. My tiny hospital in New Hampshire had even taken on overflow for treatment.

Any hospital within two hundred miles had done the same.

The Canadian government had no choice but to be honest about the terrorist attacks. Anthrax had been the method and drones the mode of deployment. No suspects had been caught. Since two locations had been hit, there were thought to be multiple suspects.

No information had been discovered on the La Ronde terrorists. Over 30,000 people had died, and many more were on ventilators and soon to be dead. Some were permanently disabled for life. 350,000 people were affected. Projected deaths were over 150,000. Cleanup was said to be impossible at the current time due to manpower and the enormous costs of cleaning up anthrax. The World Health Organization was debating what to do for Montreal as winds dispersed the spores and containment was impossible. Canada was heart broken, and action was demanded by the Canadian people. Those responsible were going to suffer.

"But if we let people into this club, into our *ideas*, then we can't keep our bug out ideas a secret anymore. And once the ATF, NSA, FBI, BLM, or any other three letter word- finds out how well prepared Northern New Hampshire is for their shenanigans, we are screwed. We have all types of unregistered guns and suppressors here."

Kyle was drunk, and he was awesome at drunk. His drinking had seemed to pick up with all the talk of the new government interventions. Alcohol did not help with paranoia. It was only second to his weed use..

"It really doesn't matter who knows. Our club does nothing illegal. *Technically.* We peacefully protest, train for end of the world scenarios, and make phone calls to congressional members. Who has what at their homes is on them, and subject to Fourth Amendment laws. Other than raising money for the local school projects, they can't even nail us through their ultimate evil minion, the IRS. The IRS has already targeted the Tea Party once, so we know as a gun club with a nonprofit status, we are sometimes on the radar. If you call sponsoring the local high school's trap shooting team illegal then we are in big trouble, but I'm sure the Libtard Anti-second Amendment types would call our hunter safety program for seventh graders evil propaganda. I don't want the Feds around here." Kyle wasn't letting up.

He sensed the people around him getting excited by someone willing to speak up. Many were fearful to do so in public because the press and government agencies would arrest, investigate, or confiscate. The new Antigun "Red Flag" laws could label anyone a possible "threat" to society and the confiscation process would begin. The Feds were now using new Israeli AI software to monitor threats across individual's entire online content. Nearly the entire gun world was on forums, Instagram, or Facebook, and with FBI informants posing as experts on topics, a list of bad apples was growing daily.

There was no due process or return of your personal property if confiscated. Red flag laws were the new feel good gun legislation. Even the Army was on board, taking away soldier's personal guns and trying to ban the purchase of firearms without a waiting period to prevent astronomical trans youth suicides and mass shootings. Add to this the largest terror attack in world history, and no one was safe from inspection.

Comments online could now even result in termination at your job. Labor bought property and goods. And labor was what this was all about. Who had a right to your labor? Could belonging to one political party determine your ability to work? The United States was out of the top ten most free countries globally and dropping faster every year. Surveillance, Palantir integration of all government systems and banks, and NSA listening devices made everyone paranoid. Guns were a second amendment protected property, bought from free labor, but it was now up to the government to decide who could work. If you held right leaning views and posted right leaning content, you may soon have no goods or property to purchase with no future job to take. Kyle listened to nothing I had to say. I knew he was right. If any three letter agency infringed into our gun club, they would find a handful of wackos to bust and make the rest of us appear as equals. If worse came to worse, they would install a few hundred child porn images onto phones and computers to make arrests. They were certainly not above doing so. The FBI's rush to catch suspects was on.

We even had some federal agents in our club. O'Reilly, as a border patrol agent, had inside knowledge on all the events ICE or the FBI were planning north of us. Keith had land, survival skills, tracking dogs, and access to the town's communications and backdoor channels. Willis, a former ATF agent, had land, land, and more land that was handed down for three generations bordering the White Mountain National Forest. Without his vast swath of land outside of Columbia, NH, we would have nowhere to train and run field exercises. He had grown to hate his former agency. Being outspoken about their actions violating protected rights had placed him under federal watch as well.

And the most important person of all in our club was EZ, an undercover Federal agent in

Canada . EZ had lots of money. Where he got it from, we did not ask. I had never even met him. He insisted on being off the radar. No attendance recorded at meetings, no records of phone calls or conversations, and he had good reasons for all of this.

Anyone with his Canadian credentials and beliefs would come under fire in leftist, antigun Canada. They would be sure to monitor his online accounts, put him under federal investigation, or entrap him at the hands of Presidential directives as a "threat to the state's interests". Canadians weren't supposed to have guns. He crossed the border regularly at O'Reilly's border crossing to maintain his gun rights and establish roots in case the shit hit the fan in Canada. Rarely did you find self made millionaires with similar interests and a deep down belief that the world was being flushed down the proverbial toilet.

EZ wished to remain an anonymous donor. Only two of us knew his Canadian citizenry, and he preferred it that way. We kept his secrets as long as he kept his pocketbook open. We were fine with providing him a new home should Canada go completely south. Billionaires around the world were buying old nuclear silos and turning them into underground survival bunkers, moving to New Zealand, or buying yachts for their family's escape plans. If I were in EZ's situation and had his money, I'd likely do the same thing.

With four houses in different areas of the country, EZ had befriended local militias, state legislators, and anyone that could help his family in a time of trouble. He was my front to power in the club. Many thought it was my money buying a lot of the supplies, but I kept my mouth shut. He had provided cash and asked for no receipts. He supported what we were doing and the cost to initiate political goals. To have someone with that kind of money on our side was a rarity, and if all he asked for in return was anonymity, so be it. If politicians could do it, why couldn't we?

EZ knew my one condition was that for my hard work, my family was his family. If something happened to me, then he was responsible for their well being. He was comfortable with that arrangement. He knew that I was smart, hard working, well researched, and would try my damndest to figure out a plan A, B, and C. If C didn't work, it wasn't for lack of trying, and I would go down with the ship. I had no intention of revealing the Canadian's origins.

Remaining anonymous for EZ wasn't fun for him. He wasn't

ashamed of his beliefs, but he had to keep his image away from the club, or there would be no club. Away from the couple of wackos that Kyle was talking about, and Wackos were what the Tri-letters were looking for. I didn't plan to be on their lists although I suspected I already was.

As an Army Reserve Officer, I had passed my background checks with ease. It was normal for police, military, and other law enforcement to belong to gun clubs, so that we could train on our weapons for qualification.   I may still be on Janet Reno's returning Veteran of Wars terrorist list, but no one believed her anymore. The use of drones to spray the anthrax would now put prior military on all watch lists however. I only knew of two people with that level of training.

"All I'm saying is that we have some kind of vetting process. Even if it's Google, Yahoo, Facebook, or paying a private investigator to do a background check. I know the Feds could set up a fake background, but with Facebook and everything else online, it's becoming harder for the Feds to fake someone's past. Even a credit history might slip their minds. If someone says they're an Army vet, let's ask them simple Army questions. Jargon. Rank questions. Unit personnel and commanders, service times, medals, etc. Easily verifiable. Then we can contact those people and see if they can verify our new members." Kyle offered.

"I completely agree with Kyle. Do what we can, when we can. We can create a committee to examine each application. Then put everyone on a probationary period. See how they vet out over time. What questions they ask, what job they are doing in the community. It costs a lot of money to fund undercover agents, and we aren't exactly big time, and if the agent isn't pulling in much intel over the period of a year, then a Tri-letter will pull them back in.

"We also need to form a biannual meeting with other clubs in the state. From this meeting, we can bring in photographs of possible agents, terrorists, or questionable people trying to establish club ties. Then share these links with each state's Presidential committee member. We'll start meeting once a year in a surprise location. If these agents aren't successful in our state, then they will be sent to another state, and maybe we can make it a little harder on them.

"There are only so many agents, and so many fake backgrounds, and so much money that can be generated. Kyle you have to remember how sloppy they were with the Fast and Furious scandal? With the Democrats controlling the White House, they will fund every department and make any executive order to eliminate what they perceive to be a threat to their political machine. O'Reilly and Willis have told you about this. He will tell you more when he comes back."

Kyle started to settle down. He was the squeaky wheel. Getting greased. That's all he wanted to see happening. He had worked hard after returning from Nam in the same field as me-Nurse Anesthesia. Half of his retirement in his measly 403b plan at the hospital had vanished in the imaginary computer universe in 2008. The same 2008 that resulted in many bankers retiring with millions, but not a single one serving a day in jail. His house was now worth half of what he had bought it for in 1998, and with all of the industry, plants, and jobs leaving the state, there was not a chance he would ever see a net gain in his lifetime. Maybe not even in his kid's lifetime. Throw in local school and property taxes and a house was a losing proposition after the Barry Sotoero double term. No jobs, no people spending. Just entitlement programs paid for by printing more fake money.

"As long as you keep this between me and you," he said, "I

don't want to look like the squeaky wheel getting greased all the time." *Bingo*.

"But, I trust you in getting this done. We've been through a lot together. I don't have much left to offer except a ton of guns, ammo, and experience. But you know I'm always here for the benefit of the group. For the benefit of the only family I have left. Now let's get out there to the rest of the guy's and call this meeting to order." I stood and walked away from Kyle having heard enough.

We left the back office at the Club and proceeded into the main room. The club was a collection of not only members, but of construction projects. Ceiling tiles from the '80s, floor tiles and white wood paneling from the '70s. The kitchen area even had a stove and coffee pot that had to be from the '50s. The only thing new were the tables and chairs which had been made for us by the high school shop class as a thank you for letting them shoot and handle one of our members automatic, vintage machine guns. There was no air conditioning, an old wood stove provided heat for those brave enough to shoot in the winter months. Major components like electrical wiring and plumbing were all exceptional because we had a lot of members in various trade professions. We just didn't have any money for fancy fluff and stuff.

"All rise and face the flag!", I said.

"I Pledge Allegiance, to the Flag, of the United States of America, and to the Republic for which it stand's, one nation, under God, indivisible, with liberty and justice for all."

"You may be seated."

All turned away from a US flag that had flown during Operation Viking Hammer, high over the mountain base at Halabja, Iraq. A town where freedom was never to be forgotten. Especially not from this large group, half of which were prior military. The same Vets who were put on a Homeland security watch list by Attorney General Janet Reno at the direction of Obama. Some of us understood that treason was occurring at the federal level, but we still would recite a pledge and defend the Republic. All had taken that oath.. It had just been banned within our local school district, and all flags were removed from campus buildings at our local college. Offensive to the left was the charge. Only Pride and Israeli flags were allowed in certain California school districts. There was to be a fight if that was going to happen in New Hampshire, and the terror attacks were making the fight as a Libertarian much harder.

"Let this meeting come to order. Because there are such a large number of you here, I am going to run this meeting a little out of order. Does anyone have questions about last month's minutes, the budget, or have any items of old business they want to address?"

"Secretary, can I please see the attendance records for tonight?"

I scanned the role. There were only two names missing. Two people who had not missed a meeting since the club's inception. Two founding members of the club. I handed the notes back to the secretary and continued on. It was clear to me now.

"Let us get right to the meat and potatoes of this meeting tonight ladies and gentlemen. We have three topics to cover. One being our new member policy, the second being our statement regarding the ongoing controversy in Concord related to Canada, and third, the fact we have terrorists embedded within our ranks."

After some gasps, you could have heard a pin drop. I saw Kyle look up at me in complete shock. He had been worried about the FBI or ATF, and now I was mentioning terrorists. He had a right to be shocked.

I couldn't understand why I had not seen it earlier. I realized I had been played the whole time. The question was why. Why had they involved all of these innocent people? Why had they involved so many great patriotic Canadians and Americans?

They were the only two people I knew that had balloons and drones. The Canadians would not be aware of that yet, but there was no doubt in my mind. The Army had always said "Trust no one." Big Green was right again. There had been terrorists in our ranks. I was going to find out a few answers for myself before the Feds really did show up. The greatest anger comes from being mad at your own mistakes.

Two people hadn't been at the gun club since the attacks. O'Reilly and Willis, and one person that I had never met in person, EZ, hadn't called me since their disappearances. He had to be involved as well.

EZ had set the club up to take the fall for this tragedy. There would be illegal transfers, unaccounted cash purchases, and more. We would be patsies for the largest disaster on the continent. Two of our members would be involved at a minimum, and what usually would have featured EZ as an undercover FBI agent setting up an illegal gun sting, would be something much worse, a foreign operative.

"Let's find out tonight who has been working with Willis and O'Reilly? And I'll say his name now, EZ. I bet some of you have seen or heard this name. We've all been set up, and if we don't come up with a plan tonight, we will all soon be arrested."

The Libertarian principals that we stood for had been shattered through violence. With the level of Canadian response, I knew the worst restrictions would come from my own government, and I wouldn't even know who this wealthy supporter was or how he made his money. I had put my trust in others. I should have known better.

And if EZ wasn't with the FBI, ATF, or Canadian authorities, just who was he working for? The Russians, Arabs, Chinese? At this point, I may never know.

I slowly approached the first table, withdrew my CZ 75 Shadow 2 Compact 9 mm from its open carry position, cocked its hammer, and stared into the eyes of the first person I would interview.

These were prior military folks in the room. They would gladly kill a terrorist. "So, as I said, have you ever heard of a man named EZ?"

Death Tolls

O'Reilly and EZ had unloaded their second matching balloon into the nearby field. He called the staff at the festival and blamed poor winds and a bad burner on his drifting off course. They returned him to his truck and trailer, so that he could return to load it for his trip back to Vermont. Showing embarrassment, he left without saying his usual goodbyes. The experienced balloon baggers, understanding his errors and offering assistance, departed without questions. Willis was sent a location and drove out to help him load the truck. EZ had hired a driver, unaware of the truck's contents, to deliver the trailer and balloon back across the border. EZ wanted no suspicion placed on his operatives for as long as possible. Eventually, the border patrol would catch on to their attack. Better to get the balloon back into the United States.

Anyone flying a balloon that day would soon be questioned.

Willis and O'Reilly had then boarded EZ's boat, the King Saul, and began their journey back to

Vermont. It would give them time to decompress. Fishing poles were placed on the boat, and EZ instructed them to stop at as many locations with cameras as possible for the return trip, wishing for them to appear as fishermen taking a week off to enjoy the river's spoils. He would meet them back in Burlington to return the boat back to Saint Jean. It was best for both of them to be off the radar.

He had reminded the two not to place calls or search the internet for anything to do with anthrax. The NSA would soon be tracking all data with that keyword. Emails and social media would be scoured on any phone that pinged a cell tower the day of the attack. It would be seven to ten days before they could assess the damage done.

Heading south, Willis and O'Reilly discussed the possible ramifications if caught, but they also discussed the possible global impact their mission would bring. The possibilities were endless, and the trip home became uneventful.

O'Reilly was an average boat Captain, and he was not fond of the water. Willis wanted to do nothing but drink beer and stress over his future. O'Reilly had taken several days to drift the river, passing Plattsburgh, New York, to the west shortly before turning east across Lake Champlain. He passed the Lake Champlain Causeway, Thayer's Beach to his south, and proceeded around Marble Island. Following the shore, he had chosen Moorings Marina as their final destination. He had attended balloon events there in the past, so if anyone recognized him it wouldn't be unusual. It also would provide a less busy boating area than the main marinas closer to Burlington.

EZ was waiting for them on arrival. He had arranged rooms for them at the Lakeshore Vermont Inn and Suites directly across from the marina. He had purchased a bus ticket from Montreal to Burlington where he had then caught an Uber to the small Inn.

"Welcome back heroes. I hope you have enjoyed my boat."

EZ took one of the ropes and helped secure the boat to a piling. Willis tied the rear of the boat once the momentum had slowed. EZ jumped onto the boat, cigar in hand, and gave each man a bear hug.

"You guys know my tradition. Let's go below, mix a drink, and celebrate with a cigar. I need to show you guys how to tend the batteries anyway. I'm sure neither of you thought of that along the way."

EZ slipped past them both, held the boat's cabin door open, and the three proceeded down to the fully stocked bar and galley. Willis took out three highball glasses and a bottle of Buffalo Trace, filling each to the rim. EZ lit each man's cigar and the glasses made their traditional clinks before he lit the cigars.

"You have made us all proud. Tell me how your trip down the river was?" EZ said after taking a long drag of the cigar.

"Other than Willis bitching the whole time, great," O'Reilly said, his drink half gone with the excitement of making it back to Vermont.

"I wasn't bitching. I was reflecting about our future. These cigars are amazing. A hint of almond almost."

Willis sat down in his chair. He was three puffs into his cigar and had hardly touched his bourbon. He felt calm, relaxed. Maybe getting home was all he needed to de stress from the events.

EZ watched as O'Reilly continued on with his cigar and bourbon. Soon, he too had taken a seat next to Willis. Both appear relaxed. They had gone from exuberance on their return to appearing as if they had just returned from a yoga retreat. Their breathing had slowed, and they both appeared to look tired and sleepy.

EZ's hand came out of his pocket where it had been on the transmitter. No violence would be needed on these two. The lipids would never leave the blood brain barrier. The tiny nanoparticles would reside there for life. Unlikely to ever be found unless a CSF sample was taken during an autopsy.

Their breathing continued to slow, and their eyes had closed, until after about five minutes, both were lifeless. He checked each man's pulse confirming death. Removing both of their cigars, he returned to the upper deck of the boat and tossed the cigars into the water. It wouldn't be good to be caught with cigars containing cyanide. Inhalation of the gas had taken just a few minutes to kill them both, and his EMF transmitter had insured that they would not panic as their minds fought desperately for more oxygen. His technology always impressed him. The power to override even the brain's will to breathe.

He turned on the fans to the galley, closed the door, and freed the boat from the dock, making the decision to take some time off. UUONE would want him to after his success. His mind would need to be fresh around ten days from now when the hospitals filled to capacity.

His vacation wouldn't be to ponder all the death and dying. He would need to be fresh to control the living. Mixed into the anthrax had been the nanoparticles. Every surviving attendee from the festival and Six Flags would now be at the mercy of UUONE's EMF array near Montreal. Canada was about to get a change in attitude. He wondered which emotion he would play with first. Linking to his Israeli intelligence for social media, they would distribute comments that "the people deserved to die" with those who thought "it was a tragedy." Combine the bots paid for by China and Russia, turn on the EMF, and Montreal would soon be willing to cheer for whatever side EZ told them to cheer for, and he knew what UUONE orders would likely say.

Divide.

EZ's Victory

The only thing necessary to create a second American Revolution had finally come to fruition. When the middle class finally decides that the valor of death is a better option than the comforts of home. When the government has absolutely failed, and no one is coming to save you.

EZ's reflection over the timeline of events humbled his abilities and accomplishments.

Two men had been discovered days after the event in Lake Champlain near the North Hero Marina in upstate Vermont. The two men were found with backpacks full of a suspicious white substance that the United States government was currently testing at its labs in Atlanta, Georgia. The two men had been identified as members of a gun club in Northern New Hampshire, where the club was now being investigated by the FBI and ATF. EZ also knew that anything beyond this investigation would lead to two Islamic fundamentalists who were deceased weeks ago. That's where the trail would end. The rest could only be found with him, and if it did, it's likely that some poor soul in Montreal would be found dead from suicide next to a small bag of more anthrax.

Division was not going away. America and Canada could only come back together with great change. Opinions were split on how that change would occur. An indentation of values, a split in public beliefs. Perhaps a new belief system or religion that could unite. Values as strong as these would need to be instilled, and even if consensus was reached, the EMF would break it. EZ beamed discontent into poor neighborhoods, and joy into the prominent. The division was powerful with so many involved.

The power of mind control has helped achieve global division. UUONE was spreading its nanoparticles around the world. Slowly at first, in no rush, to refine their techniques using the EMF. EMF frequencies could be altered and transmitted through cell phones, WiFi routers, cell phone towers, electrical lines, or basically anything close to the target. Israeli "intelligence" could also request the United States to use their HAARP, ELF, and ULF towers out of allied necessity.

EZ had helped, and those he had helped were now benefiting from America's collapse. He could care less if it was China, Russia, or America that felt as if they were in charge of the world. The Infidels would never know the level of manipulation and dedication it took to overwhelm entire societies. If Israel could manipulate the United States populace, China and Russia would be next.

UUONE was reaping great profits from his expertise. Aligning the left mind with the right was the only way to see the light, to see a pathway forward, and only those who know how to generate that light would go forward. Only those practiced enough in achieving Bentov's lessons would ever understand the true magic of the Universe. The manipulation of the human spirit had been achieved. He did not feel guilty either, as his time in Peru revealed to him life after death. These deceased individuals would be in a pathway of eternal light or subjected to eternal darkness. Being part of the Chosen ones, he knew he would become part of the light. America's fall into civil war had created opportunities moving forward. China's new power would now make them the new kid in town to divide and create profit. His people, the Jewish people, were almost universally hated, and because of this hatred, division was created even faster. It would be much harder to divide a society where all beliefs stayed in the middle. It mattered not who or where others were in power. What mattered was the financial ability or techniques needed to protect the homeland, the secrets, and the religion.

He was proud of his accomplishments as he headed back to the White Mountains in New Hampshire. Ultimate division had been achieved. It had taken many variables, tools, and techniques, but human greed was predictable. Steerable. To get Americans to fight each other, to commit to civil disobedience had needed just the right manipulation, but that division had been achieved. The balloons in Canada had secured the Northern objective. Along with the mass shooting propaganda that he had used prior to that on the Trans communities. Add some nano particles, SSRIs, depressed teens, and the weasel President Douchey could not have been any more accommodating to the mission. America would soon ban guns as civil disobedience was at an all time high. The Patriot Act would begin to look small compared to what was about to happen from the anthrax attack, and his true secret gifts were about to be put in use to make certain UUONE could control whomever decided to pay for its services. Mossad operatives were now placing chemicals across water supplies in the United States.

The media would blame AI, cell phones, and 5G towers. It mattered not. What was proven in Peru would for sure work against the general populace, steering attitudes and passion behind whatever cause was needed. The sheep followed easily. Covid had been a testing ground for world fear and disillusion. The virus itself with its mRNA technology is a study on the effectiveness of gene replication, compliance, distribution, and mind control. The first study was complete, studied, and now refined.

He was now an expert on the abilities of the mind. Abilities the world doubted. Abilities to see God, Hell, happiness, sadness, loss, fear, or any of the other twenty three human emotions he controlled in his pocket.

Because of its Libertarian base, northern New Hampshire was starting to become a hot bed of common sense. Rational opinion on turning down the rhetoric of both sides was appearing to become effective. The ability to divide the right and the left was being impeded, and that would not be tolerated by UUONE. He would be needed there to silence the voices of reason, for they were the true threat to continued chaos. Israel needed chaos so that others could fight their wars, promote a single state plan, and secure financial freedom.

He enjoyed the scenery there. The food, beer, wine, and most of all the challenges presented by the Free State Project. He believed it wouldn't be long until New Hampshire may divide itself completely from the states around it, unwilling to give up their Constitution and Bill of Right's.

Division lay to the east of the State, as well as its west. A Notch was formed.

Part Three: The Notch

<u>The Hawks</u>

The hawks used to be fun to watch. Gliding over the frigid White Mountains with ease in the gusty currents. Hawks reminded me of the summer glider club located in Franconia. Being pulled up by a single engine prop plane into the jet-stream above Cannon and Lafayette mountains, the gliders could hold two people and stay up as long as the winds allowed, drifting upwards in the jet stream, again and again. Gliding over Easton and Franconia Notch with no engine sounds. Perched in silence as you circled the earth below. Gliders were used on D-day in World War Two. Flying over the German concrete entrenchments to drop soldiers behind the front lines and to gather intelligence from high in the sky.

Hawks were now our gliders. The beautiful, wide spanned birds were a threat. Flying with tiny cameras attached to their underbellies, the Sheep's troops would use them for surveillance above the mountains. The birds flew at tremendous elevation and speed. Unless you were directly underneath the camera, strategic travel remained safe. Although, a mass troop movement only a month ago was filmed and the objective abandoned after the Notch spotted several hawks overhead, too high to reveal if cameras were attached.

Originally, the birds were shot on site, but we soon learned to use them for counterintelligence. If spotted, Notch forward observers could travel in the opposite direction and provide the enemy with a false directional assembly of troops. We had used that trick pony more than once. Soon, we sent out attachments just to induce misdirection and keep the Sheep off balance. The herd could move faster than us, so every misdirection was a necessity for our objectives. Even more dangerous than their constant surveillance, the hawks were being put to use in destroying our main form of communication-carrier pigeons. Since the sixth century under Cyrus, king of Persia, pigeon postage was a trusted form of secure communication.

Bruce, one of our most vetted members, had lived off the grid long before the Notch began. His pigeons were making him a valuable asset. No one had thought about long distance communication except him, and if you're the only guy with trained birds in a catastrophe, he bartered for nothing.

The first EMP attack had destroyed most shortwave radios. Those who had built Faraday cages were spared from the EMP's effects. Charging the handheld radios with generators became difficult as fuel and electricity were in low supply. Solar chargers would work, but even with those, we just didn't trust the fact that Big Brother might have a way of listening. Pigeons became our radios.

Bruce's birds flew back to our central base, oftentimes going over fifty miles, but Bruce said they had a range of at least a hundred. A messenger would come every other day with a couple of pigeons for flights. Some of the guys even knew the birds well from repeat exchanges, and were becoming quite attached. Feeding and playing with them. Giving them names.

It was a tough call as to whether we should shoot the hawks. If we shot them all, the Sheep would know we were on to their surveillance tactics as we constantly shifted supplies and forward movements to fictitious fronts. As far as we could tell, they didn't know we had discovered their avian satellites. We were limited on our carrier pigeon capacity and wanted to lose as few as possible. Hawks eat pigeons. Night runs were our safest flights because the hawk cameras were limited to daylight data capture, but then owls became a concern. Owls loved the taste of pigeons.

Being a George Washington fan, I applied many of his military tactics. The first being espionage. Washington's deceptions involved placing as many spies as possible within or around British military installations during the Revolutionary War. These spies would give real time feedback on strategies, troop movements, and supply routes. Those efforts changed the outcome of his war, and without our spies, we would be hopeless.

It was our best spy that noticed the hawks in the first place. No one could possibly see the cameras attached to the birds. It wasn't through seeing the cameras that the information had been attained, but rather through loose lips at the local pub. She had overheard a conversation involving their use while bartending and flirting with the Sheep. Through this one slip, we could now run the Sheep ragged over some of the hardest, coldest terrain in the United States. Washington was correct on spies. We increased pay for espionage, and recruited more women. Just like his Brooklyn Heights, our victory was going to come from luck and the enemy mistakes rather than our own capabilities. Like Washington, we didn't have thousands of troops, but we had a cause and plenty of time. The Sheep had neither. Washington believed absolutely and unapologetically in a cause that featured no future king. Our Revolution was no different. The war for individual rights was no different now than against King Richard. Freedom for the individual looked like it had a time stamp of around every three hundred years.

Fuel nationwide, particularly aviation fuel, was at an all time shortage, so fear of airstrikes had become almost non-existent. At least half of the Air Force officers had sabotaged their own equipment before departing to the hills and mountains with their families to support what they viewed as the correct cause. An air base in Burlington, Vermont, was completely destroyed with mortars early in the conflict. No planes would be landing there anytime soon as there was also no equipment to repair the runway, and those machines also had no fuel.

There were no satellites to guide munitions. The Chinese and Russians had brought down or disabled orbit GPS systems early on in order to create more chaos. Point of sight ruled. This ground game was also tankless. Tanks were sitting ducks on the steep mountain passes and choke points.

If you wanted to fight, you were coming to us with foot soldiers. Just as the Taliban proved in the mountains of Afghanistan, a small mobile force with local civilian sympathy was impossible to destroy. No superpower in history, neither Soviet nor American, with satellite munitions and an Air Force, could defeat an embedded mountainous force. It was the same in the Notch. Perhaps not at the extremes in elevation, but with very similar geography. An ingrained purpose and a well armed rag-tag militia were proving to be a little harder to shut down than the Sheep had first envisioned.

Without satellites, drones were also non-existent. Fly by wire drones were used for some amount of time, but the optic fibers needed for their extended flights were now gone as manufacturing had ceased with no new shipments arriving from China. Microchips needed for the drones were also needed for more advanced equipment, and they too were in short supply. The United States's capability to mass produce the chips required rare earth minerals which China had also ceased shipment.

The war in the Notch would be much like it had been when the British had marched through years ago. It was a battle of wit and endurance, not technology. Removing air superiority, the United States military could be humbled in ways it had not been during recent conflicts, and with so many ex-military members serving the efforts, predictions on strategies were well balanced. Take away nuclear weapons, drones, an Air Force, fuel, and it was not surprising that such a small area could maintain effective defenses. Add determination for their own freedoms, and the revolutionaries within The Notch had good odds.

<u>Duck Blind</u>

Sitting in the cold was only slightly unpleasant. I had done that many times growing up, hunting ducks in the wet Mississippi delta. It was sheer boredom that affected me the most. When constantly staring at the tree line, evaluating bushes with abstract shapes and shadows which all resembled the enemy, a mind starts to wander. The stillness was death.

Trying to fight daydreaming. Trying not to lose focus. Thinking back to the good old days before the War for Entitlement began. Pondering the future of a starving family. Contemplating the existence of a God that was supposed to return and provide salvation. The seduction of sleep would find a way to cuddle with your eyes. Luring them to close and enticing a worn body to rest. Many a soldier had fallen asleep on his watch. Waking to the sounds of this mistake. Subjugating those around him an introduction to their creator.

I was into my second 5 Hour Energy drink. The tiny bottles were light, made of plastic to limit noise, and contained plenty of caffeine, along with a plethora of other ingredients I couldn't pronounce. I had become dependent on larger and larger doses of the stimulant. Addiction to the energy drinks started after stealing a case from an abandoned gas station a year ago. Part hallucination, part psychosis, caffeine had become my drug of choice since alcohol was nonexistent. Probably as much a placebo effect as actually waking up the mind. I wondered if I drank only half the bottle if I would only be awake for two and a half hours. A smile crossed my face. My wife always loved that joke.

Nights were long in the blustery North Country of New Hampshire's winters and seemed even longer in March. Their length seemed a day unto themselves. Granite Staters were prone to seasonal affective disorder but scared of the label. They much preferred the title functioning alcoholic.

Winter was a fucking cancer, but I knew the Sheep were out there in that blurred tree line, and the desperate, metropolitan bastards always introduced themselves at night, with their functioning batteries, night vision, and fresh food. Liberated across their journey northward. The herd lacked ingenuity and belief in a cause greater than themselves, feeling entitled to everything but never joining a cause to fight anything. They fought for what they were told to, a tribe led by an immoral Chief. We would endure the fight. I half envisioned one of their lambs in skinny jeans, carrying a Starbucks coffee, on a cell phone, walking across the field in front of me. It was time for more caffeine.

One tree in particular looked just like a man with a rifle. Through my watch that winter, the tree earned the nickname Piney. When the wind would blow Piney, a sinking feeling would hit my stomach, reminding me of observing a car run a traffic light, just as you're about to go through the intersection. A moment of realization that you're lucky enough to survive towards the next light. That feeling of tucking your nuts deep into your socks. A feeling that you just defeated death. Those feelings came from the reaper's scythe, just missing above your head.

Piney in the wind always gave me that feeling, regardless of how many times I reminded myself he was simply a tree. I recalled walking next to ponds in Mississippi's hazy summers, maintaining constant vigilance over the threat of a sleeping copperhead snake. Occasionally, mistaking a root or stick for the devilish death coils, triggering the ingrained reaction of heart palpitation and vagal response. Primal epi genetics embedded for the survival of man. It was the caffeine, and that gut sinking feeling. Two things that kept me awake. To try and outlast the darkness of an overnight watch was damn near impossible. Try as you might, boredom and the cold combined into a perfect state of mental noncompliance, especially with no one to talk or keep you company. I had heard of such stories from Korean War Veterans at my old VFW. Long cold nights of misery, boredom, and below zero temperatures lulling even the most heroic into a state of despair and solitude.

My black lab used to go hunting with me in those Delta duck blinds. Bubba the Lab was an endless conversationalist. His eyes revealed stories that needed to be heard. His tales are able to provide answers to life's mysteries. His opinions are relevant. His paws shoved into my jacket, attempting to find warmth away from the snow. His loyalty is stronger than most friendships. What I didn't understand in those days was that Bubba's every thought was simply my own. His eyes never changed. His ears never conveyed emotions. . He was my conscience. Every man's loneliness and fears, dealt with through our imagining that our four legged companions contain wisdom. His thoughts were simply my soul attempting to be heard.

Probably similar things you would tell a friend if they asked for advice. A dog just lets you practice telling those beliefs before a live audience. Attempting rational vocalization is the best way to make sure your beliefs are legitimate, and sometimes that takes practice. Bubba was always a good listener.

Our practiced internal dialogues only get refined when conveyed to others. A great teacher knows their craft, having refined it enough to enable exact explanation. That poor fucking dog was likely tired of my ramblings. I wondered if this is where the word Dogma came from and took another sip from the tiny plastic energy drink.

Damn these things taste bad, I thought as I returned to a former Bubba therapy session. *Ducks are coming, time to eat, time to leave, mortgage is late, does my wife love me, why does work suck?*

Were those Bubba's thoughts? Why the fuck does this dog look at me like that with his head turned?

His bark never had a Southern accent as I can recall, but he did have Southern grit. The dog never complained about the cold. A wet duck blind was his happy place, and while miserable, he knew that going home next to the stove was worse. Boredom is always worse. Staring at Piney was worse.

A shared experience of misery brought us together for those talks. My layered Gore Tex jackets against his thick coat of fur. Bubba endured the cold and wet with me, but for what purpose? Was it really a small flying mass of feathers for a dinner treat and the practiced retrieval? For me, why was spending thousands to shoot a bird you could buy at the grocery store?

It was for the shared experience of misery. And when back home, we would talk about it around the fire, primeval in its flames, encompassing where humans had told stories for thousands of years. I'd watch Bubba as he slept, kicking his legs, dreaming of future birds to chase. Good memories always win over misery.

Thank you for the memories, good boy.

Only that lab was aware of how truly fucked up my mind was from our hunting discussions. A free psychotherapist in a duck blind. Those conversations were an easier pill to swallow, with less damage than the tequila bottle, whose dark powers I couldn't resist.

The Notch had found its value in my medical knowledge. I not only provided care to those returning from the battlefield, but I had been placed in charge of interrogations. The mental dilemma of saving on one hand, countered by the need to injure on the other. My morals were undergoing a confrontation that only Bubba could counsel. These watches gave me a chance to undergo therapy.

Without speaking, the dog's face was certainly that of the psychiatrist's office, the doctor sitting in the chair saying nothing, only letting you dig a deeper hole for yourself as that inner psyche spewed discontent and past mistakes. The ego refuses to march to its death.

Why couldn't I have made better choices? Why hadn't God been there for me? When will this end?

Perhaps God demanded I endure my life choices, to suffer through my decisions just as I now suffered the evening's cold, alone and fearful. While the retriever's face was passive, judgement was clearly being passed. His silence revealed my past choices. Life's decisions were my own, and no one was going to provide for outcome.

He sat with inquisition. Eyes as black as his coat.

Damn dog could be a judgmental little fucker.

Bubba's memories could get me through any rainy thirty degree day in Mississippi, but not here.

This was New Hampshire where ducks even refused its winters.

Icy snow pack hardened the earth, and the crunch of a man trying to walk through that evening's ice crust would be his death sentence. That's why I stayed still like Piney. I didn't move. To move was to be heard. I lived in the shadows. My ears listened more than Piney's, both of us swaying in the breeze.

The Notch Militia needed my talents. It was my caffeine. After Bubba died, The Notch was my only best friend. The Notch was who I could now talk to about my problems. It provided my therapy, and I could make no more poor choices. I could live with no more regrets. Either would mean certain death.

Bubba, I wish you could sit here with me and watch the sheep come into the pasture. It's likely I'll be seeing you soon, old friend.

Piney swayed his head in agreement.

Geography of the Notch

The Notch was composed of exactly that, Notches within the White Mountains. A notch was the proper New England term for a mountain pass or gap. The Notches were the main corridor for travel when the American Indians roamed early New England. Since most of the water had to flow through the passes, early European settlers found proximity to them useful. Commerce came through a Notch, but not over a mountain. There were twenty six Notches in the White Mountains, ten in the Northern White Mountains specifically.

The importance of the Notches was recognized early on for defensive purposes. Most of The Notch was composed of ex military, and if there is one thing ex military types loved, it was maps. Understanding the choke points that could prevent overflow from Boston, New York, Portland, Burlington, and Montreal was critical in preparation of a defense, establishing a supply route, and securing multiple headquarters. The primary Northern Notch positions were in the geographical shape of a pentagon. Surrounding state militia counterparts were on the borders, and The Notch had firm relationships with them. All depended on each other. Should one go down, all might go down.

The Mount Washington Hotel was a Northern New Hampshire landmark. The mammoth white structure had served many in its lifetime, and the historical accomplishments were as majestic as its views. Built in 1902 by coal baron Joseph Stickney, the Bretton Woods International Monetary Conference had taken place there in 1944. During that historic meeting, the World Bank and International Monetary Fund were established, as well as developing the gold standard at $35/ounce, with the United States dollar becoming the "gold" standard currency of the world.

The United States promised the world its currency would now be backed with gold. The Notch had found it quite ironic that the hotel was now our headquarters. Most of us believed that the World Bank and the United Nations had some part in our collapse, if not directly, then indirectly through bad policies that influenced legislation and banks locally. Serving as a prime example of this was the 2012 UN Arms Trade Treaty which was intended to ban import and export of firearms and weapons to international countries. Our pitiful politicians had told the Sheep that it would in no way affect their second amendment rights, but their goal was achieved.

Once three new supreme court justices were appointed by the Dutaja administration, the interpretation of the Constitution became superseded by international law. All guns were to be registered or "turned in" unless for sporting use only or needed for a farm or ranch. The Sheep had won their battle on gun right's, but the same policy had spelled their doom. Not all were agreeable in giving up rights.

Fifty trains a day used to stop at "The Mt. Wash", what locals preferred to call the place. The wealthy from New York, Boston, Philadelphia, and Pittsburgh used to travel long and far to vacation during the summer season before air travel became a reality. Mt. Washington, the tallest mountain in the Northeast United States, at 6,288 feet, was the main attraction, standing tall behind the hotel. The mountain was still a heavy tourist destination, featuring a Cog Railway, auto road, and hiking trails that beckoned tourists to the summit.

In 2006, the hotel was bought by a corporate group from Virginia who later let the Omni Hotel Group manage the property. Corporate big wigs also wanted the place to be called, "The Omni Mt. Washington", and in 2010, began to trademark the name "Mt. Washington". Everything in the whole of Grafton county had a tie to that name, and with the current economy in the North Country, no one could fight lawsuits with this giant corporation's trademark rights. Twin Mountain, the closest rural town that provided most of the hotel's workers, were quite irritated with the Omni's new demands and had started to call it "The Ominous Mt. Washington", predicting the foreboding doom that was about to cloud out the massive estate. Mt. Washington's shadow over the hotel was a constant reminder of the dark times to come at Bretton Woods.

The Mt. Wash was a perfect location to serve as headquarters for The Notch. Every direction featured high elevation and defensible positions. To the Northwest, Mt. Deception was immediately followed by Mt. Jefferson at 5,716 feet. Consisting of three peaks at its summit, Mt. Jefferson was a short drive up the Cog Railway Base Road to the Jefferson Notch Road. The Notch road provided spectacular snowmobiling in the winter and was famous for being the highest elevated road on the east coast.

Atop Mt. Jefferson, forward observers established a base camp at what was called Monticello Lawn during the summer months. Monticello's flat, grassy area provided adequate quarters, but lightning was the troops biggest fear at 5,400 feet. The Ridge of the Caps provided views to the west, considered one of our weak points, and highest likelihood of ambush. Because of this vulnerability, the Castle Ravine Trails to the North were patrolled vigilantly. Spies had been captured at both locations.

Directly North, Mt. Adams, the second highest peak in The White's at 5,774 feet, was one of the most difficult areas to patrol and offer support. With five glacial cirques surrounding the trails, Adams was a monster. The Appalachian Mountain Club, a hiker conservancy, was responsible for many of the trails and trail maintenance throughout the White Mountains, and a series of eight mountain huts had been established to help day hikers into the range. At an average interval of seven miles apart for day hikes, the alpine huts were made to withstand the toughest winters.

Madison Springs Hut sat atop Adams. Built in 1888, it was the oldest hut to top an American mountain. With a capacity to hold 52 tired hikers, the shelter was a workhorse and Godsend for The Notch. Repairs had occurred on the hut as recently as 2011, and when we took it over, needed absolutely nothing.

Furthest east, and just south of the town of Gorham off state Rt. 16, was Carter Dome. Staring over the entire width of Beans Purchase, Carter Dome was our furthest post to the Northeast before encountering The Millinocket, "The Milli" as we called them, and the Rangeley Ranger militias in far eastern Maine. Carter Notch Hut sat at only 3,288 feet, and only held 40 troops. Despite this fact, its use as an ammunition storage center for the three local militias was paramount, and also the reason it was vigorously defended.

The Notch trusted no one, and neither did The Milli or Rangley. For that reason, the commanders of all three held a meeting to entrust one another with resupply and distribution of ammunition. Because our HQ was so heavily defended to the west, and the Maine groups were heavily fortified to the east, Carter's hut was chosen as the safest site.

Former troops had suggested Carter Notch Hut for this purpose years earlier. Many had served as part of "croos" who maintained and resupplied the Appalachian Trail huts in the summer months. Often making four to five trips a shift down the mountains, these "croos" were our initial intelligence providers regarding the hut system's strengths and weaknesses. Carter

Notch had something the other huts didn't, a cave that had been used to store cheese and other perishables. Initially small, the cave had been expanded by hand and held about one third of The Notch's reserve ammunition. The rest being distributed closer to the front lines in caves behind Cannon Mountain, and the other third in current distribution.

Directly behind the Mt. Wash, Mt. Washington mountain dominated. The "Stone Pile", as it was called, was impassable, especially in the blusterous winter months. Winter could last until May this far North, especially in elevated notches. Climbing higher than its neighbors, Mt. Washington's presence was the North Country. Other than the Old Man of the Mountain, which had crumpled to the bottom of Cannon Mountain in Franconia Notch years earlier, the granite structure immortalized the region and the local's resilience. Known for the worst weather in America, holding at one point the highest wind ever recorded in history at 231 miles per hour. Based on windchill, Antarctica was the closest rival, with the peak breaking the coldest U.S. windchill record in 2023 at -108 degrees. What it lacked in height compared to the Rockies, it made up for in weather.

More than 140 people have died on the Rockpile over the years. With our backs to the mountain, a false sense of security could develop. At its peak held dozens of trailheads, a continuous weather station, and large shelters. No effort was made to staff this arctic facility in the winter, no equipment, no fuel, no food-it was impossible for rescue or resupply.

Two methods existed prior to the Sheep's grazing to support the summit in good weather. The Mt. Washington Cog Railway and the Autoroad. The Cog was a standard for tourists. Climbing slowly North over the slick, grey, granite outcroppings to the summit. Only one rail car in inventory worked on coal, and The Notch had long ago burned that for heat. A snowplow and snowcat to achieve the long journey up the mountain on the far eastern side was laughable. Two shelters were available, but only used half heartedly in the tolerable months. Between lightning, unpredictable weather, and steep ascents, Lonesome Lake Hut, located below tree line towards Mt. Monroe, and Mizpah Spring Hut, were used sparingly.

Of more importance to guarding the eastern paths through Pinkham Notch was the Joe Dodge Lodge. Named after the man most responsible for the huts and trails covering the White Mountains, Joe Dodge was quintessential New England. Over one hundred soldiers could bunk, mess, and replenish there. "The Dodge" also served as a Forward Observation Base in coordination with Milli. It was large enough to accommodate and provided downhill rapid descent into the towns of Jackson, Glen, Intervale, and North Conway where The Sheep were intent on overpowering with new lambs being brought over the 302 road out of Portland. Our biggest battles and deadliest confrontations continued to occur here. What constituted a tourist trap before The Grazing, historic, Yankee bed and breakfasts burned or molded away. Storyland park's Mother Goose was quiet, and North Conway's outlet malls were abandoned. Mt. Hitchcock, Mt. Huntington, Greens Cliff, Owls Cliff, Bear Mountain, Table Mountain, The Three Moat Mountains, The Two Attitash Mountains, proceeded in an easterly fence to Cathedral's Ledge overlooking North Conway.

On the southern faces of this fence, the famous Kancamagus Highway, The Kanc, slithered. We could not let the Kanc fall from Conway. Bear Notch road connected from The Kanc directly into Bartlett on the 302. Fuel was critical for the snowmobile troops here in the winter. Run by one of our veteran snowmobile gurus out of Twin Mountain, The Sheep were not going to get through the established perimeter from Bartlett to Carroll.

In a rickety staircase fashion, the 302 stepped twenty miles out of North Conway, going due west in Glen, north again at Notchland, an exquisite overnight outpost, through Hart's Location, the original first place to vote in America, to the impenetrable, Crawford Notch. Breathtaking waterfalls lined the tall capital "V" shape formed next to forgotten railroad tracks.

Just past the "V" was one of our biggest troop locations. Another Appalachian Mountain Club built hiker destination, The Highland Center and Shapleigh Bunkhouse sat under a watchful Mt. Willard. 122 beds existed. Bunk beds were constructed, quadrupling enlisted living quarters to almost 400. Officer's quarters compiled the Shapleigh facilities with a capacity of approximately 25 beds.

The Highland Center was a nice weapon for The Notch. Newly constructed using energy efficient walls, heating, and renewable energy sources, the ever present wind pounded across the eastern face of the Highland Camp. All forward operating bases resupplied from Highland, and The Mt. Wash was a short mile away enabling further support when the shit hit the fan.

Pemigewasset Wilderness area sprawled across the southwestern perimeter of the Mt. Wash. The Sugarloaf mountains, Mt. Zealand, and Mt. Bondcliff stood fast as the westwardly beast, Mt. Lafayette formed the famous Franconia Notch with Cannon Mountain. Close to my home, this was my front.

Franconia Notch held a shitload of hippies smoking dope, an Olympic gold winning skier heritage, and the future of my grandkids. The bottlenecked Notch impeded the disastrous flow of "Massholes" immigrating across the Massachusetts border in the south. So responsible were these fucking indigent bastards for our destruction, our imminent demise, a bounty on verified kills, "Glutton Buttons", were painted on Notch helmets, much the same way stickers were awarded and placed on college football helmets for most tackles in a game, or most touchdowns in a season. And for every Glutton Button earned, one pint of homemade apple cider was earned.

Targets were aplenty as was the only alcohol we could produce. The Notch could produce little more than grit. Battle was the only relief from the cold, and most were staying quite warm.

Necessary Surgery

"I know it's going to hurt. Just fucking do it. I'm going to die if you don't do it."

Tonsil infections normally weren't a big deal, but when there is no surgical and medical resupply, it is deadly. Group A Beta-Hemolytic Streptococcus bacteria was running rampant. While "strep throat" normally resolves in a couple of days even without antibiotics, our living in close proximity to each other with known strep carriers was causing the sicknesses to linger and to last longer each time. Troops were getting sick and staying sick. Their immune system was not able to ever completely rid the body of the bacteria, becoming host carriers themselves, and spreading the bacteria further into the barracks.

We swore that the Sheep had somehow spread it among us, but what was likely happening was the repeated use and sharing of old toothbrushes, unsanitary kitchen conditions, and lack of cleaning products. Troops constantly felt tired, had fevers, and were unproductive. The likelihood of some actually being super spreaders existed as well, and once the tonsils were repeatedly infected and cryptic, the bacteria might never leave, but rather reappear in waves. Crissy was as tough as they came, and I knew I was going to have to anesthetize her. She was past the point of recovering on her own. Anesthesia was the one skill that got me into The Notch. Prepping, and a strong gun and ammunition collection, didn't hurt my chances either.

Having a garage full of primers for reloading was also enticing to some.

I had practiced as a nurse anesthetist for twenty five years. When the downturn was coming, I started ordering the same equipment that I had used in Iraq on my Forward Surgical Team. Portable draw-over vaporizers provided the gas for anesthesia, and our unit had two, as well as the only person trained to use them.

Our hospital raids had been successful in securing other medical equipment, but as much as we tried to ration our supply, we still used too much. Most of the equipment was too bulky to transport out of the hospital, or required pressurized gases to operate. During a mortar attack three months prior, our oxygen tanks blew during the onslaught. We were glad just to have made it out with anything at all. Oxygen will produce a flame unlike any you can imagine. A heat intensity that no firefighter would ever approach

One couldn't help but try to treat your own community families after injury. If you didn't treat those around you, morale quickly went to shit. We were there to help each other, to help each other's families. If The Notch wasn't going to help you, then who was? What was the fight even about at that point? The Sheep would not give us medical supplies. We might as well have been Confederate slaves during the War of Northern Aggression. We were outlaws. Militia trash at best. The ability to believe in a cause that was not government dictated could not be achieved by the Sheep. They had to be told what to believe in. Free thinkers, free men, made their own decisions. At least they did in the old America. Our cause in this case, was to help save a fellow Patriot.

The electrical bovie was plugged into the gas generator, turned on, and ready. I slapped the grounding pad on Crissy's thigh. My draw-over anesthesia vaporizer was set up and ready. Crissy had an IV established, and I started to give her medications. There would be no need to pre-oxygenate, or de-nitrogenate as some would say. We had no oxygen. Room air's 21% would have to do, but with her youth, there shouldn't be any hiccups with oxygen desaturation. "Crissy," I said, "this is going to burn like hell when it goes in, but then you'll be asleep quickly."

It was some of the last Propofol that I had, and being that it was 3 months past its expiration date, I was hoping she didn't die from the contaminated Diprivan. Egg whites were used in the anesthetic's preservative solution, giving its distinctive white color. As back up, my only other IV anesthetic was Ketamine. Pentothol wasn't even being made anymore when the crisis hit, so my options for anesthetics were limited from the start. I was holding off on the Ketamine though. At doses over 100 milligrams without first giving benzodiazepenes, like Valium or Versed, Ketamine would cause wicked hallucinations, and that was the last thing I wanted to give Crissy.

One patient I had given Ketamine to in the past swore that her dead father was standing next to the bed, and no matter what other drug I tried to give to calm that hallucination, he still stood there at the bedside. Crying went on for hours as she talked endlessly to him, apologizing for her past mistakes. Crissy had recently seen both of her children die. Her daughter from lack of asthma medication, and her son one month later in our largest victory to date. She had not seen it as a victory. Times could be hard in the Notch.

"Take some nice, big, deep breaths Crissy. We'll take good care of you. Pick out a nice dream." "Fuck you," she said with a shit eating grin. She still had her sense of humor at least.

I pushed the Propofol in quickly. There was no intravenous tubing or intravenous bags of fluids, she just had the IV in her arm to give the meds through. I would usually give a bolus of IV lidocaine to numb the vein as the Propofol dripped in, as its preservatives caused burning sensations, but we were all out of that too. All of the other supplies had been used up months ago.

Without drug and medical equipment resupply and modern medical equipment, it didn't matter that we had surgeons. If you were shot, death was imminent. Ninety percent of wounds on the front lines were orthopedic in nature. External fixation, plates, x-ray equipment and antibiotics weren't available. Almost any injury was going to take thoughts and prayers to heal, not modern medicine.

I touched Crissy's eye lashes. There was no response, indicating that the Propofol had reached the brain. Next came the breathing tube. The laryngoscope blade was one item I had not spared with battery life. The handle took two C-batteries. We kept all batteries indoors and away from the cold to avoid depletion. Batteries were treated like gold, and since this was the one part of her procedure that was more important than the procedure itself, the intubation had to be done correctly. You could stop bleeding, but you had to breathe for the patient as well as prevent blood from entering the lungs from the surgery. Inserting the MAC 3 curved blade into her mouth, I lifted up and away, and the vocal cords appeared in view. Popping out the tube's stylet, I inflated the balloon and checked for end tidal carbon dioxide on my portable monitor. Not having "Difficult Intubation" equipment in the field, I didn't know if the procedure could have been accomplished with just "masking" her with gas the whole time, trading off breaths with cautery and the surgeon. There was always a high risk of bleeding with a tonsillectomy, as well as the possibility of the tonsils obstructing visualization on the intubation. Intubation was therefore deemed a necessity.

Next, I turned the Sevoflurane dial to three percent on my Draw-over Vaporizer which would be a conduit for the anesthesia gases to mix with air and be delivered to her lungs, mix with her bloodstream, get transported to the brain, and attach to the receptors inducing sleep. Crissy had already started spontaneous, rapid breathing. Draw-overs worked best when the patient breathed spontaneously.

"Not unusual", I told Pete, the surgeon, "She hasn't had any narcotics since we are out. She's better off breathing on her own".

Pete didn't look happy at all about that new knowledge. He had the hard job of not hitting the arteries lying just below the surface of the tonsils, and narcotics would have let her lay motionless and not respond to the bogie's stimulation. A moving target is no fun when arteries are close by.

Normally, I would give Fentanyl, a strong narcotic, to blunt the intubation response induced on her nervous system, and to prevent the pain she was about to experience, but beggars can't be choosers. Morphine was also completely gone. This was going to be gas only anesthesia. She was going to hurt like a mother fucker, both during the case and afterwards, but there was no alternative. Basically, I was just there to decrease movement and cause amnesia.

Crissy's relentless heart rate reminded me of an experience in Iraq with the Mujahedin-e-Khalq (The MEK) at their main base, Camp Ashraf, north of Baghdad. Also known as the National Council of Resistance to Iran, the group was composed of around 5,000 fighters. Half of whom were female. Because they supported Saddam Hussein, but were exiles from Iran, the MEK was considered hostile, both to the U.S. and Iran, and its tanks and soldiers bombed into submission. The MEK quickly surrendered to the Americans once they were sure the Iranians wouldn't keep pounding them. I was one of a handful who got to then go in and provide medical assistance to the injured.

After around twenty cases, no more fentanyl and morphine were available. Any time we performed an anesthetic, the heart rate leaped off the portable monitors. The body was trying to fight or flight, but was unable to leave the OR table. Although asleep and paralyzed, the body could still recognize the scalpel's incision. Once awake, the pain continued. There was nothing we could do. Save them from major injury, or they die.

The Iranians understood though, and were glad the surgeons did their jobs well. Missing an arm is better than death to most, especially in that part of the world. Any American Civil War soldier would probably agree. Almost everyone in Iraq or Iran knew a relative or a neighbor who had lost a limb to war-from land mines, bullets, or drones. Back in the States, you occasionally saw some folks on Veteran's Day who had lost limbs to combat, but those days had changed since The Notch. Most of those MEK patients in Iraq were female, just like Crissy in front of me now. Different war. Same bullshit. Same Sheep. Same ideas. Socialists were like rats in New York City, as soon as you killed one, two more would appear.

Pete went to work. I cranked the gas up to its maximum setting to try and provide a motionless operative field for him. The smell of burning tissue filled the room. Before I knew it, the tonsils were out. The whole procedure took around twenty minutes, and without surgery and antibiotics, Crissy would have never functioned again. Her repeated infections and fever had overwhelmed her immune system to the point she could no longer function in any role we gave her. We feared she may die without extraction.

We now had to worry about post operative bleeding. Pete went overboard on the electrocautery. Charring the tonsil surface to a steak-like texture. If she started to bleed significantly, and himself or cautery was unavailable, she would die quickly. Life or death decisions were being made real time in The Notch.

Her pain over the next ten to twelve days would be tremendous. She could expect heavy drooling, no sleep, and no food. There was no local prior to incision, so she would wake up with immediate pain. The swelling from the cautery would continue over the next couple of days before it would start to recede. The scariest period would be around day eight, when the charred scab over the tonsils fell off. Prime time for an unstoppable rebleed. Even in our country's better times this was a legitimate medical emergency, and often the anesthesia provider would be unable to visualize where to place the breathing tube.

Pete did all our tonsils on the same day and would return to camp in seven days to be available should a rebleed occur. Crissy was going to experience a week of painful hell, but compared to the alternative, all the tonsil patients today knew it was a surgery well worth the risks. And no one would complain. There was a greater purpose. No one tolerated complaints. Everyone was suffering in their own ways. Just like the MEK, when everyone around you is enduring trauma, loss, and heartache, a true appreciation for humbleness sets in.

Our country had lost that humbleness after every citizen's shared sacrifice during World War Two and had reached rock bottom with the Millennial "Entitlement" Generation who had sacrificed nothing but cell phone signal loss or free WI FI. The human brain needs a certain degree of humbleness to function within a free society. That brain needs a shared herd experience to keep everyone on the same playing field. 9/11 had seen some of that humbleness, but it disappeared quickly in the constant news feed of new world problems.

As society started to split before the Notch's revolution, the have's versus the have not's had grown. Only the have not's were playing on a level playing field. The playing field was funny though. It was a field that lacked for nothing, but always wanted more. Free health care, free college tuition, free everything-the most prosperous lower class in global history-and still, it wasn't enough. I liked to say I was born into the Upper Lower class, and yet, I still had a good childhood. Just how and why the world's mind and feelings were being controlled into unhappiness and discontent remained a mystery to me. It was almost as if someone had a tool to do it with.

Everyone needs a shared sacrifice. Everyone needs to experience pain or loss. To step in another's shoes and realize what your neighbor may be suffering, to appreciate what others have lost for your gain. Our surgical patients were always the first to help volunteer at the hospital after their experience. They knew what the others were going through. They shared that experience. A purpose to help a shared sacrifice.

The Sheep needed to share some of our experiences. They hadn't truly sacrificed enough.

Saving troops was rewarding, but my other job was starting to question the world's meaning. Torturing another human could lead to a Notch in the self.

The Dermatome

Everyone talked about the effectiveness of water boarding. It had it's place on the list of torture techniques. Water boarding's effectiveness was derived from the effect on the human psyche. A deep dark place within our genetic code transmitting to our brains that as humans, we cannot thrive under water.

Through the study of human embryology, we know that we developed from fish, emerging from the water. Traveling to the shore for nutrition, and eventually, the species never returning to the water. This could be easily proven through shared embryologic development and was still a favorite debate at Universities. However, that sense of knowing that we are no longer fish was an embedded code in a deep mysterious region of the brain.

The age of gills was long past human genomes, the genetic code that was passed in the womb, at the DNA level. A level that instills a fear of snakes as much as it does in instructing a newborn to latch onto a mother's breast for milk. Water boarding weaved its way inside that double helix ladder of DNA and ripped it to shreds, exposing a human survival instinct. For some, that fear was enough to reveal information others might find of value.

For other's, the cortex of the brain could override the DNA double helix's rung collapse. Areas responsible for creativity, will, and imagination could make the brain sometimes surpass fear. Captives enduring an enhanced interrogation often dug into this tool box to survive. Hostages or prisoners of war harbored the cortex's powers, and many had even been trained on how to do so. Soldiers who wanted to quit, when their bodies refused to go on, could magically carry on through the unimaginable. People who would normally succumb to claustrophobia might delve into the cortex in order to imagine themselves in another, more pleasant place. The cortex could "think for itself" per se, overriding the genetic code.

While an inherent need to survive stoked the fear when waterboarding, pain was often all that was needed to break others with torture. Punches and slaps to those who had never been roughed up were quite effective-breaking fingers, arms, and legs. Driving bamboo under nail beds. Ripping off nails with pliers. Gouging eyes. Ripping off ears. Injecting concentrated capsaicin.

Methods to inflict pain were only limited to one's imagination.

But for those who wouldn't break under either method, a combination genetic code degradation while adding pain might be necessary. The torturer had to call on his or her own cortex to get the job done, to be creative in their tactics. With all of the wars raging across the globe in the last twenty years, soldiers had heard of most torture techniques and either dreaded having certain methods deployed against them, or studied ways to make the experience more pleasant and defeat-able.

Refusing to break under certain techniques could be taught at survival, escape, resistance, and evasion schools. Keeping effective torture methods secret required originality and a lack of witnesses. Original, effective techniques required a level of repeatable murder each time, without actually killing the victim, for the victim could always be used for more information.

There was no gain in killing the hostage.

As much as pain, otherwise known as nociception in the biological world, can be envisioned through traumatic causes, much of the body's pain occurs through the mind's perception of pain. The trauma starts at the sensory levels of the skin, but the deeper levels of pain occur after the sensory pain transmits its signals from the site of injury to the spinal cord then on to the thalamus for initial processing, before undergoing the final interpretation in that most human-like portion, the cortex. One of the nociceptive pain pathways does not go towards the amygdala in the thalamus at first, but rather to the hypothalamus where the "fight or flight" response is located and initiated. Pain triggers multiple types of chemical reactions, that's why it's so hard to treat when the body experiences it. All people *react* to pain differently, and all *experience* pain differently.

Nociceptors, pain receptors, are located within the body, skin, and tissues. They are composed of free nerve endings that detect changes in the body's "senses". Pain is carried throughout the body along either A-Delta, fast, myelinated fibers, or slowly along unmyelinated, C-Fibers. Myelin acts as a conductor. Most sensory fibers in the skin areas adapt to constant triggering, such as those for pressure, vibration, or stretching, but nociceptors do not adapt. They continue to fire their signals to the spinal cord and up to the brain. This transmission is assisted by neurotransmitter chemicals, particularly glutamate. Once pain is triggered, its vicious cycle becomes never ending until something can stop the feedback loop.

Mastering the body's entire repertoire of pain anatomy and biochemistry required considerable thought and creativity. My job as an anesthetist required mastering the ability to keep a patient from feeling pain, from interpreting pain. If interpreting pain, to have the body interpret the pain in a language that it could not process. Anesthesia combines many factors when used for surgery-analgesia, amnesia, and akinesia (making the patient have no pain, forget the process, and lack movement during the surgery). So to break the best, to inflict the most pain during an interrogation, required the best efforts, both physically and pharmacologically.

To have a goal of providing non analgesia, non amnesia,

with akinesia was going against the thousands of hours spent on the trade, but I had become quite proficient. Using the same drugs from the operating room to achieve specific results for the specific receptor's desired response, was rewarding in achieving its desired effect, but disturbing when processing the morality inflicted on the participants. Bad people required worse people, and we were dealing with the worst of the worst. Highly trained military professionals, from prior US military, "contractors", and those from Russia, China, and the Middle East made up the Sheep. A mixed bag of global mercenaries, fighting for money and lack of any other professional talent other than the art of war. The Sheep used whomever they could control for their purposes. Whomever they could afford. Whomever provided plausible deniability. Those from Islamic and Communist countries of the world fit perfectly into their planned etiological flock.

As these mercenaries became more and more professional over the years, so did their training. No longer the weight lifting meat heads; but rather, cross fit, yoga, and injury prevention were now scientifically proven to extend the soldier's effectiveness and survivability over the course of repeated deployments and constant engagements. Cold water baths, strict diets, steroids. Junk food was no longer an option. Power bars, shake supplements, high protein diets, low inflammation recovery diets. There were all kinds of fads, pseudoscience, and information adrift on helping the mercenary extend their lifetime earnings.

It seemed that every returning Navy SEAL was advertising or creating a better fitness product, and a lot of the kids going through SEAL BUDS initiation were getting busted for cycling steroids. There were also readily available testosterone injections, stem cell repair, uppers, downers, pain pills, and the steady intake of ibuprofen and Black Rifle Coffee. But what science can use to help the fighter, it can also be used against him, particularly the brain's pain pathways. His accent was Ukrainian, or some Eastern European block country. Likely a former Wagner group veteran crossing the world for a paycheck. With the abundance of tattoos on his arms and back, unlikely to have come from the Muslim side of those conflicts. More likely a hire from the Russian mobs whose influence reached deep within the Sheep's cause. Funded by one of the richest and most powerful men on earth, Putin.

My colleagues had already attempted the usual rough up game to no avail. Water boarding served no purpose with a fighter of this magnitude. His genetic code had been altered during his little time on earth to endure any torture tactic he had seen or heard about around the world. But, I knew he had a cortex. That cortex held the possibility to kick off a never ending pain cycle. One that he could never control. One that he could not train to endure. That cycle was fueled by glutamate, and they didn't teach glutamate in Russian survival training.

As much as the new technology, training, and diet forged healthier, stronger, aging mercenaries, it could also be used against them if one translated the science into the outcome sought. Testosterone to get stronger. Estrogen to get softer. Steroids to increase muscle mass. Catabolic steroids to de bulk. Caffeine to stay awake and focused. Pills for sleep. Perfected diets of scaled carbs and protein for restoration of muscles. *How about a diet high in glutamate?* Much like the Miranda rights warning, "Anything you say can and will be used against you", my science would instill "Anything science can provide will be used against you."

The dipshit's name was Boris, but I called him Jeff. I called all of them Jeff. Just like I called all of the females Karen. No one likes a Karen. Just like no one likes a Jeff. Occasionally, you might like a Boris, so Jeff it was.

After his last session of pain and water boarding, which I knew would do no good, The Notch placed him in my care. He would be full of self confidence after defeating the prior techniques. My treatment was to be a little different than his prior sessions. Something Jeff wasn't accustomed to in his training. I was going to be really nice to Jeff. I needed his complete trust and cooperation. His confidence from defeating waterboarding would release a little dopamine to assist in this trust.

I brought my Russian translators into the scene, keeping them knowledgeable only to necessity, not intending on leaking any of my techniques. These were *my* techniques, and they had always worked well, especially with those East of the former Berlin wall's borders who had suffered so much under Soviet extremism. I planned to comfort the Russian when in pain, to become his new comrade in arms, and to suffer his cause with him. Jeff needed mental support, and I was happy to give it to him, and intentionally providing Russian female translators would play into that motherly role he likely never had. Dopamine is the child's blanket for the mind.

A warmer cell, warmer clothes. Hot food. Drinks. Some vodka on occasion. An ear to listen to his complaints and needs. Occasional flirting and talk of the old country. These techniques were provided by a woman he would never know, probably much the same as his childhood. Cuts, scrapes, and bruises were all treated with antibiotic shots and pills. We were different. We were there to help. At least that's what the translator told Jeff.

If he wanted to "serve his time and return to his cause, these meds would heal his wounds and keep him out of the hospital", she explained.

He had survived the prior torture, and no one could have survived that torture. Except him. He was a strong, proud Russian according to her. Rescue or prisoner trade was soon to happen. Hope is on the way. He would be laughing inside at his imminent release. Building confidence, releasing more dopamine. Wrapping him further in the blanket of comfort. He needed to believe in hope.

Death from untreated wounds was something Jeff understood from his combat around the world and in his survival training. They would have specifically instructed him to readily eat, drink, or accept anything that might increase his chance of surviving and make it to a rescue attempt or an end to the current imprisonment.

He wasn't about to say no to treating his injuries. In fact, this was a refreshing change from the cold and wind that this American Siberia provided. "The Notch" was what his American handlers called it. A wretched place, Jeff thought. He had left the Ukraine's cold behind once in his lifetime, vowing to never return to fight for another man's false promises. He much preferred the warm climate of the African and Arabian conflicts, promising himself to never take a cold weather assignment again, despite the money offered.

Jeff got a very specific diet. Rich in one of my favorite pain chemicals-glutamate-an excitatory neurotransmitter. Being sure to leave out foods rich in GABA, which was the neurotransmitter responsible for keeping glutamate in balance, causing inhibition, but not excitatory signals. I needed no balance in Jeff. He needed extremely high glutamate- super excitement at the cellular level. Too much of these excitatory chemicals would create a biome of anxiety, sleeplessness, nerve damage, restlessness, fatigue, depression, inflammation, and overall irritability. Other chemicals could also be increased in his diet that would stimulate the glutamate receptor: MSG, homocysteine, cysteine, aspartic acid, and glutamic acid. In excess, all could cause a toxic-like response in the nervous system, especially in GABA's absence. Jeff didn't know this. He munched away at what I fed him. He was just following his training as I knew he would.

Eat if they give you food. It may be your last chance to eat. Strength may be needed to escape. I even offered him second helpings.

Glutamate is responsible for the unique taste in certain foods. Often referred to as umami which is a meaty, savory, coating within the taste buds, known as Xian-Wei in Chinese. Free glutamate leads to this umami sensation and is found in cheeses, mushrooms, scallops, beef, shrimp, and tomatoes. But the nasty side of glutamate could appear in many other foods, and these were the foods he received the most. Bouillon soup broths, gelatin broths, soy protein drinks, whey protein shakes, smoke flavorings, sodas full of nutrasweet and aspartame, spaghetti sauces, cereals, corn, tofu, soy sauces, cold cuts and sausages, ramen noodles, mustards, mayonnaise, fried chicken, frozen pizzas, flour, frostings, cheap baked goods. The American grocery store is filled with glutamates, and Russians love the American diet.

Jeff was eating like a king. My favorite dish to serve him was the Americanized version of General Tso's Chicken with processed flour noodles, mixed with fried chicken and tofu, a diet version of the bottled sauce, with a side of chicken flavored tofu. All washed down with diet sodas. For dessert, cheap processed cupcakes of the Wal Mart bakery variety. Of course, all of his dishes were sprinkled with my favorite bottled glutamate source, MSG. That magical coating provides every glutamate enriched bite with Xian-Wei. As they say, you are what you eat. Jeff was excited to see his food , but he didn't know that his food was "exciting" him internally. Step two was to work on Jeff's sleep. He needed to feel as if he was sleeping, but never really reaching the true restorative parts of his sleeping cycle. Jeff went from being forced awake, to being able to sleep freely. Although, he was forced awake every fifteen minutes to an hour. His brain would dive immediately into the stage of recovery it longed for, but rudely be awakened. Never allowing him into the deep recovery phase of sleep, just the REM first and second stages. He remembered going to sleep over and over and over, but he just wasn't allowed to sleep through the night. This was nothing to him. He had stayed awake for missions all the time to get the job done. He was trained to get the job done with no sleep. They had trained him in survival school about sleep deprivation.   This training led to more dopamine release.

In addition, I only wanted him to awaken to something safe and secure. That's why the translators were Marzana and Nadia, two of our own from a Ukrainian dominated city in Florida called North Port where they had developed a deep hatred of Russians after they invaded their country.

They totally focused on his comfort. His understanding of how much love was being provided to him would be reinforced and interrupted by what I could only hope to be his maternal, Freudian attachment to his Mother, as Father's were usually absent drunkards in the Eastern Block countries, often dying from alcoholism quite young or from being sent to fight Putin's wars. Next on the game plan, Jeff's medications. I gave him a simple antibiotic for his minor cuts as well as giving Nadia topical Neosporin to rub on his injuries. While not providing any real additional benefit, the visual effect of someone healing his wounds with Neosporin would add to his mental breakdown, especially if it was maternal. What Jeff didn't know were the other injections I delivered.

First, caffeine to help disturb his sleep cycle. I had watched as Jeff skipped the coffee and tea. I knew he was trying to get to sleep, and he was smart enough to avoid stimulants. That same excitatory molecule, caffeine, would speed up that pain cycle, and I wasn't going to allow Jeff to skip his caffeine. Him thinking he was avoiding it was also powerful for he felt like he was following his training. More dopamine release.

Jeff's ripped body indicated he was quite an athlete. The injection marks also indicated he had developed a liking for anabolic steroids. Likely something he started in his forties as injuries became a common place for mercenaries, and that forty year old belly fat kept the girls chatting with his younger teammates instead of him-the old, out of shape team guy.

Estrogen supplements would have a great effect on Jeff. Both mentally and physically. He liked to workout in his cell, so to watch his mind ponder why he was only getting fatter and softer would only add to his breakdown. Work out all you would like Jeff. Your body will be tired. Your muscles will break down with little to no repair. Estrogen adding more pudge, and less violence for our guards. Estrogen would also make him more compassionate, more emotional, more feminine in his thoughts.

I wasn't concerned with his body's transformation, but rather the mental. Testosterone would increase his will to fight, his anger to resist. Estrogen would provide quite the opposite. His mind would bend from aggression and lean towards caring and forgiveness. Another play on his motherly instincts at the genetic hormone level. Nadia's familiar dialogue and stories from what was going on back in Eastern Europe would help him remember some of the good old days. His survival instincts would diminish with the new comfort found here.

Long acting Beta blockers were being crushed into his food. These Beta blockers worked on the Beta receptors throughout the body, but I was concerned about the ones specific to his heart. Once his torture began, I didn't want an elevation in his heart rate. He was already in great shape with a resting heart rate of sixty. I would begin my sessions when his resting heart rate was in the forties. With his young age, he would hardly notice the slowdown. His low heart rate to him would be further evidence that his workouts were keeping him in shape.

All the great Soviet athletes had low heart rates Jeff would likely remember. Pills found around the Notch were in great supply. The elderly left them all behind when they vacated their mountain skiing vacation homes, and almost all older people were prescribed beta blockers to decrease hypertension. Anything I could think of to provide an increased anxiety level, I gave or presented to Jeff. Surprise visits from snakes and spiders, animal torture videos, hostage interrogation videos, violent movies, and war zone sounds. Instilling hot sauce in his topical antibiotic ointment, angry conversations from strangers talking in a variety of languages he couldn't interpret, constant heat in his cell instead of cold, then switching the climate back to cold. Everything was focused on stimulation. Excitement. Famous Russian soccer games, gay porn, children in horror movies. *Anxiety.*

All were followed by the comfort of the Ukrainian women.

One of my favorite stimulants was to apply a surgical tourniquet to Jeff's extremities. While causing zero harm, the device inflicted a response on a pain receptor that was usually hard to stimulate, stretch and pressure receptors, which worked on slow un myelinated C-pain fibers. Placing the tourniquet on his upper arm, and inflating it to around twice his blood pressure, the pain would begin to pulsate at around 45 minutes, becoming excruciating at around two hours. Not a big deal when one was anesthetized during a surgery, but a very big deal when awake. The body would do anything to free itself of the tourniquet's infliction. However, Jeff's heart rate went up only to around 100 instead of the 200s usually seen without pain medication. My beta blockers were working. Pain without destruction. Mental excitation without physical harm. His body reached the flight stage mentally, but not physically.

Drop the tourniquet, and within five minutes, the body forgot that it had ever tried to avoid the stimulus. Heart rate back to forty. I always made sure that one of the females deflated the tourniquet, and that I inflated the tourniquet. Mom always made you feel better, and that's who would be asking the questions when the time came. Russian fathers were non-existent or created abuse. Mothers cared.

Jeff hated the tourniquet. Even a simple rubber tourniquet around a thumb or finger had the same outcome. Something so small inflicts such anxiety. With a father never home to help, Jeff became a man, forced to find his way on the painful path of Soviet adulthood. I didn't know this. I had only guessed, but he had admitted as much to the girls.

I was turning Jeff into an anti-soldier through science. Weak, whiney, irritable, impatient, weary, non crafty, non trusting, irrational, hyper, anxiety ridden, stressed, emotional, breakable. A true train wreck, but mostly from his own doings. He was allowed to eat heartily, sleep often, watch movies, drink unlimited sodas, have medical care, with just the occasional surprise and torture session like the tourniquet.

He thought he was winning the battle. His survival classes were paying off. He could beat these little games that I was playing. And Jeff was right, he could easily beat these games. But my game was different. My game was the excitement of neurotransmission.

Jeff's cortex was going up against Jordan in a one-on-one basketball match. Jordan's prowess was his ability to get inside his opponent's head. Inside that cortex. To throw them off their game mentally should he be evenly matched physically, all done through the brain's own use of chemical reactions and prior learned experiences to reactions. That's what made the greats great. I had to be the Jordan of my game.

No athlete wants that game of embarrassment. Everyone has experienced it. The pain of losing so badly at what you are supposed to be so good at embeds in that cortex. The Notch was depending on me. Jeff's resting heart rate had just gone to 35. Time to hit the court for some one on one with his cortex. Yesterday, I had provided some Youtube videos for Jeff's daily viewings. By this time, he was quite used to the constant stream of violence spewing from the television set. These videos showed how to use the Stryker Dermatome 40.

In the operating room, the dermatome was used to gather the grafts for split thickness skin grafting when repairing large sections of skin, such as with burn injuries or in trauma. From a depth of 0.15 mm to 0.5 mm, the dermatome would make a perfect shaving specimen of the skin, an almost Saran Wrap thick piece of tissue. This new micro sheet of skin could then be placed on the area injured, growing into new skin over the affected area. That tough waterproof outer layer of skin, the epidermis, covered the next layer, the dermis which contains sweat glands and hair follicles.

Depending on the need, the dermatome could dissect either or both of the layers. Free pain nerve endings terminated within the dermis and the epidermis. All of this science was covered for Jeff in the video- in Russian.

All day. Over and over. He couldn't really process why this

dermatome was the violent selection of the day. Just another sick video from his captors. It was at least better than the torture videos.

"Why should I care how a stupid surgical tool works," Jeff thought to himself. "These weak Americans will be destroyed soon enough. My comrades will be here to rescue me soon."

"Good morning Jeff," Nadia said softly.

She was inside his cell. Marzana was outside the cell, turning off the television that constantly played violence or chaotic American metal music videos. The sound of the dermatome's buzzing came to an end on the TV.

"Finally a break from that stupid video", he told Marzana. Shaking his head in disgust. The Ukrainian girls had really taken a liking to him, even flirting he thought. They probably enjoyed hanging around an alpha Russian male instead of the weak beta American males.

"Good morning Nadia," Jeff said.

Attempting to break the fog that was in his head. He always felt somber lately, as if he didn't care about anything anymore, and yet felt anxious. Lazy to his prayers and to his cause, unable to focus on his thoughts, and constantly nervous. He couldn't understand. It wasn't depression, but maybe this was what the American culture called anxiety.

He was getting rest and eating better than he had ever in his life. Staying in shape, exercising in his cell. Maybe it was the horrible American diet they were giving him. Frozen pizzas and Chinese food. He was growing fond of the Diet Cokes and what they called Diet Mountain Dew. He thought this must be what the lazy fat Southern Americans must feel like every day-foggy minded and slow. Worried about nothing when they had everything. Russians had no such luxuries.

"Today will be a little different for you Jeff," Nadia coaxed,

"I need you to take your clothes off for me and Marzana."

Jeff had never even considered the possibility of sex with his translators. His body had grown soft, pudgy in his chest and abdomen. His breasts even seemed to be getting larger. He thought it was likely from not getting the same quality of weights and workouts he was used to, although he had been working out, he just had seen no results. He almost felt ashamed at the idea of revealing his new disgusting body to these two beautiful women.

"Has to be the food," he thought.

He even began to feel a little embarrassed at the possibility of being unable to perform for the two lovely comrades. He had not been able to get an erection in days. Both of the girls were obviously attracted to him and his cause. These girls had no Father's, just as he hadn't. They really looked up to strong Russian men of valor. Strong men they had never been around as a child. He knew the Americans would at some point attempt to use sex as a tool to talk, but these girls were different. They were "his" people. They adored him. They understood his role in this war. He had befriended them as his training had taught.

"After you disrobe. Please place your hands together, and I will place the plastic zip ties around your wrists before we let you out of the cell for your special treat." Nadia looked towards Marzana with a wink and smile.

They seemed familiar with whatever they had in mind for him. Perhaps his captors did have a heart. He would try to enjoy his time with these beautiful women. After all, they had been extremely pleasant to him since he passed the water boarding tests. They were probably impressed with his mental strength and fortitude. Russians didn't break like Arabs. He had seen how they caved in Africa.

Jeff slid the plastic zip ties around his wrists and extended his arms towards the prison bars at Marzana. She pulled them both tight. He stepped back and towards the door to his cell. Marzana turned the key and opened the door. Jeff knew there was no sense breaching the outer doors. He had seen the level of guards and security waiting on the other side. Whatever they had planned for him, he really had no choice. He didn't want to make a stir. He didn't really feel like resisting anymore. This had been the nicest stent in a foreign jail perhaps in his lifetime. He felt anxious, but at home at the same time. He was extremely tired, yet uncontrollably excited and nervous.

Nadia guided him over to a long metal table, about eight feet in length. He could not remember having ever seen the table. There were scratch marks all over its surface. The thought of its alternative uses flashed through his mind, but he couldn't seem to focus for any length of time on important things anymore. Always awake, but irritable. Worrying for no reason. Always on edge. But, he was eating and sleeping. He was surviving.

"*Just getting old*," he thought.

He laid down on the cold shiny table as told.

At the bottom of the table were two holes close to the table's legs. Marzana placed two sets of plastic cuffs around each ankle, and then pulled up on the tabs, securing his lower extremities. Jeff tried moving his legs, but they went nowhere. He was stuck. *More anxiety.* She cut his arm cuffs while Nadia moved one arm to the side, securing it in a similar manner as his legs, but above his head. Repeating the process for the other arm. *More anxiety.* He could surely use some vodka right now.

Nadia pulled out her radio and said in English, "He is ready."

I opened the door to the holding cell. Slowly and deliberately scraping the metal latches. High pitched, ominous scraping noises that echoed around the concrete walls of the holding cell. The heavy metal door creaked on its hinges.

Straight out of a Stephen King movie was this door. I loved its sound. Its screeching always preceded the main event about to occur. To watch the outcome of a science experiment was always fun.

The metal Craftsman cart had a bad wheel, and much like a shopping cart with one fucked up wheel, it had a predictable rhythm to it's movement. *Shush-thump-shush-thump. Shush-thumpshush-thump.* Old metal tool carts from Sears were common across surgical suites in the United States. They could be easily cleaned for Joint Commission visits when they inspected the anesthesia department's tools of the trade, and this one was straight from the old hospital in Littleton. The cart slowed on the journey to Jeff. I was enjoying its sound.

Jeff's head had been intentionally left free so that he could see my comings and goings. He lay motionless and speechless on the table, unaware of what was to come. I had seen a definite change in his persona. Between the bad food, caffeine, constant itchy and burning wounds, and sleep deprivation, his anxiety was peaking. With his heart rate slowed, he was starting to tire easily. The Beta blockers working on his heart, but as a side effect, also affecting the Beta receptors in his lungs and his ability to breathe. The estrogen helping deflate his ego and will to fight. He would still have some capacity to put up a fight, but I would get all the intelligence I wanted from him. Microphones were up and ready. Cameras set up at two different angles. Back up batteries and lighting available. Jeff was a high ranking member of The Sheep. This was important for the Notch. Hopefully, he was excited enough to tell his story.

Excitatory transmitters versus inhibitory transmitters. The cortex could really make the brain its bartender.

"Would you like an espresso sir? How about some cocaine? Or, would some chamomile tea be better to rest?".

The voice in my mind switched to Tom Cruise's character in the movie Cocktail. I envisioned that sneer, confident smile, black shirt, and shaker tricks.

Nadia walked over to Jeff's flaccid, cold cock, putting her warm hand on the shaft.

"We will be here to help you today Jeff. As long as you answer some questions." She purred into his ear.

Jeff took a deep breath. Relaxing in the relief that he wouldn't be tortured, but instead pleasured. These girls would take care of him. His cock remained flaccid.

"*Odd,*" he thought.

He'd never had issues getting hard. Especially around such beautiful women he had come to trust. Who adored him. Estrogen levels were peaking too I could see. His friendliness towards the girls had increased. He wanted to bond, and yet he couldn't understand why his body hadn't cooperated to the young female's touch.

Marzana turned on the Dermatome. She had snuck in behind Jeff's head, placing the device near his ear, right next to the stapes bone and the follicles that enabled hearing. It sounded like a barber's shears scraping across a microphone. Compressed air powering its blade. Loud. Destructive. The destruction level sound of a chainsaw starting. It was a tool that you knew wasn't fucking around. A tool that held purpose. It was there to do a job of fucking up stuff.

The Dermatome demanded one's attention.

Jeff's face went from warm and blushed to white and panicked. The noise was familiar to him. It was from the last video that the Americans kept playing over and over again, except this time, it was the real tool. The Stryker Dermatome 40 video had been playing the entire last day. The sound was much different live. The monotonous instructions from the video began to play in Jeff's head. He could almost recite them after listening all day.

"....the dermis can be separated from the epidermis by using this technique…"

Musicians sounded even better live than on their albums, just as a video recording couldn't give this tool justice. Its power reminded him of the first time he had ever used a portable circular saw. You could feel the destruction it could cause.

"Be respectful or you'll lose a hand," his absent Father's voice came back to him, confused as to why at this moment.

But Jeff never had a father. Maybe it was his high school shop teacher.

"Why the fuck am I confused?", Jeff said aloud over the dermatome.

Marzena pulled the dermatome away and whispered in Jeff's ear,

"Please baby. Just answer the man's questions, so that he won't hurt you with this machine. I'm here to help you feel better. And when this is over, you know I will make you feel better." Her hand back on his shaft.

She held the button in for max speed. Making the tool scream like a handsaw. The look of utter confusion continued.

"What do they want from me?" Jeff thought.

I walked over to the steel table. Jeff wasn't attempting to move his tattooed body anymore. He knew it would be a waste of time to try, wasting his energy against the restraints. I examined the top part of his right thigh. A nice wide section to obtain a skin graft. A nice wide area to let the tool slide just under the dermis, separating the tissues efficiently.

Careful to keep my prisoner from becoming infected, I wiped the area with some alcohol.

A dead prisoner provides no information, I reminded

myself.

The alcohol's smell lingered in the air for Jeff. His imagination worked with the smell, and what limited medical knowledge he had was putting two and two together. He could lean his neck up to look down his abdomen, but the restraints across his waist prevented him from actually visualizing his thigh.

Marzena passed me the dermatome, bent over to show Jeff her cleavage, and kissed him on the lips. Staring into his eyes as they bounced around the room. The look of a teenage boy, with the fear of having done something wrong, he felt as if he had let his Mother down. A feeling he had let others down. Sheer disappointment.

"Jeff. You get no chances today at second chances. You are going to break. And if not broken, I will not kill you. But you will be permanently brain damaged enough to never cause anyone any problems again. So filled with pain, regret, and fear, that you will never work for Wagner Group again."

His fearful eyes stared at me as I continued.

"You are here to answer questions about how you breached our lines in North Conway. About how Wagner is getting supplies and troops into the United States. And who is paying you? Is it the Sheep, the government, or both. What is being promised for your success?

"We understand that you will not stop torturing our teams, so we decided to start ignoring the Geneva conventions, too. But, we really prefer to send you back to the front, so that your buddies there can see that we do not wish for you to die a soldier's death. We want to make you completely dependent on others. To make you a complete, expensive, broken human. Wanting to die, but too weak to commit suicide, and broken enough to make the Sheep forced to take care of you. You will become a burden to your own society Jeff.

"You have been a liability to your team. You were taught throughout your training that you needed to be strong in all areas for your team, an asset in all skills needed on the battlefield. Communications. Medical support. Intelligence. Fitness. Weapons. Everything you have trained for was to help the team. Working together to take on the enemy. And if hurt, your team would help you-at least get you off the battlefield until you recover to help the team again. "But not today. Today you have failed your team. You were captured. Treated well. And never volunteered to help us with what we have asked for. We made you a part of our team. Treating you, a mercenary, with compassion. Love. Food. Shelter. And for what were we rewarded? Fucking nothing Jeff. You have given us nothing. We have given you everything, and yet, you still believe you will be valuable to your country and your team again. That's not happening Jeff. You will be a crying, limp soldier, begging the people around you to help you take a piss, take a shower, to help you eat, to help put your clothes on. You don't deserve death. You deserve the inability to use your hands for your own suicide, and the inability to do anything but watch how much of a burden you are to everyone around you. You will not get death today Jeff. You will get a little more love from me and the girls."

I cranked the dermatome to max and placed it on Jeff's leg. It's vibrations rattling him. Fear causing him to piss himself. He knew what the machine could do. I slid it down his thigh towards his knee and let my finger off the trigger. Pain receptors at the dermal level firing all at once, stimulated by the glutamate.

Reaching over to the med cart, I opened a closed bowl. In it were long strips of chicken skin that I had removed earlier and stretched long and wide, allowing them to warm to room temperature.

I threw the skin onto Jeff's face.

He was screaming as loud as he could. Trying to shake the skin of his thigh from his head.

I placed my hand on his thigh again.

"Relax Jeff. The more you move, the more this will bleed. Keep this leg still for me. You know we don't want any infections. Marzena, please help Jeff with his leg."

Marzena walked over with a bandage and some tape. Quickly covering Jeff's non existent leg wound. I had removed the blade from the saw before I used it, but Jeff didn't know that. His mind was fried from the glutamate and lack of sleep. Some old red and dirtied bandages appeared in Marzena's hand. A mother's love on her face.

"Jeff. Please help me." She said, only inches from his eyes.

"Please help both of us, so that we can move on together." Her hands wrapped around his balls. "I only know that we receive gold coins from the Sheep prior to missions. Money is worthless with inflation. They pay us in gold. But you already know all these things. I am a simple mercenary. No more. They tell us nothing." Jeff was starting to talk.

"How do you get into the United States? Who does the paperwork? Who gets you from there to here?" I asked.

"We come into Montreal on trucks. We cross at a border in the Northern United States. Maybe a place called Vermont. But I don't know for sure. They just drive us during the night."

Jeff continued, "We get rifles at the airport in Canada, and they don't check us coming across the border. There isn't security like it used to be. And since we are against you, they let us walk right in."

"Who is your contact there Jeff? What is the name? Where is this crossing? You have to know. You would have been familiar with the map locations and rendezvous points if something happened. You are an experienced military guy. What radio channel was used?" I was becoming unimpressed with his answers. He wasn't lying. He just wasn't going fast enough.

I walked to his other thigh. Opening the alcohol bottle again. The smell passed under his nose. This time instead of placing the alcohol on his thigh, I splashed it all over his genitals and penis. He jumped from the cold. Trying to keep his hips still.

"Now Jeff. There is no way I can cut safely with you moving like this. If we were in the operating room, we would have to give you a little something to hold you still." He didn't like my comment.

"Fuck you American shit. I've been through all of this before." Jeff yelled.

Out of nowhere, Nadia stated in the driest of Ukrainian tones, "Well, why don't you just give him something to keep him still, and then you can cut his dick off."

Genius. Pure fucking genius. And since the idea hadn't come from me, it seemed all the more realistic to Jeff.

"Perfect idea Nadia! I love your thinking. Why don't you hand me a 10 mL syringe and needle. I got just the thing for Mr. Jeff."

I cranked the dermatome on high and put it on Jeff's balls. Piss rained. Shit came out all over my shiny dermatome. For some reason, I became angry..

"How dare you get your shit on my dermatome you fucking dickless piece of shit Russian." Although a little too dramatic, I reached in the bowl and found a heavy piece of a chicken thigh resembling the size of Jeff's cock and stuffed it in his mouth.

"You fucking cocksucker!", I laughed.

Mainly not for effect, but because it was actually funny to call him a cocksucker. He choked and gagged against the piece of chicken. I doubt he knew it wasn't his real cock. In his mind, everything was over processed. Everything was too real. Heightened.

"Jeff, you know what a dick tastes like right?" I asked him in a Dad joke voice.

"Chicken".

While hilarious to me and the girls, laying on his back chained down, he *really thought* his own dick was in his mouth, unable to lift his head far enough to see his thighs and scrotum. Another thing Jeff didn't know was that when Marzena reached down and grabbed his dick, she also put a handful of lidocaine cream all over his balls and shaft. Taking about 15 minutes to reach its desired outcome, he really couldn't feel his dick and balls, and was too confused as to why there was no pain.

Was it his superior Russian training? Where were my balls? , he thought, which was immediately replaced by the thought of the dick being in his mouth.

Nadia pulled the meat out of his mouth and threw it into the bowl. Trying not to laugh as she did so.

"I'm so disappointed I can't enjoy this later Jeff." She said sexily in his ear.

Inside my cart, I grabbed a 10 mL vial of Succinylcholine. A depolarizing neuromuscular blocker that had a special synergistic effect at the neuromuscular junction, and would act synergistically with another molecule if present- *glutamate.* Succinylcholine, which we called Sux, was given to induce paralysis in a patient. Given after they had been sedated, to open the vocal cords rapidly so that a breathing tube could be placed.

Both Sux and glutamate worked around nicotinic receptors, which were present within skeletal muscle. Sux would go to the neuromuscular junction and cause the cell to depolarize, flooding the junction between the motor end plate of the neuron with acetylcholine, causing the skeletal muscle to enter an activated state. Muscles would tighten into a flexed and locked state, contractions occurring to the point the junctions could no longer depolarize the sites occupied, thus inducing complete muscle paralysis. With glutamate present, which was already affecting Jeff's NMDA and GABA receptor levels, and thus his OCD, anxiety, and mental toughness levels, that junction was about to be supremely unaware of what hit it.

Drawing up the med into the syringe, I asked Jeff more questions.

"Jeff, who gives Russian units help here in New Hampshire? Who and where do you coordinate?" He was quiet now. Unsure what to say. He knew we were progressing to the next step.

"Jeff. This is a med called Sux. You might have seen your medics or CRNAs give it to patients after they are asleep to get the breathing tube in. Usually, you are asleep when you are paralyzed. *Usually*. Today, you will not be. You will be fully awake and aware of everything around you. We are not going to breathe for you, and if we don't, in your current condition, you may be able to go around 1-2 minutes before your brain starts to run out of oxygen. And Jeff, not to get technical, but it's really not oxygen you need. Your brain really needs to get rid of carbon dioxide. That's what makes you breathe."

He still remained silent.

"So in short, you will be awake, but unable to breathe. It's kind of like drowning would feel like in the ocean. You have filled the lungs with water, and no longer can you exchange oxygen and get rid of that CO2. For about 2 minutes you would be awake. Long enough to know that you were drowning. The good news with drowning is that your brain would shut off, and you would painlessly sink to the bottom of the ocean.

"But as you can imagine, that's not going to happen. I've been giving you special drugs Jeff, in your food. One of the drugs, Metoprolol, is a Beta blocker that has been slowing your heart down through all of this today. I didn't want you to get too worked up and have a heart attack on us-then I would never get any info from you. The bad part of slowing your heart down, is that if we give Sux a second time, your heart may not be able to speed up because it's blocked. And Sux really, really slows down your heart on a second dose.

"Now, I know what you are thinking. Why would we give it to you a second time? Well, because we are going to let you go until you pass out. Just when your brain is starting to become damaged, we are going to breathe for you and bring you back. And we plan on doing this as much as we can or as long as your heart can keep beating, just up to the point where you are either almost completely stroked out, or you are in need of someone taking care of you in a wheelchair for life, which as you know is what my goal was today anyway. More than likely, you will let us down, just like you let your teammates down." He suddenly broke.

"They have fake IDs from a girl named Amanda. She is our connection. She gets us more ammunition. She gets our food. Our supplies. She is always in your uniform though. She is on your side, an American." It was as if Jeff was on cocaine he was so excitatory. Restrained to the table on cocaine.

"She lives in Franconia or Lisbon. Somewhere near the river on the border, in an old farm house with a large barn."

Finally, some information.

"We need more than that Jeff." I pushed.

"We meet on Sunday afternoons when your troops are

usually hiding from the drones. We move freely across the Vermont border by St. Johnsbury. The people there are very supportive of us. Even before the war, the people in Vermont were on our side most of the time." True I thought. The home of Ben and Jerry's would be.

"Jeff, who else in my organization, other than Amanda, is screwing us over? Tell me the names. I know you have more than one. Who helps you on the East side of the mountains? Tell me the name."

I uncapped the syringe, exposing the needle. Jeff's eyes were bulging out of his head.

"I don't know the east side. I only do the west side. Eric and Todd do the West side. Please don't use that medicine. I have given you all of the information."

The needle went easily into Jeff's ante cubital vein. I aspirated the needle to confirm vein placement, and pushed 5 mL of the Sux into Jeff. It would be about 45 seconds until it kicked in. "You're a liar Jeff. I just gave you the first dose. In about a minute, you are going to have some of the most painful contractions across your entire body that you have ever felt. Every muscle, going to every part of your body that can move, including your eyes, are going to start to contract, all at the same time. But, the good news is, that won't happen for long. We will be right here with you Jeff. When you are begging in your mind for us to ventilate your sorry ass. You fucking piece of shit liar. We treated you so well, and all you can do is lie. Maybe we won't breathe for you."

Marzana leaned in above his face as the drug started to work.

"Please Jeff. Talk to us so we can leave this place together. I don't care if you don't have a dick anymore."

His body shook the table. Almost causing it to jump off of

the floor and tip over. Massive muscle contractions, until finally he was still. Complete lack of motion. No eye movement. No diaphragm movement. Jeff was on the oxygen clock, and only his brain could hear the ticking.

Nadia looked into Jeff's eyes. His mind was fully awake. His body unable to move. "Your brothers will have to take care of you now. You are no longer a man for me," she said, glancing at his pelvis. "You are the same as all Russian men. Worthless, dickless babies!" No response. No movement. I placed a pulse oximeter on Jeff's finger. His oxygen level read 95%. His heart rate was 70. *That damn metoprolol sure was working* I thought. An audible higher toned beep corresponded to the saturation of 95. I looked down at Jeff and began to speak.

"Jeff, I'm not sure if I will kill you today. I kinda want to see how you come back. When I wake you up, will you be unable to talk?. Stroked out? Can't move your arms? How about your legs? Someone else wiping your ass in your wheelchair? Men at the hospital having to give you baths? Russians don't have that kind of care back home. Maybe in Vermont, but not back home Jeff. We will take you across the border as a mentally sharp invalid."

The tone of the pulse ox shifted down one step. The number showed 91%. We were about a minute in. About what I expected.

"Have you ever gone to the pool Jeff? Maybe your buddies are there. You inhale and then go down under the water, and see which one of you is the last to come up for air. Did you ever do that in Russia, Jeff? Here we did. I usually got just around a minute. I had a buddy that could go about two minutes. But that's really unusual. I tell you what, Nadia, Marzena-let's all try like Jeff. Take a big breath in. Let's hold it in together. It's not fair that Jeff does this alone."

We all inhaled together. I looked down at my watch. Holding up one finger to indicate to Jeff that one minute had gone by. The pulse ox tone dropped again to 88%. *Must be the beta blockers slowing down his cardiac output and his oxygen consumption* I thought. *Maybe the glutamate wasn't all I had hoped for.*

His eyes looked lifeless now. 75% on the pulse ox. It's alarms going off incessantly telling the providers that something was wrong. I wasn't about to turn them off. Those sounds had to be unpleasant to Jeff's ears.

70%. A slight shade of blue was occurring on Jeff's face. The oxygen had been removed from the hemoglobin, having nothing else to release, the arterial blood was beginning to resemble venous. At this point, his saturation would dive quickly with no reserve of oxygen on the hemoglobin molecule. No rescue. His mind screaming for a breath. Completely aware of our presence.

Dramatically, I stopped trying to hold my breath. Bending over, I took in the biggest, loudest inhalation of my life.

"Man am I out of shape Jeff. I couldn't even go a minute. How's my tough Russian soldier doing? Ain't the same as water boarding is it bud? You know when that's over. You know you have an end in sight. But they didn't train you on Sux did they? They didn't prepare you for a slow death."

In his mind, the glutamate receptors were satiated at all nerve terminals, synergized by the Sux. An epic peak of anxiety, to a level not really achieved by any other method. It was chemically beautiful to watch.

The pulse ox hit 50%. He would start to fade now. His mind anoxic, unable to log memories. It wouldn't matter what I said or did at this point. His mind was out of his body, to the floating point. High above his body, staring back at himself.

Wondering if this was how heaven would be.

His mind had checked out of the Holiday Inn. There was no need to pay the bill. It was time to step in. The pulse ox hit 30% . The pulsatile flow of the heart slowed to almost a stop, a pulse almost nonexistent had it not been for his age and good health. Dropping much faster due to the Beta blockers inhibiting the hearts ability to increase cardiac output.

Marzena brought the oxygen mask up to Jeff's face. Prior to the first breath, she placed an oral airway past his teeth and around his tongue. She began her rescue breathing. Watching his chest rise. The pulse oximeter had already changed to 40%. Nadia unchained the restraints, and we pushed the table back into Jeff's cell. Placing him on his bunk. Cutting the zip ties. Placing his blanket over him. His pillow under his head.

Sux lasted only a short time, maybe two to three minutes at most, so he was already starting to breathe on his own, but I was unsure how long it would last because of the high doses of glutamate.

His chest began making fast, but small motions to draw air past the oral airway. Marzena assisted, but less so now. His oxygen sat at 97%. She removed the airway as he gained more strength. We exited the cell. I walked back to the cart. Cleaned up all evidence we had been in the room at all. Quickly mopping, wiping, and drying all the surfaces before wheeling the cart out of the room.

Before I left, I turned the Dermatome video back on, with the sound all the way up. Just as Jeff was beginning to regain consciousness, I closed the door behind me, trying not to make a sound. Jeff opened his eyes. He felt confused. Tired, as if he had run a race. He had been choked out before in his jiu jitsu classes, and this was a similar feeling. His sense of smell returned to him first, just like in those classes. A smell of freshness, cold. Something from childhood, but unplaceable entered his nose. Taste was next. Then vision started to emerge.

He was laying in his bed. He could make out the dermatome video. Everything had happened so fast. Not like what he thought it would be. He remembered that they had used the dermatome on him before the sux. It then occurred to him that he should look under the sheet.

Slowly peeling the sheet back, he could see his penis and balls there, and could actually feel them. They were a little cold and wet, but there. Tingling to touch, but he took a big sigh.

Thankful.

Looking at his leg, there was also nothing cut off his thigh. No marks, cuts, or bruises. *"Am I dreaming? Am I going crazy? I know they did this to me. It was all too real. They gave me this Sux medicine. I died. I couldn't breathe, and drowned in my own slow death. Or did I?"*

Jeff was unable to tell up from down, left from right. He only knew what had happened was real. Where had they gone? Where were they? None of the tools were there. The dermatome was gone. No table. But it had to have happened.

He heard the door creak, its slow distinctive sound that the sick American who had just killed him loved. He saw Marzena coming in, walking up to his bunk.

"Are you ready for me to help you with your bath Jeff?", she looked at him, winking. Pushing her lips forward to draw a sexual urge from him.

"I know you want me to help you Jeff." She put her hand on his leg, next to where he thought his cock used to be. She slowly slid it over his soft shaft. Sliding it back and forth. "One day Jeff, you will be ready for me."

Now fully awake. The Russian realized the pain and anxiety he was experiencing. *Did this happen? Did he die?* And worse than death, worse than the pain of the dermatome. He had let her down again, unable to get an erection.

He had given us one name, but I felt like there would need to be more. I would have to get a little more creative on the future interrogations.

"Marzana, get Eric and Todd ready for the Cave. We have more work to do."

Todd's Ultrasound

The blindfold was already in place. Next came the long sleeve t-shirt, placed over Todd's head. I tied and placed his arm behind his back. He was placed on a bar stool. The left arm hanging from a bungy cord, strapped to the back crossbar of the stool. Todd had been sedated in his cell.

He would have no memory of his transfer to a different room.

I had wanted to give him Versed, but because it could cause retrograde amnesia, I used Propofol instead. The short acting anesthetic depolarized the chloride channels on the GABA receptors, causing a short term loss of propagation of the impulse that would be known as consciousness. A couple small injections through the IV was all it took to get him to the next room. We always tried to leave an IV in the arms of the prisoners. Many would rip it out. Others we told it was for their own good, so that we could give them nutrients and total peripheral nutrition should they become ill from one of the Noro viruses running rampant through the camps.

Todd had to spill the beans. Prior law enforcement, and now one of the Sheep herd, he had used the good old boy system to work his way up through our ranks. Of average intelligence, but athletic, he had been able to use his family's name in the small town of Dalton to get onto the force, even befriending the local mayor and his relatives on the town council.

The piece of shit even somehow managed to get one of the high school cheerleaders to marry him, when he was a senior at the local junior college in Berlin. What a shame that such a beautiful girl could be so incredibly naive. The image of a Miller Light beer commercial came into my mind. That was Todd. Average beer. Pretending to be something he could never be.

Less filling for sure.

The muttonhead had traded local intel on our ammunition stores and fuel supplies to the bigger herd, leading to the deaths of around ten of our best soldiers. No way was he the only one who knew about this level of intel. He had to be working with others. We knew we would always have people trading intelligence for the comfort of girls or gold to stay ahead. It was expected in this volatile world.

We had also planned on using his intel against himself down the road, as we knew he would be a good source for counter intelligence, or for the spread of malicious information on our part, but he had beat us to it. One bag of weed, and five gold coins were found in his parka. There was also some type of source code and a cipher attached for an email account or computer. We wanted to really fuck with his head. And I was good at fucking with people's heads. Keeping him alive to answer questions was my goal. Keeping him alive afterwards wasn't as important. But since he was athletic, he would be a nice addition for the forced cold labor at our local landfill in Bethlehem. He would be way to stupid to plot an escape, but way too healthy to die.

Before he woke, I brought my portable ultrasound machine into the room. During my first deployment, the good old US Army had deemed it necessary to spend ten thousand dollars and acquire a portable, compact ultrasound machine so that we could do rapid assessments of abdominal injuries in the field. As an added benefit, it could be used to place ultrasound guided regional nerve blocks. In traditional army fashion, they had failed to provide us with the medications to do so.

I pushed the power button and waited for the screen to run through its preset protocols. The computer couldn't be updated, nor could it logon through WiFi to update which may give our location away. Something we were worried about with our stolen thermal vision scopes. With those, if the wrong setting was selected, uplinked GPS trackers were embedded to reveal its location to a satellite. Anyone who had served in the military knew this. Since there was almost zero internet connectivity or functioning satellites, I was probably being a little paranoid. I walked over to my med cart and pondered about what the best drugs would be for Todd's block. I wanted something intermediate acting in drug duration. We were short on Ropivicaine 0.5%. I preferred using Ropivicaine on my own troops as it was less cardiotoxic should I accidentally inject intravascularly. There was plenty of lidocaine, but it was too short acting. I wanted the block to last around twelve hours.

Opening the old, red Sears Craftsman tool chest, I saw an expired vial of 0.5% Bupivicaine. A great local anesthetic, but also one of the most cardiotoxic drugs on the planet. I didn't really give a shit if I injected in the wrong spot on Todd. Fuck him. I also knew Bupivicaine would provide more motor nerve relaxation than the Ropivicaine, another perfect choice for my needs.

I loved using pharmaceuticals to fuck with these guys.

I drew up the 20 mL vial in an old syringe with a used needle. There was no need to waste sterile equipment on the enemy. If he got infected, who the fuck cared. Piece of shit,

Todd was. If his neck or arm got infected, even more reason for him to want to leave his IV in place. Even more reason I could make him beg for antibiotics to save his worthless asshole life.

I opened the fourth drawer of the cart, only finding a couple packets of ultrasound gel. Without a gel, an ultrasound can't pass sound waves, nor receive the sound waves back to the ultrasound probe. Just like sound waves pass through water faster than air, the gel was needed for a quality image. I went over to the trash can and found a couple of thrown out packets of ketchup. Perfect. It will look like blood should he see any on his skin or clothes. Mental fornication perfection.

The old needles I had used on prior patients were never thrown away. I placed them in their original packaging after irrigating with saline, hoping to never use them again. Regional pain blocks I had practiced for years. They were magic in the field, and I could easily take away all sensation to the extremities in minutes, allowing my surgeon brethren a chance to work on a patient who didn't know that they were being cut on by the scalpel. Before I went through all of my field sedatives-IV drugs like scopolamine, ketamine, and midazolam-I thought I would try something new on Todd. He might be dumb enough to fall for it.

I turned his neck to the right, and squirted the ketchup just above his collar bone. Since Todd was an athlete, the anatomical structures of the brachial plexus appeared quickly on the ultrasound screen. I viewed the subclavian artery and vein, the clavicle, carotid artery, and the magic "traffic light" pattern between the anterior and middle scalene muscles, the C5, C6, and C7 nerve roots. Their shape is distinctive, looking like a traffic light signal-three dark hyper echoic dots resting on top of each other. C5 being the red light, C6 the yellow, and C7 the green light.

Todd never moved when the 22 gauge four inch needle slid through his neck. The needle was aimed at the side of the probe, and in plane, the glow of the needle lit up on the ultrasound screen just like E.T. 's finger from the old eighty's classic Spielberg movie. The needle's shaft was perfectly in view on the screen. I placed the needle between the red and yellow lights first, aspirated to make sure I wasn't in a vein or an artery, and injected 5 mL of Bupivicaine, watching the interscalene bundle become surrounded by the local anesthetic. The fluid appeared black on the screen, the sound waves reflecting back nothingness. Similar to Todd's future I thought. Bringing the needle back about 1 mm, I redirected it between the yellow and green lights of the anatomy-injecting another 6 mL. With 100% certainty, the block would anesthetize the phrenic nerve on his left side. This might cause some alarm in sicker, older COPD patients, or perhaps asthmatics, making it difficult to feel himself breathing. For Todd, he would just have to work a little harder to feel his diaphragm moving with each breath, creating a greater sense of panic. The interscalene block of the brachial plexus would ensure that Todd didn't feel his shoulder and upper arm, but I didn't want him to feel his forearm and hand either.

Sliding the ultrasound probe towards his clavicle, and scanning down and in, I could visualize the subclavian artery once again. A thick white line stood out revealing the clavicle and first rib. Just around the edges of the artery, I could make out three distinct vesicles. Beneath the artery I knew was the ulnar nerve pathway, to the side and top were the median and radial nerve roots of the brachial plexus. This might be overdoing the block, but this was the necessity of interrogation.

I slowly guided the needle tip towards the lower corner, and injected more local anesthetic. The ulnar nerve started to push itself away from the probe's reflection. "Eight ball in the corner pocket" as we liked to say in the anesthesia industry. I dumped the rest of the solution around the remaining two nerves, completing what was known as a supraclavicular block. Hopefully, this was enough local, and my visualizations had been accurate. Only time would tell as the anesthetic marinated around the nerve roots.

Pulling the needle out, I injected some sterile saline through its hub in case it was needed on future Todd's, washing all the clots through its tiny shaft. I wiped the ketchup off his skin, and while doing so caught a whiff of the red sauce, causing me a flashback to my high school cafeteria. Where a good lunch day consisted of as many carbohydrates that the old ladies could muster onto your tray.

Friday's were always the best. My favorite worker I remembered, Stella, would get the plastic, hospital tray and load it up. One slice of rectangular school pizza in the front space, a scrumptious 41 carbs, to its left-a hand scooped portion of crinkle fries-not freezer burned if you were lucky, but still 15 grams of carbs all the same. In the top left slot, your vegetable, or carbohydrate number three-11 grams of carb loaded canned corn-without a hint of salt or taste.

The back middle of the tray, dessert.

Not to be left out, canned peaches, in heavy syrup, 11 grams of carbs. And to drown it all down, in the back right of the plastic tray, was a minor circular indentation, indicative of a circular cafeteria cup, but no one, and I mean no one, would ever put water in that spot. Carb number five, ringing in at 13 carbs total, a boxed dairy delight, chocolate milk. In total, 91 grams of carbohydrate goodness. I wondered why the school nurse didn't give an insulin injection when you returned your tray to the tray return window. Funny how smell was heightened in times of war. It could always trigger the weirdest of times. The poor diet of America's schools was also indicative of the reason The Notch existed.

Everything seemed so over processed. As society later found out, the sheep had lied about the food pyramid back in the day. Paying off the right scientists to convince the federal government of the food pyramid, which ended up being completely wrong and inverted as to what people really needed to eat. "Only way to feed the masses", the world would continuously repeat. "The only way to prevent global warming is without all the cows and chickens." Boy were they ever wrong.

Being that one teaspoon of sugar is equal to five grams of carbs, the school lunch was like ingesting 18 teaspoons of sugar, or to put it in volumetric terms, opening 18 packets of sugar and eating them in one sitting. The same little packets that you would find in the plastic cube on your table at a restaurant for coffee. *18 fucking packets.* No wonder the sheep were fat.

I imagined opening 18 packets of sugar, pouring them into a bowl, stirring mindlessly, picking up the spoon and placing it in my mouth. Get the entire community stuck on insulin and obese as fuck. Get us all more dependent on the government for the sake of global warming or whatever other solution was profitable to corporations. All the while, the greater society got sicker and sicker from insulin resistance, particularly in the poorer communities. And with Covid's number one morbidity risk-obesity-how could anything go wrong? The government would actually arrest or throw kids out of school for calling someone fat, but completely avoid judgement of itself through inflicting certain early death through vaccines and school lunches. Free speech was like the school lunch, eat what you were served and like it.

I realized I was completely mentally side tracked from

Todd. This brain fog and lack of concentration, a side effect from my mandatory three covid injections that hadn't prevented my three Covid infections. Something had to change in our country. Ketchup presented itself as an olfactory recollection of all the lies we were told. Small memories formed a collective summation of the bigger issue. We the people should not be lied to.

I watched as Todd's arm began to loosen against the restraints on the chair top. The block was working. He slowly began to stir. I made sure that he couldn't see any part of his left arm below the sleeve. His left arm remained tied, placed behind his body, out of his vision. His right arm shackled to the bar in front of him. His waist tied to the loops on the floor. Ankles locked to floor loops. The only thing Todd could move would be his neck and his eyes. I hadn't tried this technique before, but it sure was going to be fun.

"Wakie wakie you redneck fuck." I really, really hated this guy.

Todd was almost awake. His mind still lulled in and out of the different zones of sleep. He would be fully awake in about two minutes. I pulled over my Pelican cooler, opened it, and pulled out a Moat Mountain Czech Pilsner from the North Conway brewery. Taking small sips. Enjoying what was a rarity anymore in the High Country.

Todd's eyes were open now. Staring ahead. Trying to discern where and why he was sitting in a dark, musky room. I had brought him into the basement level of the Mount Washington Hotel. Located directly under its front steps, was The Cave. This area was originally used as squash courts when the hotel was first built, but became a speakeasy during Prohibition. Before the events got bad in the Notch, the hotel was using it as a sports bar and music venue. Its basement location muted the loud bands from the high paying guests above. I had remembered my very last party before things got bad. A Fourth of July get together with the local favorite act, The Wicked Smart Horn Band. The old stone walls had muffled the band to a lull with its thick stone walls. The masonry would work effectively on Todd's screams should he decide not to cooperate. It was my favorite room in the giant hotel.

"Speak easy Todd" I said to him half joking.

The joke being lost on the redneck, not that he would have known the history of the hotel anyway.

"Where am I? What do you want from me?" His anger simmered.

I took a sip of my Pilsner, pondering what to say to the fucktard. I so much wanted to never let him die. He deserved massive suffering daily, but I knew how unhealthy it would be for my mind, let alone for poor Todd's health.

"Welcome to my Speakeasy. I'll be your bartender today. What will it be?", I said in my worst

Boston accent. "Would you like a hammer, or the dremel tool?"

I had each tool in opposite hands, holding them up for him to see. The electrical generators were on upstairs as I had requested, allowing the use of the power tools. Only the best service at The Mount Wash.

I walked over to Todd's bare thigh and placed an oval shaped gel pad. Leading back from the pad, was a plastic coated wire which I plugged into a small portable metal box.

"What's that? Why am I strapped down to this chair? Where am I?". Todd was on the last remnants of the Propofol now. Clarity had returned. Panic would soon ensue.

"Well Todd, we finally found you. And we know that you betrayed the soldiers in your unit. Because of you, ten people were either captured or tortured. Your team Todd. You have let your team down. They have all talked, and now you are here to tell us everything that we want to know."

Thank God he didn't try to deny it. Another sign of his average intelligence. His lack of military training was obvious.

"I didn't have a choice. They were going to take my family away and send them to the front in Manchester. Please don't do anything to them. They have no idea about any of the information I gave away."

The Pilsner was still ice cold. Delicious. I took a long sip from the 20 ounce can, studying the cool logo and artwork someone had worked so hard on. I could appreciate that artist's work. Many details people couldn't appreciate as an art form. My latest creation was sitting right in front of me. Now bright eyed and bushy tailed. The propofol metabolized. Time to perform my art.

"Todd. Look down. What you fail to notice is that we saved your life. You were just brought in after the IED went off. It's likely you don't even remember because of the blast. You passed out. We found you with your arm dangling. Hanging by the tiniest bits of fascia and nerves. We saved you Todd. Despite what you think of us, we are not like them. We forgive. We don't judge. And we will be here no matter what you need. The same goes for your family."

Looking down, he could see his right arm strapped to the table. His left gone. No feelings from where it used to exist-a ghost. *They weren't lying to me,* he thought. He could feel his legs struggle against the chains on the floor. Present to the tension, but unable to gain any momentum.

"We've all lost something in this war," Todd said.

"If all I've lost is an arm, so be it." He almost sounded brave.

"But Sgt. York", I said sarcastically, "Who's to say we won't take your other arm?" Moat Mountain really did have great can artist's I thought as I continued looking at the Pilsner can, acting bored and as disinterested as possible. Maybe the artist could make The Notch some T-shirts.

Todd was quiet. I reached under my chair and grabbed the black duffel bag I was keeping there. Inside, not an exact fit, but close enough, was an arm I had retrieved. Severed, and black from an explosion. It was heavily soiled but matched closely to Todd's in size. He would be too anxious to notice the details. Lifting the duffle, it was always surprising how much human extremities can weigh.

Removing the arm from the bag, its bloodied humeral shaft was visible. Tendons and ligaments crawling lifelessly out of the maroon end opposite the hand. I dropped the arm directly in front of Todd on the table. The sound resembled an uncooked steak, falling on a chopping block. Todd stared in disbelief at the arm in front of him. A sickening feeling of loss and regret bestowed his face. You could tell he was trying to process the why of what was going on and the how of his future disability.

I grabbed the electric carving knife from my tool chest. Plugged it in, and pushed the tiny on button. Two blades began slowly reciprocating back and forth, then speeding up to an indistinguishable one blade. Serrations in a whirl. All the family holiday's sprang back in my mind. Carving the "roast beast" as my wife liked to call it. The smell of the electric motor on the little device reinforced those memories.

"Todd. We are here today to allow you to talk easily and quickly about what we want to know, or to torture the fuck out of you until you have a slow rotting death. You see, we hate you. We are not going to allow you to die quickly as we would people we respect, but rather we are going to come down here daily.

Pop open a beer, and enjoy ourselves. After all, that's what a speakeasy is all about, right? Being able to enjoy what the rest of the world around us thinks is illegal?"

Wirrrr.....Wirrrrrr.

The blades glided back and forth. Todd's eyes never leaving the reciprocating blades. Not as loud as a power tool, or as powerful either. Something about the serrated edges being just enough to electrically get the job done, but with a lot of energy. Like a dull knife skinning a deer. It might take all day, but the task would be over eventually.

I grabbed the dead arm in front of me. Pinning the forearm against the end of the table. Bringing the saw up to the thumb.

Wirrrrrr....Wirrrrr....

The knife ripped through the flesh, hitting bone and began to struggle, losing its forward progress. The hinges catching and slipping on softer bone. Finally, coming out the other side of the bone, penetrating the digit. The small finger dropped to the stone floor.

Setting the knife down. I didn't reach for the thumb right away. I looked at Todd's face to see how he was taking the whole thing. Rather strange to see your own thumb cut off in front of you, even if the arm wasn't attached to your body. There was no pain. Just the idea that a short time ago, that was his arm, and someone was violating it. Showing an absolute disrespect to his body.

I took a long sip of the beer. It was starting to warm a bit. *Nothing worse than a warm beer* I thought, *especially a Pilsner.* After a long pause for effect, I spoke to him as I looked down at his former appendage.

"Todd. It's time to talk my friend."

"I'll be glad to tell you everything I know. Everything. What is it you want to know?" He was speaking faster, but I could tell he was still holding back.

"Who helped you at the ammunition dumps? Who helped you rat out the hiding spots in the mountains?"

"It was a girl named Amanda. She knew exactly where they were and how much was at each location. I swear she is the only one. We worked together several times. She was the one." He wasn't looking at me. Todd was staring opposite from me. There was more he had not told me for sure. I had a sense for the truth.

Grabbing his right forearm, the electric knife's vibrations shook down his arm. I flipped the blades upside down to their flat non serrated side, and pushed down hard against his skin. His eyes closed anticipating the pain. The vibrations shook through his shoulders and neck. The sound of the knife's weakness and lack of power was evident. Confused and full of fear, it took him a second to realize I had not penetrated his skin. It would take time to cut through an arm the size of Todd's. He had spent a lot of time in the weight room over the years.

"Tell me more Todd, or I'll flip the knife over. There has to be more than Amanda."

I knew he was telling the truth about Amanda. We knew she was in on the operation against us. He didn't know she was less than a mile away from the Cave being questioned by someone way wackier than me.

"Tell me how you got your information over to the Sheep. Where did you meet? Who did you meet with?"

"Amanda did it all. I never met with anyone on the other side. I have no clue who she talked with. That wasn't part of the deal for me."

On this, I knew he was lying. I just didn't have a name quite yet. Todd met regularly with someone. We just needed to know how and why. I grabbed his right forearm again. Tell the truth and get rewarded. Lie, and there needed to be a penalty.

I held his forearm down and began cutting his small pinky finger on his right arm. The blades screaming against bone. Blood from the tiny arteries sprayed across the room, splashing onto the lid of my beer.

"That sucks," I thought. *"Worse than a spilt beer."*

Todd was screaming in agony from the serrations ripping apart his flesh. This wasn't the super sharp precision scalpel. This knife was meant to serve Thanksgiving turkey up on a platter. I loosened my grip on his arm.

Todd tried to swing away from the pain and damage, but was tied securely to the floor. His one good arm locked to the table, bleeding profusely across the wood grains. Turning from bright red to a dark sticky mess of coagulated syrup.

"I can help stop the bleeding Todd if you just talk to me. Just tell me the truth."

He was crying now. The smell of urine evident in the unventilated basement. I held up his detached arm and stroked his face with it.

"There, there now Todd. Mommy will be here for you any second now."

The cold, stiff hand was almost like a mannequin's arm, rigid and pale. I brushed it slowly across his teared cheeks, and then used the immovable fingers to brush his hair out of his eyes. I placed the dead arm on top of his bleeding thumb.

"Poor, poor Todd. You can do this."

I picked up an old towel and wiped my beer top off, hoping he didn't have hepatitis or some other blood borne disease as many of the Sheep did, but I'll be damned if I was gonna let a little bit of Todd's mess ruin my cold beer.

The splatter of tears. Rapid, shallow breaths, mixed with moans and garbled words. Sobbing. He still wasn't telling me anything.

"Todd, do you have anything to say? Time's a wasting. I got people to do, places to see." I laughed at myself. Turning back to the box on my red cart, flipping the on switch. A beep let the room know the tiny metal box was up and ready to do its duty.

"What the fuck is that?" Todd yelled.

"Electrocautery little buddy."

I pushed the button on the electrical bovie pencil and brought it down onto his hand, cooking and searing the skin. Crackles and pops could be heard as it's current sealed the vessels it came in contact with, electrically burning shut the water filled skin, arteries, and veins on the back of his hand. The smell of burnt skin rose just under Todd's nose. Nothing smelled like burning human flesh.

He screamed and shouted for me to stop. Almost pulling his arm and skin loose from the restraints. I thought he might even pull his shoulder out of socket to escape the burn and char. "Todd, is all of this moaning really necessary? You are bleeding everywhere. Wouldn't you like me to stop the bleeding?"

I got the cautery and began carving in capital letters, T-O-D-D, into the dead arm.

"Oh sorry, how rude of me. It's upside down." I turned the arm around so he could see his name cauterized on the skin. *You definitely have more to say buddy.*

"OK...OK! We met in Burlington once near the lake at a brewery." He stated about as fast as an auctioneer selling cattle at a Friday night fair.

"I'm intrigued. You at a brewery? Was it Magic Hat? I hope you at least went to Magic Hat.

They have great beer." The liberals in Vermont did make good ice cream, cheese, and beer.

"Magic Hat 9-delicious!" I remembered for him.

"I don't fucking remember. Just put a tourniquet on my arm. Stop this bleeding. Let me go. I've told you enough."

A truth should be rewarded with a positive treatment. The bovie sparked to life again as I held it on the hole above Todd's former right thumb . The sound erupted like TV static, but louder and crunchier. Irregular. Soon, the bleeding stopped, but not Todd's cries. The bovie was a different kind of pain. Half taser, half slice. Its burn was like touching the inside of an electric socket, felt all the way to the bone. I almost felt bad for the guy. Almost.

I thought he would pass out. He was just too healthy and strong. Likely getting better food than us helped his physique.

"I'm sorry to have to hurt you, but it appears that if you have told one lie, you likely have told more lies. You for sure are not telling me everything I want to hear."

"But I have. I promised you before, but this time, that's it. I met there at whatever you call it, Magic Hat." He said this while looking me in the eyes. I was beginning to get somewhere.

"What did you discuss there?" I asked.

"We talked about ammo locations in the Notch and how I had access to them. That I could work with Amanda to get them more information. But they had to help my family first." The speed of the cattle auctioneer continued to play through my head.

I'll take two dollars, now three dollars here, and the winning bid goes to the man with one arm in the corner.

Some things are better without pain. It's the inferred mental possibilities of hurt which can change the course of an interrogation. I went once again to my red anesthesia cart and grabbed a 20 gauge catheter. With it, I returned back to face Todd and the dead arm on the table in front of me.

"Do you know what your radial artery is? Where it's

located? How much blood it can carry? It really is an impressive artery. It supplies blood to your hand on your thumb side. It's that artery you usually touch when you are checking for a pulse. You know, this one."

I put my right hand across to my left radial artery, using two fingers to check for my own pulse.

"80…not bad considering the situation you are putting me in right now." I lied.

My pulse was much higher, but I didn't want to let him know the truth.

Reaching below the table, I removed the straps that held his left arm, placing it up for him to see that it was still attached to his body. His face turned white, unable to process how this could be.

I placed the 20 ga catheter near his wrist.

"Tough to know if you are in the right spot unless you get that bright red blood return. Let's give this a try Todd."

Trying to pull away again, I grabbed his now swollen hand and flipped his arm over. He failed to hold still.

"Settle the fuck down. I am not going to hurt you. I'm here to help you. Don't make me get the bovie back out." He immediately froze his arm against the table. Not daring a move. His body going through giant lurches when he sobbed against the restraints. The memory of the electric currents changing his mind.

"That's it bud. Nice and still. I always liked you Todd. Up until a point. And you know what that point was? That point where ten of my best friends died. That point. You miserable fuck?

Tell me the fucking truth or you are going to die today."

Behind Todd I had placed a tourniquet machine. I reached under it, and grabbed a tourniquet, slapping it around his upper right arm. I turned the machine on. Its reliable squelch told me it was ready to inflate when ready.

I placed two fingers on his radial artery. It was bounding as I expected it would be. Quickly I slid the catheter into the artery before he started to squirm again. I was rewarded with bright cherry colored arterial blood, pumping up the clear hub of the needle in sync with his pumping heart. Each beat sending the cherry red fluid a few millimeters north. Dropping the needle's angle, I spun the white catheter over the needle's hub, threading it inside the walls of the artery. Once in, I pulled the metal threading out of the white catheter's center, leaving only the hollow catheter tip inside the artery. Once the needle was out, nothing was left to stop the arterial blood from shooting out. Impressive it was, shooting almost a foot away from the table.

"Relax Todd. The more you fight and move, the quicker you are going to bleed out and die." He watched as each beat of his heart spewed more and more blood across the table. It was really getting messy in the Cave now. The smell of burnt flesh and fresh coagulating blood was trapped in the dark speakeasy. It smelled like a battlefield, like copper, iron, and piss. He began to try and slow his breathing and heart rate, becoming motionless in the chair, an attempt to slow his death. The spurts began to lose some of their distance and height. Todd was a former athlete and had a great cardiac output. He could bleed out in a hurry if I really wanted him to. I watched as he started to take on a pale color.

"Once again. Information. Tell me something new, and you will get rewarded. Fail, and you will get what you deserve. But thank me this time. This is painless right? You see that I will take care of you. I'm not here to hurt you. I'm here to help. It doesn't have to be about the pain. I can let you die a slow, painless death."

I raised my beer up to my lips, but the can was empty. I let the bleeding continue as I reached back into the Pelican to grab another Pilsner. This time going with a Schilling Alexander from the brewery in Littleton, New Hampshire. Another Pilsner. Perhaps New Hampshire was learning from their Green State neighbors.

Todd began to lose more color. He had probably lost about twenty percent of his blood volume, but being healthy, he was compensating. His mind was totally fucked. The sympathetic nervous system unable to slow itself down. Awakened in a strange basement, missing one arm, tortured, and bleeding out. Too much too fast. It was all overwhelming. His breathing was getting faster with the continued blood loss., an attempt by the brain to auto regulate the changes in his blood chemistry. His body was attempting to stay alive.

"EZ. Another person was EZ. He is able to work through all of your lines from South to North. He works near the border." OK, I thought, that's new. This was of value. He had waited too long to release this information.

I reached forward and pushed inflate on the tourniquet machine. A loud buzz was followed by a beep indicating the machine had reached 300 mmHg. The balloon bladder attached to Todd's upper arm was inflated and the radial artery immediately stopped bleeding. It would be up to Todd to decide a few things now. I grabbed my beer and left the room.

"Where are you going?" Todd asked. "You can't leave me here to die."

"Don't worry. I just gotta take a piss from all this beer. I'll be right back to cauterize that artery for you."

Other than a little blood lost and a missing finger, Todd would be able to give me a little more information. I would let his blood counts increase over the next couple of days before I thought of something new to do to him, and I needed to confirm his names with another prisoner.

<u>EZ's Reveal</u>

I placed an intravenous catheter in Eric's right hand, injected some Versed, and started a Propofol drip. His eyes closed reluctantly, but he remained breathing comfortably. His mind asleep now, I went on to my next step of this torture session. They were becoming more fun for me each time, and I wasn't sure what that said about my psyche. I had become quite proficient using drugs and anesthesia to garner intelligence. Any judgement of my actions would occur after the war.

I placed a tourniquet on Eric's left upper arm, but left it deflated. Next, I turned my ultrasound machine on and scanned his lower arm anatomy. I searched for five nerves to inject with Ropivicaine: ulnar, radial, medial, medial cutaneous, and lateral cutaneous. I had done thousands of nerve blocks over my anesthesia career and was quite proficient at the technique. After identifying each nerve, I slid my block needle through the skin and directed its tip under ultrasound guidance towards the five targets. Since Eric was taking a nap, he would be unaware of the five injections. Finishing the fifth injection, I put the needle away and wiped all evidence of the block off of his skin. Next came the fun part.

I slid the tourniquet as high up his left arm as possible after cutting a slit up his uniform's sleeve. I dropped the tourniquet's cords beneath the table and out of his view. Extending his arm away and down from the table, I placed it on a support underneath his gurney.

I walked across the room and pulled a towel off of an item I had kept out of his view. Earlier, I had amputated a left arm similar in size and shape to Eric's. I was going to use the same technique I had used on his buddy Todd. I wanted to see if I could get confirmation of the same name he had given me.

I brought the arm back to his gurney, and placed it where his arm had been. These guys had been caught with the same unit, why not try the same techniques.

Cutting off his uniform sleeve, I slid it on the dead arm. In about thirty minutes, Eric would wake and only be able to lift his head a few inches off the table, see both of his arms and legs strapped to the gurney. The tourniquet on his left upper arm I placed to 300 mmHg and inflated. He would be able to feel pain around his bicep and tricep. The fact that he kept himself in shape would only help me later. Those bigger muscles required a lot of oxygen, and expelled a lot of acid.

Setting a timer, I left the Propofol running, the session would begin in about two hours. Tourniquet pain is notorious under long anesthetics that involve a limb tourniquet. Even when a patient is deeply anesthetized, and the operative surgical site pain is well controlled with local anesthesia and narcotics; over time, the tourniquet pain will be unstoppable, and usually not responsive to doses of increased IV narcotics. This can occur in as little as thirty minutes but usually takes on its own cruel personality around the two hour mark.

Two very different pain fibers carry sensations to the dorsal spinal cord relaying pain. The first is what we usually think of as "pain"-a fast, sharp, "cutting" type of pain-as when you cut yourself with something sharp. This type of pain is from what are called A-Delta fibers which are small, myelinated for speedy conduction. Myelin is a substance which helps conduct the electrical impulses faster along the nerve to reach the spinal cord. Think of insulation on copper wire in your home.

The other type of pain fiber is the un myelinated, slower

conduction, C fibers. C fibers respond to dull, achey, and burning sensations from pain. A chronic tooth ache that won't respond to pain meds, that's the C fibers at work. Tourniquet caused C fiber pain, and Eric was starting to learn about his neuroanatomy as it related to tourniquets.

Sweat was pouring off Eric's face when I returned. His chest and clothing were saturated. His body was in high gear trying to fight the stimulation of the C fibers, and only one thing stood in the way of stopping that pain. A simple deflation button on the tourniquet machine. I stopped the Propofol infusion as he was already starting to squirm on the gurney.

Every time he moved his arm and shifted, the tourniquet adapted, and blew more air into its bladder. Maintaining a constant 300 mmHg, which is quite the pressure considering that's almost three times the normal systolic blood pressure of 120 mmHg. Eric's blood pressure was way higher, and I could imagine how fast it would squirt across the room. Without the tourniquet, I knew he would bleed out profusely.

I had been gone for about two hours. I let Eric's dilemma sink into his mind as the Propofol's fog began to dissipate. Basically he had no options. His sole focus I knew would be on the tourniquet pain. Completely overwhelming to his entire being. His body was screaming at him to do something different, anything different, or face the risk of losing the limb. His brain was awakening him to the depths of hell.

The distal extremity was becoming more and more starved for oxygen, filling with lactic acids, and begging to rid itself of the toxic buildup of cellular synthesis. Something occurring on such a small scale can surprisingly build up massively over time. Eric's left lower arm was completely asleep. The tourniquet he felt on his upper arm being the obvious reason, and his brain telling him if he didn't do something fast, he may lose it soon.

"Morning Eric. How's it going?", I asked sarcastically. "Ready to tell me some more about your friends?"

He spoke. But without meaning. Without control. Completely indecipherable. Almost like a foreign language. He was ready to talk. He spoke in a loud, rapid fire succession of syllables. I brought the left arm into his view. With my other hand I turned on my battery operated Sawz All power saw. He screamed at the sound but grew silent as he witnessed me cut his arm off. I laid the arm on a table next to his gurney.

"If I drop this tourniquet, it will relieve all your pain Eric, but you will also start to bleed. And bleed faster now that your blood pressure is so high. There's a real chance I may be unable to stop the bleeding. Because Eric, I've been nothing but honest with you the entire time. It's only you who has lied to me. Over and over again. Now, do you want the tourniquet down? Do you want me to try and stop the bleeding?"

He nodded his head up and down as fast as a head could move. It reminded me of a mosher banging their head at a Metallica concert. Quite impressive was his nod's speed of affirmation. "As soon as you hear the button beep, I want to hear names. And it better be all the names. If I don't hear names, I'll let the bleeding continue."

I held the deflate button for three seconds, and the tourniquet deflated. Eric immediately began to feel a sense of relief. The ache, the throbbing in his biceps stopped, his pain decreasing quickly. Oxygenated blood flowing to the distal tissues, un oxygenated acidic blood returning to the heart to be filtered, dropping off carbon dioxide and reattaching oxygen. He now became concerned as to why his arm wasn't bleeding, but he was just too confused to process the situation.

"Names Eric. Names." I said to him angrily.

"Uhhh...OK, Ok. There were the two girls and someone

else. Someone way up the chain. Someone they only referred to with letters. An abbreviation of some sort I think." "What was this abbreviation?" I asked.

"EZ. That's it. It was EZ." Eric finally revealed the name I needed. I had heard it before, but now knew it was important. Whomever EZ was, he had to be big for the Sheep. Eric was an officer, and it was only the officers who had given this intel to me.

"That's it?. That's all you have left for me to hear? After all of this effort Eric."

I walked to his left side, making eye contact to be sure he was with me. I began to lift the left hand into the air until the entire arm was held up for him to see. I grabbed the rotting left arm off the table and threw it across the room for effect. It made a dull thud against the wall of the Cave. Eric's brain could in no way process what he was seeing. He had lost his arm. This madman had done something to him while he had been under anesthesia. Why would he have cut my arm off while I was asleep?

"I have one last thing to help you remember Eric."

I reached under the gurney. I released the restraints on his lower left arm. Since his arm was completely numb and dead to the world, he could not understand what I was doing beside him. Rotating his shoulder up and forward, I placed Eric's disrobed arm on the table next to him. His face in complete disbelief. His brain was unable to process the fact that his arm had been attached to him the entire time.

"Pretty wild right?" I asked him. "It's fucking Cave magic. Don't ever say I didn't do you a favor Eric. Congratulations. You won't be a one armed dildo the rest of your life. You'll still be a dildo, just a two armed dildo."

"You piece of shit lying bastard!". Eric didn't appear too

happy with me.

"Who fucking does this? And whose arm was that you were cutting?"

"Just another one of your sheep buddies Eric. Please tell me where I can find this EZ fellow Eric? It's extremely important to us? And as you can see, I didn't really cause you any harm. I'm not here to hurt you like you hurt our captives Eric. I've always been nice to you. I've fed you. Kept you warm."

I continued, "Eric, at Guantanamo Bay, we learned that captives would say anything during painful torture. They would make up names, lie. Anything to make the pain stop. And many would stop all cooperation after repeated water boarding. It took many years to realize the good cop got more information than the bad cop. Just let me know where he's located Eric." Eric showed some sense of relief. He was falling for all of my hard work. He just needed to reveal one last piece of information, but he was hesitating. His delay evident. Delay meant to prolong his odds of surviving.

"Since you gave me your best with this EZ fella, I'm gonna help you out with your death. I'll make sure it's nice and painless."

"What the fuck are you saying? You just said I wouldn't be a one armed dildo the rest of my life."

"You're right Eric. I reminded you though that you will still be a dildo, but you may look more like a Vegas slot machine. You'll be a one armed bandit the rest of your life." He did not like my laughter.

"Tell me now Eric. Where did you meet EZ?".

I picked up the Sawz All, placing my finger on its trigger. The little saw screaming its high pitched whine, inches from his head.

I inflated the tourniquet still on his left arm, and pinned his left hand down on the table.

Slowly, deliberately, I cut off his left hand. In my head trying to make a perfect straight slice.

His mind was not able to understand what he was seeing, but not feeling, the cut. His mind was fully aware though that this was his hand this time. I completed the cut, and held it up for him to see.

"Perfect cut Eric. Your prosthesis will fit better now. See how nice I am to you?". I placed it in his right hand, so his brain could understand that he was actually touching something familiar and real, his own hand. Still warm and heavy. "Here Eric, let me give you a hand." I laughed at my own Dad joke.

I deflated the tourniquet on his left upper arm, and since I had not cauterized or sewn the veins and arterial supply, blood poured from his fresh stub. He could lift it slightly into the air, watching the artery squirt blood into the air.

"Eric, I can turn the tourniquet back on and fix this for you. Just tell me the location." Blood was pooling off the table and around his feet at the gurney's edge. He stared at his arm.

Initially, his respirations sped up, but soon began to get shallower, with little effort.

"It was at the northern Vermont border. He knew the guards there. It was the border crossing northwest of the Notch. Now please, put up the tourniquet. Please let me live." The blood pulsed less and less from the wound until it was almost to a trickle.

No man should have to die alone. Or in pain. His lifeless body before me. His soul likely floating above us, staring down with judgement at the necessities of war. There were worse ways to die than bleeding to death. He was lucky.

"Thanks for the information Eric. EZ will be talking to you again soon in hell." I looked to the ceiling, and offered.

"Float away Eric, your death is not worth watching. The depths of hell now welcome you as they will me one day."

We had a name. It was time to find this EZ character. I had heard this name before at my gun club. I knew he was linked to the terrorism in Montreal. To Willis and O'Reilly. Could it possibly be the same guy still in New Hampshire?

<u>Moguls</u>

The impossible mogul. Fucking bastard moguls. Never a good skier, I dreaded them. Especially on a snowmobile that had been ridden more than a Kardashian sister. No suspension meant every single indention in the snow was going to be felt. Up, down, tailbone smashed-repeat. Dated, two person, touring sleds were taken from the snowmobile rental companies and were carrying a heavy burden. Ferrying supplies back and forth around alpine highways of snow and ice.

With no trail groomer to maintain the famous, albino white trail system, transport duty fucking blew. Ruts, moguls, slush, ice, tree limbs, downed trees. Everything mother nature offered in the White's was a magnet for a snowmobile trail. If it was your day for the snowmobile transports, it was also your duty to clear the trails. The White's experienced high winds and snow squalls. The only good news was that there were no drunk Massholes speeding around the blind curves of the snowmobile trails as was the norm pre war times.

Heated hand grips were a plus, but the thumb warmer on the throttle was out. The windshield had a few bullet and tree limb holes, so buffeting and wind were ever present, although we rarely reached speeds high enough for that to make a bad day worse. Seat foam was nonexistent, having long ago been squished to a pancake by too heavy ammo loads and three person transfers, but nothing was as miserable as the constant cold that overwhelmed my feet. Little worked to heat things up at minus five degrees, and there was always a wind chill, not only from the wind itself, which was constantly howling, but from the twenty mile per hour speeds reached over the trails while on the sled.

I needed a break from the hospital tent and The Cave, so I had volunteered to transport across the back pass. The cold was starting to make me regret my decision. Notch intelligence was in high gear looking for the EZ character. That would take time.

I would stop every ten minutes to warm up. Too scared to turn the sled off for fear of the battery failing, leaving me abandoned with no one to rescue me on the desolate trails. I would do fifty jumping jacks, gain some warmth in my boots, and continue on. Fear of walking ten miles in the cold back to civilization added to the insecurity of no working fuel gauge. The splattered blood on the fuel tank only increased that insecurity.

Other than horses and pack mules, the snowmobiles were one of the only ways to reliably get supplies around through the Notch in winter. There was not enough fuel to constantly battle plowing the roads, putting out nonexistent road salt, and repeating the process all over again night and day. The four stroke snowmobiles got good gas mileage and could haul some serious loads. Sometimes even towing a sled behind with more supplies, or an injured team member. Twin Mountain mechanics were known for their ability to keep snowmobiles running, and we were lucky to have them on our side.

Franconia Notch was renowned for its harsh winters. The weather changed in an instant. Complete snow blackouts. Howling winds. Rain to ice to snow to rain to sleet. There was no fear of our soldiers turning to the dark side; they couldn't get to the other side if they wanted to. Winter was a black hole in the North Country. It was also a great benefit to our defense as the Sheep did not dare enter such hostile weather conditions. Pro mountain climbers training for Mt. Everest expeditions lived throughout the Mt. Washington area because the weather was so similar.

My mission was significant, sort of. What was to be three sleds carrying ammo resupply turned into one, with half the resupply of ammo being supplemented with MREs. Both weighed almost the same in their respective card board boxes on the back of the tired Yamaha Venture Lite. I had departed at sunrise from the supply building at Crawford Depot about six hours ago.

Temperatures hadn't changed, but the wind had increased slightly throughout the day. Because I was going over Bear Notch Road to reach the Kancamagus, the wind funneled directly north into my cracked Nolan helmet. My glasses were a constant fog as I exhaled. I left my visor half cracked to allow my warm breath a place to escape the helmet for if not, a fogging on the face shield was instant.

What should have taken an hour or two during touristy times, was now going to average about eight hours, and I had only gotten stuck with the heavy sled four times today. Slow and steady was the name of the game over the pass, and any notion of the trail improving on the downhill leg was a wet dream. Cutting up and clearing downed trees from high winds was my biggest slow down. What had been the private club's duties during good times was now on The Notch. My final destination was the Jigger Johnson Campground. The Notch had been using the site as a Forward Observation Base for movements coming from the enemy controlled area of Waterville Valley. Mt. Pasaconaway, Mt. Chocura, Mt. Whiteface, The Sleepers, and Mt. Tripyramid provided insurmountable peaks directly to the South, but Waterville Valley was becoming an ever increasing threat. Its flatter nature and roads allowed the Sheep to graze for longer periods of time.

Home to the Waterville Valley Ski Resort, I found its theme at this moment a little ironic, "Escape the Outside World". Mt. Tecumseh provided the altitude for downhill skiing in the valley. With the help of the second most powerful politician in the mid sixties, Robert Kennedy, the resort began its prominence as an international "political" hotspot. John Sununu, the former three time New Hampshire governor purchased the resort later, maintaining a political feel to the town. Even advertising the resort's claim as the official ski resort of the Boston Red Sox. Most knew that professional baseball players weren't allowed to ski in the offseason because of their lucrative contracts, but it was a great draw to Massholes nonetheless .

Being one of the closest ski resorts out of Boston, a Masshole could easily travel up Interstate 93, and hit Highway 49 to Waterville's slopes. Fueling up on cheap New Hampshire liquor as soon as they crossed the border. New Hampshire even helped the intoxication by placing State Liquor stores directly on the interstate-in both directions. In 2012, New Hampshire was ranked number one in per capita consumption of alcohol, but also the number two healthiest state. Every Granite Stater knew who was funding the former statistic. Massholes buying at the border to avoid taxes. Waterville Valley seemed to be a saving grace for the Feds. Maybe the liberal heritage was its divinity.

The Feds were putting everything they had into this southern front. Concentrating on the Livermore Pass. If they were to take control of the Livermore Trail and reach the Kanc by spring, then they would have successfully divided our Lincoln to Conway resupply front lines. Because I had thoroughly hiked the area, I also knew that if they progressed due North on the Sawyer River Trail just to the east of Lily Pond, then Sawyer River Road was only a short 3.8 mile drive. While that road was closed in the winter, by spring thaw, they could easily reach the Fourth Iron Tent Site just west of Bartlett on Rt. 302-a little over 10 miles away from our HQ, and also splitting North Conway to the Mt. Washington Hotel. It was paramount to control this front line.

We were running out of troops to defend all the Notches, and the Sheep had tested every nook and cranny of our defensive network. Sometimes we would leave a route undefended, just to make another appear over defended, and reverse the scene two days later just to fuck with their intelligence. Hiking over the narrow pass of Livermore between Scaur and Flume Peaks was not easy in the winter, and they were paying the price dearly from our eastern facing snipers on Mt. Kancamagus.

But the more holes we made, the more Holes kept appearing. The Sheep could reproduce at a superior rate.

I was just crossing Rob Brook turning onto the Kanc Highway when I heard the dull, milk jug sound of bullets ripping into the plastic fairing and fuel tank of the snowmobile.

My left hand ripped the brakes as I ditched hard left, rolling the sled. Snow, steam, ice chunks, MREs, and boxes scattered into the ice covered powder, throwing more powder in the air. The cluster of debris and airborne snow acted like a smoke grenade, and that was probably all that hid me long enough to be thrown into the ice covered brook at the edge of the snow pack.

The wind howled, as if it were mad to be disturbed. Powder throughout the air adding to its call. The cold air amplifying the shots and the crash.

My right knee made clicking sounds and could move about an inch further than it should to the left-*probably my MCL ligament*-another old motocross injury coming back to haunt me.

No time to worry about that right now. My leg could move, and that was good enough.

Having been stationed one winter at Ft. McCoy, Wisconsin, during an Iraq tour, the aroma of snow percolated with gunpowder and burning fuel smelled familiar. The Army did a lot of its cold weather training over the years at McCoy, and many trainees had suffered its cold winters. What didn't feel familiar was the crack of the ice directly below my feet as it crumbled with my weight and the new weight of a 500 pound snow machine. Trying to jump with a bad knee was pointless. I knew I was about to lose my breath.

When icy water engulfs your body, the first instinct is to scream and take a deep breath at the same time. There was no time to do either. The tips of a thousand tiny icy picks shot through my Gore Tex pants and jacket. Despite anticipating the icy entrance, a silent scream was met with a mouthful of cold water.

Fuck the Polar Bear club. If I wasn't hitting rocks, I was being sucked under the top shelf of ice by the steady flow of water beneath me. Currents could suck you under the ice, and no rescue team would find you until spring thaw.

There was no pack on my back for the long journey over Bear Notch, but I did have my FN SCAR 17 rifle crisscrossed from left to right across my shoulders. I tried my best to stop from going under the ice, but it took me under regardless. I had used the SCAR in 2003 in Northern Iraq. It had been allowed with the Special Forces units to enable equivalent shot distances against the AK 47. The M16's 5.56mm rounds just didn't have the reach needed in the mountains of Afghanistan and Iraq, so the 17s 7.62 rounds had become the next best choice on those fronts. The rifle's sling caught on a rock, slowing by descent into the currents.

This felt almost like the waterboarding they put us through during SERE training, except worse, because I knew I wouldn't make it. No one was coming to save me. No one was going to call off the training exercise. There would be no medics or doctors to evaluate my chilled body. This was no longer a training exercise.

Even if I got out of the water, I wasn't going to make it with the wind chill. There was no way I'd be able to feel my fingers to operate my weapon, no way to run, no way to fight. The icy river had decided my fate. A perfect ambush had assigned my ticket to the heavens.

"Stay in the fight pussy. Move!" My ego screamed in my head.

The sling shifted and water pushed me to a deeper pocket. A gap formed close enough between me and the surface to grasp a mouthful of air, sucking in as much of its coldness as I dared. More ice pics entered my lungs. I yanked on the SCARs strap and finally released its grip on my shoulders.

A few of them were going to go down before freezing to death I promised myself. I kept moving my fingers in hopes they would work later. I refused to be Jack Nicholson's character in "The Shining", frozen stiff with his axe in the hotel's garden maze, snookered by his clever back tracking son.

"Focus on the moment, dip shit. Find a target. Shoot and move." My training kicked in. Thank you Ft. McCoy.

Turning the SCAR around as I popped into an open pool, I swung the rifle's magazine as hard as I could into the shore's ice, hoping it would stick. When that failed, the downed tree over the brook was my last hope as I drifted downstream. I threw the sling towards the hanging limb. Hanging just at the right angle was my savior limb, now attached to my sling. I came to a stop and took another breath. More shots would arrive soon once they found my position.

Because the brook was so slow and low in the winter, pulling myself along the log was easy. Although my hands and feet were completely numb, enough epinephrine kept them working to get to the bank. I would be done quickly on shore. Survival of the coldest.

"These pussies didn't like the cold. Just get to shore. Assess, shoot, move. Plenty before you have survived these conditions. You have nothing on the Korean Veteran, or the Russian at Stalingrad.

Three Sheep in snow grey Sitka camouflage were looking at the snowmobile's skis sticking out of the ice. None seemed to understand where the rider had gone, but I knew. That gave me the time I needed.

"Under the ice you warm mother fuckers." Bubba's voice from the duck blind came out in a slow drawl. My mind was in a complete smartass nonfunctioning mode. I was starting to talk to and admire my dead dog's humor.

"That's it Bubba. You always see the ducks before I do. Show them to me."   Although I had a round in the chamber, I couldn't feel the safety. Notorious for a small safety mechanism, the SCAR wasn't helping me right now.

"If you'd only switched to that aftermarket Parker Mountain Machine safety selector this wouldn't be happening right now would it? I told you this would happen dumbass". Bubba said.

"Shut up you stupid fucking dog. You know nothing about SCARs.", I yelled at him.

I couldn't help thinking, if I took off my glove, I would get frostbite, and then I realized that it didn't matter if the gloves came off. Three dudes were on shore waiting to kill me. What's a few fingers lost? My hands were a complete wet mess anyway.

Confusion was already fucking with me. Hypothermia comes on quicker when you're already half frozen from a solo six hour snowmobile trip. I threw my gloves on the ground, lined up my Trijicon ACOG to the 100 meter cross hair, and prayed to any God in the universe that the rails had held the optic's zero during my roller coaster ride.

There was no indication that I had hit the guy I was aiming at until I saw the bright red blood that splattered the white camo of the Masshole directly behind him. It was much more gratifying than paintball. The immense splatter reminded me of those white disposable bunny suits the professional painters wear that usually have different colors of paint all over them. Except this painter had just accidentally spilled crimson from head to toe.

The SCAR had a fourteen inch barrel with a Gemtech suppressor attached. Usually, the first shot out of a suppressor on a 7.62mm rifle is quite loud, sounding a lot like an unsilenced .22 rifle. However, although the company didn't recommend it, adding water to the suppressor prior to firing a first shot helps deaden the initial shock wave that gases would normally provide for subsequent bursts.

I didn't just add a little water, I added a fuck ton from my little swim in the creek. Masshole two and three had no idea where the round had come from, the suppressor was doing its job. They began looking up and behind them instead of down river.

Expecting return fire, I dove to my belly in the snow. In a perfect prone sniper's position, the ACOG locked onto its target once again. It's zero having been proven, the reticle almost seemed to smile. Its glowing green horseshoe lighting up against the white snowy backdrop.

Breathe. Slow pull. Follow through. Move. Repeat.

I kept the trigger back as I watched through the scope. The round ripping the carotid of Masshole two. Blood spurting out at all angles and his body frozen from the round's kinetic energy released into the spinal cord. I released the Timney two stage trigger back to stage one.

Feeling the practiced "click". Readying myself for my last target.

Assess. Move.

Knowing the Feds had top quality body armor, head shots were a must, and Hole three got two of them. Instead of what the Army had taught me on body shots, I started aiming all shots at the mouth, and if recoil brought the barrel up, then so be it. At a hundred meters, these fuck nuts were closer than most of my targets on range days. The first round entered dead on. Teeth exploded out the Hole's cheeks from the 7.62s massive energy, and the second round pushed the left eye into and out the rear of the skull. Everything was extra colorful with the snow. Bob Ross would have been envious.

"*Happy little trees.*" I laughed aloud to myself.

"*Now add a happy little tree to this spot, and a little color here.*" Said the Bob Ross voice in my head.

"*Those feet aren't going to be happy.*" Same voice. Same Bob Ross. Same smartass.

"*Gotta move*", Bob said. "*Or you're going to freeze.*"

 Protocol begged me to shoot and move. Seek cover. Scan. To place a few more rounds into the bodies and seek intel, but my shriveled blue balls begged for warmth. Because the campground was less than a half mile away, I knew it was my only hope.. I ran all of one minute before another target appeared in front of me.

As I raised the SCAR on a bouncing run, my buddy Zeb appeared in the glass with ten friendlies behind a snow machine.

They had been out on patrol and had heard the gunfight. I had probably saved all of them from being surprised by a Hole attack.

I had never been happier to see the douche bag.

"Looks like they were a forward patrol," Zeb said after looking through their gear. "Came right over the Bolles Trail from Wonalancet. They were either out to get intel and return, or they're the tip of a spear headed our way. Need some coffee?"

They took me to their cabin, and I passed out from exhaustion. Apparently, I dozed for over an hour in front of the fireplace before awakening to the smell of coffee.

"I'd prefer some iced Black Rifle Coffee if you have any asshole." I replied sarcastically.

Shaking uncontrollably.

I was on my third cup of luxury. Their last bag of Black Rifle Coffee. While my feet still burned, and my knee was in disarray, I was drinking fresh brewed, just ground coffee. Not some shit caffeine product from a plastic bottle. Life was good. Enjoy this moment for at least a little while.

"*Pretty cup of coffee*", the Bob Ross voice continued.

"A Big Cat Coffee truck's last stop was at Redeke Cabin. The driver took one to the head. His misfortune is our gain. We keep it a secret here at Jigger's Java House," Zeb said sarcastically. Zeb filled me in on the action occurring on the Mid Kanc. It had not been going well, but he did have one piece of good news.

"We captured one of the guys who attacked you earlier today. We noticed tracks away from the main group. He was likely an officer. Didn't want to engage in the fight. Once you warm up, maybe you'd like to have a chat with him. I know it's your specialty."

"That's awesome news! I thought you guys killed all of

them. How'd you keep one alive?" I asked.

"Well it was quite easy." He laughed. "At least that's what he says his name is anyway. He was carrying a bunch of digital equipment, some sort of chemicals, and a portable antenna. We aren't sure what its purpose is. Never seen anything like it."

"EZ? No fucking way. We have been looking for him. We think he's the leader of a lot of what's going on around here. Send him as fast as you can back to the hotel. I'm going with you."

Maybe the cold of transport duty wasn't that bad after all. Looking towards the fireplace, he noticed Zeb's black lab come around the corner. He laid close to the fire, turned his head, and looked into my eyes, reminding me of my old lab. Almost as if the dog knew something I didn't. The dog was trying to tell me something important. EZ was important. No way this couldn't be the same guy that had gotten Willis and O'Reilly involved with anthrax. The Notch was a small place. Everyone knew everybody else's business.

<u>Creative Solutions</u>

Blindfolded and cuffed, the Sheep known as EZ was loaded onto the snowmobile. We dressed him for warmth as I didn't want him cold when we arrived back at The Notch. I planned on interrogating him as soon as possible.

While making the journey, my mind raced over the possibilities of capturing information. This was no ordinary mutton. He spoke perfect English, but with an accent that was hard to place, so he was obviously fluent in other languages. His skin was dark in appearance, so somewhere in the Middle East was my best guess. He was fit, muscular, and calm at all times. His capture seemed to reveal no stress, almost as if he was on some form of medication or had some special meditation ritual to remain calm. Intimidation tactics did little to instill fear, as he remained calm to the threats we made against him.

EZ had experience from someone. Who that was remained a mystery.

I felt that most of my prior medical experimental interrogations may not work on a man of his caliber. He was not going to crack on a first go around, but the good news was, this meant he was important. His name had come up twice in regards to operational planning in former interviews. The Notch needed a break, and they would be counting on me to get the job done. We were low on supplies, ammunition, and reinforcements. The herd was just too big for the small pockets of resistance across the United States. With other countries offering to help the liberal government, we would only be able to fight for our freedoms for a short period going forward. We had tried our best. The anthrax in Quebec had instigated the last straw of division, leading to absolute control over the Republic. We would never see such freedom again, and I didn't care about living as part of that new society.

The brain washing and lies out of Washington, D.C. had reached epidemic proportions. Somehow, no matter the message, it appeared the herd followed. It was almost as if they were brainwashed, or that the government had complete control over the hearts and minds. Were people this stupid, or did they have some way of controlling the populace? If they did, how would that even be possible? If we were unable to figure out how the corruption was achieved, our cause would cease to exist. This very well could be my last interrogation, so I better make the best of it.

EZ was off loaded and brought below to the cell just outside of the Cave. Marzana and I sat and debated our possibilities.

She had been loyal and a good learner to my methods- understanding the implied thoughts of no harm to continue further questions to a confused but comfortable client. She also understood that a soldier of his caliber would not fall for the female entrapments. He would not fall for sleep deprivation or water boarding. Withholding food and water would also let him retain his secrets. A new method had to be developed. Something he would not have trained for.

If EZ had no fear of death, I began to think, then perhaps the only way to break him was to make him think he was already dead, and therefore safe to tell those around him his darkest concerns. To openly confess about his goals, and his accomplishments. But how do you achieve mental death with the ability to not kill the patient? I only knew of a couple drugs that could perform at that level. But how was I to keep his brain functioning, to keep his lungs working, but not allow him to perceive his bodily senses?

I could think of only one method. It would be all that I had left to try. After that, the torture would begin out of necessity, and if anything else, we had removed a top commander from the field.

We also needed to understand the equipment he had been captured with. That would require some of our specialists. There had been a journal that was written in either Hebrew or Arabic. It contained what appeared to be formulas, but for what, no one knew. There was a transmitter of some sorts and pint containers of a white tinted liquid that we were scared to touch. Could this be the source of the anthrax in Canada? Was this anthrax in the liquid that he was coming to use against the Notch? Our interpreters were limited due to the geographic location. I doubted we had an Arabic translator, but I knew we had a Hebrew one.

Bethlehem, New Hampshire, functioned as the summer vacation area for most of the Hasidic Jews from New York City. It had been for years, when the diamond trading Jews sought clean air in the hot summers of the city, prior to air conditioning and modern medicine. They would fill small cabins throughout the summer months, throwing large parties on Friday nights that continued until the Sabbath. Their houses and rentals were easily recognized by the wire that circumnavigated the boundaries of their yards called the Eruv.. Only certain activities were permitted beyond the wire, and I had seen the same wire surrounding their neighborhoods in New York City.

Walking through the town in full length coats and large beaver pelted hats, with their distinctive beards and curly side burns, the men were mysterious and spoke only in Hebrew. The women wore long black dresses, seeming subservient to the commands of their husbands. The town of Bethlehem had endured their teenage drivers and arrogance for decades. I only hoped that one of our own had learned enough Hebrew to possibly read EZ's journal-if this was even the language of record.

Knowing what the journal contained may enable a better outcome for my interview, so I headed straight to Michael who had catered hundreds of their events in the North Country. I found him smoking a joint behind the kitchen when we arrived.

"Hey buddy. I need your help. Can you read this?"

Michael glanced through the journal before speaking. I knew he took his time before usually offering his thoughts on any subject of importance. He finally closed the journal, took a hit of his joint, and looked off to Mt. Washington in the distance.

"I knew they were using something on us. We are so fucked. This is Hebrew."

* * *

Eruv

Marzana brought water in for our new prisoner. He appeared to feel confident and safe within his cell, so he did not object to the food and water placed before him. I was going to do my best on this round of medications. I had few options left to try should he pose a problem. I had left Michael to translate EZ's journal for round two should it become necessary.

EZ had been trained to eat and drink when offered. The soldier never knew what his captors were up to, but starvation could be their next motive. Never turn down the opportunity to nourish the body. After a full day in the cold, he felt he needed the calories as well. The journey back on the snowmobile had been jolting and cold. The cold and snow were foreign to his upbringing. He had gotten used to the cold of Canada, but add the snow and wind, and he prayed that his next assignment for UUONE would be in Latin America. He had been trained in the Mossad's version of survival school. These rednecks from New Hampshire would not present anything he had not seen before in Israel. The Mossad was the best in terrorist negotiations, and through those had learned what to teach their own so as not to reveal information. He would ride this out, reveal a few facts, and wait for a rescue from UUONE. His plans had been left in Canada prior to his departure, so those with rescue capabilities would be on their way soon.

There was no way they would crack him in one day.

I was waiting to give Michael some time to decipher the journal we had caught EZ with. He didn't appear happy with its contents, and that put some fear into me. It wasn't his first language, but he knew the importance of getting it done quickly. I had also taken the transmitter into a Faraday cage and turned it on. I feared that it would emit some sort of satellite tracking and lead to a rescue attempt. Despite the fact we knew most satellites were disabled and destroyed, I couldn't be sure that what now appeared to be an Israeli had some sort of alternate communications ability.

The device was quite small and had an antennae that screwed into its top. It did not appear to be a radio or shortwave. No preset phone numbers were stored. The face of the unit had around twenty buttons. Each was labeled in sharpie with three Hebrew symbols or letters. I could not tell the difference, so Michael would need to translate these as well. The Faraday cage was encased in foil around the ceiling and walls. We had stored batteries, radios, and other electronic equipment to protect against EMP attacks. We had learned our lesson early in the conflict about those, having much of our communication tools destroyed from the electromagnetic pulses. I pushed one of the labeled buttons, and nothing happened. No noise and no signal seemed to be emitted. Turning the power off, I proceeded to the small quart size canister we had found in his backpack. Fearing it could be anthrax or some type of biological agent, I was extremely careful in my approach. I poured a small amount into a stainless cup which would later be bleached and burned. The chemical held a hazy, milky appearance, but was opaque. I shined a light through the liquid and could make out very small reflective particles. Its consistency reminded me of the Goldschlager liqueur we used to take shots with at the bar in Bethlehem, Rosa Flamingo's, which I had heard sold more of the 24 karat gold leafed cinnamon shots than anywhere in the country. These gold flakes were the size of salt flakes. I poured the contents back into the container and disposed of the cup. Perhaps the journal would reveal more on the liquid's purpose.

Proceeding back to the Cave, I gathered my equipment. I would try my best on the Israeli. It was time to find Michael and hope his translation was accurate.

Journal Contents

Michael was waiting for me when I returned to the Cave. "What did you find out?" I asked.

He stood from the bar, and I noticed he had helped himself to a tequila. Shaking his head, he started on his dissection of the journal.

"It's all starting to make a little more sense. I just need your ideas on if I'm right. I'm one hell of a conspiracy theorist, but this goes beyond that. I'm just not sure I even believe myself. I've translated, and I think I have the bulk of the information for you. But I may need another tequila before we dive in."

He walked behind the bar, grabbed a bottle of G4, filled shot glasses for himself as well as me. Raising it in the air, he passed me mine, waiting for me to do the same.

"To the right to be left the fuck alone," he cheered, tipped the glass back, and closed his eyes. I did the same, feeling that bad news was on its way.

"The journal appears to contain a recipe of some sort. A dosing guideline based on weight, and dosages over time. I don't think what you have in the container is poisonous or will injure us. The directions do not state what the chemical is, only how much to start with based off of a kilogram of body weight. Page one's chart gives weight in one column and dosage in the other. As you progress, the charts reach to day seven, at which point the doses remain the same with a warning that states something to the effect about possible kidney damage, pineal gland dysregulation, neurotransmitter disruption, and lab levels needing processed for higher dosing. Further in the journal, another chart listed human emotions, 27 to be exact. The journal is handwritten elsewhere for what appears to have been some type of training retreat." I was a bit confused.

"So what is the chemical solution for? And what could it possibly mean involving emotional states? What do you think the training was for?" I asked.

"This is where it gets a little more intense. A little more conspiracy theory oriented. I can't be absolutely sure, but I can make a good guess based on my history of spending time in New Orleans."

He walked around the edge of the bar and took a seat next to me, letting out a sigh.

"There's a lot I've never told you about my past, but let's just say it was quite shady, involved a lot of interesting characters, and the consumption of lots of drugs. Since you're a Libertarian, a true Porcupine believer, I don't think you'll judge me, but I don't want it to get out to the rest of the guys here. They might be a little more judgmental."

"Of course not. What you say stays here. You know I've had my own past too. I'm not an angel by any means. Tell me what's on your mind? Do you want a beer and a Zynn?" I reached into my pocket pulling out two of the tiny lip pillows and grabbing two beers.

Whatever Michael had to say, it was going to be important for my interrogation.

"The dosing guide and the chart are one thing, but the other notes definitely were taken during some kind of drug ceremony, likely psychedelics. I saw the term ayahuasca several times, DMT, and although I didn't have time for a thorough translation, this has to be a journal from a ceremony. Years ago, I attended one in Costa Rica for the fun of it. Ayahuasca is kind of like mushrooms but far more intense and long acting. It can open up visions of the universe, the soul, and crush the ego. It can lead to profound changes in addiction, depression, and anxiety, but it can also lead to many participants fearing life or having bad visions-for life.

"It's not a drug to take lightly. The military veterans were trying to get it legalized for PTSD prior to the Notch. Politicians labeled it as a Class One drug, so an FDA reversal was needed in order to do treatments legally in the United States. Veterans were traveling out of the country to seek the drug's messages, and many returned with no further depression or suicidal tendencies. Before our little revolution took off, suicides were as high as twenty five a day in Vets, even with those who had not seen combat. The government was fully aware, but as is usually the case, the VA and the pharmaceutical companies stood the most to lose through its legalization.

"What could be a wonder drug was dragged into committees by politicians hoping to put off votes until the next election cycle, especially by the Conservatives. They didn't want to be seen in their districts as legalizing drugs that had been placed on a list to help Nixon reign in the Hippies back in the Sixties and Seventies as the Vietnam War raged on. Many claimed then, and it has been proven since, that the CIA was involved in distribution and control going forward after the illegal label had been placed. By controlling the narratives in churches, papers, and nightly news, the war on drugs became a central focus, all while they were selling and distributing to pay for their own interests. It was never about damages caused from the chemicals, it was about the ability to control the populace."

I let this sink in for a moment. Having heard a lot of this before, I wasn't surprised, but what did it have to do with EZ and the journal, with the war.

"So we have a journal of a ceremonial experience. The journal also contains charts that determine a drug by weight, and another that lists every emotion possible in the human mind.

Why does that have you so concerned?".

Michael opened the journal and turned to the inside of the back binder. On it, I recognized the transmitter's face plate I had just held. I was wrong on the buttons, but close. There were thirty buttons in all. Labeled 1-30 on this chart, with writing appearing above each number as I had seen them on the transmitter in the familiar Hebrew lettering.

"Each button on this chart is labeled with an emotion. Numbers 1-27. I did translate this because I knew the symbols were on the device, and you would want me to. The last three buttons are ON, OFF, and Transmit. I believe if I keep reading, it won't matter what I find in the journal.

"I believe this is an electromagnetic device of some sort, and that chemical can somehow be given to control emotions based on the button pushed. The journal comes from wherever this EZ guy learned how to use this evil thing, but he was likely worried he would forget the dosing. Perhaps he wasn't the brightest, or maybe he didn't want to overdose the people he intended to use this on.

"Whatever the case, I could see adding a psychedelic like ayahuasca into the process to confuse the victim into not thinking these thoughts were real, or to more easily break into the psyche. We used to call it "Syncing Up" when we used those drugs. The mind was able to see and hear things unimaginable when conscious. Once again, all of this stuff was studied and researched for decades by the CIA, British, Russian, and Israeli intelligence. To have the ability to read a person's mind, travel to the past or the future, or to steer a population into believing a narrative. I believe that is what this chemical, combined with this device, can do. If they have figured this out, then they may have been steering the course of political thought-hell, all thought-for who knows how many years. There have always been conspiracy theories relating to 5G towers, ELF and HAARP towers. It was proven years ago that the Russians beamed frequencies into American embassies. Combine this with the other propaganda-Meta, Twitter, Instagram, news cycles, and you could easily get an entire population to feel a certain way about what was going on in the world. We may have found the very method of how all this shit started."

I knew he wasn't wrong. He had also had more time to consider its ramifications. Demonic ramifications, as to who would decide when and what emotions to place into another's mind? Who was working together for what goals? Was it money? Power? Religion? Whatever it was, it was about control. Determining the outcome in order to provide a solution.

There was only one way to determine if this was actually what the device was used for, and I just so happened to have a guinea pig for my experiments. I didn't have ayahuasca, but I did have something almost as good, and if my initial tries were unsuccessful as I thought they may be, then I may just have to try out this little transmitter.

"Want to go have some fun? I may need your expertise on some things. Your past life may come in handy if this goes down a different rabbit hole." I was offering an opportunity that I knew he would jump on.

"Let's go to the Mardi Gras doc." Michael raised his beer.

"As long as I get to hear Trombone Shorty." I finished my beer and knew this was bigger than the both of us.

EZ's Cell

Four guards were assigned to EZ, and I had security doubled around the hotel. Someone at some point would be looking for this guy. I walked past his holding cell. He looked rather normal. Not a Navy SEAL physique for sure, but muscular, little to no body fat, more of a gymnast's body. There would be no Krav Maga attempts from him though. Now that I knew his background was likely Israeli, he would have known some form of the self defense techniques. The four guards all had stun guns, and EZ's legs were placed in double plastic zip ties, just loose enough to allow him to stand.

I wondered what his story was. The history of what appeared to be a normal looking guy from a country that was supposed to be our strongest ally in the Middle East. I did know that the Israelis were quite conceited in their politics and had a history of using the United States to serve its best interests. Intelligence had revealed numerous plots over the years of deception, bugging, double agents, and spy missions against their supposed "ally". I'm sure the CIA was equally as active in Israel's politics. Both were guilty of doing what was necessary to achieve deception for the greater good of their existence.

The prominence of Israeli interests in the United States congress was evident. Based on religious percentages of the general population, Judaism was far over represented. With activist groups like AIPAC, the American Israel Public Affairs Committee, Israel was suspiciously always involved in our countries decisions affecting Israel. Politicians all visited Israel, received large donations yearly, not from AIPAC, but from private donations, thus AIPAC avoided the need to register with FARA, the Foreign Agents Registration Act, only claiming to be a domestic lobbying group to benefit Israeli interests.

It was all quite controversial, appearing as if NGOs or USAID backed non for profits could bypass restrictions to fund nefarious motifs. The United States had been equally banned across other countries including China and Russia after many

NGOs were determined to be shells for the CIA, NSA, or other intelligence entities. Israel, although what some perceived as a conspiracy theory, was even mentioned to have perhaps had knowledge about the events of 9/11, had intentionally sunk the US Liberty in 1967 to obtain uranium, and knowingly provided false information that led to many conflicts in the Middle East at the expense of the US soldier and taxpayer. Whatever the case, where there was smoke, there was likely fire.

Could Israel be behind this EZ character's device? Could they have helped control the minds of Americans? Or, did the CIA directly participate with a supposed ally in an attempt to steer their control over the people?

I didn't put it past the Israeli's any more than I did my own government. We had been lied to repeatedly and treated like minions. From the cause of World War Two, Vietnam, Iraq, Afghanistan, election fraud, Covid, drugs, USAID, the American citizen had been lied to for the benefit of whatever cause the American politician deemed necessary. Those lies had not been voted upon by the people, for certain they would have not been passed had the evidence been clear.

The lies had been sold in order to provide a war and solution based economy as manufacturers and large corporations had left the United States, Europe, and the West, to greater profits for their share holders. To be at war was to make a dollar. The United States no longer could survive without a war based economy, and we had deserved our collapse. Those that assisted this collapse were just as guilty, often providing the false narratives which enabled a sell to the tax payers.

The situation we now faced in the Notch was a final chapter in the outcome of the continuation of such lies. We viewed it as good versus evil. The corruptness revealed by whistleblowers like Edward Snowden had revealed we no longer lived in a society that protected the Bill of Rights. We survived in a society that more resembled George Orwell's 1984. A government produced society of slaves.

Looking at EZ, I saw him as the evil part of my society. Not because of his religion, but for his support of what only he determined was my cause. He felt he had the power to decide what I deem as important to my family, to my society, to my country, and through whatever means necessary, he would attempt to enforce his mission to achieve those goals.

It was now time to enforce my goals. The goal of the individual's right to make their own decisions. The possibility that he had a device to control emotions just made my hate grow. I needed that hate to avoid sympathy in the interrogation room.

He made eye contact with me, and I did not look away. For a brief second, I could see a lonely man. Vulnerable, before his face hardened once again.

You are vulnerable EZ. All humans are. That vulnerability stood to be protected.

This Israeli may think he was in Amalak, but he would be forced to learn that we took care of our weak, cripples, and exiled. All religions were protected here. The Founding Fathers' principals had been mismanaged for the profits of other nations, and for the enrichment of a corrupt political system. They would be protected here, not abandoned to his army.

Our message from God had been received just as clearly in The Notch. It was time for EZ's own *yetzer hara.*

The Journal

Opening the journal, I turned to one of the last pages, it was the only page with a phone number. I hadn't recognized it initially. Phone lines and the internet were down, so I couldn't look it up, but I had copied it. Something told me it was important. I knew I would remember at a later date.

With curiosity, I read Michael's translation. He had time to complete the entire journal's translation. He had transcribed its contents into a notebook, page for page matching EZ's entries. The notes started with descriptions of locations in Peru's history, continuing on with tourist sites and their importance to native history there.

After the Peru section, it appeared that he had taken notes on a special diet, mental preparation, self questions, and expectations for an ayahuasca retreat. He had answered the questions describing his current health and state of mind. He revealed goals to overcome current obstacles to life and joy, love and hope. From this section, it contained a timeline for specific food and medications to stop before the ceremony, items to bring to Peru's Amazon, and expectations for during the ayahuasca ceremony. He continued on with a list of intentions to be set for his journey, and how to safely navigate the intake of the medicine. This portion ended with how to integrate his experience back into his daily life, outline common themes, and what to discuss with loved ones after his trip. There was a blank page before the next section started. I could only assume that these were notes taken from the actual retreat. He began each page labeled in order of ceremonial days. The first described his arrival and food intake for the day along with a description of his housing and instructors. Day one involved a process called Vomitivo. Day two through four went into great detail of his actual ayahuasca ceremonies. His handwriting was almost illegible, likely composed while still under the influence of the plant medicine. Another blank page, and then the formulas were charted. Another blank page, and a page telling him to read a book.

Stalking the Wild Pendulum, Itzhak Bentov.

The rest of the journal was empty until the back cover where we had found the transmitter image. Flipping through the empty pages of the journal, I had missed the phone number written in small print, next to the creasing and glued backing. That's where the phone number had been. Obviously one of importance since he made an effort to not have it discovered. But it still bothered me. Where had I seen this number? And why did EZ have it in his journal? I went back to my room at the Mt. Wash and found my phone. The battery had long ago died, but I plugged it into an outlet that had generator power. Sparking back to life, the iPhones bright screen was a forgotten antique of my past. To me, they had expedited the ruin of our society. I almost wanted to shut it off.

Opening the phone icon, I started typing in the number. As I entered the first four digits, a name came up from my contact list.

O'Reilly.

I had proof. This was the same EZ that had paid for much of our gun club's existence. The same EZ who never returned my calls after O'Reilly and Willis's disappearance. The same EZ who I suspected had been involved with the release of anthrax from drones and balloons. I now had definitive proof that this was an important guy. He would not know that we knew each other. I worried that anthrax could be what was in the canister he brought. But that didn't make any sense. He carried no special equipment to handle its use. He could have been vaccinated, but he still would need antibiotics after being exposed, and those were in short supply. The canister had to hold something else. And what about the transmitter? Why was it in the back of the journal?

Why were there twenty plus emotions labeled on the buttons?

There were a few Vermonters who had been at the balloon festival that day. I decided to seek them out. Perhaps let them meet EZ. Maybe one of them could make a connection to this guy. They were part of a lucky few who survived the terrorist event, being in good health and taking antibiotics.

Grabbing the journal and transmitter, I went to search for my friends from the Green State.

__The Epidural__

My team had placed EZ into a chair with his chest touching its aluminum back. His arms were strapped around the back, then placed and secured in front to the vertical metal spindles. His feet were secured to the lower rear rail which made his lower back arc into a soft curve as he lay sedated from the Propofol. I had placed his IV in his right inner upper bicep to prevent him from trying to dislodge it should he become too awake during our session. He had been stripped bare. There were no tattoos to help identify his home country, although we suspected Israel from all of the Hebrew written in the journal we had found in his possession.

I brought over a small table and carefully opened the epidural tray using sterile gloves. In a 3 mL syringe, I drew up 1% Lidocaine to numb his skin. Any movement during the procedure might result in a "wet" tap with the large 18 gauge epidural needle going a bit too far into the subarachnoid space, ejecting clear cerebrospinal fluid. He would then be worthless from a splitting headache until the hole healed itself from the leak.

Next, I aspirated normal saline into the 5 mL glass epidural syringe. Its plunger sliding effortlessly within the barrel. The syringe was designed specifically for epidural placement since a "loss of resistance" technique would be used. Opening the micro catheter from its plastic packaging, I laid it to the side of the tray for easy access once his epidural space had been located. It would then be advanced past the hub of the needle around 3-4 cm. Lastly, I opened a sterile window Opsite dressing to secure the catheter in place once the needle was removed. Marzana opened and sterilely handed me a Chloraprep stick to clean his skin.

Unsure of how much information he would provide, I wanted to remain as sterile as possible to prevent him from obtaining an infection. After prepping his lower back and applying a windowed drape, I felt over the drape to identify his iliac crest at the top of his hips. Guiding my thumbs towards midline, I should be between lumbar space three and four. Wanting a faster result with less medication for my intended purpose, I then went two levels higher to space L1-L2, making an indention with my thumbnail to help identify the site on the skin. The local syringe pierced his skin with a small 25 gauge needle. The Lidocaine formed a small wheel. He didn't move during this bee sting, so I was happy with his sedation level from the Propofol.

Placing the local syringe back into the tray, the epidural needle would come next. Guiding the needle through the skin wheel, I slowly advanced towards his spine until I felt the needle held firmly in place with ligaments and muscle tissue. A metal stylet with the needle was removed. I then connected the glass epidural syringe to the needle. This is where an epidural became challenging, and yet fun to place at the same time.

Advancing by feel, I would advance 1-2 mm at a time, pushing on the plunger of the saline filled syringe. This continued as I began to feel a crunchiness with the tip of the needle. This meant I was getting close to the epidural space as the needle was passing through the dural ligament. Just as the crunchiness stopped, I pushed the saline, and it passed easily forward, indicating a "loss of resistance" and the space itself. Taking the glass syringe off of the needle, I observed the needle's hub to see if any clear fluid emerged. Seeing none, I was happy not to have gone too far into the subarachnoid space where a spinal anesthetic would have been dosed.

The plastic micro catheter was then advanced slowly through the needle as it faced no resistance. I could feel the catheter take its turn at the end of the Tuohy needle, thus enabling the catheter to continue in an upward direction towards his upper spine. Once I had advanced the appropriate distance, I began a push and pull method with the needle and the catheter, being diligent to not pull the catheter out of the space as the needle was removed from his back.

Start to finish time, two minutes. Experience helped.

I coiled the micro catheter next to the insertion site, and placed the Opsite over the coil. The last step was connecting a syringe connector so that medications could now be given through the catheter into the epidural space.

Originally, I had wanted to perform a spinal anesthetic on EZ, but that would come with some restrictions. Only having Spinal Marcaine, at best I would get three hours of time, and unless I placed a spinal catheter I could not give repeated doses. Even with repeated doses, I may not be able to control the spread and rise of the medication up his spinal cord resulting in a total spinal, apnea, or even seizures if the medication went to his brain. The epidural solved these issues. I would use Marcaine 0.5% through the catheter, and with repeatable small doses, I could achieve whatever height level desired. I could also leave the catheter in should I need to use the technique for another interrogation.

Marzana handed me a 30 mL syringe of medication as I pulled the sterile drape off of his back. I wanted to take my time, so I began with a 15 mL bolus through the catheter as she turned off the Propofol infusion. He would gradually emerge from the IV anesthetic in around five minutes. I connected a BP cuff to his left arm and placed a pulse oximeter onto his right middle finger. Baseline vital signs were taken every five minutes because the injection would drop his blood pressure. Medications to treat this drop were readily available.

We then leaned his chair forward onto the floor. Spinals and epidural dosing levels could be adjusted due to the specific gravity of the medication. This Marcaine was hyperbaric, meaning that it was heavier than the CSF, so placing EZ in a head down position would start the medication towards his upper torso as it sank higher towards the head.

Going to my anesthesia cart, I obtained a nerve stimulator. The small plastic device held two metal prongs at one end with digital adjustments in the middle. After turning the machine on, I placed the prongs onto EZ's temple and hit the tetanus button. His head immediately shot upwards as he let out a loud groan.

"Yep. It's working.' I laughed at Marzana.

I was teaching her as much anesthesia as I could in the Notch. I loved teaching, and if something were to happen to me, I hoped that she could one day take my place, but what I was about to do was the opposite of a textbook. It was highly dangerous, and if I should give too much of the medication, I could push past the cervical 3-5 levels that enabled the diaphragm to work. At thoracic level 10, EZ would be unable to feel his chest rise with the contraction of the diaphragm. Going north of that would be the art of this anesthetic.

"C 3-4-5 keeps the diaphragm alive." Marzana said proudly. I was glad she had been reading her textbooks.

EZ began to stir. His respirations became stronger. His head lifted itself from the down position as gravity pulled it towards the floor. I had brought Michael in for this interrogation just in case EZ reverted to his native language under the stress. I didn't want to miss any important confessions.

"EZ, time to wake up? Are you awake?"

I was close to his ears, speaking quite loudly. He opened his eyes and turned his head towards me attempting to orient himself to his current situation.

"Nope. You haven't been trained for this one buddy. I came up with this all by myself," I said proudly. "And, with Marzana's help. Thank you Marzana."

Michael was sitting close behind him. Ready to give us a hand should we need his expertise.

"What have you done to me? Why am I attached to this chair?" EZ said.

"We wish to obtain some information from you EZ, and this was the best way I could think to do it. Are your legs feeling any different." I asked him.

"I can't feel my legs or my butt." EZ replied.

I placed the nerve stimulator onto his thigh and hit the button again. I could hear the machine dispersing its electrical current, but he did not respond to the painful stimulus. I slowly walked the nerve stimulator up the side of his torso getting a response at his belly button level.

"OK Marzana, where are we?" I inquired.

"We are at a T10 level. Perfect for groin or leg surgery, " she said.

"2 for 2 Marzana. Why don't you give the next dose. Let's try 10 mLs this time." She connected the meds, and slowly pushed 5 mLs. We waited for around five minutes, checking his vital signs before administering the next 5 mLs. Another five minute wait before we assessed his level again.

"I'll let you do the honors this time as well."

She placed the nerve stimulator at T10 and slowly crawled up his torso before she reached just above his nipple line.

"T4!" She stated with some confidence. "Perhaps T3 as we are just above his nipples."

"3 for 3 Marzana. Let's flatten his chair out now and start here."

Michael helped us as we placed his chair against a table. His spine in a flat line with the table's top.

EZ couldn't feel his entire body. No feeling from chest to toes, and soon he would start to sense that he wasn't breathing. My pulse oximeter would tell me when he had actually stopped getting oxygen to his brain. Marzana wasn't ready for the next lesson in anatomy, so I didn't ask her. It would be quite unfair.

EZ's fight or flight response would originate from the spinal nerves along the Thoracic one level to the Lumbar three level, near where I had placed the epidural. Pushing my epidural dose higher up his spinal cord would risk blocking his cardio-accelerator fibers. His body's usual response to his situation was already being visualized by his pulse on the pulse oximeter rate.

His heart rate was not going up, but rather down.

The levels of T1-T5 could result in arrhythmias or even cardiac arrest since the spinal cord could no longer adjust the brain for fight or flight. The release of norepinephrine to increase heart rate to the receptors needed at the spinal cord level would be unable. Just as if we were performing a Cesarean Section, the body would not care if a large incision had just occurred across the abdomen. The spinal cord was unaware of the incision, despite the brain being fully aware that the stimulus was in fact occurring. A surgeon could be seen. A scalpel could be seen. The incision watched. The body was disconnected from the brain.

He was physically safe, but mentally in a very tough spot having no way to fight or flee.

The pulse oximeter read 94% oxygen saturation with a heart rate of 85. His blood pressure was 88/60. Perfectly fine for an athlete or a soldier. His brain would perfuse just fine. If he began to drop lower, phenylephrine, ephedrine, and epinephrine were in my cart. I had a few things to do before I started my session. EZ could marinate in his stillness until my return.

The Transmitter

Walking up from the hotel to the AMC Highlands building, I found who I was looking for. Barb had been at the balloon festival in Canada the day that the anthrax had spread. She was an active New Englander, raising chickens and turkeys with her husband Kevin, who wasn't as lucky to have survived the anthrax. She could always be spotted easily with her beagle, Ben Beaglesburger, whom she had named after her favorite Pittsburgh Steeler quarterback. Kevin and Barb had moved to the North Country to escape what had become the chaotic steel town of their youth.

"Barb, how are you doing?". I reached down to pet Ben. He was treated as a celebrity in the Notch. Without him, there would be no rabbits in our stew. His nose was worth more than our pigeons.

"I've been doing well. Just canned some tomatoes, beans, and apples. Helping teach the younger kids how to do the same. To what do I owe the honor of your visit?"

"I hope I don't bring up bad memories, but I need to talk to you about the balloon festival. I've found something that I'm not so sure how to interpret, and I wondered if I could ask you some questions."

"I would love to. Anyway it will help me castrate the men who did this will make me and

Kevin's ghost happy."

" I sure hope you have that opportunity. We all miss him, the Notch isn't the same without him. He taught me so much about hunting bears and rabbits, along with this little fella."

I tried to lighten her anger. I reached down and rubbed the ears on the little beagle. He wagged his tail, remembering my smell I'm sure, wondering if I was going to take him on a hunt. I continued.

"Barb, does the name EZ ring a bell with you? He's a prisoner we just obtained. I have heard his name going all the way back to O'Reilly, Willis, and the gun club. I had never met him, but I know he was quite wealthy. With Kevin's connections, maybe he had mentioned him in the past."

"That name doesn't ring a bell. Doesn't mean that Kevin didn't know him. He seemed to know the whole county. What's the book for?"

She pointed towards the journal I held. I passed it over to her, and she scanned quickly through the pages.

"I've heard of ayahuasca. Never done it, just mushrooms and some weed. I'll stick to my Iron City if I can get some. What's this drawing on the back page?" She had reached the back binder, displaying the transmitter.

"It's an image of this transmitter that we caught him with. I can't figure that out either. Each button is labeled with an emotion of some sort."

I handed her the device to allow her to see the Hebrew letters, telling her EZ was likely from Israel.

"That's interesting. I always went to church with Kevin. We would always get strange looks from the Hasidic's on Sundays when we would leave our church in Bethlehem. I think they were into that religion Madonna was-Kabbalah. Kinda felt like they didn't like us much. What's it do if you turn it on?".

"Try it, just push that button towards the bottom and hold it. It should be charged enough for you to use."

I watched as the device's digital screen brightened, waiting for a command.

"So the buttons here are associated with emotions? Wouldn't it be funny if this thing actually controlled emotions? Turn to that back cover again. Which button controls Romance? Maybe

I'll feel some of that since Kevin's been gone for so long."

She laughed and matched up the button from the book to the transmitter. Pushing the appropriate button. I noticed Ben looked up at the antennae and headed straight back to the Highland Center.

Perhaps he could sense something I couldn't.

I watched as her face changed. First to a smile, then to a big grin. She tilted her head to the side in a flirtatious manner, adjusted her hair, and inched closer towards me.

"Well I'm not sure, but I certainly do feel a lot different all of a sudden. Have you been losing weight?"

I stood in absolute shock. It couldn't be true. There was no way this could be how this worked. I grabbed the controller from Barb, looking at the chart, I found an emotion that may be easier to spot. I selected confusion and hit the button. Barb's expression changed slowly. She seemed at first reluctant to change her disposition, but I could tell a new one was there.

"Barb, do you know why I'm here talking to you today?"

"Yeah, something about Israel or the balloons, but I'm not

really sure why you would be asking me. I'm no expert on either."

I cycled immediately: admiration, adoration, appreciation, amusement, anxiety, awe, awkwardness, boredom, calmness, confusion, craving, disgust, empathy, entrancement, envy, excitement, fear, horror, interest, joy, nostalgia, romance, sadness, satisfaction, sexuality, sympathy, triumph.

Twenty seven emotions. Twenty seven versions of Barb. I then turned the unit off.

"Barb, how are you feeling?".

"I feel confused, but overall OK. Like I said, I'm here to help you as much as possible, but I'm not sure I can connect this EZ guy, his notes, and that transmitter." She was back to her baseline.

"Believe me Barb. You connected more than you'll ever know. Do you know any others who survived the attacks that day?".

"We have about three of us here in the Notch. Would you like me to find them for you?", she asked.

"I would love for you to Barb. Please send them up to the hotel as soon as you can. Tell them it's important."

I began my descent back to the hotel. As I did, I could see Ben at the center looking towards me. I turned the transmitter back on, and hit a button. He looked towards the ground and ran further behind the building.

He could sense electromagnetics.

Ayahuasca, Bentov, human emotions. I think I knew what was in the canister now, and I thought I had figured out that there was more in the Canadian drones than just anthrax. Maybe even all those chemtrails people kept talking about.. It was time to start EZ's interrogation. I had some new tools to work with.

I opened up the journal again, turning it to what EZ had

revealed about his personal life. His troubles. His desires of what he wished for from his ceremonies. I read every ceremonial description in detail. It was a roadmap, drawn by himself, that held the directions to his problems and happiness. His expectations and his goals were all written in full.

Finishing his Ceremony Two experience, my game plan was ready. EZ's purgatorial abyss lay deep in his brain, and I now had the tools to find it.

<u>EZ's Refusal</u>

No longer needing the restraints, we cut the zip ties off of EZ's legs. Michael and I lifted EZ from the chair and moved him over to the old bath tub we had found at the landfill in Bethlehem. We placed him into the tub with his legs over hanging the sides which allowed his torso and head to float. Marzana was holding his head cupped in her hands. She reached below her and placed an inflatable pool float beneath his neck. His entire body was submerged except for his face. His ears rested just above water level.

I wanted him to feel a sense of weightlessness above the epidural block with his life dependent on those around him. There would be no pain inflicted physically. His training would be ready to endure pain, but I was hoping he might not be ready for the mental aspect. Feeling helpless, dependent, and with an absolute sense of numbness. He needed to feel alone with the possibility of drowning should we choose that fate for him.

"EZ. I hope that you are comfortable. You were in dire need of a bath, so I hope you don't mind if we knock out this chore at the same time we get some information from you."

I sat next to the tub so that he could see me talking. Michael sat opposite of me with Marzana at his rear, available to control his head.

"You have no idea of who I am. I am irrelevant to your cause. I came through this area to seek you. No one else," EZ said. Obviously he had time to create a lie.

"I don't think that is true EZ. We found your journal. We have translated it, and we are prepared to let you live if you tell us what it means. What is contained in the canister EZ?" I presented the canister to remind him of his backpack's contents.

"You will never know what is in there. Nor should you. It is beyond your expertise. I can give you a contact in Vermont. I am very valuable, and they will be happy to trade prisoners or supplies for my safe return."

He looked into my eyes. I could tell this was true. He was valuable. Whatever he was carrying was valuable.

"EZ, two of your team members were captured here and revealed your name. We have been waiting for your arrival. You don't know how powerful we have become for our own cause. No one sought to protect you. Your team could care less if you were caught and if you were tortured. They have since left this Notch. We returned them safely because they did tell us everything."

This was not true at all. We had killed both of them with no remorse. They became food for the pigs.

"I know you are lying. I have not seen or heard of their return. You would have killed them. You are a sick group. You refuse to listen to our country's peace offers. They are much too big for your small numbers. How do you expect to fight the US military? As well as all of the United Nation's peace keepers that are now on your soil? You should be joining your own country's military to fend off this invasion from other nations."

Smug. Arrogant. While true, our cause would never live under any man's beliefs unless they provided absolute freedom.

I knew if the most powerful nation could not take over Iraq or Vietnam, how could they expect to quell a citizenry with millions of guns. They would first have to remove the guns, as Canada had done, before ever thinking about a takeover. Unless they had some other type of powers, they would forbid the use of nuclear weapons. The world's most needed farm land, water, oil, and minerals would be contaminated by a nuclear strike.

"No EZ. Your friends are in the hands of the units to our South in Massachusetts. We would never have sent them back to Vermont. We told them to go there and keep going South. If they reach the American Deep South, they won't stand a chance. They are much more violent than we are. They have no sympathy there to change. Their poor have learned to deal without since the Civil War. That's why rednecks from the South can prevail in so many special forces units. Where are you from? I see the Hebrew in this journal. Are you from Israel?"

"It doesn't matter where I'm from. I will tell you nothing. These dumb methods will get you nowhere. My mind is much too capable. I have been trained for much worse."

"OK. Sounds good EZ. I offered you to freely tell me. So, let us begin today's session. Be forewarned, we will now never allow you to go. We have placed an epidural in your back. We do not plan on letting you ever walk again. You will remain an invalid, dependent on the three of us to wipe your ass, feed you, and help you with the bed sores that will become infected. We will let you die a slow death. Slowing down the medications to allow you to feel the pain, but not enough for you to offer resistance or put up a fight. Then, I'll give you antibiotics to heal those infections, and let the process start over again. We will let you sink into death, save you, and make you die again. Eternal hell has begun EZ. Marzana, remove the pillow."

Marzana removed the small inflatable air pillow, and EZ's

head sank beneath the water. He would instinctively hold his breath. When he did attempt a breath, the blocked T3 level would not allow his body to feel his diaphragm expand. He would not even know if he had taken a breath. Water would enter the lungs, and he would drown passively, only his mind knowing he was close to his maker. All repeatable of course as I had placed an Ambu breathing bag next to the tub, and if need be, I would intubate him, raise his oxygen saturation levels, and start the entire process over.

His head sank beneath the water. We waited about ninety seconds before I could see his head start to move about, his mind racing from the carbon dioxide it needed to rid from the body. Bubbles emerged from his mouth. The protective pathway from the tub's water now open into his lungs.

"Raise his head Marzana. Let's see how he's taking this." I said.

She cupped his head bringing his eyes and ears above the water. He coughed responsively from the water that surrounded his vocal cords. Innervated by cranial nerves nine and ten, the glossopharyngeal and vagus nerves, which carried further into his superior laryngeal nerve. These would not be affected by the epidural, but he could only hear his dilemma, not escape or feel it. His eyes were in panic. I checked his pulse ox levels. 85% and rising with his fifth breath. Heart rate to 100. He was in better shape than I imagined. He would do fine on repeated drownings.

"Welcome back EZ." I whispered into his ear.

"Slow deep breaths. You are in a safe place. Relax and breathe. We have you. That's it....breathe."

He slowed himself. Pulse ox increasing to 95% again, heart rate to 90. His eyes darted around the ceiling. His mind came back into focus as he exhaled the poisonous carbon dioxide.

Where had he heard this before?

"It's OK, EZ. Do you have anything to say to us? You know why you are here. Just tell us." "Fuck you." He said in a low struggling gurgle.

"Marzana, make him comfortable again please. Let him experience death. Feel yourself floating. Let your brain relax. We won't let you die. We will be waiting patiently for you in a few minutes, and I promise that we will save you. Have fun on your journey, and remember to breathe when your mind tells you. This will expedite your next experience. You are going to die a thousand deaths EZ. The more you breathe, the bigger breath you take, the quicker you get to experience this again. Over and over EZ. Purgatory awaits. Go ahead, Marzana. Become his angel of death."

She let his head submerge once again.

We waited and watched the pulse ox drop into the seventies before the bubbles began. Marzana, being the good student she was, lifted his head back out of the water. His color was a slight turquoise. The arterial blood depleted from oxygen as his hemoglobin had released all the molecules it could hold. His coughing sputtered back once more, and his breathing recommenced. I waited for his eyes to open again and placed the nerve stimulator to his temple to which he provided a scream.

"EZ, what's it like down there? Every time you drop into the abyss, you will see more levels that you can fall, more levels of purgatory to experience from all of the bad things you have done. Your God wants you to stay there between heaven and hell-let you experience all of the pain you have inflicted in others."

Leaning close to his ears, I whispered to him again.

"Breathe EZ. That's it. We are here for you. You are in a safe place. Breathe. That's it. Calm your mind. Don't let it

race. Use your training, I'm sure you can beat this. Be strong EZ.

Breathe."

Pulse ox at 92%, heart rate under a 100.

"I will ask you no questions EZ. You said yourself you wouldn't reveal anything. So, I trust you. This time, I want you to trust me as we let you fall further into the abyss. Weightlessness. Falling rapidly. I want your mind to look beneath you at all of the levels you have to fall. You will notice that this time, there will be a thousand more than the last. You will open your eyes up and see the light above you, and you will feel the eternal layers of darkness below you. We will be here for you though, don't worry. We will be here for the next breath when we pull your head above the water. *Breathe EZ.* Take a nice deep breath this time so that you can stay on your journey longer. Perhaps you will drown this time and make it to hell to escape us. I know you think you will rise towards the light, but remember, we are the light EZ. We are now your heaven. We are now your cause. It's OK, EZ. Use your training now. Don't listen to me. Don't listen to your mind. Listen to God as he determines how far you will fall this time."

Marzana let his head fall again. The oxygen level dropped much quicker this time. I let it get to 60% before I heard Michael next to me.

"This is kind of fucked up man. Isn't this against the Geneva conventions or something? I may need a joint before I watch anymore of this."

I was kind of having fun fucking with EZ, but I didn't have time for his resistance. I would ask him questions this time upon his return from the dead.

"Up you go Marzana."

She leveled his head once more. His face blue. His mind

not wishing to take another breath. I placed the Ambu bag over the bridge of his nose and covered his mouth, administering slow breaths. His color changed from blue to white. Saturation levels from the sixties to the eighties.

I began to assist his breathing as his brain took over his will to survive. He went very deep this time and took around five minutes to return to a level where he would listen to me.

"That's it EZ. Breathe. It's OK. We are here for you. You are in a safe place now. I'm here next to you. To protect you. I would never let you die. Calm yourself. Breathe. That's it. Deep breaths. *Shhhhhhh. It's OK."*

His eyes were staring straight ahead, and his head remained still. I turned the nerve stimulator down to a smaller charge and shocked near his lower jaw. It responded with a snap as he let out another groan.

"EZ, tell me about your experience this time. Please tell us. We have never been to purgatory. Who was there with you? Family? Friends? Could you see many more levels this time? I bet instead of a thousand levels, there were a million. What a treat! Next time, there will be even more levels. Maybe a billion!"

I only spoke in whispers, close to his ear. I could tell he was present with me.

"I bet you feel like having a conversation now EZ. You know that I will repeat this all day. It's time you told us a little about why you are with us." He coughed, and finally began to speak.

"I am from Israel. I only work for Israel. My mission was to assist the CIA in finding intelligence about the Notch. Without satellites or cell phones, both of our countries cannot collect like we used to do. It is only with human intelligence now. Boots on the ground. Interrogating your captured. Hiking into your mountains. This is why I was sent." His eyes remained open and lifeless. Staring blankly at the ceiling in the Cave.

"Very good EZ. Now tell us about your journal. Tell us about the transmitter and the canister.

What are they for?"

I continued in a whisper. We were in a good spot.

"The journal is from a yoga retreat I did in Peru. It is meaningless. The canister is only a sports drink. The transmitter is for radio communications. I promise all of these things."

"This doesn't appear to be a true statement EZ. Michael here translated your journal. It has dose guidelines for something, and the transmitter has human emotions labeled on each button. Tell me why these are there. Remember EZ, you are safe. Breathe. You are in a safe place." He took a bigger breath.

"What I say is true. Please believe me. I am nothing but an Israeli soldier sent to work with your CIA. I'm nothing more. I am not even smart enough to understand your needs. The chart was for a protein mixture at the retreat. That is why it is in this journal. They showed us how to mix our energy drinks."

I was a bit angry at this lie. His mind was still strong enough to deliver it. "Marzana, I think he may be ready to see the darkness again." Michael stood.

"That's it man. I need a break. I'm going outside. That's enough for me right now. I'm a chef not a Nazi."

He walked out of the Cave. Lighting a joint on his exit.

"Take a break EZ. I'll be back. Marzana will let you rest on your pillow again. I'm sure you have a lot on your mind. Memories from your past are now fresh in your mind to contemplate.

I'll be back with you soon, but this time, I will have a surprise for you."

Leaving the room, I grabbed his journal and proceeded out to the smoking area. Michael was there smoking his joint. I handed him a beer.

"I'm sorry my friend. None of this is easy for us. Get it- *EZ for us*." He looked at me and laughed.

"You are one fucked up dude, man."

"I'll need you one more time Mike, but know this, without your translation, none of this would have worked. Let me tell you why."

Michael listened as I told him about Barb, the journal, and the transmitter. I told him my plan for the next step of the interrogation. Continuing to the bottom of his joint, he just kept shaking his head in disbelief.

"I need your help on this last chance Michael. You see now why I was doing it the way I was. It's not my ideas that will break him. It's his own. Those were his darkest fears on the ayahuasca."

"I've done a lot of acid and mushrooms in my life brother. Let's go give this guy the worst trip of his lifetime. Give me a second to make his trip more memorable."

Janitor's Closet

Michael was gone for around two hours. This gave EZ some time to think about his choices. We laid his chair in a flat position, and I turned an IV pump on to continually bolus the epidural. Going to my drug supply, I picked up a bottle of Ketamine. The 10 mL bottle was labeled Ketamine 100 mg per/ mL. With it, I grabbed a 5 mL syringe and headed back to the Cave to wait on Michael. I wasn't sure what he was up to, but if it helped in the interview, then I was all for it.

I heard him open the old wooden door to the Cave. He

waved his hand and told me to follow him. We walked through the basement of the hotel until we arrived close to the basement exit. He opened the door to a room labeled "Janitor's Closet". I had never been into this area of the hotel, but Michael was down here frequently to receive cooking supplies and garden tools. The entire room from floor to ceiling was adorned with psychedelic patterns that looked familiar to me, but I couldn't place where I had seen it. The pattern was composed of repeating parallel squares. Inside of each square were intricate symmetrical swirls of varying color. All of which were in perfect symmetry. The borders surrounding the squares were of a white and dark blue pattern, also in perfect symmetry.

Michael had then turned the squares at a forty five degree angle making them appear more as uniform diamonds. The room smelled of some type of glue to hold the designs to the wall. He had lit candles in all four corners to mask the smell, and once he closed the door, they provided an eerie ambience that only candlelight can do. The colors waved with the light causing the patterns to come and go. Near the rear of the room, he had brought in two speakers placed opposite of each other, speaker wires leading back to an old Kenwood amplifier.

"Pretty trippy huh? It's the hallway carpet from the third floor. We had some left in storage. If you are planning on getting him to have one hell of a trip, this may help a little. Looks similar to my old college dorm room. I'm hoping he sees the machine elves."

I asked, "What's with the speakers? Are you planning on playing some Pink Floyd?"

"Have you ever heard of binaural beats? They are best played through headphones, but this was the best I could do. My phone will connect to the receiver. I have some downloads on it for when I do mushrooms. One speaker will play at one frequency, and the other will play at a different frequency. What his brain will hear will be the difference of the two frequencies. For today, he will hear what's called the Earth's heartbeat frequency at 7.83 Hz. This is called the Schumann resonance, and it comes from the low electromagnetic vibration between the lightning sound waves that bounce down from the ionosphere into the Earth's crust. We won't hear it, but if he's on a psychedelic, he may open up what's called the Third Eye when his left and right brain sync together. I used to listen to some pretty trippy podcasts about it. The CIA used to use it as well. There's a place called the Monroe Institute where they would train remote viewers for warfare, and these beats would help them get to that Third Eye quicker. So, what do you think?"

"This is genius. I never would have thought to do this. Thank you. Might make the interrogation go a little quicker for sure. Are you sure these binaural beats won't affect us while we do this?", I asked.

"Back before The Notch, you were influenced by them everyday. Every intelligence agency on Earth, especially the CIA, were broadcasting EMFs to try and affect the public. The Israeli's even had a secret electronic warfare unit called Unit 8200. People thought it was a conspiracy theory, but I bet they don't now.

"Ever notice how divided we have all become? With the right repeated messaging, add the EMF waves, and people were being bombarded with discontent. That's why I switched to grounding sheets and wore a tinfoil hat. I would even move my phone to another room at night and shut off my WiFi router.

"Why do you think they were making everyone dependent on cell phones, 5G towers, WiFi, and electricity? Control the mind, and you could control the population. At least that's what all those Alex Jones shows used to say. They called him a conspiracy theorist at first. Ended up he was right on about 95% of all the stuff he said."

"With what I've just figured out Michael, you will understand that Alex Jones was right about everything. I figured out what the transmitter does, as well as what's in the canister. Today, you will see first hand what the world has been doing to us all. Why we are so divided, and why people are always upset at things that should have no significance in their daily lives. The Intel agencies like Unit 8200 have been running a psyop on us for years. Today will be the first day we get the chance to use it on them. The Ketamine, binaural, and visuals will get that Third Eye to open, but what's in the canister will get us the truth. We will not need him to relax his body, or to regulate his breathing consistently, the epidural will do all of that for us. Let's get this thing done."

"Right on man. I love watching people on Ketamine. Let's do this!"

Purgatory Abyss

We brought EZ into the janitor's closet blindfolded on a stretcher, and closed the door. Marzana placed a towel across the door's lower crack to prevent any outside light from entering. The room felt even smaller with the four of us and the wheeled stretcher. Candlelight flickered and shifted the patterns on the carpet that Michael had installed. Two tones, almost sounding like static, were coming out of each speaker at a volume loud enough to block any external noise of the hotel. I had told all workers to vacate the building. Mainly out of fear of the transmitter. There was no telling who may also be infected with the chemical contained in the canister which rested in the corner.

I had guessed EZ's weight. Following his journal

guidelines, I mixed the appropriate dosage of the chemical into a syringe. EZ had been dosed with a 100 mg of Ketamine before we left his holding cell. It took less than two minutes after administration for mydriasis to occur, his pupils widening. His eyes did not remain in a fixed location, but rather darted in small circles. The ketamine would also decrease his pupillary light reflex allowing the candlelight and patterned carpet to come alive. I checked his heart rate, and it had increased from his baseline.

Ketamine was a dissociative anesthetic that I knew binds to the NMDA receptor in the brain. It could cause mild analgesia and breathing wasn't affected, even at larger doses. It was the drug of choice for The Notch when trauma was involved, and its use dated back to the Vietnam War. It was safe to use on bleeding patients with low blood pressure, burns, and also patients who had inhalation injuries since it caused the lungs to dilate, making it easier to breathe.

The drug at higher doses would cause dysphoria, euphoria, and sometimes hallucinations. Colorful dreams, near death experiences, and dissociations were what I was after today though. I wanted EZ to enter a dissociative state, detaching himself from reality. Floating out of his body, detached from the reality around him. I had to be careful with this "Special K" drug to not take the dose too far, putting him into what was called the "K Hole", causing him to hallucinate and have illusions.

To prevent this, I had treated him with 2 mg of Versed, a benzodiazepine, and would limit my dosing to less than 100 mg of Ketamine. The Versed would also cause retrograde amnesia, so if EZ did tell us something, he wouldn't remember that he did. This would be perfect as he would think he had never revealed his secrets.

Once the Ketamine and Versed were working well, I slid a nasal gastric tube into EZ's right nose. This would be the pathway for the canister concoction. I had brought along saline to inject after the mix, pushing it into the stomach for absorption. I knew EZ wouldn't swallow it on his own. He did not react to the transmitter when I had tried. Perhaps the agencies had figured out a method to neutralize the chemical, or there was a way to block its effects. I felt confident they would have used it on their own to show its effectiveness.

We removed the blindfold. EZ's eyes darted from place to place. We had worn all black clothing to be as non reflective to the candles as possible. Lifting his NG tube, I injected the slightly white mixture into EZ's stomach and flushed saline behind it. I wasn't sure how long the chemical would take to react, so we waited while the binaural beats played.

Working from EZ's journal, I had memorized with great detail the worst of his ayahuasca experiences. Everything from his visualizations, sounds, smells, touch, instructors, pain, and especially on what his trip had revealed. This had been the ceremony for him with the most fear, a deep, dark journey into the depths of purgatory. The land of waiting before entrance into hell. Heaven could be seen above, and the journey to hell was exponential in length. These types of trips would occur in a K Hole, with LSD, and sometimes ayahuasca.

I had attempted some of the trip's details with his first interrogation without success, but now with Ketamine, binaural beats, Michael's carpet patterns, the epidural, and lastly, the canister mix, EZ would be guaranteed purgatory abyss. I had even found a red LED flashlight.

Confession

We waited about twenty minutes for EZ to adjust to the room and medication. His mind dreaming. His body floating. Unable to feel his body from his chest down. His fight or flight blocked at the spinal level. Only his mind would be free to try and escape his situation. Chemically restrained, that escape would never happen. He was going to be forced to go on his own worst trip a second time. His head no longer moved about the room. His eyes could not be examined in the darkness, but I assumed his pupils were at maximum dilation.

Michael's binaural beat music had a relaxing effect, and I found myself wondering if I was starting to hemi sync my own cerebral hemispheres. I focused on the task to come, trying to avoid where my mind seemed to be going. Marzana sat on the floor remaining silent and motionless. Michael seemed to be watching over EZ with the presence of a New Orleans voodoo doctor.

I leaned into EZ's right ear.

"Relax EZ. We are here with you. You are in a safe place. Take some big deep breaths. It's time for you to go to the place that you fear. The place where you like to avoid the darkness. The pit of blackness where your descent is never ending. Let your mind open that third eye. The eye that will let you travel about the Universe. Let the mother of the Universe take you to where your fears are. *Deep breaths EZ.* Take us with you. There is someone in the darkness who needs to ask you questions, and perhaps, he will let you rise into the bright light, away from the darkness resting in your soul."

"You remember the white light EZ. Your family was there. Your old dog. Your Father, and Grandfather. The warmth of heaven, of God. Your connection to all of the animals and plants around you. The pathway to all of the knowledge of the Universe is there where Mother Ayahusaca has shined for you before. That's where you can go EZ, but only if you confront the darkness. Confront your fears. Do not be scared. Confront those who ask you questions on your journey for they are not real. Only illusions, placed to better your soul if you seek to enter the white light. Listen to the sounds around you. Let your mind take you to the abyss. Nothing there is physically real. Leave your body and travel with your mind. You will be safe here. You are surrounded by those that care for you. Do you wish to travel with Mother Ayahuasca today EZ?".

"Yes. I feel like my mind is dropping. I can hear the waves of the music opening up to you Mother. Please let me see the light above."

EZ's head shifted up on the table, almost as if he was looking at something above him. He had made the connection. This third eye was opening to allow him into the threads of the Universe where for thousands of years, cultures all over the world went regularly.

"Tell me when you have entered the darkness. Mother will show you the way. She is all knowing. She knows what we all wish to seek. Envision your intentions EZ. Let her take you there."

I whispered this time into his left ear.

"I feel her presence. She is beautiful. I am flying with her now. She is guiding me through time. She is warm and loving. I remember how to talk to her now. She is telling me to go to the darkness. I feel it now. I feel myself dropping."

He looked towards his toes, letting out the sound of fear. A hushed scream lasting seconds came just above the sound of the speakers.

"Mother, I am here. Please don't let me fall any further. Please don't make me breathe. I don't want to drop further into more death. I know what will happen."

"*It's OK, EZ. Slow your breathing.* Let your mind escape the breathing. Who is there with you?".

"My mother is here. I see a black and blue butterfly. It's flying around the diamonds and jesters.

It's going between the matrix of colors. *I can hear death.*"

"Slowly EZ. Go to your Mother. She is ready to ask you some questions." Back in his right ear I spoke.

"Mother, what is it you wish to know? I am sorry to be here. I have done something wrong. I've done something for which you are ashamed. I am so sorry Mother. I love you so much." I tapped Marzana on the shoulder. It was her turn to ask the questions. The soothing sound of a woman's voice may rest his mind.

"EZ, where are you from? And who did you work with there?"

"You know this Mother. What a silly question. Our homeland, Israel. I was with the military before they sent me off to Peru for UUONE."

UUONE? What the hell was that? I motioned for Marzana to pursue the question.

"What is UUONE EZ?"

"Mother, you know I can't talk about the secret things we do. Where we go. It's all to protect our homeland though. You would be proud of how much I have done for us. To further our religion. To keep us safe from the infidels around the world. I have made a difference, Mother."

"Tell me EZ, how did you kill all of the people in Canada?".

"You would be proud of my work Mother. I was able to convince not only Arabs, but the dumb Americans to do the work for me. I didn't actually kill the people Mother, they did. They had no idea how many they would kill with the anthrax spores. It was beautiful to see my mission come to a completion. No evidence of Israel. UUONE was very proud of me. Especially being able to mix Nanemo within the drones as well. Everyone suspected the anthrax Mother, but that wasn't the real goal. NanEmo was."

Marzana continued.

"I'm sorry EZ. Please tell your Mother what NanEmo is. Your work is always confusing to someone as old as your Mother."

"I understand Mother. I could tell no one else but you. You are safe in the hands of God now, so you can't tell anyone here. Mother Ayahuasca told me to answer your questions, so that I can be in the light with you one day. NanEmo is a tiny lipid molecule that goes into people's brains. The lipid coating allows it to attach to cell membranes, eventually crossing to the other side. Inside the lipid coating, are small metallic particles. Over time, the lipid shell dissolves, leaving the particles behind. Dr. Bentov taught me how to use it. He was an amazing man. He was my mentor in Peru. I'm sure he is in the light with you if you want to talk to him, Mother."

I pushed Marzana aside, and whispered to EZ.

"EZ, can you hear me? This is Dr. Bentov. I am here with your Mother. I have missed you EZ. Tell me, how is my invention working out? Has the transmitter been effective?"

"Bentov. I have missed you. You have taught me so much for our cause. It has worked so well. Your genius is changing the world. With it, we are able to control whomever we choose. The technology has only gotten better since you left us. You would be amazed at what we can do to the mind now. Even from great distances."

"EZ, where are they making NanEmo now? Is it still made in Peru?"

"Of course not silly doctor. You know we would never

make it anywhere else than Israel. It is far too important for us to reveal to anyone else. Our teams with the CIA bring us the components, and we mix it there. Our control over the American Congress has enabled us to fund as much as we need to make. We give them the NanEmo when they come to visit Israel with AIPAC. It's with the American tax dollars that we fund our projects now. You would be so proud of us."

EZ was smiling now. Enjoying his pride of bragging to his mentor.

"How about the reversal agent EZ? Has it been effective? This would make your old professor proud."

"Bentov, you know that I could never tell you that. UUONE said I couldn't even tell you. Not even my Mother."

Marzana spoke into the opposite ear from me.

"It's OK now, EZ. I am here with you. It's safe. Remember what Mother Ayahuasca told you. You have to tell the people on your journey the answer to their questions in order to go to the light. It's OK son, Bentov deserves to know. He taught you so much. He has led to your success EZ. You owe this to him."

EZ remained quiet on the table. Seeming to not want to reveal this one last secret. I turned on the transmitter. I had memorized some of the buttons, and I hoped the mix from the canister, NanEmo, had made it to EZ's brain.

I felt down and across the buttons, hitting the button for anxiety. I alternated between anxiety and fear. Cycling the buttons every thirty seconds.

"EZ, you seem to be headed towards the darkness. What is the reversal? Where is it found? Don't fall into the darkness EZ. Head towards the light. Can you feel the light?" I pushed the buttons for admiration and joy.

"I feel you Mother. I feel the light. I want to be with you. I no longer want to be in this darkness. The Stoico is made in

Montreal. That is why UUONE has me living there. You would be so proud that they trusted me and no one else. We get the chemicals from the Chinese. Because they sneak so many components for Fentanyl into the ports there, we never are suspected. Even if the authorities were to find them, we have infected everyone from their President on down through their Parliament. Are you proud of me, Mother?".

I had enough of what I needed for now. I could always get him to confess more when we needed it. He may even admit more once we told him he had let down his cause, breaking to an American, an Infidel no less.

Looking at Michael, I pressed the button for horror.

"EZ, you have let us all down. You have let Bentov down, and your Mother. You have revealed too many secrets. It's time for you to understand your mistakes. *Take a breath EZ. Breathe. It's OK, EZ. Breathe. Feel the darkness.* You are dropping further and further into the darkness. Only we will decide when it is time for your return. With each breath, you will fall into exponential darkness. You must be taught a lesson from Mother Ayahuasca."

I handed the controller to Michael. He was in charge of the trip now, and he had been on many. I no longer cared where EZ's mind traveled. He had been part of destroying our world. He had been helping a cause that had led to the greatest division in human history.

I heard EZ take another breath, and scream as he fell further into his own hell. A trip to his own personal hell. Even if the Ketamine wore away, we now held the power of his emotions. There was no Stoico reversal in the White Mountains, only an endless K-Hole.

We now knew who was responsible for the endless division, and The Notch it created.

* * *

Prologue

<u>The Gold Room</u>

Fourteen chairs surrounded the rock maple table, its ten legs holding the wood's enormous weight. It had come from Carolyn Stickney's private dining room at the Mt. Washington Hotel. She had inherited the hotel after her husband Joseph Stickney's death in 1902, having only one year to enjoy the dream property before passing. They had been together for a decade. There were twenty seven years between them. He had married her when she was only 25. She had designed the table to match her poster bed, now occupying her personal room, 314, a short walk up the stairs in the front lobby.

The light turquoise blue fabric on the chairs had once held the fourteen power nation representatives at the International Monetary Conference in July, 1944. Their gold-colored framework was symbolic of the agreement that was enacted that day with the final Articles of Agreement establishing the US dollar with its gold backing standard as the currency of choice for the newly established International Monetary Fund. A fact now displayed on the door entering what was now called the Gold Room.

A fireplace with intricate white molding and a mirror sat behind the table. A display case of miniature flags, representing all of the countries in attendance that day lie opposite two green and silver striped chairs and a small maple secretary's desk. Golden framed photos of famous attendees adorned the walls. People such as Secretary of Treasury Lord Halifax,

French Ambassador Henri Bonnet, Treasury Secretary Henry Morganthau, U.S.S.R. Chairman S. Stepanov, and Economist J.M. Keynes now looked over the famous table that changed the world. I had summoned the heads of The Milli, The Rangely, and The Waterville Valley Militias. I had also requested the heads of the Quebec, Vermont, Maine, and Massachusetts oppositional forces to come to the historic room to negotiate a truce. I could see them outside through the large window behind the table, waiting on the front porch.

Behind me, I heard my other guests arriving. Barb, and three others from the balloon festival, EZ, Michael, Marzana, and Crissy. EZ's plastic cuffs were loose enough for him to make his way towards a chair next to the fireplace. Crissy took out her video camera, computer, multiple zip drives, and microphone. Michael brought a backpack which I knew contained NanEmo and the EMF transmitter.

Today, we would sign new Articles of Agreement, and I could think of no better room at the hotel to perform this historic task. What had happened there over a century before had changed how the world functioned, and what we were about to record would do so as well. Displaying the use of EMF technology and submitting this evidence around the world. Believable only if our enemies could see it with their own eyes. With today's AI, no one would believe us otherwise. A new Fenian Proclamation was being written by a Provisional government with aims at a liberty of conscience, remembering the past, looking well to the future, and avenging ourselves by giving liberty to our children in the coming struggle for human liberty. O'Reilly would have been proud.

www.ingramcontent.com/pod-product-compliance
Lightning Source LLC
Chambersburg PA
CBHW020736020826
48980CB00018B/480/J